For some, death is only the beginning

SPECTRAL GALLOWS

Mark W. Danielson

Night Shadows Press

ISBN 978-0-9846044-7-0 (pbk.)
ISBN 978-0-9846044-9-4 (ebk.)

Night Shadows Press
8987 E. Tanque Verde #309-135
Tucson, Arizona

Library of Congress Control Number 2013948672

1 2 3 4 5 6 7 8 9 10

Books by Mark W. Danielson

Danger Within
The Innocent Never Knew
Diablo's Shadow
Writer's Block
Spectral Gallows

markwdanielson.com

To my late father, Bill, whom we dearly miss.

First and foremost, I would like to acknowledge my beautiful wife, Lyne, whose patience allows me to create, and keen eye provides constructive criticism.

To Proof Reader Valerie Johnson, thank you for your red ink spots. I owe you a pen.

To Michele Gerbrandt, thank you for another outstanding cover. I knew it would be brilliant.

To Editor Helen Ginger, thank you for your first look. I truly appreciate your remarks.

To Long Island Paranormal Investigator Rob Levine, thank you for lending your expertise in paranormal phenomena. It was most useful in developing the storyline.

To TCU Physics Professor Magnus Rittby, thank you for validating my use of Quantum Theory. It is noteworthy that you and everyone in your family have performed at the Scott Theater featured in this tale.

To my family and friends, thank you for your unwavering support of my conscious and subconscious writing. You know who you are.

Finally, to my little doggie, Maxx, who never leaves my side. Like your namesake character, you are extra special.

SPECTRAL GALLOWS

Fort Worth, Texas
Late October

One

EIGHTIES ROCK MUSIC SEEMED odd for a dive called the Chuck Wagon Diner, but that was nothing compared to its photo-packed walls. As Maxx Watts and partner Blaine Spartan took their seats, Watts noted every picture was of military personnel either in the field or their official portraits. Studying the Vietnam War shots, Watts overheard someone say *murder*. Being a homicide detective, he craned his neck to find the person who made the comment. The bearded, pony-tailed hulk of a man was easy to spot because he was still arguing with a fair-skinned redheaded man sitting across from him.

"Why do you keep saying that?" Red fired back.

"Because it's the truth, goddammit!" said the sixty-something bully with driftwood-toned skin. When Watts reached into his pocket to start his Sony recorder, Hulk fired a gaze that made the detective retreat into his menu. A follow-up peek confirmed Watts' dad had an Army jacket identical to this one, clear down to his two stripes and black-horse shoulder patch. Hulk's black Tee, bunched-up denim jeans and scuffed black ropers suggested he drove a motorcycle, but Watts hadn't seen one outside. If the stranger's cologne was supposed to mask the cleaning solution smell on his soiled clothes, it wasn't working.

Not to be outdone, Red countered with equal ferocity. Sporting neatly trimmed hair, a similar oversized black Tee, and gray Nike's hiding under pressed denim jeans, Red's only similarity to Hulk seemed to be his wardrobe.

A woman's voice took Watts by surprise. As he looked up, the gum-smacking waitress said, "Are you gentlemen ready to order?"

Watts looked up and then back at his menu. Annoyed by her

noisy gum and more interested in eavesdropping than ordering, the detective shook his head hoping she would leave. Red's next rebuttal came when the dark-rooted blonde waitress turned away.

"Travis," said Red, "After forty plus years, why do you keep insisting it was murder?"

"Because the goddam police ignored the evidence and ruled it a suicide," said Hulk, AKA Travis. Travis then settled into his seat and sipped his coffee. He downed half a cup before continuing. "Marv, I knew Jeremy Delouse, and I assure you he was too much of a wimp to take his own life. Of course, his sensitive tendencies probably made him a good actor."

Unable to jot notes, Watts burned the names and physical descriptions of the men into his brain. Travis and Marv were obvious, but he had no idea who Jeremy Delouse was.

"Sensitive tendencies?" Marv heatedly said. "What's that supposed to mean?"

Travis tucked in his chin and drew in a breath. Frowning, he stared at Watts until he looked away and then leaned over the table to speak more softly. "Don't get all pissy, Marv. I'm just saying Jeremy was more in touch with his inner feelings than most men, and the stage allowed him to express them – and before you interrupt, he wasn't gay. He definitely loved the ladies."

Marv nodded, folding his straw into three equal segments. When he released it, it squirmed like an earthworm on a dry sidewalk. Grinning, he picked it up, re-bent it, but didn't let go. "That makes sense because according to Dad, Jeremy was always having girl trouble."

"Girl trouble? How so?"

"They'd lead him on and then stomp on his heart," he mumbled at his straw. "Dad also said lots of people kill themselves over their lovers."

Travis' frown deepened. "Listen, Marv, Jeremy loved those drama queen actresses, and any of them could have planned his final exit, if ya know what I mean." When Marv failed to respond, Travis rubbed his eyes, heaved a sigh, and pushed himself from the table. "I gotta hit the head. Be right back."

Marv nodded and resumed his straw playing.

About then the detectives' waitress returned. Hoping some idle chat might make up for his earlier rudeness, Watts smiled at her. "I'm curious – what's the story behind all these wall photos?"

"Hon," said the woman, smiling back, "Anyone that's been in the military is welcome to bring in their photos. Did you serve?"

Having spent his entire adult life in public service, her question made him pause. Realizing she meant the armed forces, he slowly shook his head. "Did you?"

Beaming now, she pointed to a much younger version of herself. "That's me right there," she said, admiring her portrait. "I wasn't in long, though. In fact, my Army time was like a bad pregnancy – nine months, two weeks, one day, and three hours."

Dressed in a gray suit and striped blue tie, Spartan snorted. "If you don't mind my asking, why so short?"

"Well, Hon, I guess I didn't care much for takin' orders."

Grinning at the irony, Watts pointed to his menu selection. "I'll try your Wagon Burger, medium, with sweet potato fries."

She nodded, then looked at Spartan without writing anything down. "And you?"

"I'll do the same, please."

"Okay – two Wagons headin' your way. I'll be right back to refill your drinks."

"Thank you, ma'am."

Always one to ogle the ladies, Spartan studied the waitress' photograph while Watts pondered why Travis favored one leg as he walked. The old man's gait reminded Watts of how he walked in bare feet because his left leg was slightly shorter, but since Travis' soles looked to be the same height, that couldn't be it. His partner's nudge took him by surprise.

"Hey, Maxx. Let's talk to Marv while he's alone."

Watts shook his head, thinking they were better off remaining seated. "Let's see how this plays out. They've been talking about actors, so maybe they're rehearsing a scene."

"Well if that's the case, the big guy's pretty damned convincing. I wouldn't want to face him in a dark ally."

"Yeah, I know what you mean," he said, figuring Travis had at least twelve inches on him.

Soon, Travis was making his way back to the table. After sitting down, he used his fork to sift through his leftovers. Suddenly he stopped and pointed his fork at Watts until he looked away, then turned to his friend. "Sorry for the lapse, Marv, but with age comes weak bladders."

Shaking his head, Marv released his straw. "Don't kid yourself,

3

Travis. It's the coffee that's making you pee, not age. What's with you, anyway? You look like a zombie."

While nodding his agreement, Travis waved his waitress over. Like a well-trained monkey, the woman refilled his mug and left. He then ripped open a sweetener, dumped in the contents and stirred noisily. "So, where were we? Something about Jeremy's women?"

"Yeah. You were implying that any of them were capable of killing him, and since this is my dead uncle we're talking about, how about explaining yourself?"

Blinking hard, Travis cupped his mug with both hands. After a long sip, he dragged his sleeve across his mouth. "Marv, forgive me for not making sense, but I can't remember the last time I slept." He paused to drink but then set it aside. "Let me ask you something," he said, slurring his words. "You ever been drunk on sleep?"

Scratching his head, Marv allowed his hand to slide down to his neck. A moment later he fingered his ear like he was attacking an invisible foe. When he stopped, he said, "What the hell are you talking about, drunk on sleep?"

The old man shrugged, downed more caffeine and slowly looked up. "Drunk is how I feel most of the time, Marv. When I lie down, my numb body vibrates like I'm ridin' the rails. At times it feels like someone's sittin' on my chest, driving nails into my eyes. Other times I hear voices when no one's around. My stomach burns like I've downed a fifth of Crown Royal, but I haven't tipped a bottle since I passed out ten years ago. Honestly, falling asleep scares the hell out of me, but I keep going 'cause there's no other option."

"Dude, I had no idea. That's an awful existence, and I'm sorry. But can you forget about this drunk-on-sleep thing for a minute and get back to your point about Uncle Jeremy? Why do you keep insisting he was murdered?"

Travis gulped his beverage until it was gone. Following a nasty belch, he set his mug aside and started digging into his pants pocket. "Treasure your youth, Marv, and pray you'll never end up like me." With that he tossed three singles on the table, then stared at the money. A moment later he took one back and replaced it with two quarters.

"What are you doing, Travis? She was an excellent waitress."

"Yeah, she filled my mug four times, but three bucks is too much for coffee." Using the table, he steadied himself as he stood. When he reached vertical, he drove his finger into Marv's chest. "Think about what I said, kid. The answer's in there somewhere." He then cordially patted Marv's shoulder. "Catch ya later."

"Yeah, see ya."

Knowing they would lose Travis if they didn't confront him, Watts and Spartan stepped into the old man's path. Seemingly unimpressed with their badges, he smugly rested his arm on their table. "Get outta my way."

"Sir, we just want to talk," Watts quickly said. "We're homicide detectives and couldn't help overhearing you mention murder. Could we speak somewhere in private?"

The bearded man looked down on Watts like Goliath sizing up David. For a moment it seemed like Travis would talk, but then he straightened himself and quietly lumbered toward the door.

"Sir?" said Watts, trying to lure him back. "We'd really like to speak to you."

Ignoring them, Travis exited the restaurant without ever looking back.

Feeling his anger rise, Watts turned his attention to Marv. "How about you? Mind if we ask a few questions?"

The redhead surprised him by stretching out his legs and inviting them to join him. Watts sat in Travis' seat while Spartan pulled up another chair. Seeing that Marv was busy fiddling with his straw again, Watts broke the ice.

"Thanks for your time," he said, then made their introductions. "I'm sure you can see why homicide detectives would be curious about your conversation. We overheard you mention the stage. Are you actors?"

The Goth redhead smiled, sectioning his straw. "Actors are stupid. I have nothing to do with them."

Spartan squinted at the man. "Why is that?"

"It's not important."

Watts moved his lips around while exchanging glances with his partner. He then covered his mouth and breathed heavily through his nose. A moment later, he crossed his arms and leaned back in his seat, trying not to wrinkle his sport coat. "Forgive me, but I like knowing who I'm addressing. What's your name?"

"My given name is Marvin Delouse, but I go by Marv. Not Mr. Delouse, not Marvin, just Marv."

The response triggered grins from both detectives. "Pleased to meet you, Marv," said Spartan, extending his hand. "And what's your friend's name?"

Marv refused the hand-shake, but did raise his head. "Why?"

Watts shifted in his seat, hoping his partner wouldn't turn Marv off like he did Travis. For now he would let Spartan handle it as he was better at remaining calm.

"Marv, your friend seemed quite disturbed by your uncle's death ruling. Why is that?"

Marv released his straw and watched until it had slithered back to its original shape. Then he began stirring his coffee as if deciding on whether to talk or not.

The redhead tested their patience with long sips, but Spartan hung in there. When the silence had gone on long enough, he spoke again. "Level with us, Marv. What's your relationship with the big guy?"

With a shrug, the man hid behind his coffee mug.

"Look, Marv, we're not here to make any judgments or otherwise harass you. As Detective Watts said, we were eating lunch, and thanks to your loud-mouthed friend, we couldn't help overhearing him say the police ignored evidence involving your uncle's death. Now, whether you admit it or not, you seem to have an interest in this matter and with your help we might be able to clear this up.

When the redhead failed to respond, Watts stepped in. "Come on, Marv, humor us. Share what you know. Either that, or we'll turn our backs like the other cops did."

Finally the man lowered his mug and stared back with cold eyes. "Frankly, I don't care what you do. My uncle died before I was born and nothing will ever change that."

Spartan shook his head, staring at the ceiling. He held his gaze for a moment, and then looked back at the man. "Can you at least tell us how he died?"

Marv mangled his plastic straw and tossed it on his plate. Mimicking Spartan, he looked up and sniffled. It was impossible to tell whether he was experiencing waves of emotion or toying with them like he did the straw, but when he finally met Spartan's eyes, he wore a look of determination.

"How he died depends on who you talk to. Some believe his soul is trapped inside the Scott Theater where he was found dangling by a rope, and then there are those like me who believe he was a fool who took his own life over a woman. But my friend refuses to believe that. He thinks my uncle was hanged and now he haunts the theater's dungeon. Of course, nothing he says will ever change my mind. As you could probably tell, it's not the first time we've had this conversation, and it always ends up the same way with him walking out on me." After saying that, Marv wiped his straw clean and started bending it again. Without looking up, he added, "The media turned Uncle Jeremy into a folk legend, and now so-called paranormal experts claim he is indeed haunting the place. Sadly, that story has lasted over forty years. If you want to know more, you should visit the Scott Theater. I'm sure whoever works there would be thrilled to tell you about it."

Spartan nudged his partner's arm. "You know, it didn't dawn on me until now, but one of my kids just read about this while researching haunted places in Fort Worth. Funny how Halloween always sparks interest in ghoulish subjects."

Marv grinned at Watts. "Seems your partner's way ahead of you."

In his high school days, Watts might have reached across the table and hit the man, but now he just smiled back. "With All Hallows Eve only days away, this is definitely a good time for ghost stories. But so we're on the same page, can you confirm your Uncle Jeremy is the presumed ghost in the Scott Theater?"

"I'm not gonna confirm anything. It's that crazy old man who believes it."

"Oh, right. And what did you say his name was?"

Marv set his straw free and it lunged at Watts. Clearly amused, he spoke while re-bending the straw. "We both know I never mentioned it. However, I did say that anyone at the Scott Theater could recite the fabled story." He then raised a brow at the detectives. "I watched you take notes. How could you miss something that obvious?"

Grinding his teeth, Watts pretended to review his notebook as adrenaline raced through his veins. "Ah," he said, tapping his notebook page. "Just like you said, no name mentioned." His comment left an awkward void as Marv quietly stared back. "I don't get it, Marv. If Jeremy was your uncle and there are suspicions about his death, why wouldn't you want us looking into it?"

Marv shrugged again. "As I said, it happened a long time ago, and that ghost story is as stupid as my uncle." With that, he grabbed his check, rolled out of his chair, and like his cohort, walked out without looking back.

Two

Soon after Marv left, Watts approached the cashier to pay his bill. He showed his badge to the skinny woman while handing over his credit card, hoping his official position would persuade her to talk. Instead, she flatly told him they didn't give discounts to law enforcement officers.

"You misunderstand," said Watts with a smile. "I'm looking for information, not a cheap meal. I don't suppose you know anything about the man who just paid his check?"

Smelling like smoke, she shook her head and swiped his credit card.

Spartan leaned on the counter because he was taller than his partner and slid his tab over. "Did your last customer use cash or a credit card?"

"Cash," she said, handing Watts his credit card and receipt.

After totaling his ticket and signing it, Watts gave her the merchant's copy. "Have you seen them before?"

She shrugged and was about to swipe Spartan's card when she stopped and placed her hands on her hips. "Let me ask you somethin'. Do I look familiar to you?"

Watts studied her and shook his head. "I don't think so. Why?"

"Because unless you're exceptionally beautiful or hideously ugly, we're all just faces in a crowd. I only know who you were talking about because he paid his bill right before you came up. In the five years I've been working here, only four people stood out – the two SOBs that tried to rob this place and the two off-duty cops who were eating in the back room. If they hadn't heard what was going on and called for backup, the robbers might have hurt people and gotten away. Instead, both robbers got shot and one died. The diner was closed for a few days and I lost some pay, but I remember their faces like it was yesterday."

8

"I remember that case," said Spartan. "And you're right – it was a miracle no one else was hurt."

She nodded, waiting for Spartan to sign. "Like they say, the Lord works in mysterious ways."

"Amen." After signing and separating the receipts, Spartan slid over his business card along with her copy. While tucking his wallet away, he added, "If you happen to see him again, would you please give me a call?"

Watts elbowed his partner and pointed out the security camera. "No need for that," he said to the cashier. "Can we please speak to the manager?"

She hesitated, but then disappeared in the back. Moments later she emerged, grabbed a fresh coffee pot and made her rounds. Watts expected an older man would eventually step from the room, but instead a shapely woman in her late twenties appeared in a tapered white shirt and black slacks. Her nametag read Becky, but her expression looked as dull as the Hershey bar shine on her black pumps.

"I'm the manager," she said, keeping her clutched hands at her side. "May I help you?"

Watts raised his badge. "We're hoping your security tapes can identify two men who left within the last few minutes. There's no problem, but we'd like to talk to them. Your discretion would be greatly appreciated."

Becky eyed them warily. "What are they wanted for?"

Spartan adjusted his tie and smoothed his dark hair. "We're not at liberty to discuss that," he said. "We just need your cooperation."

She sighed and said, "Follow me."

Watts followed her into the office, squeezing into a corner so his partner could fit. Both detectives were physically fit, but the small space was barely adequate for one visitor. On Becky's desk, a split screen monitor showed live footage from four security cameras. In the top left corner was the cashier and a customer. Top right showed the back of the restaurant. Bottom left scanned the main dining area. Bottom right focused on the front door. Watts found this level of security extraordinary for a simple diner, but it made even less sense when no one was monitoring the images. Becky must have sensed his concern for she offered a quick explanation.

"Cameras can't stop robberies, shootings, or fraud, but their footage can help nail the bastards afterward. Cameras also help keep honest people honest. But let's face it, what's someone gonna steal from a diner besides money? Pancakes? Tableware? Napkins?"

Watts grinned, realizing she was right. She was much more attractive when she smiled back. "Becky, can you reset your video to thirty minutes ago? It shouldn't take long to see what we're looking for. Only a few people paid their bills during that time."

"No problem," she said, doing as he requested.

With all three of them watching the monitors, Watts had her stop the tape when Travis and Marv appeared. Looking at his partner he said, "If we can get these images to Forensics, Ms. Woods should have no problem identifying them." He shifted his gaze to Becky. "It's not her normal line of work, but she can do most anything to break a case. Can we borrow this?"

"No problem," she said, drafting a custody note. She blushed when her hand accidently slid over Watts' arm. "Sign this and it's yours."

"Thank you very much, Ms. —"

"Knolls," she said, handing him the DVD. "Becky Knolls."

"Well, Becky Knolls, we certainly appreciate your assistance."

"Anytime," she said, batting her eyelashes. "By the way, how was lunch?"

"Fine," said Watts, dropping the disk in his coat pocket. "I'll get this back as soon as possible."

"No rush."

She surprised him by waving as they left her office.

"Careful," Spartan whispered as they headed outside. "She has eyes for you, and Daisy wouldn't like that."

Watts chuckled at the irony of how many times he had warned Spartan about his own roaming eyes. Yes, Watts had noticed Becky's flirting, but this was hardly the same situation as a married man's gawking. Watts and Forensics Technician Daisy Woods had something special, and he wasn't going to blow it by philandering with a diner manager. Approaching their unmarked Crown Victoria, he said, "Trust me, Blaine, ever since Daisy came into my life, I've never had eyes for another woman."

Spartan's head spun around. "I hope so, Maxx, but by the time we left, Becky was like putty in your hands. You sure you weren't flirting with her?"

Watts didn't speak until they were in the car and his partner had closed his door. "Blaine, I was not flirting, and you know my heart belongs to Daisy. She's perfect in every way, and in the most literal sense, we see eye-to-eye."

"I see," said Spartan, fastening his seatbelt. "Then why can't you two make a commitment?"

Watts rolled his eyes. "Look, Blaine, you and Sandy have a great marriage and it shows in your kids, but it's complicated when both people work for the same police department. Besides, we've only been dating a few months."

"Translated, I assume that means you're not sleeping together."

Ignoring his partner's toothy grin, Watts twisted the key and gunned the engine. "Don't push it, pal. Let's get to the lab and find out who we're dealing with. While Daisy's doing her thing, I'm gonna see what the Scott Theater has to do with this case."

"Right – assuming there *is* a case."

"Exactly."

Three

Watts kept thinking about Daisy as he pulled into the police headquarters lot. She was perfect for him. Athletic build, not an ounce of fat, neatly trimmed cocoa brown hair, and in heels she might have a half-inch on him. He could live with that.

Headquarters was located at 350 Belknap in downtown Fort Worth, so the cops affectionately called it "350". Doing so saved air time because everyone understood what it meant. Every Fort Worth detective worked out of this building because of its central location. It helped that the forensics lab was in the basement. Otherwise, dating Daisy might not have been doable.

Watts had often invented reasons to see her, but today it was legitimate. As he approached the building's parking lot entrance, he tried to focus on his job more than his girlfriend. Travis' accusations made the Delouse hanging an extremely delicate matter, therefore probing into a closed case required extreme discretion. With his boss' fuse shorter than his inseam, he thought it would be best to wait until the case had merit before mentioning it.

Once inside 350, Watts headed directly to the lab while Spartan went upstairs to check his messages. Lately, the homicide business had been slow, but with Halloween fast approaching, it was only a matter of time before things went awry, and they'd be assigned another murder case.

Daisy beamed when Watts entered the room. Crossing her arms, she leaned over the counter showing more cleavage than usual. "Hello, detective. What brings you to the dungeon?"

"Interesting choice of words," he said. He then spent the next several minutes filling her in on the diner conversation about Jeremy Delouse and the Scott Theater, adding that theater personal referred to their basement as the dungeon. "So I'd like you to put a name and history to Travis and Marv so we can see if the old man's story has any merit."

She abruptly stood and stared at him like he was crazy. "Let me get this straight. You want me to run down two people who had lunch in a diner because they were talking about a suicide that occurred in 1970?"

Managing a straight face, Watts nodded. "Except Travis swore this guy was murdered, which is why it got our attention." When her bewildered expression never changed, he added, "Blaine was there, too. Call him if you don't believe me."

Then her stern expression melted like spring snow. "Fortunately, things are unusually slow right now," she said, taking the disc. "I'll see what I can do."

"Thank you, Ms. Woods. I really appreciate it."

Of course, sticking to formalities was a game because everyone in the building knew they were dating. However, since visitors and supervisors could drop by unannounced, they agreed it was better to keep up the charade than risk a reprimand. Watts left the lab without looking back, knowing he would be seeing her this evening, if not sooner.

He skipped up the stairs like a ten year old, and when he arrived at Spartan's cubicle, he found him staring at his computer screen. Standing behind his partner, Watts said, "Find anything interesting?"

Spartan glanced over his shoulder and then went back to his computer monitor. "I've been reading about the Scott Theater. Seems the suicide story is legit."

"What about the haunting?"

"Maybe. According to this article, a young actor named Jeremy Delouse hanged himself from a pipe in the theater's basement, and his ghost reportedly haunts the dungeon-like corridor where he died. One wardrobe woman got so frightened from unexplained noises she ran from the building screaming and never came back."

Watts smiled. "Old wood creaks and cracks as the temperature changes."

Spartan swung his chair around, looking annoyed. "Clearly, you've never been to the Scott Theater."

"Nope, can't say that I have."

"Well, it's right across from the Amon Carter Museum and its concrete structure means no wood-creaking noises."

Contemplating that, Watts grabbed a tissue from his pocket and blew his nose. After wadding it and tossing it in the trash, he said, "Since I'm the one that got us involved in this mess, I recommend we drop it and pretend it never happened."

Spartan's jaw dropped. "Are you serious? Right now we're at an all-time low for homicides so it's the perfect time to look into this. What could be better than a ghost story at Halloween?"

"Oh, I see what this is about. You want this for your kids, don't you?"

"No, not at all. I'm just saying this haunting has merit. Besides, why are you trying to back out after you got me interested?"

"Blaine, I just want to make sure you're willing to look as stupid as me, because this thing could get real complicated.

Spartan pursed his lips, rocking his chair hard. "I can't say I'm fond of your word choice, but yes, I am committed to this case." Pointing to his computer monitor, he added, "Anyway, an *Apparition Hunters* psychic named Marla Caine visited the theater as part of the supernatural investigative group. Having no prior knowledge of the theater's history, and having been born in 1974, she had no prior knowledge of Jeremy Delouse or his hanging. When she and the others met in the theatre to discuss their planned evening investigation, she almost immediately had visions of the play *My Fair Lady*. Soon after, her vision changed to the stage production of *Paint Your Wagon*, so that set the time period somewhere in the late 1960s or early 70s. She reportedly sensed a spirit was trying to show her this. She also felt the presence of young children, and sensed a lot of activity in the dungeon area, located directly below the stage. Though primarily used for storage, the dungeon also has rehearsal rooms."

Watts nodded, amused, but unconvinced. "Blaine, you do realize that anything can be published on the Internet, right? I mean, a well-written article about an 8.0 quake in Japan can convince people it could shift the Earth's axis and cause world climate change."

"Ah ha," said Spartan, looking unusually perturbed. "Anyway, Ms. Caine also sensed a male spirit she believed was once a janitor. According to the *Apparition Hunters* report, the suicide victim, actor Jeremy Delouse, could easily be mistaken as a janitor because he was also a stagehand, and stagehands do a variety of jobs including clean-up."

Watts grinned in disbelief. "Blaine, this is a great Halloween story, but I still don't believe in ghosts, and from what you're describing, it sounds like these investigators manipulated their findings to suit the myth. When did this so-called investigation take place?"

"*Apparition Hunters* was here in 2006."

"So, we're talking thirty-six years after Jeremy's death."

Spartan nodded. "That's how I add it up."

Watts stood there staring at the floor, his grin gone, no words coming to mind. His partner's disappointed look made it worse.

Spartan swiveled his chair and palmed his cheek. "Once again I must remind you that you were the one who got us into this, and now you mock me after I give you some legitimate information that supports what we overheard at the diner. So what gives, Maxx? Are you afraid to admit that ghosts really do exist?"

Watts wrinkled his face, disturbed by the question. "Ghosts don't scare me half as much as Captain Ryder. I mean, I've gotten away with pushing a lot of his buttons, but if all we have is hearsay and some bozo Internet reports, his bird's nest is really gonna flare."

Spartan's face suggested he was thinking about the bald spot on the back of Captain Ryder's head that once resembled a robin's nest. But stress and age had evolved it into an eagle's nest whose center turned red whenever Ryder got mad. Ryder had become so self-conscious about his bald spot that whenever Watts and Spartan were in the room, he avoided turning his back to them.

"I hear ya," Spartan finally said, tenting his hands. "And it's good to know you're looking out for us." He paused, gazing at nothing in particular. Slowly, his eyes drifted back to Watts. "What did your lady friend say about that surveillance video?"

First off, please don't refer to Daisy that way. Second, she said she'd work on it. Knowing her, we'll probably hear something in the next hour or so."

"She's a great catch, Maxx. I hope you two never break up."

Watts smiled. "I'll pass that on. Anything else you want to tell me about this Scott Theater and its ghost busters?"

"It's *Apparition Hunters*, Maxx – but then you already knew that."

"Oh, yeah."

"Anyway, listen to this," said Spartan, swiveling his chair to recite from the web article. "From 1967 to 1970, actor Jeremy Edward Delouse worked as a stage hand for the Fort Worth Community Theatre. After volunteering his services for two years, he was hired as a salaried employee. According to the *Fort Worth Star-Telegram*, Jeremy suffered from depression after his girlfriend broke up with him, probably around Christmas or New Year's. On January 15, 1970, Jeremy committed suicide in the dungeon hallway by hanging himself from a pipe." Spartan then swung his chair to meet his partner's gaze. "I think we should visit the theater so we can meet the spectral version of Mr. Delouse."

"Perhaps," said Watts, backing away. "Any idea if the theater's been remodeled since 1970?"

"That should be a matter of public record, since it would require a building permit."

Watts felt antsy and couldn't explain why. His hands felt cold so he stuffed them in his pockets. "Anything else we should know about Jeremy's spirit?"

Spartan returned to the article. "Many entities who died from taking their own lives still linger in this world because suicide didn't resolve their issues. In other words, they're still miserable after death."

"And who is saying this? Ghosts?"

"Maxx, I'm just the messenger. You really should read this article."

Watts skeptically leaned over his partner's shoulder to skim the report. When he finished, he stood as tall as his 69 inch frame allowed. "Is this the only story about Jeremy Delouse?"

Spartan shook his head and returned to a previously visited site. "This one claims some Scott Theater workers encountered cold spots in the dungeon area, and power tools turned themselves on in the equipment room. They also heard strange noises like thumps and footsteps. The area under the stage is a maze of hallways and rooms that frequently flood from spring rains, sometimes accumulating as much as a couple of inches of water. To clear the water, janitors push the water into the sump pump. One day, a worker was trying to squeegee water down the hall when he heard a loud bang as if someone slapped the door as he went by. The worker flung the door open to catch whoever was playing a joke on him, but no one was there and the water in the hall remained perfectly still."

Watts tossed his head back, willing himself not to laugh. "And you believe it?"

Spartan cast another angry gaze over his shoulder. "As I said, I'm just the messenger."

"Yeah, right. Anything else?"

"Actually, yes. They say Jeremy isn't the only spirit haunting the theater. Supposedly, the theater's namesake roams the halls straightening paintings, and there are also women and children spirits roaming, though no one can explain why."

Watts nodded, rubbing his chin. "So far we have women, children, the theater's namesake, and our suicidal janitor/actor. How about flying monkeys? Big Foot? Seabiscuit?"

"Mock me if you will, Maxx, but a lot of people have reported odd things, and since I have no idea what lies beyond our realm, I'm gonna keep an open mind."

Four

WHEN THE PHONE RANG, Watts quickly answered. He was expecting Daisy, saying she had the surveillance video results, but instead it was Captain Ryder. Had his boss somehow overheard their conversation, or did someone from the lab call him when they saw Daisy reviewing the videotape footage? Watts learned long ago never to volunteer anything, and he had never found a good reason to change. If his boss wanted to discuss the Ghost of Halloween Past, he would have to pry it out of him.

"Hey, captain," he innocently said. "What's up?"

"I have something that might interest you and your partner."

Not one to procrastinate under such circumstances, Watts said they would be right down. As he cradled the phone, he considered the captain's peculiar tone. He didn't sound upset, but he wasn't normal, either. Most importantly, whatever he was calling about didn't seem to concern the Scott Theater, and that eased his mind.

Tapping Spartan's shoulder, Watts said, "The boss wants to see us, and whatever you do, don't say a word about this ghost investigation. I'm dead serious about that, Blaine."

"Dead serious," Spartan repeated, chuckling. "Good one, Maxx."

"Whatever. Come on, let's go."

When they arrived at Ryder's office, Watts gently tapped on the glass door. Ryder looked up and promptly waved them in. Watts was nearly overcome by the smell as he stepped inside. His over-refined nose identified it as reheated Tex-Mex. Perhaps that was the reason for his boss's sour expression.

Ryder gestured for them to sit across from his desk and waited until they complied before speaking. "Maxx, I realize you have no love for Officer Mulberry, but he's on his way to the hospital with a gunshot wound. I thought you'd want to know."

A shot of adrenaline blasted Watts' veins. "Porgy's been shot?

Where? How? How bad?" His sudden concern for his nemesis surprised him.

"He'll be fine because his Kevlar vest protected him from what would have been critical wounds. He did take one in the shoulder, though. Went clean through from what I hear. The good news is the shooter was using roundheads instead of hollow points, so the damage wasn't as bad."

Watts looked stunned so Spartan spoke. "Who was the shooter? How did it happen?"

"Well, that's why I called you both in. You see, Officer Mulberry pulled a rust-bucket pickup over because its loud exhaust fit the description of the vehicle used to kidnap your Dairy Queen kid."

"Tony Fazelli," said Watts, cutting in.

"Yeah, Fazelli," said Ryder, tossing his hands up. "Anyway, Officer Mulberry reported the shooter was a muscular man with a shaved head, barbed wire tattoos on his arms, jeans, heavy boots and a white tee."

"That's the sonuvabitch, all right! And what about his buddy, Minnie Me?"

Ryder hiked his shoulders. "One man, one shooter, he got away. That's all I know."

"The shooter got away?" said Spartan, now equally red-faced. "In broad daylight?"

"Apparently. Anyway, now you know as much as me. And by the way, that doesn't mean you're on the Forest Park double murder case—"

"Which remains unsolved," said Watts, interrupting.

Ryder's chair squeaked as he leaned back. He pulled out a drawer to rest his foot while he eyed his detectives. "Two months is hardly a cold case, Maxx. Skip Parsons is still running down leads, and I want you to stay away from him because he's still fuming over the airport bust. But feel free to say hi to Porgy if you want. I figure since his shoulder wound is similar to yours, you might have something in common. Maybe now you can bury the hatchet."

Watts felt his skin warming. Although his history with Porgy could never be erased, he did notice that his disdain for him had been diminishing ever since he assisted him with Tony Fazelli in Forest Park. He quickly stood, hoping to be dismissed. "Anything else, captain?"

"Nope, that's it. Get back to work."

"Yes, sir."

Watts turned and walked out the door, annoyed at his left shoe. He didn't like its mushy sound, but its custom sole leveled his hips. Living pain-free should have overridden any embarrassment, but the noise always reminded him he was different.

"Are you okay?" said Spartan, struggling to keep up.

"Physically, yes. Mentally, not so much. Let's check out the river." From that, he expected Spartan would know he wanted to talk in private.

Watts headed outside and led his partner north on Taylor Street. It was a beautiful day for a walk. Now that the massive wildfires had been extinguished, the air was clear again. At a perfect seventy-two degrees, Watts was enjoying himself so much that he didn't want to speak. He spotted an empty bench overlooking the Trinity River and took a seat. Once Spartan joined him, he said, "Thanks for being patient, Blaine."

"No problem. Now would you mind telling me what's eating you?"

Watts snorted and swiped his index finger under his nose. "Hmm, where do I begin? First, the Skinheads that carved swastikas into Tony Fazelli's chest are either back or never left town. Then Barbed Wire shoots a patrol officer. Granted, I don't care much for Porgy, but I hate it when police officers get shot. Thank God he was wearing his Kevlar, but it still takes time to recover from a shoulder wound. Call me selfish, but I always figured I'd be the one who nailed those bastards. Either that or they'd nail me. If they were looking for me in Leroy, they wouldn't have a hard time finding me."

"I agree. There aren't many lifted green Dodge Ram monster trucks like Leroy."

"Hey, Leroy's one-of-a-kind, and his exhaust sounds way better than that rust bucket's."

Spartan shrugged. "Okay. Now that we've established that, what else is bugging you?"

Watts closed his eyes, bunched his fists, and arched his back. Twisting in both directions helped him relax. After lowering his arms and opening his eyes, he said, "Doesn't it bother you that Ryder is still distancing us from the Forest Park double murder case? I mean, if Skip and his cronies haven't figured it out by now, why not give it to us – especially since we have reason to believe Tony's kidnappers were involved?"

"No one's ever been able to prove that, Maxx. No DNA or

fingerprints. Only the similarity between Tony's wounds and the swastikas carved into those Chinese guys' chests. We've been through this a hundred times, and I'm sure you and Daisy have had private discussions about it. We're not in a position to get involved in that case, and the captain specifically said to stay away."

"Yeah. And that's what bothers me the most. But you're right. For now, all we can do is hope that someone nails Barbed Wire. Maybe the FBI will get involved now that one of our own's been shot. It shouldn't be that hard to find this pickup."

"I don't know," said Spartan, bending over to pick up a stone. He tossed it like a pitcher, but the drought-stricken tributary was so low it barely reached the water. He eased his back onto the bench and glanced at his partner. "It's one thing if a federal officer's been shot, but quite another when it's a lowly cowtown beat cop. I doubt the FBI will get involved."

Watts nodded and then tossed his own rock. His made it a third of the way across the river before it skipped. He figured the difference in distance was his pent-up frustration. "Blaine, you ever have one of those days where nothing makes sense?"

"Plenty," he said, searching the ground for another stone. "Why do you think I turned to drinking?" He tossed it, but it dropped well short of his partner's. He didn't pick up another one. Instead, he draped his arms over the seat back. "It took rehab to get my head straight and I've never craved beer since, but your problem has nothing to do with drinking. And before you start, you'd better accept the fact that the world is screwed up and nothing's fair."

Watts listened while picking up another rock. He let it fly and this time felt it in his shoulder. Though he was two years from forty, the strain made him feel old.

"Don't worry, Blaine. I'm not gonna hit the bottle, but I'd sure like to smash Barbed Wire's face. If he or his buddy had tried something stupid at the Dairy Queen, I could've taken them down, Tony Fazelli never would've been kidnapped and Porgy wouldn't have been shot."

"It's all shoulda', woulda', coulda', Maxx, and you can't change any of it. Look at the bright side. Porgy is so large the shooter couldn't tell he was wearing Kevlar. Good thing, too, because had he known, he might have shot him in the head."

"Noted. Besides, who couldn't use some time off? I can't imagine how many donuts Porgy will devour while he's recovering. If you think he resembles the Michelin Tire Man now, just wait until he's had a few weeks off without any exercise."

Spartan grinned, tossing a flat stone. This one skipped off a submerged rock and nearly reached the other side, and that made him smile. "I'm not sure exercise is even in Porgy's vocabulary." He picked up another stone and examined it. Holding it in his palm, he said, "Looks like a gold vein, doesn't it?"

"Yeah, but it's better off in the river. Only a fool would think it's real gold." Watts then stood and brushed off his pants. "You ready to head back?"

Spartan dropped his stone and got to his feet. "Ready when you are."

Once they were underway, Watts nudged his partner's back. "Thanks for listening, Blaine. I appreciate it."

"I'm always here for you, partner."

"I know, and so is Daisy. With luck, she will have identified Travis."

"Let's go find out."

Five

WHEN WATTS RETURNED TO his desk, he found a manila folder with a rubber band around it to keep it from coming open. The attached sticky note said, "You're welcome." Recognizing Daisy's handwriting, he picked it up and got Spartan's attention. "Let's find a room."

Spartan grinned looking over his shoulder. "Shouldn't you buy me lunch first?"

"Very funny. Let's go."

They found an empty interrogation chamber and closed the door for privacy. Although the room had been vacant for hours, the musty smell of sweat still lingered. Watts dropped the folder on the stainless steel table and sat in one of the two chairs in the room.

"Considering the sensitive nature of this case, I figured we'd be better off discussing this here. Hope you don't mind."

"Normally I wouldn't, but if Captain Ryder sees us in here, he may think we're working on the Forest Park murders against his orders."

"That's a risk we'll have to take," said Watts, examining the folder's contents. Inside, a divider separated the two men from the diner so he handed the info on Marv to Spartan and kept Travis for himself. "Computer recognition has identified the old man as Travis McLean, age 66, with no current address. The name matches what Marv called him at the diner. He served two years in the Army in Vietnam, was honorably discharged, and has no criminal record."

"Okay," said Spartan, preparing to read from his sheet. "It identified the other man as Fort Worth resident Marvin Delouse, age 42. He never served in the military, has no criminal record, no speeding violations, not even a parking ticket." Spartan set his paper aside and looked at Watts. "These guys are as exciting as milk toast. So, now what? Do we invite them to lunch?"

Watts grinned, staring at the cinderblock walls that were painted pale green to calm suspects. Perhaps that color choice worked on some people, but it seemed unlikely it would have any effect on a cold-blooded killer like Barbed Wire. He spotted smudge marks on the two-way mirror and soon realized they were from someone's lips. Apparently whoever was in there last was sending a message to the people watching from the other side. Watts pondered that for a moment. Criminals with nothing to lose will often play mind games on their victims to keep them from testifying against them. Then again, it could have been one of the detectives messing with the building's custodian. Stranger things have happened.

Spartan snapped his fingers. "Yo, Maxx. You still with me?"

Blinking brought Watts back. His mind alive again, he gathered his papers and tucked them back in the folder. "Before we talk to any persons of interest, we need to visit the Scott Theater to get a sense of what happened."

Spartan blew out a breath. "I seem to remember suggesting that a while ago so I'm all for it, but are you sure you don't want to find Travis McLean first?"

"First off, we don't have his phone number or address, so that could be difficult. Secondly, we tried talking to him at the diner and he took off, so no, I think we'll hit the theater first."

"Okay, so when do you want to go?"

"Now, assuming that there's someone to let us in. I'll call the theater and then see if Daisy wants to go with us. We could use her forensics expertise. Who knows what we'll find?"

Spartan rose and headed out the door. "I'll be at my desk."

Watts went back to his desk and searched on line for the W. E. Scott Theater. In seconds, he had a listing and map location. Before dialing, he read that William Edrington Scott, a descendent of a Tarrant County founding family, willed three million dollars to help develop Fort Worth's cultural district. Even though he died of lung cancer in 1961, five years later his dream was fulfilled when the doors to the five-hundred seat live theater named in his honor opened. Since Mr. Scott never saw his theater, it seemed unlikely that his spirit would linger there straightening its paintings, but as Spartan said, it was best to approach this with an open mind.

A woman with a smoker's voice answered the phone. She sounded like she was in her sixties, but he was wrong more often than not. Her bubbly enthusiasm weakened when he introduced himself as a homicide detective.

"What does this concern?" she anxiously said.

"A ghost tale," said Watts, expecting a chortle. Instead, there was only silence. "Before I go on, may I have your name?"

"I'm Betty Cerin, and your manner suggests you're not a believer. I assure you we take our hauntings seriously."

Watts was stunned. It seemed everyone picked up on that except him. The more he considered it, the more he questioned why he was wasting his time with Jeremy's death. Perhaps his oversensitive nose would benefit most from a theater visit. It had smelled death often, but that was usually within a few hours of a victim's demise. Unless some spirit was guiding him, it seemed unlikely he would smell anything of significance. He pushed the thought aside, listening to her breathing.

"So I hear," he said, recalling Marv's tale.

"Detective, I'm no expert, but several paranormal investigators have visited this theater over the years, and I've picked up on what they were saying. Every one of these people had different paranormal experiences. One of them went to a janitor's office after hearing a strange noise that sounded like a squeaky faucet turning. When he went in, the water was turned on, but no one was in the room, and he had entered through the only door. They also recorded a low voice saying, 'help us' as well as some unintelligible whispers. Their data confirmed it wasn't from anyone on their crew."

"Spooky," he said, trying to sound interested, even though it seemed remarkably close to what his partner had already told him.

"Oh, there's more," she said. "They also took photos of manifestations in several places. They called them orbs, which I believe is an energy ball. Some orbs were in dressing rooms while others were spotted in the theater. They also recorded a voice saying, '*Let me out of here.*' Mind you, the investigative group was careful not to make assumptions and quickly pointed out a nearby vent which may have influenced their readings. They left saying it was virtually impossible to assure that what they *believe* these voices were telling them were actual words or sentences."

"And yet *you* believe them."

"Yes, I do, actually."

She started coughing. When it continued for several seconds, Watts grew concerned. Finally, she cleared her throat and resumed her spiel.

"Detective, I'm not a tour guide, and we don't use this theater as a haunted house. I'm only telling you this because I've met so many non-believers that I feel compelled to share our spirits' stories."

"I'm still listening, Betty."

He was taking notes now, not that his beliefs had changed, but they might be of benefit during his theater visit.

"Well, the investigative team also found some unusual EMF readings just outside the janitor's closet."

"EMF readings?"

"I'm sorry. I'm used to talking in abbreviations. EMF stands for Electro Magnetic Field readings. Scientists believe that virtually everything in life emits high-level EMF readings. They use Milligauss Meters, commonly referred to as mG meters, to measure these magnetic fields, or more technically their flux density. MG meters can detect up to several times the strength of Earth's field. Ghosts tend to be in the 1.5 to 6.0 mG range"

"Wow," said Watts, clicking his pen, eager to meet this woman. "Betty, are you sure you're not an expert?"

She laughed. "Hardly. I just know how to listen."

Watts smiled. "Sorry," he said. "Please continue."

"Thank you. Now, where was I?"

"You were talking about mG readings."

Following a brief pause, she said, "Frankly, I'm not sure where I was going with that other than to say these investigators used digital meters in addition to taking video and audio recordings."

She cleared her throat again. Watts hoped it was due to allergies and not cancer. Tempted as he was, he didn't ask.

"Oh, now I remember," she said, sounding happier. "I was telling you how investigators always use disclaimers, like how blowing vents can also influence the mG readings. But nothing has explained the popping and clanking noises they recorded in the dressing rooms and stage areas. They did state the musty smells in the basement probably came from rainwater seepage. You know how fierce those Texas gully-washers can get."

"Yes, I do. I've heard of storms washing cattle away."

"Me, too, but storm phenomena are different from Electronic Voice Phenomena, or EVPs. Most investigators don't hear EVPs while they're in the field, but instead pick them up on playback. After ruling out other possibilities, paranormal investigators believe EVPs are spirits trying to communicate with the living. Ever since the investigators told me this, I've been hooked on those paranormal TV shows. Granted, they ham it up, but they consistently say the same things so they must have some merit. Of course, I have no idea what any of their qualifications really are.

"I do remember them mentioning an EVP that sounded like a woman saying, '*It's cold again*' in the Green Room, and then another EVP saying the same thing in a whisper. Yet another said, '*Come back*', and there were whispers they believed said '*noose*' and '*murder*', though they were less certain of them. They also photographed several orbs in a rehearsal room as well as in the shop area, although subsequent investigators have disputed these orbs as being dust spots on the camera's lens. Anyway, in the theater, they captured an EVP saying '*Raven*' in a haggard voice. Raven was the name of an actress from the theater's early years so any spirits inhabiting the area from that time period would have known her.

"The costume shop produced whispers too faint to be understood, but they recorded strong EMF readings in the 1.5 to 2.0 region at the waist-high level. Those numbers increased to over ten as they lowered the meter to the floor. They could never explain these readings, particularly at the floor level, but some believed the pipes in the floor may have affected the numbers. Still, they only found those readings in one small area of the costume shop.

"When they ascended the stairwell from the dungeon to the stage's left, they recorded an EVP of an unintelligible woman's voice a couple of times. In the stage area, they photographed several more orbs. I'll be the first to admit this theater has its share of naysayers, detective, and I've never personally heard or seen a spirit, or knew of one interfering with a live performance, but there is certainly ample proof of spectral events here at the Scott Theater."

Watts smiled into the phone, scanning his notes. "Betty, I'm amazed at your recall. I can barely remember what I did last week. Is there a time when my partner and I can tour the theater? We're in the process of conducting an informal investigation, and I'm reluctant to say any more about it until it has merit."

She paused as if looking at her calendar. "If you'd like to come by today, I'll be here until six."

"That's perfect. Let's shoot for two o'clock. I'll let you know if we're running late."

"Sounds good. And I won't mention this to our spirits. I wouldn't want to spook them."

Watts chuckled. "Thanks, Betty. See you soon."

Six

As soon as Watts ended the call, he went into his partner's cubicle. He stood there for a moment, watching Spartan's fingers hammer the keyboard. Still unnoticed, he wondered if these spirits Betty spoke of shared his frustration of invisibility. He even squished his shoe a couple of times by rocking back and forth, but apparently his partner had become so accustomed to the noise that he no longer paid attention. Spartan finally turned around when he loudly cleared his throat. He looked surprised, but not startled.

"We have an appointment at the Scott Theater at two," said Watts. "I'm gonna see if Daisy can come along to help search the suicide site. Whatever we find will determine whether we pursue this case."

Spartan moved his mouth to one side, seemingly considering the options. Finally, he said, "As intriguing as this is, what can you possibly hope to find at a site from so many decades ago?"

Watts placed his finger over his mouth, weighing Betty's and his partner's comments. It took several seconds to formulate a response. Finally, he said, "Who knows what we'll find, but the woman from the Scott Theater is convinced that ghosts reside there, and if that's the case, why wouldn't Jeremy Delouse be among them?"

Spartan raised a brow and then lifted his head to stare at the ceiling. He didn't do this often, but when he did, it either meant he wasn't convinced, or he didn't like the plan. In this sense, it was his polite way of saying, *You're on your own, Maxx.*

"Come on, Blaine. Spit it out. What's on your mind?"

Spartan's expression never changed, even when his gaze dropped from the ceiling to find Watts.

"I was thinking about Captain Ryder, wondering what face he'll make when he gets wind of this. What color his bird's nest will be should he dare turn his back on us. Of course, there's always the possibility he'll break into a hysterical laugh. If that happens, he'll probably give us time off without pay for being so gullible."

Watts hiked his shoulders and showed his palms. "It's okay, Blaine. You can stay behind, but I have an appointment to keep, and as best I recall, there's no statute for murder."

Spartan's eyes narrowed. "Thanks for the reminder."

Hearing his partner's sarcasm made Watts realize he had been skeptical until he spoke to Betty Cerin. Then he realized he should have asked for her maiden name. He was getting sloppy. But since she was neither a witness nor a person of interest, asking that might have turned her off. God, he hated second-guessing himself! Feeling his ears warm, he said, "So, are you in or not?"

Spartan tossed his hands in the air. "Sure, why not? I haven't heard a good ghost story since I was a kid at a campfire."

"Good. Now here's the deal, and I don't even know if she can come yet, but if Daisy is with us, don't say a word about this case. I need her there as a forensics technician without any preconceived notions. Got it?"

"Got it. But how are you going to explain this to her? So far, you've asked her to identify people without giving a reason, and now you want her to visit the Scott Theater with us. It's just a thought, but you might be better off asking her to a theater performance and then snoop around while you're there."

Watts adamantly shook his head. "You can't mix pleasure with business, partner, although you deserve some brownie points for thinking that up. I'm afraid I'm still learning about this dating thing. Fortunately, she's as naïve as me. Anyway, I'm gonna call her to see if she can go. Let's plan on leaving at 13:40."

"Okay, one-forty it is. Should I bring a cross or wear garlic?"

"Funny, Blaine, but we're chasing ghosts, not vampires."

Spartan's impish grin told Watts he had been duped. Without further comment, Watts turned his back on him and went to his desk to call the lab. Daisy didn't answer the phone, but after a brief pause she came on the line. He spoke as if his conversation was being recorded, which for all he knew, it was.

"Ms. Woods," he said. "Detective Spartan and I need to visit the Scott Theater this afternoon, and I was hoping you could accompany us. We're checking out whether a murder may have occurred there in 1970. It's unlikely we'll find anything, but I'd like you to look for any forensics evidence that might give this rumor some merit."

"Let me check my schedule and I'll call you back."

"Thanks. I'd appreciate that."

Watts hoped her "check-her-schedule" response was because someone was nearby. Ever since their co-workers learned they were dating, it was critical that they maintained their professionalism. Neither needed any accusations of them flirting while on duty. Of course, in a very real sense, having Spartan nearby had the same effect on romance as a garlic necklace.

Daisy called back ten minutes later saying she could take a couple of hours off. To minimize rumors, Watts told her to meet them at the Crown Vic. It seemed unfair to be so secretive when the department employed several married couples, but thoughts of marriage weren't on Watts' horizon. Wishing everyone would mind their own damned business, he tapped on Spartan's thin cubicle wall. "Blaine, Daisy's gonna meet us at the car in a few minutes. Are you at a good stopping point?"

Spartan stopped what he was doing to glance over his shoulder. "Ready when you are."

"Okay. I'm gonna hit the head. I'll be right back."

By the time Watts returned, Spartan had shut down his computer and was leaning against his desk, arms crossed, gun bulging from his waistline. He looked eager to go, checking his watch twice before Watts managed a word.

"So, you ready to chase ghosts?"

"Absolutely," he said, pushing himself from the desk. "Let's go."

Soon after Watts had unlocked the Crown Victoria, Daisy climbed into the back seat and set her kit bag on the floor. The temperature inside the car was quite warm, so he rolled down the windows for ventilation.

Spartan looked over his shoulder at her. "Hey, Daisy. How are ya?"

"Fine," she tartly said, her tone suggesting she wasn't thrilled about being there. So long as it was just the three of them, they agreed to address each other by their first names. She leaned over the front seat to look at Watts. "I'm still not clear on what you expect me to find some forty years after this guy's death. Don't get me wrong, I'm happy to get out of the office, but this seems a bit of a stretch. What's Captain Ryder's take on this?"

Her question pierced him like an arrow. Clearly, she knew him too well. Perhaps this was why couples shouldn't work together. "While Captain Ryder is aware we are looking into a possible murder, he doesn't know many details because we haven't had anything worth passing on. Thankfully, things are amazingly slow, especially for being so close to Halloween, but that's why we have time to check this thing out."

When she finished running her fingers through her hair, she shrugged and looked up. "Oh, what the hell? I'm in."

From the way she said it, Watts knew he was better off driving than debating. At times Daisy could be moody, but he wouldn't know what was bothering her today until after work. He calmly set the car in gear and drove out of the lot.

It didn't take long to reach the community arts center where sunlight bleached the Scott Theater's walls. Stylish and definitely sixties, whoever designed the building certainly borrowed from Frank Lloyd Wright. Watts figured he should take Daisy to a play there some night. He wondered if she was thinking the same thing as they headed toward its entrance.

To make identification easy, Watts made sure his badge was visible as they walked inside. An attractive gray-haired woman immediately approached them with her hand extended.

"You must be Detective Watts," she said, shaking his hand. "I'm Betty Cerin. We spoke on the phone."

Her body was thin, her hand cool and limp, but her smile was warm. Her features had softened with age, but her blue eyes still shined. He gently shook her hand and said, "It's nice to meet you, Betty. This is my partner Detective Spartan and Forensics Technician Woods. I doubt we'll find anything, but could you give us a tour and show us where Mr. Delouse ended his life?"

"Of course," she said, leading them down the carpeted foyer toward the stairway.

Watts appreciated her slow pace, for it allowed him time to take in the theater. Drawing in a breath through his nose, he smelled spilt wine and a variety of cleaning solutions, but no death. He didn't know what ghosts smelled like, but after sniffing in every direction and detecting nothing unusual, he assumed none were stalking him.

"Betty, on the phone you mentioned you hadn't seen any ghosts or heard any unexplained words, but have you ever experienced any chills or weird smells? Maybe had some kind of premonition?"

She stopped and turned to look at him. "I suppose that depends on your context, detective. I've experienced chills on a pier overlooking a foggy San Francisco Bay, and weird smells often emit from chemical warehouses and oil refineries. I've also had premonitions of bad things happening that came true, but I'm not sure where you're going with this. Exactly what do you mean?"

Her question caught him off guard. He wasn't expecting an elderly lady to be so sarcastic. Unsure whether to smile or frown, his lips chose something in between. His partners' expressions suggested he was on his own.

"I was simply referring to any odd things you might have experienced here."

Smiling knowingly, Betty started walking again, her chin held high. "Detective, thousands have walked these floors and most have experienced nothing more than whatever event they came to see. This is because our spirits choose who they want to contact. They know who is receptive and who isn't. They don't wander the halls wearing sheets or manifest themselves in ghastly forms to scare people. I have no idea how many spirits live here, but I do know they exist. Whether I've communicated with them or not is neither important nor pertinent. What matters is that you leave here with the answers you were seeking."

While contemplating her response, Daisy chimed in to keep the momentum going. "Betty, is it possible to have some alone-time in the area where the suicide occurred once we've toured the building?"

Once more, their guide stopped and turned around. "If you're hoping that Jeremy Delouse will say hi, you'll probably be gravely disappointed because most hauntings have either occurred close to the curtain calls or well after hours." With a stiff face, she added, "Personally, I don't like the term *haunting* because it implies evil spirits. I assure you I would have left a long time ago if any fit that category."

Spartan smiled, scanning the interior. It appeared he was going to say something, but then shook it off and tucked his hands in his pockets.

Daisy ignored him by looking at their hostess. "I'm sorry, Betty, but I'm not sure if that was a yes or a no to my question."

Watts raised a brow, concerned that Daisy might have offended their theater guide.

Betty's smile broadened. "To answer your question, yes, I will arrange for whatever it takes to satisfy your curiosity. I'll also make sure you know where the light switches are, but be aware that darkness and preconceived notions can trick your mind into believing things that don't actually exist. You may also find yourself so drawn into this that you are convinced you made contact with a spirit. You may even dream about it when you're asleep, but that doesn't make it real. As I said, the chances of you making contact, or hearing or sensing something unusual is as likely as you winning the lottery."

Daisy stared hard before allowing a smile. "I'm sure you're right, Betty. We do appreciate your cooperation."

Spartan hunched over with his arms folded. "Betty, I'm curious, and I ask this is only because you seem to avoid answering the question, but have you had any unusual encounters that you aren't willing to discuss?"

Through narrow eyes, she said, "I've already stated that my experience here is of no consequence. Feel free to explore the theater for as long as you like. There aren't any performances tonight, so should you care to return after we close for the evening, let me know and I'll make arrangements for our custodian to let you in." She then struck a pose with her hands raised to the ceiling and gazed at the three of them. "Like water finding its way to the sea, so shall you in your quest for the truth. That was one of my favorite sayings when I was young. I hope that answered your question."

Spartan moved his mouth from side to side, nodding. "Yes, ma'am."

Betty spent the next few minutes leading them through the building, during which time no one experienced anything unusual. The air was heavy, the only sounds coming from their shoes. More than once, Betty looked over at Watts' shoe, trying to discern why it made noise when he walked. Seeing no point in explaining, Watts kept quiet. He was ready to head back when Daisy asked if they could return to the scene of the hanging.

"We'd also like to be left alone," she added.

Betty calmly looked at her, palms together, fingers intertwined. "Certainly, dear. You know the way. My only request is that you check back with me before I leave."

Watts smiled. "Thank you, Betty. We appreciate your help." He moved closer to Daisy to nudge her out of the way, but Daisy stood her ground, her finger pressed against her lips. She didn't speak until Betty was walking away.

"Before you go, can we get a ladder that can reach the dungeon's ceiling? I'd like to check out the pipe where Jeremy hanged himself."

Sporting a parliamentary smile, Betty turned once more. "Certainly, dear. I'll send someone down to help with that. Anything else?"

"Actually, some flashlights would be helpful, too."

"I'll see what I can do."

Watts was confused. On their dates, Daisy was so gracious and kind, but today she was like a machine. While he valued her forensics expertise, her harsh tone was unexpected. Seeing this side of her took him outside of his comfort zone. Perhaps this was why the department frowned on co-workers dating.

Seven

It was logical that Daisy wanted to return to the scene of the hanging. After all, that's why she came along. But Betty had also warned that the dungeon could muddle minds, and it didn't help when one of the two hall light bulbs blew after they turned on the wall switch. Watts tentatively moved forward into the dimly-lit space, realizing his anxiety stemmed more from watching horror movies than any real danger. Nothing had changed in the dungeon since Betty had given her tour, but it felt different now that she was gone. Watts' shoe seemed louder, and his heart throbbed in his ears, but he, Daisy and Spartan walked the hall like the Tin Man, Dorothy and the Cowardly Lion.

Sliding his palm along the concrete walls as he walked, Watts wondered how many times this area had been used as a tornado shelter. Did people huddle here when the big twister ripped through Fort Worth several years ago? If so, whoever was here probably never heard a thing.

He didn't recall the air smelling as musty when Betty was giving her tour, but at the time, he was paying more attention to her describing Jeremy's hanging. Now looking around, he feared the dungeon's lack of windows could turn this place into a death trap should fire break out. Along the way, he felt several reference points that could help them escape in the dark.

Spartan was also palming the wall, but his actions were more like he expected his hand to pass through it. Watts smiled, figuring he had been watching too much *Harry Potter* with his kids. He eased closer to Daisy.

"Any thoughts?" he said to her, breaking the silence. At the time, he thought it was a neutral question. He was wrong.

Arms crossed, her eyes traced the overhead pipe that ran perpendicular to the corridor. When she finished, she looked at Watts. "Yes, detective, I have several thoughts."

"*Detective?*" he said, tilting his head sideways.

Her eyes quickly returned to the pipe. "Isn't that what you are? A *detective*?" She paused to exhale loudly. "Geez Louise, how long could it possibly take to get a ladder?"

Her terse demeanor surprised him. He had never seen her like this. Was it PMS or the dim light that was making her so irritable? Then again, maybe an evil spirit had taken over her body. As soon as that thought surfaced, her head angrily snapped around as if she had read his thought. He moved as close as he dared, keeping his voice low so Spartan couldn't hear.

"Daisy, are you okay? You seem edgy."

"I'm *fine*."

With her words warning like a rattler's tail, he took a step back. "Okay, well the maintenance man should be here soon. Remember, Blaine and I are here to help, not hinder you."

"I hope so – on both counts."

The approaching footsteps ended their conversation. At first they were barely audible, but as they intensified, a door creaked, and then came a loud *bang!* As the indiscernible shadow slowly emerged, there was another *clank*, and then the ladder's silhouette became identifiable.

As Watts' heart raced, Spartan and Daisy grinned like they had known it was the maintenance man all along. He smiled back and was about to comment when a husky voice came from down the hall.

"Did someone ask for a ladder and flashlights?"

"Yes sir," said Watts. "We're in the hallway."

The shadow nodded, unfolded the ten-foot ladder, and left it several yards from where they were standing. After setting the flashlights on the floor, the voice said, "When you finish, leave the flashlights here and I'll put everything back. No need to fold the ladder."

"Thank you," said Watts, as the shape merged with the darkness. Only when he was gone did Watts realize he never saw the man's face. Whether he had intentionally hid behind the ladder or not was difficult to say, but it was a moot point now. Watts quickly returned his attention to his partners.

"Well, now that we have a ladder and flashlights, shall we check out this pipe?"

Already working her hands into a pair of Latex gloves, Daisy didn't answer. Instead, she grabbed the ladder and positioned it under the pipe. After pulling some things from her kit, she slid her wrist through her flashlight cord and ascended the ladder. Watts and Spartan quickly moved on either side to steady it.

Looking up, they watched her lean into the pipe and examine it from various angles. The ladder creaked, but no one paid attention. As she moved to different angles, her light beam sabered the walls and ceiling.

"Well?" said Watts. "You see anything?"

"Dust and spider webs, which I doubt are the same ones from forty years ago." She let her flashlight dangle from its strap and clung to the ladder while she looked down at them. "Frankly, I'm not sure what I'm supposed to find, but before I touch anything, how about turning off the hall light so I can see better?"

"You got it," said Spartan, heading for the light switch.

"God, it's cold in here," she said, aiming her flashlight beam down the pipe. Then suddenly everything went dark. "Stop it!" she angrily yelled.

While Spartan ran for the light switch, Watts looked at Daisy. "Stop what?"

Still clinging to the pipe with her head inches from the ceiling, she fired a gaze at Watts. "You touched my thigh!"

Watts made a face at Spartan who was now near his side. In response, Spartan hiked his shoulders, saying nothing. Watts then gave Daisy a curious look. "Would you mind showing me where I supposedly touched you?"

Grabbing her thigh an inch below her buttocks, she said, "Right here, you pervert."

"Okay, that's enough. First, this is an official police investigation and I would never touch you or anyone else inappropriately. Second, the only way I could touch you there is if I had climbed the ladder, and since I never moved from this spot, that makes it impossible. Third, you're the one who turned off your flashlight, so what's going on here? You've been acting strange ever since we arrived."

Rather than answer, she toyed with her flashlight, flicking the switch on and off. As expected, the beam properly reacted to the switch position. "I swear I never turned it off."

In unison, they both looked at Spartan; he promptly raised his palms. "Hey, don't look at me," he said. "I was nowhere near the ladder when she yelled."

"And if I had moved," added Watts, " you both would have heard my shoe, which as you can see, is still attached to my foot."

Spartan rested a hand on the ladder. "So what are you suggesting, Maxx? That this was our first ghost encounter?"

Watts stared at his feet, having similar thoughts. "I won't even go there, Blaine. Most likely her Chinese-made flashlight cut out." A couple of breaths later, he said, "Daisy, exactly what did it feel like?"

"Cold, like a hand that had been skiing or shoveling snow. I had goose bumps."

He nodded, extending his hand toward her. "Take it."

She held it for a brief moment and then climbed down to sit on the lowest step. When she buried her head in her hands, Watts moved in to console her, his arm around her shoulder.

"Hey, kiddo, you're worrying me. You want to get out of here?"

Slowly, she lifted her head toward Spartan and then twisted it to see Watts. In the process, her neck popped. "I don't scare easily, Maxx. I was leaning against the ladder and the only thing near it was you, so if this wasn't your idea of a Halloween prank, what touched me?"

Once more, silence hung like the plague. Were the spirits mocking them? "I have no idea, Daisy, but if a ghost was responsible, then it must have a sense of humor."

Spartan loudly cleared his throat. "How about if I turn off the lights again, everyone keeps their flashlights ready, and we'll see if anything bizarre happens."

Watts was the first to answer. "I'm game, but first let's space ourselves at least ten feet apart."

"I agree," said Daisy. "And everyone stays clear of the ladder."

"Sounds good." Spartan then took his position near the light switch.

Daisy and Maxx moved five feet from the ladder in opposite directions, with Daisy being the farthest away from Spartan. Once Daisy raised her thumb, Watts nodded and everything went dark. At first no one said a word. Under total darkness, five minutes passed. Then ten.

"Is it me, or does it feel cold in here?" said Daisy.

Suddenly, the ladder squeaked.

"What was that?" said Spartan, cycling the light switch.

Still five feet from the ladder, Watts and Daisy stared in astonishment.

"This is creepy," she said. "Leave the damn lights on."

"I concur," said Watts. "Anyone ready to leave?"

"Hell, no! I said it was creepy, but I'm not giving up right when it's getting interesting." She then turned to Spartan. "Blaine, could you get me some wet paper towels from the restroom so I can clean this pipe?"

"Sure." He quickly took off.

Watts met Daisy at the ladder. "Did anything touch you this time?"

She shook her head, shaking the ladder. "I would have screamed bloody murder if anything had." The ladder squeaked, but it was a different sound from before. "What would make this thing squeak when no one was near it?"

"I have no idea, but twice you've mentioned the cold and I've never felt it. Are you feverish?"

She backed away from the ladder, gawking at it. "No, Maxx, I'm fine. And thanks for bringing me along. This is turning out to be very interesting. It's like being in a carnival fun house, only more captivating. There must be a logical explanation for this."

Her comment took him back to his first and last fun house experience where ghouls and zombies clawed him in the darkness. He hated it, but this was completely different. Here, they were experiencing real unexplainable spectacles. Thinking about that, he blinked a couple of times, fearing the next time the lights cycled off and then on, he might see a body hanging from the bar.

Knowing nothing about his thoughts, Daisy climbed the ladder again. Curiously, it didn't squeak until she was three steps from the top. From there, she surveyed the space for any vents that could have blasted air over the ladder to cause it to move.

"There's nothing here except empty space and stale air."

Watts nodded, watching her. "Well, if Jeremy's responsible for the noises, it's too bad he won't show himself."

"I agree. At least then we might know if it was murder or suicide."

"Jeremy Delouse," said Watts, seeking the ghost. "Are you here? Can you show yourself?"

"I don't know about Jeremy," said Spartan, emerging from a room, "but I'm here with paper towels."

Daisy dropped a few steps to grab the cleaning supplies, thanked him, and then scaled it to clean the pipe. Soon, dust clumps were dropping like bat guano. With the ladder positioned in the center of the hall, she could only reach a few feet in either direction, but they all agreed it was sufficient since that's where the hanging most likely occurred. With the pipe now clean, she was ready to examine it.

Looking down on them, she said, "Before I get too far into this, how do we know this is the same pipe from 1970?"

Good point. Scratching his chin, Watts looked for his partner. Once more, Spartan responded by shrugging his shoulders and showing his palms. Taking that to mean silence was safer than suggesting they were in over their heads, he said, "All things considered, I think Betty would have told us if it had been replaced. For now, let's assume it's original. We'll confirm it later."

She nodded as she shined her flashlight on the clean section of the rusty pipe. "I'm really not sure how to proceed with this, guys. I mean, there won't be any fingerprints now that I've wiped it down, and I don't have any dye with me, not that there's anything to see. Did either of you review Jeremy's case file? I mean, surely the police would have noted anything unusual."

Spartan looked at his partner. This time, it was Watts who was showing palms, so he glanced back at Daisy. "I can't speak for Maxx, but I haven't seen Jeremy's file."

Watts stared at the floor, avoiding Daisy's *you've got to be kidding me* look. When he figured it was safe, he said, "Remember that we're only here to look around, but as long as our schedule permits, I'd like to resolve this. I hate having people think cops bury evidence."

"I agree, but what do we tell Captain Ryder?"

Watts thought for a long moment. To brief Ryder now would be like walking over hot coals, and he was pretty sure that would ruin his custom shoes. His partners were waiting, so he said the first thing that came to mind. "We'll talk to him when we're ready."

Eight

WATTS WOULD NEVER ADMIT it, but he found the dungeon creepy. Betty Cerin still had ninety minutes on her shift, so there was no reason to hurry, but their echoing footsteps and the thought of facing Captain Ryder raised the hair on his neck.

"Guys, I think we've done all we can until we can devise a solid plan. Daisy, I need you to find a dye that can reveal rub marks on steel that might not have been available in 1970, and Blaine, I need you to examine Jeremy Delouse's file and determine whether his hanging could have been staged. With luck, Jeremy's death photos will confirm this is the right location and it's still the original pipe. I'll be running background checks on Marv Delouse and Travis McLean. Any questions?"

He was relieved when none came.

When they arrived at 350, they dispersed to their respective work stations. Watts settled at his desk and turned on his computer. Finding information on Marv Delouse was easy. He quickly learned he was employed as a loan officer, had never been married, and had no outstanding warrants. Travis McLean was a different story. His last known address was in Fort Worth, he was a Vietnam vet with two campaign medals and a Purple Heart, and his driver's license expired over three decades ago. Since then, everything was blank as if Travis no longer existed. Without Marv's assistance, finding him would be a challenge.

Marv told them Jeremy Delouse was his uncle, but he never mentioned his parents. Then again, with their time short, it was hardly a complete interview. Reviewing his Sony's recording from the diner helped formulate more questions, but they would be worthless if Marv didn't volunteer answers. Based on their last encounter, Watts had little faith that would happen.

Feeling like he hit a wall, Watts checked his watch and realized it was quitting time. While locking everything in his desk, he considered himself lucky that Ryder hadn't contacted them all day. He got up and stepped into Spartan's cubicle where his partner was studying images on his computer. Watts gently tapped his cubicle's siding.

"It's quitting time, Blaine. You ready to head home?"

Spartan checked the time and then glanced over his shoulder. "Guess it is that time. You have any luck with your research?"

"Not really. One's a banker, the other a drifter. One's easy to find and not talkative, the other may as well be a ghost."

Spartan nodded, sliding on his coat. "Doesn't sound very promising. Any thoughts on Captain Ryder?"

"Yeah, we'll ignore him. If he wants an update, he knows where to find us."

"Okay, but what about Daisy?"

"Different boss, and I haven't heard of any problems."

"No problems? Really?"

Watts frowned. "I meant she didn't allude to any problems with her boss. As for why she was in such a foul mood today, I have no idea. It's not like her."

Spartan chuckled. "Welcome to the real world, Maxx. It's easier to give women space than to understand them. If you see her tonight, go easy on her. Push the wrong buttons and she might kick your ass."

Watts thought for a moment. Although he had shot and killed a woman before, Dad taught him to never strike one, so if Daisy wanted his ass, it was hers to kick.

"Judging from her mood this afternoon, I'm not sure she even wants to see me again."

"Oh, please," said Spartan, sliding his chair under his desk. He then took a moment to adjust his tie and button his coat. "Maxx, I can't tell you how to live your life, but I will say you need to learn some empathy. It doesn't matter whether you and Daisy end up together or you find someone else, everyone always has good days and bad. Good partners provide balance, even when things get ugly and you're both in foul moods. With women, you're usually better off admitting you've had a rough day so they know to give you some space." He drew in a breath and blew it out like he was dousing a candle. "What I'm trying to say is, don't let today's events ruin your chances with Daisy. That dungeon has some strange vibes. I think we were all a bit on edge."

Watts stood there gazing at his partner. Not long ago Spartan was drowning his sorrows in booze, but with the department's and his

42

wife's support, he overcame his addiction and found new love in his marriage. His experience gave his advice merit so Watts took it in, but he still needed to confront Daisy to see what was bothering her.

"Thanks for your concern, Blaine. Have a good night."

"Anytime, partner."

Rather than head to his truck, he went downstairs to check on Daisy and was surprised to learn she left ten minutes ago. The news stung, for over the last two months she had never once left without calling him first. Making the assumption that she didn't want to talk to him, he kicked some pebbles on the way. He climbed into Leroy and thought about what his partner had said. Maybe there wasn't a problem, and a message would be waiting by the time he got home. Clinging to that thought made it easier to drive off the lot. Killing his radio gave him time to reflect, and his thoughts returned to the theater. Betty had warned the dungeon could twist minds, and Spartan's comment tended to support that. Still, they all heard the ladder squeak and Daisy swore something touched her thigh, so as far as he was concerned, the dungeon was haunted. Oddly, these strange events only increased his cohorts' determination, and while thinking he might be the odd man out, Daisy phoned.

"Maxx!" she frantically said. "I need you here—now!"

He had no time to react before the phone went dead.

Nine

WATTS GUNNED LEROY'S ENGINE and peeled onto the street, his heart pumping faster than his truck's pistons. His white knuckles squeezing the wheel, he couldn't imagine what was wrong. Staying alert for patrol cars, he weaved through the commuter traffic, still hearing the fear in Daisy's voice.

He spotted Daisy the moment he pulled into her parking lot. Even before she climbed in, he could see tears streaming down her cheeks. Thinking that one of her parents had died, he released his seat belt and leaned over to calm the waves that were rippling through her body. A horn honked and he checked his mirror. Only then did he realize he was blocking the entry to her apartment complex. Waving an apology, he moved his truck and the car zoomed past. Now parked in a legal spot, he killed the engine and cracked his windows open to allow some air.

Years ago he might have said something like "what's wrong" or "are you all right" and whoever he was with would have smacked him. But he remembered one of his old flames telling him, "Sometimes I just need a hug." That seemed like pretty good advice, so he held her until she backed away knowing she would speak when she was ready.

It took some time before she regained her composure, and even though she wasn't talking, he forgot his own problems. When they parted, she held onto his arms and laughed nervously as she wiped her running mascara.

"I must look hideous."

It seemed any answer could lead to trouble, so he quietly lifted Leroy's console lid and offered a tissue, which she gladly accepted. She went through five tissues before clutching a spare. Finally, she seemed ready to speak.

"Thank you for coming over."

"You know I'm always here for you, Daisy, although you scared the hell out of me."

"I'm sorry," she said, her eyes slowly meeting his. "Can we get some coffee?"

Considering her smeared makeup and tousled hair, her request surprised him. Not that she was a fussy woman, but she always looked meticulous in public. Her frazzled appearance didn't disturb him half as much as the panic in her voice.

"I'll take you wherever you like, but first tell me what you're running from."

Staring at the floor, she snickered sarcastically. "Oh, yeah. I forgot you're a detective."

She stopped talking after that. She briefly glanced at her apartment and then looked back at her feet. Watts figured if the tissue in her hand had been a chunk of coal, she would have squeezed it into a diamond. But once more he did the smart thing by leaning over and putting his arm around her and waiting for her to speak.

"Okay, *Columbo*, since we're obviously not going anywhere until I talk, here it goes." But before she explained, she bunched her fists again. "God, it's no wonder Kat Coulter broke!"

Watts thought about the woman they recently put away for murdering her husband. Kat was the first person to ever call him Columbo, referring to the bumbling TV detective, because he repeatedly made surprise visits to her, and as in the TV show, his instincts proved correct. He and Daisy worked hard on that case, but right now her Columbo reference didn't sound very nice. He listened carefully, hoping to understand where she was coming from.

"I think I'm losing my mind," she said, rubbing her temples. "I admit that at first the dungeon kind of spooked me, but then I asked myself if I was going to let some weird thing keep me from doing my job? You already know the answer to that one, so by the time we left, I was quite determined to see this through. By the way, I did find a metallurgist who told me about a dye that should show even the slightest scratches, so assuming the pipe is original, I should be able to confirm whether the hanging occurred there."

Watts nodded his understanding, but didn't interrupt. He noticed her hands were trembling again.

"Everything was fine until I got home. As I climbed the stairs and pulled out my keys, I spotted a hangman's noose above my door. It scared the hell out of me so I called you and ran down the stairs. I'm not sure what it means, but I think it has something to do with this investigation."

Watts' face tensed and head cocked, staring at her ghastly makeup. Soon, people would be paying makeup artists to look like this for Trick-or-Treating. Relaxing a bit, he said, "Could it be someone's Halloween decoration?"

Daisy adamantly shook her head. "I admit I've seen a few Halloween nooses, but never at my place, and never hanging over my door. This was like a warning – like something in the theater followed me home, except this was hanging before I ever got there. Only something from another dimension could do that. Something like Jeremy Delouse's ghost."

Watts bit his tongue to keep from grinning. "Daisy, think about it. While we experienced some strange things this afternoon, I hear ghosts can only manifest as silhouettes or energy balls. Since I can't see an energy ball having the dexterity to tie a noose, either someone's playing a prank or they're trying to scare you."

Nodding, she flipped her visor down and used a moist tissue to erase the steaks from her face. After straightening her hair with her fingers, she said, "I'm sure you're right. Can we get that coffee now?"

"Absolutely," he said, "right after I check out your apartment. May I have your key?"

Reluctantly, she handed it over. "Don't go searching through my dirty clothes."

"I promise," he said, opening his door. Most likely she was trying to be cute, but he wasn't about to ask for clarification. "Stay put and lock the doors." He then headed across the parking lot.

His special shoe sounded like a quacking duck as he ran toward the stairs. Most of the time it didn't bother him, but after today's experience with it echoing in the dungeon, he was noticing it more than usual.

The noose was easy to spot. Made of quarter-inch nylon rope with the opening perhaps two inches, it could barely string a rat, but it was nicely fashioned and suspended by a single staple. Had the perp used tape instead, there was a chance that he or she had left some prints.

After taking several pictures with his camera phone, he carefully removed the staple, tucked the noose in his coat pocket, and entered her apartment. Everything inside looked as it had the last time he was there. Recalling her pervert reference when she thought he had groped her while in the dungeon, he wondered if she had ever been abused. One thing was certain. Now was not the time to ask.

Ten

THE NOTION OF DAISY being physically abused stirred new thoughts, particularly since she had recently transferred from another police department. But how could any mistreatment be tied in with the toy noose, and was this toy linked in some way to the Jeremy Delouse hanging? Watts' head pounded as he sought answers.

Right now, he was as confused by his personal relationship as he was the theater's dungeon. It seemed the closer he got to women, the less he knew about them, and Daisy was no exception. No doubt this was why he preferred romantic baby steps to diving in head-first. He figured Daisy had similar thoughts because there had been no mention of the "L" word so far. At the rate things were going, it could snow before anything happened between them.

He had intended for his cursory look through her apartment to be nothing more than a security check, but now he found himself looking for photos of old boyfriends. Thankfully, the only one of her with another man was one taken in the Stockyards stage coach, and since they were sitting on opposite sides and the man was significantly older, he presumed the guy was either a relative or a friend. Satisfied, he quickly headed outside, locked her door, and headed down the steps.

He leaped down the steps twirling her keys on his finger and climbed in Leroy's cab. "Good news, Ma'am. Your apartment's secure, and there's no underwear in sight."

She swatted his shoulder harder than usual.

"Hey, Lady, I'm a sworn officer of the law. I could take you in for that."

Finally smiling, she clung to his arm and leaned into him. "Will it help if I cooperate?"

Testing the waters, he leaned into her and tasted her lips. The surprising depth of her kiss told him she was better now. When they parted, he fastened his seatbelt and started his truck.

"So, where do you want to go?"

"Well, I'm pretty hungry. Are you up for Tex-Mex, or do you want to stick with coffee?"

"Actually, Tex-Mex sounds great. Hopefully we can get a quiet booth."

Before backing out of his parking space, he checked Leroy's fuel gauge. His truck drank gas like a thoroughbred gulped water, but he felt certain he could make the round trip. During the drive he kept pondering his abuse theory, but this was her time to talk, so he would only discuss it if she brought it up.

Soon after delivering chips and salsa, their waitress set peach margaritas. One sip told Watts he made the right choice. By the time the waitress returned, they were ready to place their orders. The young woman smiled warmly, thanked them, and left.

"She's a great waitress," said Watts. "She really knows how to pace things."

"I agree," said Daisy, lifting another chip.

They talked for an hour without mentioning the theater or toy noose. When they finished their meals, they ordered coffee, as neither was eager to leave. Once the waitress cleared their plates, she reached across the table.

"Thanks for coming to my rescue," she said, holding his hand.

With her staring into his eyes as if to say, *It's your move*, Watts covered her hand with his and smiled back. "I'm always happy to help, Daisy, and if you can't reach me by phone, have the mayor send the Bat Signal."

She smiled and let her eyes fall to the table before meeting his again. "I thought you were Columbo, not Batman."

"Columbo by day, Batman by night."

"I see, and with Halloween right around the corner, you can be whoever you want."

He gently squeezed her hand, gazing into her eyes. "Daisy, all I want is to be with you. You gave me quite a scare today. I've never felt so anxious over someone, even my mother."

She gently pulled her hand away to sip some water. "How can that be?"

"Mom had to be strong to put up with my father, and she constantly told me not to worry. I always figured she'd out-live me, but I was wrong. I guess God needed another strong woman at his side. I really miss her."

"I wish I could have met her. I bet we would have hit it off."

"Trust me, she would've loved you."

He downed some coffee and set his mug down, amused at how she had turned the table on him. So much for getting her to open up. No sooner had he finished his coffee than the waitress refilled it again. He hadn't planned on drinking a third cup, but what the hell – it prolonged their time together.

Feeling the noose in his pocket, he figured neither of them would sleep until they confronted the issue. After fidgeting for a moment, he said, "Going back to what happened at your apartment, I'm really not sure what to make of it. I mean, on the surface it's a miniature noose stapled to the overhang. Prank or decoration, it was carefully positioned, and I don't see how there could be any prints. So, what are your thoughts, Daisy? Has anyone threatened you? Do you know anyone who would leave it as a decoration?"

She leaned forward, propping her chin in her hands. She stared for a moment and then used her knife to slide the chip crumbs from the table onto her plate. When her eyes roamed the room, their waitress appeared with their check. Watts presented his credit card and the waitress took off. Finally, Daisy spoke.

"I've been pondering that noose all evening, Maxx. I've never decorated for Halloween and no one has threatened me. I have no idea who would do this."

"Well, that certainly makes it harder, doesn't it?"

She paused to sip her coffee, then said, "What about Betty? She had the time and knew we were interested in the noose."

"And why would she do that?"

"To keep us from proving anything. Think about it, Maxx. The Scott Theater is a certified haunted building and probably brings people in because of it. Maybe she did it to scare us off."

Watts laughed so hard people were staring. Glancing their way like Travis did at the diner, it also reminded him how they got involved in this case. How he wished he and Spartan had chosen a different restaurant that day.

"Okay, let's say Betty did it. Care to explain how she knew where you live? It certainly didn't come from me or Blaine."

She allowed her eyes to roam the room and then searched the table for more crumbs. Seeing nothing, she smiled and looked at him.

"When you put it that way, naming Betty sounds pretty stupid, but when you're grasping at straws you take whatever comes your way. The truth is Betty was the first person that came to mind so I spit it out. End of story."

He her hand was cooler than before. Her margarita had worn off and now reality was setting in. Her face told him that going home alone was a concern.

"Daisy, would you like to stay at my place tonight? I'll sleep on the air mattress bed. No hanky-panky, I promise."

"You mean no hokey-pokey."

The way she said *hokey-pokey* implied interesting possibilities, but he feared sex would change their relationship. Rather than flirt, he faced her matter-of-factly.

"All I'm saying is you might feel safer sleeping in my bed tonight. I washed the sheets yesterday and I don't have bed bugs or hang tiny nooses outside."

She grinned, thinking about it. "Okay Mister Maxx with two x's, I accept your offer, but I'll need to pick up a few things, as well as my car. It won't take long. If I don't show up within thirty minutes, you'll know something happened."

Watts shook his head. "No, I'll go in with you and then follow you to my house."

"Thanks. I appreciate that."

Eleven

Watts' mind wandered as he tailed Daisy to her apartment. It was barely nine PM when they left her parking lot, but it felt much later. Staying three car lengths back, he hit the speed dial on his cell phone. His partner answered on the third ring.

"This must be important if you're calling me at home," said Spartan.

After bringing him up to speed on Daisy's situation, Watts ended with, "She's pretty shook up."

"Hmm. Where's the noose? Do you have it?"

"Yeah," said Watts, holding it in his palm. "I'm gonna lock it in Leroy's glove box so she doesn't see it again."

Spartan hesitated. "I don't get it, Maxx. How could she get so upset over a toy noose? I mean it's gotta be a joke, right?"

"Perhaps, but who's the joker? Outside the three of us, no one in the department knows we're investigating Jeremy Delouse."

"I wouldn't bet on that. Some of her co-workers might have overheard something, or Betty could have called someone."

Watts shook his head. "Daisy and I already wrote her off."

Feeling the nylon rope between his fingers, he knew tracing it would be impossible. Oddly, the rope felt cooler than it should for having been in his pocket. Rather than risk making the day crazier by mentioning it, he tossed the snare in the glove box.

"Forget the noose, Blaine. I called so you wouldn't say anything stupid the next time you saw Daisy."

"Don't worry, partner. I'll be careful. Keep her warm tonight, okay?"

"Ahah. I have plenty of blankets. See you in the morning."

Shortly after ending his call, they were turning into his parking lot. She pulled into the visitor's spot while Watts returned Leroy to his stall. As soon as he hit the parking brake, he leaped from his cab to help Daisy with her overnight bag. Assuming she stayed, it would be the longest time they had ever spent together. He didn't care that most of it would be spent recharging their batteries.

While Daisy got settled in his bedroom, Watts turned on the TV and flipped through the channels. He paused for a paranormal show, but changed it before she came out. He didn't think she needed another ghost story before going to sleep.

When she came out in her cotton pajamas, he figured all they needed now was popcorn and hot cocoa and they'd be twelve again. Smiling, he patted the sofa for her to join him. Once she was next to him, he offered her the remote and then slid his arm around her.

Holding it like it was the Holy Grail, she said, "You trust me with your remote?"

"Yup, because that's the kind of guy I am, so either pick something or I'll start singing."

She quickly hit the menu button and started scanning the options while Watts pulled the queen-sized air mattress from the closet. Once he had spread it on the floor, he hooked up the air pump and the living room was instantly swallowed.

"This is ridiculous," she said. "Unplug that thing before it buries us. We're sleeping in the same bed."

"Okay," he said, pulling the plug. "I promise I'll stay on my side."

"That's good to know. Besides, it will also tell me if you snore."

"Likewise," he said, smiling back.

He didn't intend his stretching during Leno's monologue to imply that he was ready for bed, but she suggested it anyway. After tucking his air mattress away, he brushed his teeth and slipped on a pair of gym pants because the satin boxers he normally slept in were too risqué.

Lying in bed, they stared at the dead bugs in the ceiling fan's globe with the covers hugging their necks. The blades were probably filthy, too, but she wouldn't notice unless she turned it off. He wondered what she was thinking, and whether she was looking for photos like he did in her place. Did she wonder why his only photos were of longhorn cattle? Did she notice him watching her? If so, she did a great job pretending not to notice.

He desperately wanted to brush her hair from her face, but instead reached for her hand. "I'm glad you're here," he said. "And I hope this isn't too awkward."

Smiling, she said, "Everyone else would think our being dressed was awkward."

Feeling a stirring in his mid-section, he turned on his side to face her. "As much as I'd love to take this further, this isn't the right time. You're vulnerable and I don't want to spoil it. Whenever we decide to make love, I want it to be perfect for both of us."

She rolled on her side toward him, resting her head in her hand. "I see. And do you always decide what's best for your girlfriends?"

Whatever was happening down below suddenly died. "Do you think I'm controlling?"

She took his hand and placed it over her heart. "Not at all. In fact you're the sweetest, most considerate man I've ever met, and I love you for it."

Hearing the "L" word got his blood flowing again. The only problem was she didn't say I love *you*, but rather I love you *for it*. He took that to mean she thought he was a good guy, and there was a significant difference. He slid closer and kissed her, gently at first, but more passionately when she didn't resist. His hand cupped her warm breast and she didn't pull away. But suddenly the words "I love you *for it*" shot through him like the bullet did his shoulder two years ago. The pain was less intense, but it was still a game-changer. He rolled onto his back, faking a smile, desperate to take her in his arms.

"Are you sure we can do this?" he said.

"What? Make love?"

"No, sleep together *without* making love."

She smiled, fluffed her pillow, and turned away from him. "Good night, Maxx."

Watts looked at his alarm clock. The last time he was in bed before eleven, he was sick with a fever. He turned off the light, kissed her neck, and said, "Good night, sweetheart." *I love you.*

53

Twelve

WATTS AWOKE TEN MINUTES before his alarm was set to go off. Seeing Daisy next to him warmed his heart. He quietly canceled the alarm and snuck into the bathroom for a quick shower before she awoke.

She surprised him by coming in the bathroom while he was toweling himself. As he quickly covered his mid-section, she waved while yawning and closed the toilet door as if they had been living together for years. Unsure about what she saw, he quietly slipped out of the bathroom to put on a robe.

When she came out, she said, "Nice butt."

"Nice, but what?" he said, grinning.

Her eyes crinkled as she came over and planted a kiss on his lips. "Good morning, sweetheart."

Though tempted to drop his robe and climb into bed with her, he instead let his lips explore her minty mouth, fresh from the toothpaste, glad that he brushed before showering.

She pressed her body into his and then smiled wryly. "I can tell you're glad to see me."

"I am," he said, feeling the blood drain from his brain. "Did you sleep well?"

She nodded, still pressing into him. "I can't remember the last time I slept this well. Thank you for having me over."

Aware that his robe had become a circus tent, he felt the sudden need for a cold shower. Moving closer, his body screamed, *Go for it!* but his heart said no.

"You know you're welcome to sleep over anytime."

Moving her hands to his shoulders, she whispered, "I look forward to that," and kissed him again. She then returned to the bathroom and closed the door.

Since the circus had left town, the devil in him wondered what the hell went wrong. Here he was with this beautiful woman who was probably naked by now and practically inviting him in, and all he could do was gaze at the closed door. It would have been easy to strip off his robe and join her in the shower, but his conscience held him back. The only reason Daisy spent the night was because she was upset and she trusted him, and even though she had made some suggestive advances, it still wouldn't be right to take advantage of her. Suddenly a thought came to him. What if she hung the noose and this was all a ploy to get him sleep with her? She had the opportunity and means to do it. Stranger things had happened. But as flattering as that seemed, it was also deeply disturbing. True or not, there was no way he could confront her because if he did and he was wrong about her, he would lose her forever. As with everything that had happened recently, it was best he kept his thoughts to himself.

Listening to the shower run, he imagined the water caressing her skin. He pictured himself soaping her and then watching the lather trace her beautiful curves. Cupping her jaw, he leaned into her, kissing her deeply while the water warmed them. He became so involved in his dream that he didn't notice the shower was off. He quickly slipped on some pants and a shirt from his closet. When the door opened, she emerged in a towel with wet hair glued to her neck.

"I don't suppose you have a hair dryer to you?"

Embarrassed, he barely shook his head while tucking in his shirt. "Sorry. You want me to check with a neighbor?"

She laughed, shaking her head. "If someone knocked on your door at six thirty in the morning, would you answer it?"

Smiling back, he said, "Probably not." *Note to self: Buy a dryer to keep on hand!*

"That's okay," she said, ducking back into the bathroom. Before closing the door, she added, "You're the only one I need to please."

She emerged ten minutes later, hair still damp but combed, and grabbed some clothes from her bag. "How are we doing on time? I don't want to hold you up."

"Lady, you can hold me up anytime," he said, admiring her shape.

Studying his expression, she teased him with her grin. "You know, Maxx, one of these days I'm gonna grab you."

He looked up and smirked. "Oh, I look forward to it, and since we got up earlier than normal, we can stop for coffee if you want."

"I'd love that. I'll be ready in five minutes."

Soon after, Watts led the way with her overnight bag over his shoulder. Crossing the threshold he half-expected to find another nylon noose, but instead, he saw a dead cricket. Kicking it away, he welcomed the crisp morning air. Fall was his favorite time of year. Mild temperatures, no thunderstorms, too early for snow, but Blue Northerns were always a possibility. Those Canadian cold fronts could drop the temperature ten degrees per hour, but that wasn't going to happen today. With a high predicted of seventy-five and his favorite girl at his side, nothing could ruin it.

After walking Daisy to her Nissan Tundra, Watts climbed in his pickup. With a twist, Leroy's turbo boosted engine growled like a cougar. Enjoying the sound, the detective opened the locked glove box to examine the noose. Suddenly the hair on his nape stood up. The noose was gone!

Thirteen

Daisy was preparing to back out of her parking spot when Watts stepped from his cab. Pretending to examine his tires, he walked around his truck wondering how someone could have broken in without setting his alarm off and also open his locked glove box without leaving any marks. Seeing no damage to the windows or door frames made it even more peculiar, especially since Leroy's spare key was buried in his sock drawer. For a brief moment, he wondered if Daisy had snuck out while he was asleep, taken the noose, and then climbed back into bed. The notion quickly vanished since she never knew it was there.

She pulled up next to him and rolled down her window. "Is there a problem?" she said.

"No, I just have this crazy habit of looking my truck over before I move it. Every morning I check it to see if I have a door ding or scratch."

The ease of his fib surprised him, for he had never lied to her before. He climbed back in, raised his thumb, and waited for her to move her truck. Soon they were on the street heading toward Daz Good Coffee.

They parked in the lot and followed the welcoming aroma inside where a dozen people sipped coffee while surfing the web on their computers and smart phones. Six empty burlap bags hung from the ceiling like banners, their stenciled sides identifying their origins. The elementary school artwork in the corner drew smiles from Daisy while they waited to place their order.

They seated themselves at a bar table that faced the drive-through and watched a young woman nearly drive into the wall while dialing her cell phone. The next car in line had a joyful dog sticking his head out in anticipation of receiving a doggie bone. As the next vehicle pulled up, their order was called and Watts went to retrieve their coffees. "For my special lady," he said, setting hers down in front of her.

She smiled, tapping her drink to his. "To my special man."

They each took a sip, fixated on each other. Watts had never been happier. Her smile erased any fears of her leaving him. After ten minutes of small talk, they needed to part ways. He told her Leroy was hungry, but his real reason for wanting to stop for gas was to check out Leroy's alarm system. Once she was gone, he double-checked the cab for the noose or signs of a break-in, but came up empty on both counts. When he arrived at the gas station, he rolled down the windows and climbed out. While trading dollars for fuel, he locked the cab, waited a moment, and then opened the driver's door from the inside. Leroy's bellowing drew inquisitive looks from everyone within a two block area. After canceling the alarm, he repeated this from the passenger side. As expected, it produced the same result followed by more stares. Thinking someone might call the police, Watts made a point of dangling his keys. Once the gas pump reached his wallet's breaking point, he cradled the nozzle and printed his receipt, still bewildered over the missing noose. The more he thought about it, the more he wondered if last night's margarita might have caused him to dream this whole thing up. After all, he rarely drank alcohol, and it wouldn't have been the first time it generated odd dreams. He might have even believed it, had Daisy not spent the night at his place.

He felt emotionally drained by the time he got to work. No sooner had he tossed his keys on his desk than Spartan invaded his space wearing a smug look. While checking his IN basket, Watts acknowledged his partner with a verbal greeting hoping his lack of eye contact would send him away. Instead, his partner moved in closer and leaned on his desk.

"So, how was it last night?" said Spartan, pogoing his eyebrows. Did you two finally —"

Watts lowered his papers to stare at him. "No, Blaine, but thanks for asking. She was upset, and I was trying to figure out why there was a noose over her door. As innocent as that sounds, it's the truth."

"Sorry, man. It'll happen someday. Everything still cool between you?"

"Absolutely, and since you like puzzles so much, here's one for you. How does one break into a locked vehicle, remove something from a locked glove box, and leave it untouched?"

Spartan frowned. "What happened, Maxx?"

"You remember that noose I told you about last night?"

"Yeah,"

"Well, it's gone. I had it locked in the glove box, and when I climbed into Leroy this morning, the alarm was on, the glove box was still locked, and nothing was forced open. It's like it just vanished."

"So, what are you saying? That one of your ghosts took it?"

"Don't be a smart ass. I was merely telling you this to see if you had any ideas on how someone could steal it. Leroy's alarm works fine, so does the glove box lock, and before you suggest that Daisy had anything to do with it, she didn't know it was in there and has no idea it's missing."

"You thought *Daisy* had something to do with it?"

Watts leaned into his partner. "Do you have a hearing problem? I just said there's no way she could have possibly had anything to do with it."

Spartan grinned, admiring his shoes. He lifted his left pant leg, rubbed his right toe on his sock, and then reversed it so both shoes were polished. "Maxx, I consider myself a pretty good detective, but I'm no expert on car alarms, glove boxes or ghosts. If you don't want to confront Daisy about it, then why not have another lab tech examine your truck? Who knows? Maybe they'll find something you missed."

"Good idea, except I don't want her to know the noose disappeared, and there's no way I can get the lab to help without providing specifics."

"Oh, yeah," he said, stroking his chin. "That's quite a dilemma. Sorry, dude."

"Look, Blaine, if we hadn't experienced those weird things at the Scott Theater yesterday, I'd drop this like an anchor and pretend it never happened, but the fact is, we can't do that now. So before Ryder dumps some milk-run case on us, we'd better find whatever we can on Betty Cerin, Marv Delouse and Travis McLean. I don't see how any of them could be involved in this noose thing, but we still need to pursue it."

"I concur. I'll run Marv and Travis through the databases again to see if I missed anything and also do a background check on Betty. What do you plan to do?"

"Buy some rope."

Fourteen

WATTS' INTERNET SEARCH FOR local nylon rope vendors was predictably long. It came in twenty-five, fifty, or one hundred foot lengths, was washable, guaranteed to hold up to two hundred pounds, and had an endless variety of uses. Contemplating the noose, he recalled the demonic girl from his childhood who lived down the street that hanged her Barbie dolls by the neck. That was his first memory of a slip knot, and the doll size was similar to the one found above Daisy's door. Even as a kid, he wondered who fashioned Barbie's noose because the girl was in his third grade class. He couldn't remember her name, but he distinctly remembered her cutting Barbie's arms and legs off, shearing her hair, and painting her eyes red. At the time he was certain she was doomed to a pitiful life, but a few years ago he recognized her in a photo where she was receiving a humanitarian service award while serving as the head librarian at the Granbury Public Library. In the most literal sense, it proved you shouldn't judge a book by its cover.

It would have been easier to match the cord if he still had Daisy's noose. Now, he had a better chance of matching hay sticks in a cow's mouth. He was still pondering that when his partner came in.

"Okay, here's what I came up with," said Spartan, reading from his notes. "Betty Cerin is a widow and has been with the Scott Theater for over forty years. Cerin is her maiden name. Her married name was McLaughlin. She was working there as an actress but gave it up right after Jeremy Delouse died. Since then, she's been working in a variety of administrative positions at the theater with occasional supporting roles."

Watts leaned back in his chair with both feet propped up, twirling his pen. "That's good stuff, Blaine. I can't believe you got all that from the National Database"

"Actually, it came from Betty. I just got off the phone with her. She was very pleasant."

Watts glanced over his partner's notes, thinking about Kat Coulter, whose deceits nearly kept her from jail. Actors are deceivers, he reminded himself. Even former ones like Kat and Betty. Never rule anyone out. He pursed his lips, looking at his partner.

"I don't suppose you asked if she had any connection to Jeremy Delouse."

Spartan's head shook. "At the time, I was seeking basic information, and she seemed open to discussion. I figured mentioning him might distract her thoughts."

"You're probably right. We need to go back anyway."

"When?"

"We'll set up a meeting as soon as Daisy gets the metal dye. Did you find anything new on Marv or Travis?"

"Not really. No phone number for Travis and I left a message for Marv. Based on our last conversation with him, I'm guessing he won't be calling back anytime soon."

Watts nodded, dropping his feet to the floor. "Considering how long Betty's been working at the theater, she's still our best resource. She must have known Jeremy, so the odds are good she knows something about Marv."

Spartan squinted. "Why is that? Jeremy died before Marv was born, and I'd think that since Marv's father was Jeremy's brother, he would have told him about his uncle."

Watts sighed, straightening his desk. Over the years, he found that tidiness helped restore order when things got out of kilter. A moment later, he handed Spartan his notes. "So, what do you know about Marv's father?"

"Nothing, really. I can't do a search without a name."

Watts nodded, stretching his neck. He was far too young to feel this old. "Keep trying to reach Marv. Tell him we'll meet him anywhere, any time. Maybe there's a murder motive in his family history." He closed his eyes and leaned back in his chair. "I still can't believe we're doing this."

"I can't believe we haven't had another homicide."

"Yeah, I know. That's almost as spooky as the missing noose." Getting to his feet, he said, "I'm gonna check with Daisy and see when she'll be ready. I'll be back in a few."

"I'll be waiting."

Fifteen

Daisy met him at the counter but didn't look as spry as she had at the coffee shop. She wore a hint of worry, but the enduring scent of his shower soap made him smile. Foregoing any small talk, he got right to the point.

"Any word on the metal dye?"

She nodded. "It should be here within the next couple of hours."

"Great. Should I call Betty to make an appointment for this afternoon?"

Daisy stopped to look around the room. A couple of techs were working on projects and the phones were quiet. No one was paying any attention.

"Since Betty will probably be there all day, why not wait until I have it? I can call you when it arrives."

"Sounds good."

He smiled, tapped the counter, and left, unsure what he would do to fill his day. Things got worse when he saw Captain Ryder talking to Spartan. His attempt to deviate into the break room was foiled by his boss's keen eye.

"Not so fast," said Ryder. "Forget the coffee. You and Spartan, in my office, now."

His stomach suddenly in knots, Watts nodded and joined the procession, his left shoe making a farting noise, one step at a time. Today he found its nuisance noise surprisingly amusing. Images of his shoe farting while he served as a pallbearer brought a grin. Picturing Ryder's body in the casket made it even funnier. Not that he expected his boss to pass into the netherworld anytime soon, but he couldn't stop his subconscious mind from sparking the thought.

With his boss holding the door open like a rancher leading his cattle to slaughter, Watts saw no reason to make eye contact as they entered his office. Carefully avoiding the captain's prized Indian rug, the detectives stopped shy of his cheap metal desk, chins up, hands at their sides.

Ryder slid behind his desk and seated himself, taking a moment to study his detectives. Finally, he said, "Have a seat, gentlemen."

They did as he requested, sitting mannequin-still with their feet planted on the floor.

The captain pulled out a drawer, rested a foot on it, and leaned back. He looked unusually upbeat, as though he planned to send them back to Patrol. That seemed to have been his goal for some time, but it was difficult to do when their case-solving ratio exceeded the average. He picked up a pencil and started tapping, keeping his eyes on them. When he set his pencil down, he dropped his foot and leaned forward like a judge ready to give sentence.

"Care to tell me what's going on?" he said.

"Sir?" said Watts.

"Don't play dumb, Maxx. I got a call from the lab supervisor this morning. He told me you took your girlfriend to the theater yesterday and he wanted to know why. Since I was clueless, I told him I'd get back to him and started asking around. Imagine my surprise when I heard that someone spotted The Three Musketeers leaving in a Crown Vic. So, now that we're all together, how about telling me what's going on?"

At that moment, all Watts could think of was Jack Nicholson's *You can't handle the truth!* line from the movie *A Few Good Men*, but rather than risk a demotion, he simply said, "It's complicated."

Playing Good Cop/Bad Cop, Ryder promptly shifted his gaze to Spartan. A master at intimidation, the captain's eyes narrowed and his face tightened. With his hands folded, his gaze burned a hole in the detective's head.

Watts watched, hoping his partner remembered the lessons he had taught him over the years. First, that their record was above reproach. Second, that they were free to investigate leads anytime there was opportunity. And third, that both of these things justified their actions. Spartan seemed to be recalling this as he calmly looked at his boss.

"Sir, I agree with Maxx. It *is* complicated, and it would be in your best interest to allow more time before having this discussion."

Ryder nearly snapped his pencil in half. "Am I hearing you right? You're saying I shouldn't know what's going on with two of my detectives?"

Watts crossed his legs. "Sir, it's not that we're hiding something from you, it's just that we need something more definitive before we can discuss it. I can tell you that we're running down leads in an old case, and they may produce nothing. Right now we have the time, so I'm asking that you trust us with autonomy."

Ryder closed his eyes and rubbed his brow. When he opened his eyes again, he said, "Okay, spare me the details, but tell me what case you're working on."

Spartan glanced at Watts. Upon receiving his approval, he said, "That's where it gets complicated, sir. You see, there isn't a murder file on this guy."

Ryder immediately switched his focus back to Watts. "I'm getting real tired of you two speaking in riddles. Start talking or you're both facing two weeks of unpaid leave."

Watts slowly uncrossed his legs and leaned forward in his seat. "Okay, Captain, here's the deal. We overheard a conversation where a guy was claiming a suicide was actually a murder. Naturally, that piqued our interest, so we've been running down leads ever since. We haven't discussed it until now because everything's been hearsay. We solicited Ms. Woods' assistance to help verify the death occurred where it was described. She's supposed to get some metal dye this morning which can confirm that. We plan to head back to the scene as soon as the dye comes in. You're welcome to join us if you like."

"No thanks," he said, as if revolted by their presence. "Things have been eerily quiet around here, and I can't explain why, so for now I'm gonna let you slide. However, you'd better have something substantial in the next forty-eight hours or I'll have your badges."

"Yes, sir."

They quickly stood and filed out the door before Ryder had second thoughts. Once out of earshot, Spartan glanced at his partner.

"Maxx, I must say I had no idea how you'd save us from that whirlpool, but nice job. What were you gonna do if he wanted some real justification?"

Watts confidently patted his coat pocket. "Not to worry, Blaine. I came prepared. The tape from the diner would have won him over. My Sony's never let me down."

Sixteen

Spartan and Watts spent the next two hours tracing Marv Delouse's blood line. Since they still hadn't been able to reach him, they had to improvise. By inserting the information from his driver's license into Geneology.com's form, they learned that Marv was the only child of Grace and Warren Delouse. Running Warren's name through the National Database told them he was two years older than Jeremy, and he died in 1985. Such dead ends were frustrating, particularly when the clock was ticking.

Soon after, Daisy called saying the dye had come in. Her voice tensed when Watts mentioned his conversation with Ryder.

"Are you sure we should continue pursuing this?" she said.

"Positive," said Watts. "We still have forty-six hours to come up with something, and if we can convince the captain it's a worthy case, then time becomes irrelevant. The only question is whether your schedule allows another trip to the theater."

"It's not a problem because things are slow here, too. I fear some mass murderer is about to start shooting from a bell tower."

"Let's hope you're not a soothsayer," said Watts. "In the meantime, I'll call Betty to see if we can get access to the dungeon this afternoon."

"Will Blaine be there?"

"Of course. He'll be controlling the lights just like the last time."

"So no hanky panky."

"Or hokey pokey."

When she paused, her teasing took him back to high school when he and his buddies would sit outside checking out the girls, talking about seeing them naked. Back then, a glimpse of cleavage was enough to tense his body, and even their harshest gazes couldn't deter him from thinking about sex. But now he found Daisy's innuendoes more flattering than sexy. *What's wrong with me?*

"Maxx?" she said. "You still there?"

"Of course," he said, her voice drawing him back. "I'll call you once I talk to Betty."

"I'll be ready whenever you are."

Her tone left him wondering whether her comment contained sexual overtones or if his brain was stuck in his high school fantasy. He was contemplating that while dialing the Scott Theater. He expected Betty to answer, but instead a male voice came on the line, said she was having tea with a friend, and that she would be back in an hour. Watts thanked him and left a message asking that she call him. He hung up without getting the man's name, but decided it wasn't worth calling him back.

Unsure what to do next, he rested his head in his palm thinking about Daisy. He yearned to feel her naked body against his. They came close last night, but his insecurity held him back.

"Maxx?"

Watts practically leaped from his chair. "Christ, Blaine, you scared the hell out of me! What's up?"

"Sorry, dude. You okay?"

"Yeah," he said, straightening himself in his seat. "Just thinking about the case."

"Aha. Anyway, I haven't found any obituaries on Travis McLean, nor have I found anyone except Marv who has heard of him. Not sure about you, but it makes me wonder if that's the guy's real name."

"He served in Vietnam, is not a ghost, and like many troubled vets has chosen to drop out." Watts then swiveled his seat so he could see the whiteboard they were using to trace Jeremy Delouse's bloodline. Unfortunately, the depicted lineage had more cavities than an eight year old kid.

Spartan's look concerned Watts. It was as if he wanted him to pull the plug on this case but wouldn't come out and say it. That annoyed him. "Do you think the Mormon Church would have a more detailed record of Jeremy Delouse's ancestry?"

"Beats me, but would they share that information with the police?"

Watts placed a finger over his lips, thinking nothing good could come from getting the Mormons involved. "Let's forget about Jeremy for now and concentrate on his nephew and the elusive Travis McLean. If the only way to find Travis is through Marv, then so be it. Let's do whatever it takes to find him."

"As in put out an APB?"

"I doubt Marv's that hard to find."

"I'm sure you're right. I'll keep digging."

No sooner had Spartan left than Marv Delouse's caller ID showed up on Watts' phone. "It's him," said Watts, waving for his partner to come back. Holding the phone so they could both hear, he said, "Hello, Marv. This is Detective Watts. Detective Spartan and I were just talking about you. Thanks for calling back."

"Well, after a dozen messages, I figured I'd better call before you had me arrested."

Watts grinned at his partner. "Marv, we're still trying to determine if there was any foul play in your uncle's death. Maybe if we put this to rest, his spirit will cross over into the next dimension."

"If you believe in such things."

Marv's response was expected. Watts only said it to provoke cooperation. "Marv, can we meet somewhere to talk? It shouldn't take long, but I'd rather not discuss this on the phone."

"I don't know. I'm at work and my schedule's pretty full."

"Would you prefer to come down to the station? We're right next to the court house."

"No thanks. Police stations aren't my thing. Just tell me what you want to know."

"Two things," said Spartan, chiming in. "Your family tree starting with your grandparents, and where we can find Travis McLean."

"Why would you possibly need to know my ancestry?"

"Humor us, Marv," said Watts. "We're investigators. It's what we do."

"I'll think about it. That's what I do. And as for Travis, I have no idea. Sometimes he'll call me out of the blue and I meet him. Frankly, I'm not certain he has a home. He always smells like he's been sleeping on the sidewalk, and his eyes always look tired."

"Why is that? Do you know where he works?"

"Haven't a clue," said Marv, his voice trailing off.

Watts feared he was losing him. "You said he smells like he's been sleeping on the sidewalk. Can you describe it?"

Marv's answer followed a brief hesitation. "You know that musty scent you get when you've been outside for a while? But what difference does that make? Do you plan to sniff him out?"

Though it might be possible with Watts' sensitive nose, he kept it to himself because Marv sounded ready to end the call.

Spartan leaned into the phone. "Where do you live, Marv?"

"You're the investigator. You tell me."

Watts jumped in. "We're only asking because we could swing by since it might be easier to talk in person."

"No thanks. Besides, as I already said, I'm at work and I don't like people who butt into other people's conversations. And who needs more ridicule when your last name's Delouse? God, I hate that name. I really should change it. As for this charade of clearing my uncle's name, I do believe you're wasting your time."

Exhaling noisily, he said, "I see your point, Marv, but one never knows when a suicide might turn out to be murder. That's why homicide is always sent out to investigate."

"Well in that case let me be clear about something, detectives. First of all, Travis isn't my friend, and second, I believe he's senile. Had you been eavesdropping earlier, you would have heard him say he communicates with ghosts."

"You mean like a medium?" said Spartan.

"No. More like a large."

The detectives smiled even though this wasn't a laughing matter. Yesterday the notion of anyone communicating with ghosts seemed ludicrous, but then they experienced those phenomenal events in the theater after Betty Cerin said spirits lived there. Marv seemed irritated that they weren't talking.

"It was a joke," he said. "Medium, large, as in a large drink? Geez, you guys really need to lighten up."

"We got it," said Spartan. "It just wasn't that funny."

"Oh, that's cold. Now you sound like Travis."

Hearing the name sent Watts back to the Chuck Wagon Diner where Travis said, "... *the police ignored the evidence and ruled it a suicide ... he was too much of a wimp to take his own life ... those sensitive tendencies probably made him a good actor ... he loved the ladies ... any of them could have planned his final exit.*" And regarding these women, Marv stated, "*they'd lead him on and then stomp his heart.*"

His flashback prompted more questions. After popping his knuckles, he said, "Marv, let's go back to the Chuck Wagon Diner for a moment. When your father said your uncle was always having girl trouble, did he happen to mention any names?"

"Look, detective, I just told you Jeremy was an embarrassment to our family, so no one ever spoke of him. Besides, Dad passed away before he ever discussed him with me. What little I know about Jeremy came from theater docents and Internet accounts. Should you care to look, I'm sure you can find the same information." Marv paused as if checking the time. "Guys, I hate to be rude, but I need to get back to work. Good luck with whatever it is you're doing."

When the line went dead, Watts was sure he would never hear from Marv again. Now it seemed that the entire case depended on Daisy's metallurgy results.

Seventeen

SINCE THEY WERE STILL waiting to hear from Betty, Watts suggested they all go to lunch. Daisy seemed willing and Spartan never turned down a meal, so they were out of the station within minutes. With mild temperatures making it a perfect day for anything except work, Watts suggested they grab sandwiches from a nearby deli and eat outside.

On their way to the deli, Daisy offered her face to the sun. "It's so beautiful. What a nice change from this summer."

"Amen," said Spartan as his stomach rumbled loudly.

Watts looked at him funny. "Dude, it's like you're feeding a tapeworm. What gives?"

Spartan shrugged. "What can I say? I'm blessed with a high metabolism."

"Yeah? Well, let's hope you're not blessed with high cholesterol, too."

Watts mentioned that because anything else would suggest he was envious, which he was. He chose this deli because it didn't offer fries, but Spartan didn't need to know that, either.

Daisy huffed. "Can't you boys just enjoy the sunshine?" Instead of an answer, she got stares. "Okay, how about we take our sandwiches to the river? There are plenty of places to sit even if the benches are taken."

"Fine with me," said Watts. As he opened the door, the smell of fresh-baked bread had him salivating. "Man, that smells good!"

"That it does."

It was early, but the deli was packed. When their turns came, they each ordered their favorite sub, then grabbed a drink and bag of chips and paid for their meals. Watts was surprised when the mustached cashier dropped a cookie in his bag.

"It's my son's birthday," the man explained as he took their money. "Everyone gets a free cookie today."

"Well, thank you," said Watts. "Tell him Happy Birthday for us."

"Will do." Then the man smiled and dropped a cookie in someone else's bag.

He didn't need the calories, but who could resist a fresh chocolate chip cookie? He was biting into it before they were out the door.

"Put that down," said Daisy. "We're having a picnic."

"Yeah," Spartan snorted. "Save it 'til we're there."

Knowing he couldn't win, Watts dropped his half-eaten cookie into his bag.

It didn't take long to reach the Trinity River that ran behind 350. The low water level reminded Watts of the inlet where they found Tony Fazelli. He couldn't believe those bastards would dump him there. The more he thought about it, the deeper his frown.

"Man, what's with you?" said Spartan. "Was your cookie tainted?"

Watts grinned. "No, there was nothing wrong with my cookie, and I'm fine, thank you. I was just thinking about Tony Fazelli, wondering why we can't find his kidnappers, especially after one of them shot Porgy Mulberry. I mean, every cop in the U.S. has their descriptions. Why is it so hard?"

Daisy rested a kind hand on Watts' shoulder. "Why is it so hard for you to let go?"

Watts sighed, nodding at her. "I'll try. I promise."

"I hope so because it's hard to see the world through mud-covered glasses."

"I guess," he said, mulling the thought.

Daisy finally settled on a spot where the cool breeze climbed the riverbank. Though the mildewed smell of the low river was unkind to Watts' over-sensitive nose, he didn't mention it. Instead, he seated himself next to her and bit into his sandwich.

"Maxx," said Spartan, chewing a mouthful, "If it's any consolation, I've never stopped thinking about Tony or those Skinheads. In fact, I can't get those Forest Park murders out of my head, but whether those Skinheads were responsible for both crimes remains to be seen. Even so, when I look at my kids, I have no idea what I'd do if someone cut one of them like they did Tony. I mean, I really have no idea."

Watts nodded his understanding. "Thankfully a plastic surgeon sewed Tony up, and from what I hear, he made a great recovery – at least physically."

Daisy was about to bite into her sandwich but suddenly set it aside. Her sad eyes roamed the river as if searching for a corpse. She finally took a bite and chewed slowly as the water lapped the shore. In

71

the distance, the Stockyards' steam engine blew its whistle while three nearby blackbirds chased off a raven.

"I'm always thinking about Tony," she finally said. "Sometimes I feel his head in my lap like when we were waiting for the ambulance to show up. I'll probably remember him for the rest of my life, but I can't stop living because of what happened. As for the Forest Park murders, their case is cold, and I refuse to lose any more sleep over it, because I know I did all I could. I love my job, and sometimes it sucks, but I'm not going to let it consume my life. Right now I want to enjoy this setting. We can't change what happened, but we can sure change what's going on here and enjoy our lunch."

Watts wrapped his arm around her and leaned his head against hers. "You're right. Sorry I mentioned it."

The wind brought the locomotive's pistons closer, starting with a slow chug, moving faster as it picked up speed. The engineer blew its whistle as it neared an intersection: two long bursts followed by a short burst, and then another long one. It was Morse code for Q: a warning to make way for the Queen, a remnant from the past still in use today. Watts followed its smoke trail picturing the smiling faces riding inside its cars. Daisy was right. They had to live their lives, and at that moment, he hoped Daisy would always be in his.

Eighteen

A SUDDEN WIND GUST served as a reminder it was time to get back to 350. After gathering their trash and tossing it in the can, they made a beeline for their building. Daisy went directly to the lab, while the detectives headed back to their desks. Watts searched for a note saying that Betty had called but found none. His voice mail was empty, too. He considered calling her again but decided against it. Like Daisy said, this was his job, not an obsession. Seeing nothing new on the whiteboard, he invited Spartan in to share his thoughts.

"I'm stumped, Blaine. We have until tomorrow night to find something. What have you got?"

"Like you, I have nothing. Maybe ghosts can pull things out of thin air, but I can't."

Watts nodded, twirling a pencil. His phone rang and he checked the ID. "It's Betty," he said, smiling again. "Detective Watts, homicide."

"Hello, detective. This is Betty Cerin. You wanted to speak to me?"

"I do, and thanks for returning my call. We'd like to visit the dungeon this afternoon so our forensics technician can run some tests. Maybe we can talk while she's doing that."

"Of course, but why did you insist on talking to me? Anyone working here would gladly let you in and fill you in on what took place."

"Perhaps, but no one tells stories like you."

Suddenly all was quiet. He could hear her breathing but had no idea what she was thinking. When her silence continued, he said, "I meant that as a compliment, Betty, and we love your company. You have a certain flair for the theater."

"Well," she said, "I *was* an actress, once upon a time."

"Is that right?" he said, pretending not to know. "How long ago was that?"

"Long before you were born."

Watts smiled. Hoping praise would help his cause, he said, "I'm sure you were superb." When she didn't respond, he added, "Could we drop by in about twenty minutes?"

"I don't see why not. You know the way and the hours."

"Great. We'll be there shortly."

The glow on Watts' face was bright enough to light up the dungeon. He tucked his phone away and rose from his chair. "You heard her," he said to Spartan. "Let's go find Daisy."

Twenty-five minutes later, The Three Musketeers entered the Scott Theater. What Ryder intended as a joke had become a term of endearment to them. They spotted Betty immediately and greeted her with handshakes.

"You certainly are punctual," she said. Her eyes locked onto Daisy's forensics kit before returning to the lab tech. "So, tell me, Ms. Woods, what are you expecting to find today?"

"Well, yesterday I wiped off dust, so today I'll probably find less."

Betty laughed with delight, the way an actress would on stage. "You're so cute," she said with her hand over her heart and head tilted back. "I love people with a sense of humor. Laughter is so important, don't you think?"

"Absolutely," said Daisy, nudging Watts. "Anyway, we need that ladder again."

"Actually, it's where you left it, because our maintenance man hasn't been in yet."

Spartan turned to face her. "When does he normally come in?"

"He should be in later today," she said, looking around. Lowering her voice, she moved closer toward them. "Unlike the rest of our employees, his schedule remains flexible. If word got out, some of the other employees might get upset, so please don't repeat that. He's been here a long time, and as long as everything is ready for the performances, the boss is fine with it. Anyway, you had some questions for me?"

Watts nodded, surveying his surroundings. At one end of the reception area, a couple of women were talking. At the opposite end, a middle-aged man in slacks and a dress shirt glanced at them, his posture and attire suggesting he was a manager or perhaps security. The detective acknowledged him with a nod, and the man walked away.

"Betty, would you mind accompanying us downstairs so we can talk while assisting Ms. Woods? Also, I'd like to record your remarks if that's okay. On occasion, it's proven to be more accurate than my notes."

Betty's eyes lit up. "I haven't been recorded since I was on stage," she said. "Just don't ask me to sing, okay?"

Daisy's eyes widened. "You sang on stage? How wonderful."

"Oh, I was in a few musicals back when," she said, basking in the memory. "First I was a supporting actress in *My Fair Lady*, but then I got the role of Elizabeth in *Paint Your Wagon*. I had a magnificent time, but that was so long ago I can't even remember the words."

Watts eyed the man at the end of the hall who had yet to move. "Our time is limited, so let's continue this discussion downstairs." He said that hoping to gain more privacy.

The dungeon seemed darker than before. As Betty had said, the ladder and flashlights were exactly where they left them. Watts and Spartan eased the ladder into position while Daisy prepared the dye. While Spartan assisted Daisy, Watts and Betty continued their discussion, his Sony recording their words.

"Betty," said Watts with his back to the others, "you were describing your role in *Paint Your Wagon*. I'm not familiar with that play. Can you tell me about it?"

"Oh gosh, now you're making me feel ancient." She briefly glanced at Daisy before continuing. "*Paint Your Wagon* was an Alan Lerner and Frederick Loewe Broadway musical comedy, but in 1969, a movie version starring Lee Marvin and Clint Eastwood came out and hit it big. It was a privilege playing Elizabeth on stage. I'll always cherish that role."

Watts glanced over his shoulder to make sure his partners were okay and then went back to Betty. "You must have been quite good to get the leading lady role. How long did the play run?"

"Let me see," she said, moving her mouth from side to side. "I believe it opened in October and ran through December, so it must have been three months. I felt like a star."

"I'm sure you were. What happened once the show closed?"

Suddenly she deflated. "I decided the theater wasn't for me after all."

Watts was thinking about that when the ladder squeaked. He quickly turned and saw Daisy reaching from the ladder's upper steps to apply dye to the pipe. The subsequent chemical reaction left an acrid odor that only seemed to bother him. He re-checked his Sony recorder to make sure it was working before facing Betty again.

"Forgive me for stating the obvious, Betty, but you were a star performer, and stars don't normally quit."

Without explaining, she bowed her head and started humming a tune. After a few bars, she stopped and looked up. "Sorry," she said. "I was reminiscing and missed your question."

"Not a problem. I was asking why you quit acting."

She smiled gently. "Sadly, stars fall as fast as they rise. I was fortunate to have had my time in the spotlight."

Daisy grabbed the pipe to steady herself and the ladder squeaked again. "Here," she said to Spartan, lowering the dye can to him. "Don't spill it."

"Relax. I've got it."

Once the can was safely on the floor, Betty looked at Daisy. "Find anything, dear?"

"Actually, I have," she said, shining her flashlight over the pipe. Climbing down, she replaced the lid on the dye can and lifted a camera from her kit bag. "There are some interesting marks on the top and sides but nothing on the bottom. I can't be sure what etched the pipe, but it could be from a rope."

"Well, at least it sounds like your trip was worthwhile. Stay as long as you like, but I have work to do. I'll be upstairs if you need anything."

Watts nodded his thanks, skeptical about any success. As of now, Daisy could not confirm the hanging took place here, and he didn't recall any mention of pipe marks in the 1970 police report. In this regard, did these marks have any impact on the suicide ruling?

He let his flashlight beam bounce off every corner, wondering if any evidence survived. Other than a few spider webs at the ceiling and water marks near the floor, the dungeon area looked restaurant clean, which seemed unusual for restricted space. The persistent cleaning solution scent suggested the area had been scrubbed since their first visit. But why? Was someone afraid of disproving the legend of Jeremy Delouse? If so, what could they possibly benefit? After all, Jeremy wasn't the only spirit claimed to be living here.

"Hey, guys," he said, lifting the Sony from his pocket. "I can't help thinking we're missing something's so let's all listen to this."

After rewinding the tape, he played it back with everyone gathered around. Every sound was remarkably clear, including the ladder squeak when Daisy leaned on it.

"There! Did you hear that?" he said, stopping the tape.

"I heard something, but I'm not sure what," said Daisy. "It was pretty muffled."

"I agree, and it didn't come from any of us so it must be an EVP. I'm turning this up as loud as I can. Listen carefully."

He played it back and Spartan's eyes shot open. "Noose and murder?" he said.

Watts stopped the tape and wiped his brow. "Thanks for confirming it, Blaine. It's barely audible, but that's exactly what I heard."

Nineteen

AFTER LOOKING TO MAKE sure no one had overheard them, Watts suggested they go into a small room and determine exactly where everyone was when this EVP was recorded. He started recording when they followed Betty into the dungeon and stopped shortly after she left, because his primary objective was to record her conversation. Curiously, there was nothing unusual until Betty left the dungeon.

After listening five more times, Spartan nodded his agreement. "I definitely hear *murder*, but I'm not as certain about the other one."

"I agree," Daisy skeptically said. "I mean it could be *murder* and *noose*, but we could also be hearing that because of expectation bias. You know how those paranormal TV shows capture weird sounds on their recorders, and then they try to make sense of it just like we are now?"

"Yeah," said Watts. "Go on."

"Well, it seems like they tend to hear what they want to hear, rather than explain it as some other phenomena. More than once I've tried to figure out what this faint voice is saying, and before I can get it, they'll dub what they think it is saying at the bottom of the screen. Once they do that, my objectivity is gone and I start hearing what they want me to hear."

"Which is exactly why I didn't want to say anything until someone else did."

Spartan leaned against the wall and looked around the room. "I'm confused, Daisy. Are you saying you don't believe this is an EVP? What about the pipe marks? Did you only mention them to provoke Betty?"

"No, that's not it at all. In fact, I'm quite certain that something heavy hung from that pipe, but how do we know it was Jeremy? For all we know, it could have been anything from a piñata to a sofa."

"A sofa?" said Spartan, raising a brow.

"She's exaggerating," said Watts. "Let's go back in the hall and re-check that pipe."

Arms crossed, Daisy pouted. "All I'm saying is the only way we'll find out about the pipe is to compare my findings to the 1970 police report. As for the strange voice, maybe the lab can provide an answer."

Watts stared at his recorder. "I admit it's easier to see and hear what we want, but expectation bias has no place in any police investigation. I also agree that Daisy discovered something, but whether it's related to Jeremy's hanging remains to be seen. Of course, this mystery voice is something else entirely. I'm hoping Captain Ryder will give us more time if we can confirm it's a legitimate EVP."

Suddenly the light went out and the temperature dropped rapidly. Instinctively, Watts planted himself against the wall searching for a hint of light. His breathing quickened and felt goose bumps on his arms. When Spartan flipped on his flashlight, he could see his breath. For the first time he saw panic in Daisy's face.

"What the hell's going on?" she said.

Watts reached out for her hand. "I wish I knew. Blaine, get the light."

"I'm on it," he said, following his beam. "It's warmer over here." Then he flipped the switch up and down. "Nothing's happening. Is it still cold where you are?"

"Not like it was," said Watts, checking the area with his flashlight.

Daisy rubbed her arms firmly. "This is creepy. I'm ready to leave."

"Me, too," said Spartan. As he started walking toward them, the light flickered for a second and then came on.

Watts anxiously looked around, the only sound his pounding heart.

"Jeremy, if you have something to say, now's a good time to speak up."

No one answered.

"All right, guys, spread out. Let's find whoever's messing with us."

Going in different directions, they opened every door and inspected every room but saw no one or nothing out of place, and there were no vents where someone could have whispered *murder* or *noose*.

Totally frustrated now, Watts angrily said. "Jeremy, are you trying to tell us you were murdered? We're here to help you." Having allowed sufficient time for a response, he added, "Jeremy, if you were murdered, make some noise." His head snapped around when the ladder squeaked.

"Sorry," said Spartan, backing up with his hands in the air. "My fault."

Casting an angry gaze, Daisy repositioned herself directly under the pipe. "Is this where you hung, Jeremy? Did you die here? Did someone murder you?"

When the ladder banged again, no one was near it.

"Dear God!" she said, clutching her chest. "Maxx, can we leave now?"

Watts shook his head, shushing her with a finger over his lips. Before stepping back into the hall, he had turned his recorder on again. Whatever was happening added credence to the EVP he previously recorded.

"Jeremy, I spoke with your nephew," he said. "He came into this world after you passed, and he seems to be a fine man. For some reason he wants us to forget about you, though. He says you're folklore and doesn't believe your spirit exists. Care to respond to that?"

The room went dark again and the temperature felt like it dropped twenty degrees. Their breaths became visible with each exhale. Within seconds, a small orb appeared at the end of the hall and pulsed brighter as it moved toward Watts. Staying long enough to illuminate the detective's face, it then accelerated down the hall. Reaching the end, it vanished and the hall light came back on. The orb's departure warmed the temperature, but Watts was still shivering.

"Goddam! Did you guys see that, or am I imagining it?"

"It was real," said Spartan, mopping his brow. "When the lights went out, I grabbed my phone. I snapped a photo when I saw the orb, but I'm not sure I got anything."

"Either way it's on audio, and no one can deny it. God, I can't wait to see the expression on the Captain's face when he hears this tape. I'm certain he'll give us more time."

Spartan shook his head. "More likely he'll say we fabricated it."

"And he'll also say the pipe marks only verify what the police already knew," said Daisy.

Watts threw his arms in the air. "Well, if you want to give up, so be it, but this place is mind-blowing, and I'm not gonna quit until I find some answers."

Daisy exchanged glances with Spartan and said, "Who said we were giving up?"

"Yeah," said Spartan. "This is just getting interesting."

Relieved, Watts stared at where the orb disappeared. "Well, Jeremy, what about you? Are you in?"

This time Jeremy didn't answer.

Twenty

THE THREE MUSKETEERS WERE emotionally drained by the time they reached the lobby. Each made a quick visit to the restroom to wash up, and by the time they met up again, Betty seemed to be hovering near Jeremy's framed story. They said their good-byes without mentioning anything about what happened downstairs and headed out the door.

They were all squinting as they stepped outside, but no one was complaining. The air was clear, the sky alive with swarming blackbirds. After what they had been through, their conversation was limited to the beautiful sunset the clouds would make.

Walking into 350, Watts contemplated his upcoming meeting with his boss. Addressing Daisy he said, "Do you think the lab can confirm my tape's authenticity? I don't want any claims of falsification."

"I suppose, but it will take time. Didn't you need to see Captain Ryder right away?"

After puffing his cheeks he quickly expelled the air while nodding. "Guess we'll have to do that later." Turning to his partner, he said, "Did you e-mail your orb photo?"

"Yeah, I did it while you were driving."

"Thanks. I'll check it on my desk computer. Daisy, I'll call you before we go in."

"I'm pretty sure I'll be busy," she said with a grin. "Feel free to go in without me."

"For now, please make a copy of the tape, and we'll talk again before the meeting."

Before she could reply, Watts rushed upstairs to open his e-mail. With his partner hovering over him, they viewed the photo.

"Well, Blaine, I can't say much for the clarity, but it does show faint illumination in my face from a single light source."

"Yeah, but the black background makes it look Photoshopped and this is the only one out of three I took that had anything on it. Whether it will mean anything to the boss remains to be seen."

"I hear you. Make sure you bring your phone with you so he can see the original."

"Don't worry. My phone is like jewelry to me."

"Ah ha. You might want to keep that one to yourself. Let's get to work."

Once Spartan left, Watts sat with his fingers suspended over the keyboard. He typed "paranormal investigators" into the Bing search box and hit Enter. Numerous listings from around the country soon appeared. Intrigued by Long Island Paranormal Investigators, he clicked on their link, and a professional-looking website sporting a dozen or so smiling faces filled his screen. He was smiling, too, after reading their services were free. He quickly sent them a query and then went into Spartan's cubicle.

"Blaine, I'm sorry for being so abrupt outside. Daisy's remark made me a little edgy."

"No sweat," said Spartan without bothering to turn around.

Standing behind his partner, he checked out his computer monitor. "So, what are you working on?"

"This is Betty Cerin's history. I'm hoping it will tell me why a successful leading lady would go from the stage to administrative work right after her leading man died."

Watts barely nodded. "She's probably the only one who can answer that."

"Maybe, but I'm searching databases anyway."

Spartan stopped talking when a woman's photo appeared on his monitor. He clicked for more information and seconds later, another page came up.

"Jackpot!" he said, reading the facts. "Betty Cerin, born in 1949, married Travis McLean in 1969, dissolved marriage in 1970, no outstanding wants or warrants, has two speeding tickets to her name, and has used the same Fort Worth address for the last twenty-one years."

Watts leaned over his partner's shoulder studying the page. The image was taken years ago, her hair then blonde and eyes brighter, but she was definitely the same Scott Theater actress. "She was married to our Travis?"

"Apparently."

"This is huge. We've been so focused on Marv and Travis that we, or at least I, have completely blown off the obvious. I always got a strange vibe from her. Pull out your notepad and read what she said."

Spartan flipped through his notes and stopped on one paragraph.

"Betty Cerin is a widow and has been with the Scott Theater for over forty years. McLaughlin was her married name."

"But in 1970 her name was McLean, and Travis is very much alive." Taking his seat, he gestured for Spartan to continue.

Shaking his head, Spartan nonchalantly said, "She stopped working as an actress when Jeremy Delouse died."

"Yeah, we know that, but it's the timeframe of her marriage that's important. If she got an annulment, maybe she didn't think her marriage to Travis counted, so she didn't mention it."

"Maybe. But what if she didn't get it annulled? What if she didn't want us to know about her first marriage?"

"There's always that possibility, I suppose. What else do you have?"

Spartan scanned his notes and shook his head. "Nothing new. She quit acting and then started working administrative positions at the theater. Been doin' it a long time."

Watts sunk deeper into his chair, rocking it hard. "I can't believe we missed this detail."

"Maxx, we haven't missed anything. Betty has been polite, cooperative, and I'm sure there's an explanation for the omission of her marriage to Travis."

"Perhaps," said Watts, straightening his posture. "It's just that I never expected Travis McLean would be her ex-husband."

Spartan raised his hands. "Me neither, but that's how it is."

"You're right. Did you find anything new on Travis?"

Spartan scanned his computer and said, "Nope. Looks like the same information we already have."

Watts moved closer to the screen and began reading aloud. "Drafted into the Army in late 1968, Honorably Discharged with a Purple Heart in 1971, no wants, warrants, or driving tickets, his driver's license expired in 1975, never drew any VA benefits, no employment record since the Army, isn't drawing any social security, and has no known address." He then backed away and folded his arms. "Geez, if I didn't know better I'd think he was dead."

"Hey, maybe he is dead. I mean we're the ones assuming he's the same Travis McLean from the diner."

Watts heaved a sigh. "The only problem is, nothing shows he's deceased. Can you call up his Army record?"

"No, but an FBI buddy of mine probably can."

"Great. Find out everything you can about Travis and Betty. She was acting weird this afternoon, and I think she knows more about Jeremy's death than she's been volunteering."

Spartan glanced at Watts. "Are you thinking Betty had a fling with Jeremy while her husband was in Vietnam?"

"I do, which is why I want to see his military record. Think of how he'd feel if he learned Betty was fooling around while he was sloshing through leech-infested rice paddies."

"Especially being newly married."

Still imagining how a combat-hardened vet would take news like this, Watts shook his head. "I think we need to see Betty again."

Twenty One

Eager for answers but still uneasy about Daisy's irritability, Watts called the lab. She answered and informed him she had copied the tape, printed her pipe photos, and would deliver them when she had time. Though her response was professional, it was also icy, and that frightened him more than any paranormal activity. While his gut told him to confront her about her attitude, his brain couldn't handle it yet.

She showed up minutes later and bombed his desk with a large manila envelope. "Here you go, *detective*. Have you faced Captain Ryder yet?"

He shook his head once. "Right now we're investigating some ties between Betty, Travis and Jeremy. Hopefully, Blaine's FBI friend can get his hands on Travis' Army record."

Spartan poked his head out of his cubicle. "No luck on that yet, but my buddy seems confident he can get it. I'm sure Travis' Army fingerprints will prove the man from the diner's true identity."

"That's great," said Daisy, "but it doesn't explain why you haven't talked to Captain Ryder yet."

Watts sighed, tiring of her constant second-guessing. "Forget about him. We still have another day. Any idea how long it will take to verify our EVPs?"

Following her head-shake, she added, "If you don't need anything else, I should get back to the lab."

Still wondering what he had done to upset her, he reminded himself this was how she sounded when they first met at the Forest Park crime scene. Maybe her detached, matter-of-fact demeanor was her way of maintaining professionalism while working a case, so it wasn't him at all. Seeing that he had no reason to take this personally made him smile.

"I think we're good, Ms. Woods. Thank you for your help."

For a moment she stared back and twitched her brow, but then she said, "No sweat," and hurried away as though she was cramping. At least he hoped that's what it was.

Seeing her this way was unsettling. Feeling responsible for her foul mood spun worse-case scenarios in his head. Was she trying to ditch him? Could they still work together if their relationship went awry? For that matter, could they even finish this case? He was so preoccupied with Daisy that he failed to notice Captain Ryder leaning over his cubicle. Clumsily getting to his feet, he grinned at his boss.

"Hello, Captain. Have you and your kids carved any Halloween pumpkins yet?"

"They're too old for that and it's none of your business. Your clock is ticking, Maxx. Got anything yet?"

"Actually I do, but there's nothing I want to share yet."

"You sure about that?" he said, scanning the office like a submarine captain searching for targets. The only noise in the immediate area came from Spartan, who continued typing as if he didn't know his boss was one cubicle away. Ryder's eyes found Watts again. "Maxx, do you *try* to piss me off?"

"No, sir, I believe that comes naturally." He held his grin for as long as he dared, then sat down so Napoleon didn't have to look up anymore.

"Don't keep me in the dark, Maxx."

"Okay, how about if I tell you we have some serious leads that suggest Jeremy Delouse was involved in a love triangle? And before you say *that explains why he killed himself,* I'd like you to wait for our formal presentation." When Ryder made a face, Watts added, "Captain, yesterday you gave me two days to make a case. I'd like to take advantage of whatever time we have left rather than spend it debating."

Ryder drew in a breath and slowly blew it out his nose. "If you weren't such a capable detective, I'd have you directing traffic before sunset, but I suppose a deal's a deal. Just make sure you give me a full briefing before you go home. Are we clear?"

"We may need to leave to follow a lead. Can I brief you over the phone? If you'd prefer, we can videoconference so you'd know I wasn't in a bar."

"Funny, Maxx, but that's the last place I'd look for you or your partner." He then swatted the top of the cubicle with his palm and stormed off, not in goose-step fashion, but Hitler still would have been proud. Annoyed by Ryder's interruption, Watts returned to his partner's cubicle.

"You can relax now, Blaine. He's gone."

"I know, and I must say you did a great job of blowing him off."

"Years of practice, my man. Find anything new with Travis' military records?"

"Afraid not. My friend in DC reminded me that things there always move at the speed of government. I didn't need to ask what he meant."

Watts nodded, feeling their time slip away. So far all they had were pipe photos and audio recordings, all of which would be challenged. Then it occurred to him they may be going about this the wrong way. If they were investigating this as a new crime, they would be comparing autopsy to crime scene photos.

"Blaine, since we're both at an impasse right now, how about we take a trip to the ME's office to see what we can find on Jeremy?"

Spartan promptly shut down his computer and got up from his chair. "Let's go."

As they left the station, Watts figured getting out would accomplish three things. First, their boss couldn't show up unannounced to harass them. Second, it gave Watts some time away from Daisy. Third and most importantly, a new ME review might reveal previously overlooked evidence. Thankfully, Dr. Morton didn't keep them waiting long.

The detectives followed Morton into his office and seated themselves across from him. "Thank you for seeing us on such short notice," said Watts.

"That's why I'm here. So, you're investigating a cold case murder?"

Watts leaned forward with clasped hands. "Actually, it's a potential cold case," he said. "Back in 1970, the police listed it as a suicide, but it's possible it was a murder."

"I see," Morton said, adjusting his thick black-framed glasses. And where did this event take place?"

"At the Scott Theater. The vic's name was Jeremy Delouse."

Seeing Morton turn pale made Watts leap toward him. "Doc, you okay?"

The ME nodded and slowly removed his glasses. After pinching his eyes, he blinked a few times and blew out a long breath. "Jeremy Delouse, eh?" His color returned once he slipped on his glasses. "I remember him because he was my first autopsy. I couldn't believe it when his name surfaced in the theater hauntings. My wife and I have been to several performances there and never experienced anything out of the ordinary, but who am I to say his spirit isn't hanging around – no pun intended."

"Jeremy was your first autopsy?" said Spartan.

Morton eyed him suspiciously. "I can see your brain calculating the years, and yes, I really am that old, but my memory is still sharp. Whatever you want to know I can probably tell you off the top of my head. Some things you never forget."

"I'm sure that's true," said Watts, "but with all due respect, we'd like to see his file."

"Well, I could probably find you the microfiche version. Everything was converted many years ago to save space. That decision turned out to be a good one, because hundreds of files were destroyed in a warehouse fire several years ago."

"Arson?" said Spartan.

"Of course. But before you review the microfiche, what questions do you have?"

Watts settled into a chair, pressed the record button on his Sony, and flipped his notepad open. "For starters, can you describe the scene?"

Morton leaned his head back and placed his right hand over his mouth. He kept that pose for a while, seemingly organizing his thoughts, during which time, he breathed heavily and gazed at nothing in particular. Every time he shifted in his seat, they expected him to speak, but his words never came. Finally, the ME's hand fell to the arm rest.

"Jeremy was young," he said, as if he could see him standing in the corner. "Twenty-three, if I remember correctly. Clean shaven, strawberry blond hair, nice build, and a face that belonged on stage. Few bodies ever leave an impression, but I remember feeling very sad for this kid because he seemed to have it all. Imagine what it was like, staring down at someone the same age as my brother. My hands were trembling as I examined the rope marks on his neck. I had hoped it was a quick death for him, but it wasn't. Instead, he suffocated for several minutes. I'm certain I listed his cause of death as asphyxiation."

Spartan nodded. "Were there any marks on the body besides rope burns?"

"Not rope burns, but rather bruises and impressions. The difference is significant. Rope burns require rubbing while impressions are stationary. Either way produces bruising."

Watts considered that for a moment. As impressed as he was with the doctor's recollections, it seemed likely that instincts would have taken over and the noose would have rubbed while Jeremy struggled to free himself.

"Dr. Morton, can we see the microfiche on Mr. Delouse?" he said.

Morton smiled as an old man would at his son who didn't believe him. He pressed the intercom button to reach his secretary. "Megan, can you please show the detectives the microfiche on Jeremy Delouse from January, 1970?"

Her pause implied confusion. Watts wondered why.

"Certainly," she said.

Morton grinned, folding his hands. "Megan will take care of you," he said in a tone suggesting their conversation was over.

Spartan rose from his chair and extended his hand. "Thanks, Doc."

Watts quickly followed suit. "Keep up the good work, Doc. We're nothing without you."

"Well thank you, detective. That's the kindest thing you've ever said to me. Now that my life's complete, perhaps I should retire."

Watts burst out laughing, knowing he was kidding. He and the ME had worked a lot of cases together, and it was nice the circumstances were different this time. Like Morton, he remembered the victims long after their cases were over.

He wasn't expecting the ME's secretary to be so shapely. Her long brunette hair caressed her chest, and her skirt seemed to share the same length as her heels. Ignoring their obvious glances, Megan led them to a locked office. As she bent over to unlock it, her skirt slid up her thigh stopping just shy of her buttocks. Noticing his partner's gaze, Watts jabbed him in the ribs. Spartan's eyes immediately fell to the floor.

Megan searched for several minutes before handing them an envelope containing Jeremy's history. "Do you know how to work the microfiche viewer?" she said.

Watts flipped the ON switch, slid the flat film under the reader's lens, and Jeremy's data appeared on screen. "I think we're good."

"Okay. Let me know if you need anything else. The door will remain locked from the outside so no one should disturb you."

"Thanks, Megan," he said, wondering how many other guests had a pulse.

Spartan admired the fiche viewer, shaking his head. "Man, it's been years since I've seen one of these. I'm surprised you knew how to turn it on."

"I spent a lot of time in the library growing up." While maneuvering the film under the machine, he added, "On a separate note, I thought you were past the ogling stage."

"Seems we were both ogling."

"I see. I'm sure Sandy would accept that for an answer."

Spartan's face reddened. "Moving on, what are we looking for?"

"Photos."

Using the reader took Watts back to the third grade, where his favorite librarian let him review whatever he wanted once he had demonstrated his ability. "Did you know one fiche can hold up to 98 document pages?"

"Can't say that I did, Maxx. Find anything of interest?"

"Not yet, but you can imagine the space savings. I remember the librarian saying it had an estimated five hundred year shelf life in dry climates."

"I imagine that was a major selling point to the medical profession."

"Yeah, especially since it produced an exact image of the original documents and photos. And unlike today's digital media, microfiche doesn't require any software to decode stored data. But as you can see, finding what we're looking for is much easier on a computer than moving film around under a reader's lens." He paused, and moved it a little more. Suddenly, he said, "Eureka! We have autopsy photos!"

Studying the images, neither saw anything more than the rope marks on Jeremy's neck, which did not appear broken or deformed. Close-ups revealed broken capillaries in his eyes.

Spartan leaned over Watts' shoulder to see better. "Is there a close-up of just the rope?"

Watts shook his head. "Not that I've seen, but then this is just the ME's file." Thinking about that, he looked at his partner. "I wonder if Jeremy's police file is on microfiche."

"Beats me, but we can check once we get back to the station. Of course, Captain Ryder is certain to ask whether we learned anything from this visit, and I don't want to leave without an answer."

Watts climbed out of the seat and gestured for his partner to assume it. "It's all yours, Blaine. Knock yourself out. I need to use the restroom."

He left the door cracked so he could get back in without disturbing the secretary. On his way, he wondered if any spirits lived here. His understanding was that spirits tend to remain where the person was killed, but the morgue felt much creepier than the theater. He took his time exploring the facility while he was there. Dr. Morton waved as he passed his office, but it was more like a "howdy" than an invitation to come visit. Eventually, he meandered back to the microfiche room, hoping his partner had come up with something in his absence.

"Find anything?"

Spartan shrugged, staring at the reader. "I've gone over every inch of this and didn't see anything that could be considered a match for the pipe marks in the dungeon. About all I found was a note describing the rope as one-inch twine." He paused, studying the fiche again. "You remember Dr. Morton saying the cause of death was asphyxiation?"

"Yeah."

"Well, it wasn't. According to this, the cause of death was cerebral edema followed by cerebral ischemia due to obstruction of venous drainage of the brain via occlusion of the internal jugular veins. Vessels were engorged and cyanotic through lack of oxygen. Classic signs of strangulation: petechiae, burst blood capillaries in the eyes, protruding tongue. I was reading that, by the way. I won't pretend to understand all of it."

"I hear you. What's petechiae?"

"I called Megan and she said it's plural for petechia, which is small red or purple spots on the body caused by a minor hemorrhaging."

"In other words, marks from broken capillaries like we saw in the ME's photos."

"Exactly."

Watts nodded, wondering what else he might have missed. "Any other findings?"

"It says compromise of the cerebral blood occurred by obstruction of the carotid arteries. Rope marks on his neck were consistent with a slow death caused by strangulation. After death, the body typically shows marks of suspension: bruising and rope marks on the neck. An intact hyoid bone suggests no manual choking."

Watts nodded, tapping his lips. "I'm not sure it makes any difference, but why would Dr. Morton say Jeremy died from asphyxiation?"

"Beats me. Why don't we ask him?"

They left the door open and moved as quietly as Watts' shoe would allow. In the background, Dr. Morton was dictating the kind of autopsy no one liked – a fourteen year old girl who overdosed on drugs. From what Morton was describing, she wasn't a regular user, either. Experience told Watts she was probably a normal kid that caved under pressure. Morton stepped away to blow his nose and then resumed his dictation.

The ME's voice carried more emotion than usual. Considering the number of teen deaths he had seen over the years, that seemed odd. Regardless, it was clear that now wasn't a good time to confront him about a death that occurred in 1970. Watts signaled to retreat and led the way to Megan's office, thinking she might be able to help.

Busy with paperwork, the secretary barely looked up when they came in. "Are you gentlemen finished?"

"Not quite," said Watts. "I was wondering if you knew anything about the teen that's undergoing an autopsy right now. The doc sounds unusually sensitive."

She smiled wryly. "If you're referring to his nose blowing, he's been fighting allergies for weeks, probably a result of the drought. He does his best to hide it when he's in the field, but here, he honks with no remorse."

Watts nodded, glancing at his partner who seemed fixated on the medical magazine on Megan's desk. A moment later, he realized that the magazine was in line with her cleavage. Spartan's roaming eyes must drive his wife crazy.

"I know this sounds silly, but have you ever heard of a hanging victim arriving at the morgue with the rope around the neck?"

"Can't say that I have, but then I'm just a secretary. My only involvement with dead bodies is through the reports."

"I suspected that was the case." Watts looked around, trying to come up with some other questions, but nothing came to mind. "I suppose we should get busy. Sorry to have bothered you."

She glanced up to fake a smile. "No problem." Instantly she went heads-down.

The morgue was unusually quiet as they walked back to the microfiche room, which made his shoe squishing seem three times louder than normal. When they arrived, they found the door locked. Watts frowned at his partner, thinking he had pulled it shut.

"Don't look at me," said Spartan. "I didn't close it."

Watts shook his head and sighed. In the distance, Morton was dictating again. Leaning into his partner, he whispered, "It's a heavy door with a smooth latch. It must have shut on its own. Would you please get Megan to open it again?"

"You bet. I'll be right back."

Spartan's eagerness was predictable. Any excuse to see an attractive woman was a good one. While waiting, Watts contemplated the dead girl on the examination table. He couldn't imagine the torment her parents were going through. As a beat cop, he had to remove several kids from their homes after they had torn the place up. As a homicide detective, he saw some of these kids become victims of drug-related crimes. The teen girl on Morton's slab no longer suffered, but her actions sentenced her parents to a lifetime of grief.

Watts heard footsteps and looked up. Spartan was waving the key like it was an Olympic medal. After unlocking the door, he gestured for his partner to enter.

"That's great, Blaine, but how did you get the key from the Iron Lady?"

Spartan chuckled. "Would you want to walk in those spike heels? Trust me, I didn't have to beg."

Watts smiled. "Well, now that we're in, let's get back to business." But as soon as he sat down at the desk, he noticed Jeremy's microfiche was missing and the machine was turned off. He looked underneath the machine and on the floor but didn't see it. "I don't know what in the hell's going on, but I know I left the fiche in the machine. How about checking the cabinet?"

Spartan checked the spot where Megan got it from and didn't find it. After several minutes of searching and coming up empty, he frowned at his partner. "I have no idea where it is, but it's not where she pulled it from."

Watts squeezed his eyes shut. "Unreal. I'd ask Doc Morton, but he hates interruptions. Let's return the key and have Megan ask him when it's convenient."

"She's not gonna like this."

"Well, that's how it is."

Watts timed their walk to her office, which took just under three minutes. They had spent less than five minutes with her before returning to the microfiche room. Assuming they kept the same pace on their return trip, they were away for approximately eleven minutes. Eleven minutes would have been plenty of time for anyone working in the morgue to enter the room, remove the fiche, and lock the door. Though the time table made sense, who else would want Jeremy's file?

With the thought hanging like stale air, Watts tapped on Megan's door to get her attention. She acknowledged them by raising her index finger, not making eye contact until she had completed her task.

"Are you heading out?" she said.

Shaking his head, Watts slowly approached her desk. "We wanted to discuss a discrepancy with Dr. Morton, but he's busy." He had hoped to see what she was working on, but she minimized her screen before he could see anything.

"Would you like me to leave him a note?"

"Maybe," said Spartan, butting in, "but first, does the Records Room door normally close on its own?"

Her expression soured. "I'm not sure what you mean, since it's always supposed to be locked. Is there a problem?"

"No," said Watts, Watts quickly said, surveying the office. "Megan, where did you go after you let us in?"

Her eyes narrowed. "Here, of course. As I said, the paperwork is endless."

"I'm sure," said Spartan. "Who else is in the building right now?"

Crossing her arms, she gave a scornful look. "What are you asking, detective? Should I do a roll call for the twenty-some people on day shift, or should this body count include the dead?"

Watts smiled as Megan pondered her answer. Twenty-some employees sounded reasonable for a department with multiple functions. Resting his hand on a vacant desk he said, "Megan, who else uses the microfiche room?"

Her face wrinkled like something was amiss. "Anyone with a need," she said, "but you're the first I've ever let in. Mind telling me what's going on?"

Following a long pause, Spartan broke the silence. "Jeremy Delouse's microfiche is missing. Someone took it while were looking for Dr. Morton."

Her eyes danced like angry bees. "His file is gone? How can that be if you locked the door? I mean, it was locked, right? Tell me you came back for the key because it was locked."

"Yes, we came back because the door was locked," said Watts, stopping his partner from spewing more details.

Megan placed her hands on her hips and paced. A moment later, she threw her hands up and glared at them. "Well it's not here. Feel free to look around. While you're at it, check my phone records. I've had two calls since I let you in and I broke a nail typing a report. Here, take a look," she said, raising her middle finger.

Ignoring her clever gesture, Watts copied the numbers from her phone log while searching for the missing film. He wasn't surprised when nothing turned up.

"Getting back to the fiche file, is it possible someone cleaned the Records Room while we stepped out?"

Her nostrils flaring now, she said, "Detective Watts, I will personally hold you accountable for any security breach."

"I will accept full responsibility for any missing items," he said, hoping to avoid further confrontation. "Is there a duplicate by chance?"

"Detective, the microfiche *was* the duplicate," she said, still shaking her head. She paused to look at her copying machine and then held out her hand. "I need to see your badges for my report."

Without hesitating, Watts lifted his shield and dropped it in her palm. Once Spartan followed suit, she scanned them into her computer and handed them back. Her matter-of-fact approach reminded Watts of Daisy Woods, whom he still hadn't heard from. After typing their names and saving the document, she minimized the screen.

Watts tucked his badge away and looked at her. "Now that that's out of the way, could you help us look for the missing file?"

Groaning at her IN basket, she logged off her computer and marched through the door stomping her heels. Her silence was probably intended to show her annoyance, but she couldn't help huffing as she keyed the lock.

"I don't see how anyone could have gotten inside since I'm one of the few with a key." Pushing the door open, she said, "Of course I'll have to accept the blame, because I failed to emphasize it should always be locked."

Walking beside her, letting her vent, Spartan said, "Detective Watts already told you, we will assume responsibility. No one's gonna blame you."

"That's easy to say when your job's not on the line," she mumbled, searching the shelves.

The detectives exchanged glances before beginning their own search. Watts put little effort into it, since the dusty layers confirmed nothing else had been disturbed. That didn't keep Megan from sorting through all of the files, though.

Suddenly her arms dropped. "Sorry, guys, but it's time to quit when my limbs go numb. Search as long as you want, but my gut tells me it's not here."

Watts nodded his agreement. "Who else knew we were looking at his file?"

Her first response was to pout and stare at the ceiling. Following a brief pause, she said, "Dr. Morton and I were the only ones who knew you were interested in Mr. Delouse's file, and that means I'll get blamed for what happened." Pausing to roll her eyes and grit her teeth, she added, "Anything else? My IN basket requires my attention."

"No, Megan, but thanks for your help. Remember, I'm the one that left the door open. Make sure you put that in your report."

"Count on it," she said, hurrying away.

Spartan made a sour face. "Well, here's another nice mess you've gotten us into."

Watts grinned, recalling the Laurel and Hardy episodes he watched with his mom. Someone gave her a VHS set many years ago, and she loved having him at her side. "I agree, Ollie, and unfortunately all we've learned is the microfiche contents are inconsistent with the ME's reported cause of death. Of course, we can't prove that without Jeremy's file in our possession."

Spartan looked doomed. "How will we explain this to the captain?"

"I have no idea, Blaine, but since Dr. Morton's credibility is at stake, maybe he'll keep this to himself."

"By which you mean you have no intention of telling the boss."

"Only if word gets out," said Watts, guiding his partner out of the room. "As I've said so many times, never volunteer information." After pulling the door shut, he added, "What do you say we head back to 350 and see what Daisy's come up with?"

"Sounds good."

Twenty Two

WATTS CALLED DAISY FROM the station's parking lot, unsure how things were with them. Her tense voice meant either she was still angry, or a co-worker was within earshot. He hoped it was the second option because Spartan was listening in. His anxiety eased slightly when she started with talk about EVPs.

"I've been listening to a lot of paranormal examples to get a better sense of what you recorded," she said. "Some were quite difficult to understand, but others were clear like your passive session."

Head tilted, arms crossed, he said, "What do you mean by passive session?"

"In paranormal lingo, a passive session is an unsolicited spirit response like what we recorded at the theater. At the investigator's recommendation, we ran our EVPs through a computer program that chopped the recordings into analytical segments. Then we attempted to rule out non-spectral sounds by comparing them to our voices. We also used a filter to remove background noise, which in our case was minimal, since we were in the nearly soundproof dungeon. We ended up with an unexplainable voice that definitely seems to be saying *murder* and *noose*. Maxx, I can't help thinking about that noose I found above my door. Do you think it's somehow related?"

Watts rubbed his forehead, thinking about that. "I doubt it, but we just got back to the station. We'll be right there." After hanging up, he turned to Spartan. "I assumed you were coming with me, but if you prefer, you can head upstairs."

"Are you nuts? I'm not taking a chance of Captain Ryder seeing me."

Watts snickered, picturing their boss roaming the halls on a witch-hunt. Then again, he tended to show up at the most inopportune times, so maybe there was some truth in it.

Daisy was waiting for them at the counter and welcomed them with a smile. "This way," she said, and led them into a small room filled with electronic equipment, technical manuals and printed graphs. She seated herself in front of a computer and clicked the mouse. A new graph instantly appeared.

"This is an electronic portrayal of the sounds taken from your Sony recorder. Note how it spikes where the word *murder* appears. Digitally comparing this voice to ours showed no matches, meaning none of us uttered *murder* or *noose* as a joke. As far as the lab is concerned, our EVPs are legitimate."

Watts cast a worried look. "Playing Captain Ryder's favorite role as the Devil's Advocate, how can you be certain about what this mysterious voice said? In other words, are we hearing this because of the expectation bias we discussed earlier?"

Spartan's face sank. "How can there be expectation bias when we never expected to hear a voice in the first place?"

While Daisy stared at the computer screen, struggling for an answer, Watts replayed the EVP three more times using a headset. Each time, he pressed a little harder over his ears to hear better. He then paused the recording and removed the headset. "Blaine, none of us expected to hear anything down there except our own voices, and what I'm hearing sure sounds like *murder* and *noose*. These EVPs are the break we were hoping for."

"I agree," said Daisy. Looking around, her co-workers seemed preoccupied with other duties. No one nearby was paying attention. Still, she kept her voice low. "How did things go at the morgue?"

Spartan's head dropped so Watts took over. "Let's just say it could have gone better."

Squeezing her chest, she switched her gaze to Spartan. The detective responded by stuffing his hands in his pockets and shuffling his feet until he broke.

"Fine," said Spartan. "In a nutshell, Jeremy Delouse's autopsy showed he died from blood loss to the brain rather than asphyxiation like Dr. Morton told us. It turns out Dr. Morton conducted the autopsy. We tried to ask him about it, but he was busy, so we talked to his secretary. Somewhere in that brief time, someone stole Jeremy's records."

"Jeremy's records are gone?" she said, glancing at Watts for confirmation.

He frowned back, nodding. "Which means not only are we in trouble, but we can't prove Dr. Morton's cause of death ruling was inconsistent."

Spartan looked at Watts. "The autopsy had a statement about Jeremy's neck bone, but I can't seem to recall it."

Watts scanned through his notes. "I believe you're referring to his intact hyoid bone supporting the suicide ruling. Of course, none of that matters without Jeremy's records to back it up."

"That makes sense," said Daisy. "Since the horseshoe-shaped hyoid is located above the thyroid, it normally breaks if the vic's been strangled."

"I understand that," said Spartan. "But why didn't it break when he was hanged?"

"Geometry," said Watts. "Due to the angle of the noose, the chin takes the brunt of the fall, whereas hands normally crush the hyoid."

Daisy smiled. "I'm impressed, and you are correct."

"Thank you," said Watts, smiling back. "Geometry was one of my better subjects in school, but I'm no expert."

"No offense, but you really should ask Dr. Morton."

Watts pinched his eyes, concerned about Ryder's deadline. "Morton can wait. Were you able to get the tape transcribed?"

"Of course," she said, sliding a manila folder over. "I meant to give it to you before, but I got sidetracked showing you the digital depictions."

"No sweat." He then opened the folder and tabled the contents for review. "I'm only concerned with the last few minutes of the tape."

Watts: "Forgive me for stating the obvious, Betty, but you were a star performer, and stars don't normally quit."

Betty: "Detective Watts, stars can fall as fast as they rise. I proved that."

Daisy: "Here, take this. And whatever you do, don't spill it."

Betty: "Did you find anything, dear?"

Daisy: "Actually, I have. I found some interesting marks on the top and sides, but nothing on the bottom. I can't be sure, but it appears that fibers etched this pipe."

Betty: "Sounds like it was worth the trip. Now if you'll excuse me, I have work to do. Stay as long as you like. I'll be upstairs if you need anything."

Soon after, the faint voice heard only on the tape said, *"Murder"* and *"Noose"*.

End of tape.

Watts glanced at Daisy who kept staring at the transcript. "This transcript confirms that the EVP occurred right after Betty left the room."

"That's how I see it," she said, her eyes locked on the paper.

Spartan scratched the back of his head, squinting. "The dungeon was so quiet we could have heard a pin drop. How could we have missed the voice on this EVP?"

"Beats me," said Watts, dabbing a Kleenex to his nose. "I guess that's why they call EVPs *phenomena*."

Wadding his tissue flashed him back to the morgue where Dr. Morton kept sniffling while he examined the body. Over the years Watts had seen countless teens that matched this girl's description, any of whom could have died this way. He could never rid them from his head. How did the ME cope with such tragedy?

Daisy's voice brought him back. When he opened his eyes, she and Spartan were staring. He quickly said, "We need to get back to work. Daisy, thanks for the help. I truly appreciate it."

"You're welcome." Almost as an afterthought, she reached into a drawer and pulled out his audiotape. "Here's your original. We made copies, so do whatever you want."

Do whatever you want? Hoping he wasn't reading too much into her words, he dropped the tape in his pocket and left. His emotional baggage weighed him down as he climbed the stairs, and when he arrived at his desk, he plopped in his chair, exhausted. When rubbing his forehead did nothing to ease his headache, he closed his eyes trying to empty his brain. Lately, nothing had been going right, and he felt certain Daisy was the reason. Having doubts about paranormal activity didn't help. When nothing eased his mind, he stepped into his partner's cubicle.

"Blaine, I'm thinking we should postpone our meeting with the boss. Right now all we have is a pipe scratch, concerns about the ME's statements, a person of interest we can't locate and know nothing about, a man who refuses to speak to us about his uncle's death, and a ghost we think might be talking to us. If we go to Captain Ryder with this, he'll burn us at the stake."

Spartan grinned, shaking his head. "He won't burn us at the stake, Maxx. He'll just say we're both crazy and kick us off the force."

Watts snorted. "Thanks, Blaine. That's much better. Meanwhile, tick-tock."

He heard footsteps and recognized them as Captain Ryder's. Like Watts', Ryder's shoes had a unique sound. He carried more weight on his left foot, which meant more noise when that heel struck the ground. When the sound stopped, Watts looked up.

"Hello, Captain."

The flimsy cubicle panel rocked as Ryder leaned on it. Quickly backing away, he pointed to his watch, and then headed for the closet they called a break room. Even though he never uttered a word, his message came through loud and clear. *Your time's up, boys!*

Spartan waited until he saw Ryder enter the break room before speaking. "I believe he delighted in that display."

"Yeah, it's called taunting. He probably used the same tactic when interviewing suspects. If they didn't break from his ugliness, his breath would send them over the edge."

Spartan grinned, making sure Ryder hadn't reappeared. "We still have a few hours. What do you want me to do?"

"Keep looking into Travis McLean and Jeremy Delouse. Find whatever you can on those two and get back to me. It's time I checked in with the Mormon Church."

"Say what?"

Watts turned his head to sneeze, the pressure from the spasm thrashing his brain. With so many things on his mind, he had to forget about Daisy and concentrate on the case. Aware that Ryder might stop by again, he was careful about what he said.

"The Mormons are genealogy experts, and I need to know more about some family trees. We're obviously missing something, and I'm hoping they can provide answers."

"Fair enough," said Spartan. "Keep me posted."

Watts returned to his cubicle and stared at his computer monitor, wondering how to delay their meeting with the boss. The EVP recordings would be a tough sell, but they might buy them more time. Ryder kept his promise and had assigned last night's homicide to another team, but nothing would keep them from moving up the list. Since all other records had failed to produce any history on Travis McLean, he typed *Mormon genealogy* in the computer's search engine. Almost immediately, a list of various search options appeared on screen, the top one being The Mormons (LDS). He filled in the blanks for first name, last name, and hoped Travis truly was 66 for his age. When he clicked on the *Trace my tree* image, over thirty people with the same name appeared. Only one was in his sixties. He was sixty-nine and from Iowa, which made it unlikely he was the same Travis.

When he clicked on *This is me*, it said there were nearly 140,000 McLean records in their database and gave an option for a free seven day trial. Cursing under his breath, he kicked over his trash can.

Before anyone appeared, he bent over to clean up to make it appear an accident. The so-called free trial required his name and e-address and he wasn't willing to do that, especially on a police computer. Frustrated over wasting time with the Mormon Church, he logged into the National Database which confirmed Betty Cerin had indeed been married twice.

"Hey Blaine, check this out." He began reading once his partner was there looking over his shoulder. "Betty Cerin married Travis McLean on January 26, 1969. That marriage was annulled on February 27, 1970. Then on August 2, 1971, she married Justin McLaughlin and became a widow the following August first. She never re-married after that."

Spartan's forehead wrinkled as he leaned into the computer screen. "Where'd you find that?"

"National Database, Bro. Maybe it updated after you checked."

Spartan cleared his throat several times. "Maxx, I refuse to believe this database just uploaded information from the seventies. The bottom line is, I missed it."

"Forget it, Blaine. What matters is this confirms Betty was married to Travis when Jeremy died."

"Again, maybe she didn't think annulments counted."

"Perhaps," said Watts, scratching his neck. "Or is she hiding something?"

Spartan hiked his shoulders. "I don't have an answer for that one."

"Okay. Got anything else in your notes?"

After double-checking, he shook his head sideways.

Discouraged, Watts leaned back in his chair and rocked it hard. "I'm worried how the boss will take this."

"Don't worry, Maxx. We'll face Captain Ryder whenever we need to. In the meantime, I'll see if I can get Betty back on the phone and ask about her marriages."

"Good idea, and this time I'm going to record it."

The number Betty gave was the Scott Theater's, and no one was answering the phone. Spartan hung up and re-dialed, but again, all he got was a recording giving theater information and a referral to their website.

Spartan set his phone aside. "What now?"

"Now I go home and bury my head under the covers."

But Spartan wasn't laughing. Instead, he calmly sat next to his partner with folded hands.

"Okay, Maxx, I'm not your therapist or confidant, but I need to know what's bugging you if we're gonna keep working together. This isn't like you, man. You're usually the driving force behind our investigations. The one who inspires *me*. You're forgetting we're trying to solve a case that isn't even a case, and I'm not willing to throw my career away over it. I'm not sure what you're trying to accomplish by harassing Betty, but we could find ourselves in deep kimchee if she complains to the chief. So with this in mind, how bad do you want this?"

Watts closed his eyes and inhaled through his nose. His eyes stayed closed a long time before blinking. "As always, I want the truth, and not just a piece of it. It concerns me when people of interest make themselves scarce. I can't help thinking we're getting the run-around like she's protecting someone. So yeah, I'm feeling a bit anxious, but it's only because I'm willing to go the distance. I hope you're with me, Bro. I really hope you're with me."

"I don't know," he said, rubbing his eyebrows. "I mean, I understand your frustration over the case, but I also think you have other issues. So man up and spill it. I'm all ears."

Watts gazed at his desk, wishing he could display Daisy's photo that was tucked away in his drawer. Thinking of her started his heart banging like an engine with a fouled plug. He needed to talk, but not here.

"Walk with me, Blaine."

"I take it we're doing another grounds inspection?"

"You got it."

Watts didn't speak until they had approached the river. He loved going there, especially on days like this. As falling leaves crossed their path, the sun warmed their skin. Soon, the rippling water had blocked out the street noise. After tossing a stone in the river, he glanced at his partner.

"First of all, thanks for being patient."

"No sweat, man. It's what partners do."

Watts passed a grateful nod. "Picking up where we left off, and I swear to God I'll beat the crap out of you if you utter a word about this to anyone, I don't know what's happening with Daisy. I really thought we had something special, but now all I'm getting are mixed signals. She's an amazing woman, Blaine. I don't want to lose her, but I'm not sure what to do.

"Ease up, Maxx. She probably has a lot on her mind."

Watts' head cocked. "Are you her confidante now?"

"No, not at all. All I said was she isn't trash-talking you. Why are you so worried?"

Squeezing his hands until his fingers turned white, Watts hoped the pain would stimulate his brain. Instead, the blood rushing through his ears muted all sound, including his partner's words. His hearing improved when Spartan touched his shoulder. Pulling away, he said, "Let's not talk about her anymore."

"You know, Maxx, you're driving me crazy. First you drag me away from my desk, then I tail you like a puppy, and now you don't have the decency to hash this out. What's wrong with you, man?"

Watts showed his palms. "Like I said, Blaine. I don't want to lose her."

Spartan turned his head toward the station. "You're on your own, Maxx. I need to get back to work." He started to walk away but then stopped to glance at his partner. "You know you're gonna blow it for everyone if you don't pull yourself together. Give her enough space where she won't feel smothered, and don't come back until your head's clear. I'll take care of Ryder if I have to." After that he walked away.

Watts stared at the river as his partner's words sunk in. He tossed another rock and watched it plunk into the mud bank. A wind gust caused a sudden chill. After ten minutes of pondering his life, his love, and this crazy case, he accepted that most of his stress was self-induced, and that the world's fate was not dependent upon him solving the mystery behind Jeremy Delouse's death. Right now all that mattered were his job and his girlfriend, and he would do whatever he could to keep both.

Twenty Three

WATTS' ANXIETY LEVEL HAD eased somewhat by the time he returned to his desk, but when he sat down, he felt the need to apologize to his partner. Spartan must have known he was there, but he made no attempt to acknowledge him. Watts tried to lighten the mood by leaning into his partner's cubicle. He didn't speak until he made eye contact.

"Blaine, I'm sorry. You're a good friend and I always appreciate your advice." When his partner continued to type, Watts took the hint and retreated into his cubicle.

Deciding to focus on his meeting rather than his partner, he sat at his computer and started to document the Jeremy Delouse investigation. Less than one sentence in he realized Daisy had been instrumental in authenticating pipe marks and EVPs. That had him thinking about her moods swings, which he then connected to when she first spotted the toy noose. While he remained convinced the dungeon's paranormal activity increased her anxiety, it was a stretch to think there was any correlation between her nylon noose and Jeremy's hanging.

A noise made him look over his shoulder. Thankfully it was Spartan and not the boss.

"What's up, Blaine?"

"Maxx, when you came in I was in the middle of something that couldn't wait. Now that it's done, I thought we could kiss and make up."

Watts shushed him and then poked his head outside. Seeing no one he whispered, "Keep your voice down, dude. People might get the wrong idea."

Spartan's grin faded. "It was a joke, Maxx. A way to say I'm sorry. Anyway, have you sorted things out?"

"If you're referring to a lady friend the answer is yes, and thank you for your concern." A glance at his watch confirmed the minutes were vanishing faster than a dungeon orb. "Should we try calling Betty again?"

"Sure."

Watts readied his Sony when Spartan dialed Betty's number and began recording once she answered the phone.

"Hi, Betty, this is Detective Spartan again. Sorry to bother you, but I have some personal questions to ask. Should I come down to the theater, or can we speak over the phone?"

"I have nothing to hide, detective. What's on your mind?"

After verifying his partner's Sony was recording, he said, "Could you please provide some details on your marriage status?"

""No problem, and hello Detective Watts, I assume you're listening in."

Watts waved at the phone, rolling his eyes. "Hello, Betty. Yes, I'm here, too."

"Now that we have that out of the way, I married Justin McLaughlin on August 2nd, 1971, and became a widow one day before our first anniversary. He was on his way back from a jewelry store when an illegal T-boned him at an intersection. They found a necklace in his car along with an anniversary card. I've never taken this necklace off, because Justin was the love of my life. My happiness died that day. I hope the driver that took his life is riddled with guilt."

"I'm sorry for your loss, and your bitterness is certainly understandable." He paused before getting to his point. "Betty, weren't you also married to Travis McLean?"

"Yes, but to tell you the truth, I could never call that a marriage. We exchanged vows on January 26, 1969, and then he left for the Army on February 7th. On April 4th, he landed in Vietnam to be part of President Johnson's surge. Then I received word that he was injured on June 21st, but I had no idea about his condition. A week later, I was informed that he was at Fitzsimons Army Hospital in Colorado, so I drove there. Other than his leg, he looked fine, but he was terribly angry and told me to leave. I stuck around for a day or two, but he treated me so horribly that I went home. The next time I heard from him was in a letter saying he was rehabilitated and had landed in Vietnam on August 3rd. Needless to say, he was more interested in the Army than me, because I'm certain he could have received a medical discharge. I didn't see him again until December 26th, and since we spent most of the time fighting, he left to stay with his parents. Then on January 23rd, he said I deserved better and returned to Vietnam."

"Sorry to interrupt, Betty, but I just want to clarify that was January 23rd, 1970."

"That's correct. Anyway, he agreed to have our marriage annulled while he was over there. Later, I heard the fool opted for a second tour. I had only one true husband, gentlemen, and after two attempts at love and a tragic loss, I decided I was better off dedicating my life to the Scott Theater. It's been a wonderful home to me. I have no regrets."

Watts passed him a note wanting him to ask why her second marriage didn't show up in the database. Spartan paused for a moment and said, "Betty, where did you and Justin get married?"

"On a cruise ship in the Caribbean. The Caribe Princess, I believe. Why?"

"Did the ship's captain marry you?"

"Yes. Why? Is that a problem?"

"Not at all. In fact, it sounds quite romantic." He paused again to re-read Watts' note. "Did you ever change your last name?"

"I did the first time, but once that marriage was annulled, I went back to my maiden name. Justin knew what I had gone through, so neither of us thought it was important to change it again. Ironically, after he died I seriously considered changing it to McLaughlin in his memory, but never did. I still quiver when I approach his gravestone, so there's no way I would feel comfortable sharing his name. I guess that makes me weak."

"You're not weak, Betty. Just a grieving widow." Stopping to clear his throat, he said, "On a different note, did you ever hear from Travis McLean after you separated?"

"We went our own ways, detective, and I've never had any reason to contact him."

Watts was about to stop the tape when Betty asked him a question.

"You've been surprisingly quiet, Detective Watts. You were always the curious one. Don't you have any questions?"

"Not right now, Betty, but thanks for asking. By the way, you might like to know that we documented some interesting EVPs shortly after you left the dungeon. The tape revealed a paranormal voice saying *murder* and *noose*. Has anyone else reported this before?"

"No," she said without hesitation. "Is there any way to identify the voice?"

"Not that we know of, but since you're more in tune with the spirits than us, do you have any idea why one might say either of those words? I mean, isn't Jeremy Delouse the only one who died in that theater?"

"We've had some people collapse and hurt themselves over the years, and plenty of actors have faked death on stage, but Jeremy is the only one that actually died on the theater premises. Do you think Jeremy's saying he was murdered? Is that what this is about?"

Using a hand gesture, Watts quietly deferred her question to his partner.

Spartan nodded and said, "Betty, this whole thing is so far out of our league that we have no idea what we're getting into. If we get any answers, we'll be sure to let you know. Thanks again for your cooperation. We really appreciate it."

"I'm always happy to answer your questions. Good day, gentlemen."

Watts stopped the Sony when Spartan hung up. Wearing a smug expression, he ran his hand through his hair. "Well, Blaine, any thoughts?"

"Of course we'll have to see if her story checks out, but it could explain why her second marriage's documentation was flawed."

"As in her marriage license was lost at sea?"

"Something like that. I mean, think of all the paperwork cruise ships must have dealt with before computers. If her marriage license wasn't properly filed, it wouldn't show up in the database, and the fact that she never changed her name means she would have received her husband's life insurance payoff whether they were married or not. In other words, it's plausible she was married twice and isn't covering anything up."

Watts bobbed his head as he spun around to use his computer. "I'm gonna run Justin Laughlin's name through the database to see what happens."

The results came back with forty-one names. Three quarters of the way down the list, he found the man he was looking for. "Justin McLaughlin. Born July 6, 1949. Died August 1,1972."

"Poor bastard," said Spartan. "Barely twenty-three years old."

"You're obviously forgetting that tens of thousands of teens died in Vietnam. Every time Dad got drunk, he'd start ranting about all the buddies he lost over there. Several of the kids he went to school with came back in flag-draped coffins before their twentieth birthday."

He stopped talking when Justin's profile came up.

"McLaughlin graduated from the University of Texas in 1971,

which explains how he avoided Vietnam. Dad said all you had to do was make basic grades to evade the draft."

"But wouldn't he have been eligible once he graduated? I mean, the war didn't end until 1973 or 74, right?"

"That was long before my time, but who knows? Maybe he was about to be drafted when he died. All that really matters is Betty's story checks out."

Spartan nodded, gazing at the ceiling.

Watts gave him a curious look. "What's with you?"

"You're gonna think I'm perverted, but I was thinking how attractive Betty must have been as a young actress. Can you imagine her getting married twice within a couple of years and then becoming a widow at such a young age? Guys must've hit on her all the time. I wonder why she never married again."

"Beats me, but I'm not about to ask her anything that personal."

Spartan nodded. "You're probably right. So, where does this leave us? Are we gonna give this case up or beg for more time?"

Watts raised his hands. "It's your call, partner." He didn't mean that, but then he couldn't do this alone, either. While waiting, he pictured the cogs spinning in his partner's brain. Still without an assignment, he was hoping Spartan would want to continue their pursuit. Whatever decision he made would be honored. Finally, Spartan met his gaze.

"I believe we still have loose ends," said Spartan, "so I think we should press on until we're told to quit or assigned a new case."

Watts smiled. "I was hoping you'd say that. So, what do you see as loose ends?"

"No different than before. Marv Delouse and Travis McLean."

"Exactly, and I also believe Marv knows where he can find Travis."

"Maybe. So what do you want to do? Tail him?"

Watts' grin widened. "I like the way you think, Blaine, but before we do any stakeouts, we'll need to run it by Captain Ryder."

"Say what? You're going to ask permission?"

"Sometimes it's for the best. So, what do you say? Shall we meet our fate?"

"I can't see any benefit in waiting."

"I agree," he said, gathering his documentation. "Off we go."

They were ten feet from their boss's office when Ryder stepped into the hall. "Well, well," he said, holding an empty coffee mug. "What do we have here?"

"Sir, we'd like a few minutes of your time," said Watts. "Better now than later."

"Go on in and take a seat. I'll be right back."

Watts made sure his captain entered the break room before entering the office. Sniffing the air after sitting down, he quickly concluded the musty smell was coming from that old Indian rug. For years, the fake potted plant in the corner Ryder's wife gave him had been gathering dust. He assumed this rug received the same attention. He noticed Mrs. Ryder's desk photo was facing the plant. He had commented before on how ridiculous it looked. Maybe he positioned the photo so she could see it. Perhaps she was the reason he was angry all the time.

Thinking back to this case, he saw it was gaining momentum and wanted to finish it with dignity. To withdraw now would be a travesty. He felt his partner nudge him and immediately heard Ryder's footsteps. He barely got to his feet before Napoleon entered the room with a full coffee mug.

Ryder plopped in his chair, set his cup on the desk and folded his hands together. "Okay, boys, start talking."

Watts smiled confidently. "This case has turned out to be quite interesting," he said, spreading Daisy's data on Ryder's desk. "Sir, as difficult as this is to believe, we're dealing with multiple realms. These are digital depictions of Electronic Voice Phenomena known as EVPs. They were recorded on my Sony in the same place they found Jeremy Delouse's body in 1970. As you can see, *murder* and *noose* were both recorded on audiotape. The lab filtered the background noises and ruled out any human intervention. Independent paranormal investigators validated these EVPs as being legitimate."

"Besides this," Spartan interrupted, "Forensics Technician Woods had some odd experiences while looking for scientific clues in the dungeon."

Ryder's eyes swung back to Watts.

"It's true, sir. Something physically touched her leg when no one was near her. She also found a small noose hanging outside her apartment, and we're trying to determine if there's any correlation between the knotted cord and the EVPs. Now here's where it gets freaky. I locked her toy noose in my truck's glove box and then locked the truck, but the next day when I looked for it, it was gone and there were no signs of a break-in. I'm sure you think we're nuts, but I truly believe these odd events make Jeremy's death worth investigating.

There are too many weird things happening and we don't believe it's a coincidence."

Ryder quietly leaned back tapping his fingertips together, his gaze alternating between the detectives. Eventually he sipped his coffee, but then resumed his previous position.

"Sir," said Spartan, breaking the pause. "We believe the only person who can provide proper insight into this matter disappeared after separating from the Army in 1972. His name is Travis McLean, and he is friends with Jeremy Delouse's nephew, Marv Delouse. Travis was also briefly married to our contact at the Scott Theater, Betty Cerin. There are too many coincidences to believe everyone isn't somehow involved. I cannot explain the spectral voice saying *murder* and *noose*, but we cannot rule out the possibility that Jeremy's ghost is seeking our help in solving his death."

Ryder's belly laugh made his chair squeak. As he calmed down, he gulped more coffee and then leaned back with his mug in his hands.

Fearing the worst, Watts stepped in. "Sir, with all due respect, we're not crazy, even though if I were in your position, I'd probably think that, too. But the fact is, we don't really know what happened in the Scott Theater the night Jeremy was hanged, and we discovered some intriguing discrepancies in his ME file. It turns out the doctor who performed Jeremy's autopsy was none other than our current ME, Dr. Morton. Unfortunately, someone removed Jeremy's microfiche before we could confront Dr. Morton with our finding. All things considered, we believe there are plenty of reasons for you to keep us on this investigation and let Marv Delouse lead us to Travis McLean."

Ryder's seat clunked as he leaned forward to place his hands on his desk. When his fingers started a drum-roll, Watts wasn't sure whether his boss was pondering their plea or playing a song in his head. Finally, the noise stopped and he brought his tented hands to his lips.

"I've got to hand it to you two," he said. "You're not only my best detectives, you're the most persistent. I've always liked that about you, and since we're not swamped right now, I'll grant you more time. But promise that if I need you on another case, you'll accept it without protest."

"Agreed," Watts said, exchanging nods with his partner.

"Sir," said Spartan, "Do you have any problem with us tailing Marv to find Travis McLean?"

Ryder's head dropped. "Show me your badges and read the words out loud."

Spartan complied, staring at his badge. "Detective, Fort Worth Police Department."

"Exactly, and the way I see it, tailing a person in the interest of solving a crime or potential crime is *detective* work. Don't you agree?"

"Yes, sir," he said, tucking his badge away.

"Is there anything else?" said Watts.

"Nope, other than you guys owe me big time for this. Good luck and get out of here."

Twenty Four

WATTS NUDGED HIS PARTNER as they walked back to their desks. He had planned to tease him about what the captain said but decided things were going too well to stir the pot. Spartan was sensitive and too often took such matters personally. So instead, he smiled and said nothing. Spartan's rumbling stomach reminded them they had missed lunch.

"I know it's late," said Watts, "but you want to grab a bite?"

"Absolutely, and I don't care where."

"Well, we haven't been to Whataburger in a while, and since Marv should be at work, we might have time to drop in on Porgy to see how he's doing. After that we'll stake out Marv at his last known place of employment."

"Sounds good."

They climbed into the Crown Vic and headed to the burger joint. Lately, every time Watts went there, he started thinking about their meeting with the woman who turned out to be a murderer. And just before he began his interview with Kat Coulter, he heard the custom pipes of that rust bucket F-150 he had been searching for, the one the kidnappers drove Tony Fazelli away in, and likely the one that carried Porgy's shooter. It takes guts to shoot someone in cold blood, but people that shoot cops are either on drugs or the Devil's slaves. His flashback reminded him how dangerous those rust-bucket suspects were. The memory stayed with him as he placed his order.

After a quick lunch, they pulled up to a Krispy Kreme before heading to Baylor All Saints Medical Center. The receptionist looked up Officer Mulberry's name and then directed them to Porgy's room.

Watts eased the door open and peeked inside. What he saw was a lump resembling a beached whale, complete with blood stains. He and Spartan approached the bed where Porgy lay on his side facing the window, his left arm in a sling. Spartan bumped the bed and Porgy's eyes slowly opened.

"Hey, Porgy," said Watts, seating himself in the empty plastic chair. "Howya doing?"

Porgy grinned faintly. "Well, if it isn't my two favorite detectives." Easing himself onto his back, he pushed the controls to raise the bed so he could see them better. "What brings you here?"

"We came to check on you," said Spartan, handing over the donuts.

Porgy smiled as he peeked in the bag. "Hot damn! Now you really are my favorite detectives. And I seriously love glazed Krispy Kremes."

"That's good, because there weren't many flavors to choose from. We picked these right off the assembly line."

Porgy selected one and took a bite, unconcerned about any sugar glaze falling on his bed. "Oh, God, if this is Heaven, then let me stay."

Watts laughed. "Nice to see you smile, Porgy. How's the shoulder?"

"You know what it's like, Maxx. It burns. Where'd yours go in?"

Watts pointed at his wound. "I made a full recovery, but the scar still hurts sometimes.

Porgy nodded. "Guess we're twins now."

Spartan laughed with them. "Glad you're okay," he said.

"Yeah. Me, too."

Watts' expression turned serious. "Porgy, what happened out there? I mean, the APB warned everyone that these morons were armed and dangerous. Didn't you think about that when you approached them?"

The officer set his donut aside. "First, there was only one guy in the truck. Yes, he was big with wire tats around his biceps, but he was still only one guy. I was prepared to draw my weapon as I approached the truck, and when I got within six feet, I asked him to step out of the vehicle. He raised his hands and was calmly getting out when he grabbed a pistol off the seat and fired three times before I could react. He was a damned good shot, too," he said, pointing to where he was hit. "I took two to the heart and one to the shoulder."

"Consider yourself lucky he didn't know you were wearing Kevlar or he might've put a round through your head for good measure."

"Frankly, I'm surprised he didn't, because this dude was mean as a snake. I played dead when I went down, but what saved me was all the blood spilling on my uniform. Don't get me wrong, my shoulder's killing me and I have some serious bruises where the Kevlar stopped the bullets, but I'll take pain over death any day."

115

"We're glad you're okay," said Spartan. "Maxx was particularly upset when he heard you got shot."

Watts and Mulberry both stared at Spartan. True or not, the remark made him uneasy.

"Of course I was upset," said Watts, trying to diffuse the tension. "I hate it when any cop gets shot." He paused to face the window where colorful leaves swirled in the courtyard below. A patient was being wheeled past a young woman on a bench eating her sandwich. Looking at the officer's reflection, he added, "Porgy, I don't suppose you know where Barbed Wire was heading? I really want to nail that sonuvabitch."

Porgy laughed so hard he screamed in agony. He closed his eyes until he settled down and then took a sip from his water glass. "Apparently you didn't hear they found the pickup a few hours later, torched and abandoned on the side of the road. The hood was up and the radiator had bullet holes in it, so either it had an engine fire and the guy shot it, or it quit and he torched it. Either way, unless we get lucky, the bastard got away."

Watts met Porgy's reflection and slowly turned to face him. An expression harsh enough to ward off evil spirits had replaced Porgy's smile. "Porgy, we'll get him sooner or later, and when we do, we'll both have the pleasure of seeing him behind bars. Until then, try to take it easy."

Porgy stared out the window. "I hope so," he said. After an awkward silence, his smile reappeared. "Before you go, could you hand me that magazine?"

Watts reached for it and gawked at the cover. "Since when did you read *People*?"

"Normally I don't, but it was there when I woke up. What else am I gonna read?"

Watts raised his brows. "What do you like? Mysteries? True crime?"

Mulberry shook his head. "Honestly, I don't read much."

Watts nodded, pulling Spartan aside. "Can you hang out with Porgy for a minute?" he whispered. While Spartan bobbed his chin, he said, "I'll be right back, Porgy. I need to make a phone call."

"I'll be here."

Watts left the room and made a beeline for the gift shop. Quickly scanning their limited selection, he recognized a book and took it to the cashier. After making his purchase, he hurried upstairs to give Porgy his gift.

Porgy looked genuinely surprised as he read the title. "*Velocity,* eh? Can't say I've ever read Dean Koontz."

"I guessed that from what you told me, but it's a real page-turner. I bet you finish it before you get out of here."

"I doubt it. They're talking about sending me home tomorrow."

"Even so, if you start it, I still say you'll have it read before you leave. Speaking of which, Blaine and I need to beat feet."

Spartan nodded, heading for the door. "See you around campus, Porgy."

The Patrol Officer nodded his chin as they walked out.

Back in the car, Watts pulled out his notepad to review his notes. "According to Marv's IRS return, he works for Wells Fargo Bank. Considering where we spotted him with Travis, it's logical to believe he works at the Main Street location near the stockyards. Before we go there, I'm gonna make a quick phone call to be sure we're not wasting our time."

Watts' smart phone immediately connected him with the Stockyard branch. When someone answered, he said, "Hello. This is Mr. Demitri with Chase Bank. We are reviewing a credit card application for Mr. Marvin Delouse and need to confirm his employment."

"I'm looking at him right now," the woman said. "Would you like to speak with him?"

"That's not necessary. We prefer keeping these things confidential. Thank you for your assistance." He quickly ended the call.

Spartan grinned at him. "That was pretty slick. I take it he's there?"

Watts twisted the key and set the car in motion. "Yeah, he is, but I have a feeling whoever I spoke to will tell him, and he might leave before we get there. Fortunately, we're only a few blocks away. You remember what he looks like?"

"Of course. I'm a detective, remember?"

Watts chuckled. "Yeah, I do. Nice of Captain Ryder to remind us."

"I hate to admit it, but that was a pretty cool way to say go for it." Spartan smiled, gazing out the windshield, then added, "Do you have any idea what time he gets off work or what door he'll come out of?"

"Nope, but I thought we'd look for an employee entrance out back before you go in to inquire about a checking account. Since I did most of the talking at the diner, Marv is less likely to recognize you. When you get a chance, ask the service rep about their hours."

"Great plan, he coolly said. "And what happens when this service rep wants me to sign up for an account I don't want?"

"Just tell them you're not happy with your current bank and wanted to compare programs. This isn't rocket science, Blaine. Roll with it."

"Yeah," he mumbled. "Roll with it."

Watts turned into the Wells Fargo parking lot, amazed that in all of his visits to the Historic Stockyards, he had never used their ATM even though it was right across the street. Other than its heavily-sloped roof, the building was unremarkable. Its parking lot looked large enough to hold a hundred cars. A sign warned that parking was for bank business only, and that violators would be towed. But since the lot surrounded three sides of the building, it was impossible to cover every exit.

Parking where he believed the bank employees would park, Watts issued his final instructions. "Keep your cell phone on, pretend to scan your apps while the rep is talking, and nod and smile once in a while. Do whatever it takes to look inconspicuous. If you spot Marv, avoid eye contact with him. "

"Got it," he said, climbing out.

Watts watched him enter the bank. Ten minutes turned into twenty, and he was getting concerned. For a stakeout twenty minutes was nothing, but he couldn't imagine what was taking his partner so long. While waiting, Watts sized up every man who left the building, but Marv wasn't among them. In fact, no one even came close.

He sensed his partner had some reservations about going in alone. Spartan probably would have preferred they go in together, ask Marv where they could find Travis, and leave. But Watts believed Marv had a stronger connection to the Vietnam vet than he implied. Casual friends don't have emotional conversations or mention relatives without reason.

To counter his boredom, Watts scrolled through his Mp3 app until he found a *Zac Brown Band* album. When *Chicken Fried* came on, he thought about Porgy, wondering if he had turned the first page of *Velocity* yet. Regardless, he was glad he gave him the book. What Porgy did to him when they were kids was unforgivable, but Watts saw this as a step toward burying the hatchet.

He thought about Barbed Wire and how he destroyed his own pickup. He doubted it was an engine fire. More likely, Wire realized the truck's unique sound and rusted red and white color is what got him pulled over. Surely he knew that after shooting a cop, the authorities would step up their man hunt. More than ever, the Dairy Queen security photos of him and his sidekick were cycling through the media. But what concerned Watts was Wire didn't leave town after Tony Fazelli's kidnapping, and that made him and Minnie Me as notorious as Al Capone. So why didn't they kill Tony rather than dump him in the creek with superficial wounds? That part never made sense.

Watts noticed the noticed the snowballing traffic on North Main Street and checked the time. His phone rang and Spartan's name showed up. "Well?"

"He's still here. I'll be out in a second."

Soon after, Watts saw his partner emerge from the same door he entered. He waited until Spartan was inside the car before asking for a report.

"Sorry it took so long," said Spartan. "Marv works in one of the side offices so he must have something to do with loans. There were several people waiting to speak to a rep, so I took a seat and caught up on e-mail so I wouldn't draw attention to myself. If Marv spotted me, he paid no attention.

"I waited for twenty minutes before the lady invited me into her cubicle, then another fifteen to explain their services and why I should choose Wells Fargo over their competitors. Since my back was to everyone else in the bank, I couldn't see Marv, but when I left, he was still in his office sorting papers."

"So, what did she look like?"

"Who?"

"The woman who detained you for so long – and don't lie to me."

Spartan's face reddened as he stared out the window. Eventually, he faced his partner. "Okay, I admit she was an attractive brunette, but I swear I'm not gawking like I used to."

"I sure as hell hope not," said Watts, recalling his previous lectures on the hazards of roaming eyes. "Did you see any employees slip out another door?"

Spartan shook his head. "As far as I can tell, everyone uses the same one."

Watts nodded, agreeing that one door would be easier to guard than several. "Wait here."

He climbed out to inspect the building and found an emergency exit that hadn't been opened in a while. Since the remaining side was the drive-through, he returned to the car. After pulling his door shut, he said, "What was Marv wearing?"

"A typical banker's uniform – white shirt with black tie. I have no idea about his pants or coat since he was sitting behind a desk."

"Judging from his restaurant attire, I'm guessing they're black, too."

Spartan nodded. "Thankfully, strawberry blonds are easy to spot."

Watts agreed and started the engine. "Since Crown Vics don't exactly blend in, I'm moving to a less conspicuous spot. After all, we want to tail him, not talk to him."

"I agree."

Watts found a spot where he could follow Marv out either exit. Surveying the remaining cars in the lot, he speculated on which one was Marv's. His fondness for the dark side suggested something grungy like the black Jeep Wrangler, but he could just as easily own the silver Prius. As it neared closing time, most customers were using the drive-through.

"If Marv's a loan officer, he should be leaving about now." No sooner had he spoken than Marv came out wheeling a bicycle with a backpack over his dark suit. "Crap!" said Watts, sliding the car in gear. "His bike changes everything."

He then hit the gas and cut Marv off. Marv flipped him off before realizing who it was.

"What the hell was that?" Marv angrily said. "You nearly hit me!"

"But I didn't," Watts countered. "Would you mind giving us a few minutes of your time? If you promise to follow us, I'll move the car so we don't embarrass you."

Marv exchanged glances with Spartan through the windshield before going back to Watts. "If you wanted to talk, all you had to do was come into my office. Your partner was in the bank for at least thirty-five minutes, so it would have been easy. What do you want?"

"Right now I want you to walk your bike over to where I park the car. We'll talk once you've done that."

Marv reluctantly complied, meeting the detectives in the far corner of the lot. Suspecting they were being videotaped, Watts had made a point of presenting his badge in case bank security people were watching. Since no one came out, he assumed he was good to talk there.

After climbing in the back seat, Marv leaned forward. "All right, I'm here. Now what's this about?"

"Marv," said Watts, looking over his shoulder. "All we want to do is talk to your friend Travis McLean, but he's as elusive as a mountain lion. We're not looking to arrest him, and we don't believe he's committed any crimes. We just want some answers, and you seem to be the only one who knows where to find him. So, what do you say? Can we count on your cooperation?"

Marv glanced at his bank and back at them. "What are you going to do if I refuse? Tail me?" When they didn't answer, he said, "Look, I'm not stupid. I'm sure that was your plan, but you weren't expecting me to have a bike. Am I right?" He started to sweat when neither detective spoke. "Okay, you win. I'm supposed to meet Travis at the Chuck Wagon Diner for lunch tomorrow at eleven-thirty. We go there so often the waitress holds that table for us. You should get there early and have an order coming. Travis may not talk to you, but I promise I'll get him there. In return, you need to promise me you'll never pull a stunt like this again. Another incident could cost me my job."

"Fair enough," said Watts, offering his hand.

Rather than accept it, Marv got out and pedaled away.

Spartan shook his head. "I do believe you pissed him off, Maxx."

"I don't care, so long as he delivers Travis."

"You really think they'll show?"

Watts shrugged and started the car. Pulling onto Main Street, he said, "Everyone has to believe in something, and right now I believe Marv's gonna do what he said."

Twenty Five

It was past quitting time, so Watts and Spartan parted ways at the station. Watts admired the sky as he walked to his pickup. For a brief moment, the sun seemed balanced atop a skyscraper. Soon after, it was skewered by the tower on its journey to the horizon to mark the end of another day.

Leroy growled as Watts fired him up. Even on bad days, his truck's throaty exhaust made him smile. Knowing that the rust bucket pickup, his biggest competition for best pipes, was now in the scrap yard broadened his smile. *Chicken Fried* was playing on the radio, so he cranked it up. Right then his phone rang. He thought it would be Daisy, but instead the caller ID showed Porgy Mulberry's name. Disappointed, he turned the music off and put him on speaker.

"Hey, Porgy. What's up?"

"I wanted you to know I finished the book."

"Really? It's only been a few hours."

"I read a lot faster than I run, and I really enjoyed it. I just wanted to say thanks."

For a moment Watts was speechless, not only because of the speed at which Porgy read the book, but that he would think to call him. "You're welcome. One of the characters reminded me of you."

"You mean because the cop ends up dead?"

"No, it's because you share some of that character's good qualities."

There was a long pause. It sounded like Porgy had set the phone down and was reaching for something. Watts heard him blow his nose and pick up the phone again. At times he wished phone microphones were less sensitive, and this was one of them.

"I'll take that as a compliment," Porgy finally said. "I'm still groggy from the medication so I'll talk to you later. Make sure Spartan watches your back, Maxx."

"Thanks, Porgy. Now, get some rest."

It was a relief ending the call, as things were starting to get awkward. Watts turned up the radio and Alan Jackson was crooning a love song. He changed the source to CD and Zac Brown's song, *Toes* put him in the mood to sit on a beach with the waves tickling his feet. He dreamed about doing that with Daisy in Hawaii one day. She had been there. He never had. Right now his dream seemed farther away than summer.

When he got home, he searched his pickup again for the missing noose thinking that maybe it had slid between the seats or seat back. Running his fingers between the crevices and peering under the seats with them slid forward and back produced nothing. He finally gave up and went into his apartment. Before meeting Daisy, he would have plopped down in his oversized chair, turned on the TV and started flipping through channels. But now he wanted no part of it. Instead, he hung up his coat and tie, slipped off his shoes and tucked them neatly in the closet. And rather than sit in his chair, he chose the love seat. Daisy's perfume lingered there. He missed her deeply.

Time may heal wounds, but not when you're in Purgatory. That's how she made him feel, anyway. He desperately wanted to call her but wasn't sure what to say. Hoping she would call only made things tougher. He wondered if she were having similar thoughts.

He finally resigned to eating solo. His apartment was tidier now, but his pantry was still bare as a baboon's butt. He spotted one box of mac and cheese in the corner and expected an army of cockroaches to flee as soon as he lifted it. When that didn't happen, he turned on the stove and set some water on to boil. After dumping the macaroni into the churning water, he read the directions and realized he had neither butter nor milk. Oddly, he had lived in this apartment for over two years and had never bothered to introduce himself to either of his neighbors. To his left was a woman in her forties who he suspected was a divorcee. She seemed nice enough, but like him, kept to herself. He had never even seen the neighbor to his right, but judging from the variety of women's voices he had heard wailing through their common wall, he assumed it was a single man keeping busy between the sheets. Seeing no alternative to begging for milk and butter, he took a mug from his cabinet and went to the lady next door.

When the woman answered the door, a wonderful aroma flooded his senses. A sniff identified it as one his favorites – spicy beef. Greeting him warmly she extended her hand. Standing with his empty cup, he awkwardly switched it to his left hand so he could shake hers.

"Hi," he sheepishly said. "I'm Maxx from next door. I was making some mac and cheese and wondered if I could borrow some milk and a tablespoon of butter."

"Of course," she said. "I'm Annie. Come on in." Leading him through the entry, she looked at him over her shoulder. "If you're eating mac and cheese, your girlfriend must not be around."

Watts flinched. How could a woman he had never met know anything about his girlfriend? All he could manage was to shake his head from side to side, hoping his jaw didn't fall off.

"Well, if you don't have any plans, why not join me for dinner? I made a big pot of stew, and there's no way I'll eat it all even if I freeze half of it."

Watts hesitated, feeling tense. Annie was attractive and single, and that could complicate things if Daisy dropped by unannounced. But since she had never done that and his mouth was salivating, he quickly accepted Annie's invitation. "Just let me turn off my stove, okay?"

"No problem. I'll leave my door unlocked."

Not surprisingly, the water was boiling over when Watts returned. He removed the pot from the burner, turned everything off, and didn't bother to clean up. He then searched his cabinets for something, anything he could bring, but a bottle of wine had yet to materialize. Without wasting any more time, he went next door and politely tapped on her door. She answered quickly, as though she was standing there waiting for him.

"I told you it was unlocked," she said, pulling him in.

Feeling like Hansel stepping into the witch's cottage, Watts followed her into the kitchen. In the brief time he was gone, she had somehow managed to set the table and light a candle.

"I'm sorry, Annie, but I couldn't find anything to bring. This is very kind of you. My girlfriend will probably send you a thank you card for taking care of me."

Annie laughed, dishing out the stew. "Don't worry, Maxx. As fit as you are, I'm not after your body. You knocked on *my* door, remember? It's dinner and nothing else."

But her comments didn't help him relax. Torn between his obligation to dine with her and his overwhelming desire to leave, he managed his best grin to assure her he already knew that. When she gestured for him to take a seat, he nervously complied.

"I really appreciate this, Annie, and I'm sorry we've never gotten to know each other since we're right next door. By the way, I hope my music or TV isn't too loud."

Shaking her head, she took a seat and forked a bite. After swallowing, she said, "I've never heard a thing from you, but the guy on the other side of me plays non-stop sports and yells whenever someone scores. I've never met him, but I assure you I'd never invite him over for dinner." She quickly stuffed in another mouthful.

Watts matched her bite for bite, interjecting as little conversation as possible while doing all he could to keep his personal life personal. Annie, on the other hand, divulged volumes about what it was like being a high school teacher, how demeaning teens could be, how most had no clue about what they wanted to do, and how she had given up on men, but her phrasing made her last topic seem open for debate. Eager to get back to his apartment, Watts took his dish and utensils over to the sink.

"I hate to be a party pooper," he said, rinsing the dishes, "but I have some business I need to complete before morning. Again, thank you for having me over. It was really good."

Smiling graciously, she walked him to the door. "It was fun, Maxx. Thanks for putting up with my blabbing. I hope I didn't bore you."

Watts shook his head as he stepped outside. "Not at all. See you around, Annie."

He hurried to his door, unsure why he felt so uneasy about sharing her dinner. Not once had she come onto him or asked about Daisy. For that matter, she never even asked his profession. Perhaps it was because she was too busy lecturing about the Arabian horse's stamina while he smiled and nodded. He guessed she didn't get much company, so she seized the opportunity to yap. He wasn't sure he could handle a repeat.

He spent the next few minutes cleaning up his messy stovetop, thankful that salt dissolved as quickly the second time around. At eight-thirty he sank into his favorite chair and picked up the remote. Rather than turn the TV on, he readied his cell phone but never called Daisy. Finally, he dialed.

"Hello?" she wearily said.

Watts swallowed hard. "Hey, kiddo. How are you? I miss you."

"I'm fine. What took you so long to call? I ended up fixing mac and cheese."

"No way."

"Yes, way. It was either that or scramble an egg, and I wasn't in an egg mood."

"Well, believe it or not I was also fixing mac and cheese, because I thought you were mad at me. The only problem was I didn't have any milk or butter, so I went next door to borrow some and instead of giving me some milk, my neighbor invited me in for stew."

"And was this neighbor a she?"

"Yes – a high school teacher. I'd never met her before."

"Well, I hope she didn't teach you anything."

"Okay," he said, feeling more relaxed. "It's time to get your mind out of the gutter." But rather than laugh with him, she got quiet. After a brief pause, he added, "I didn't get many words in, but I did tell her about you."

"As in what?" she said, sounding skeptical.

"Right off the bat I told her I had a girlfriend so she knew it was nothing more than dinner."

"I see. So, is she pretty?"

"I suppose, but since you're the only one I think about, I was very uncomfortable being there. I know it sounds horrible, but I couldn't wait to leave."

Daisy giggled out loud. "Well, as cute as you are, you sound awfully paranoid about a neighbor who took pity on you and fed you dinner."

"You're right. I mean, she never came on to me and probably loved having someone listen to her stories."

"Absolutely. It was very nice of her to look after you. And while you're out shopping for thank you notes, perhaps you'll pick up a few groceries so you're not starving. I don't know how you'd survive a disaster."

Smiling he said, "I'd be working, so it wouldn't be an issue. So what's your excuse for having mac and cheese tonight?"

"It was quick, easy, and I had milk and butter to go with it."

"Touché." Watts paused for a moment as his stomach tensed. "Daisy, are we all right? I mean, lately it seems like you've been pushing me away."

"Maxx, you're the most important man in my life," she quickly said. "No, scratch that. You're the *only* man in my life. I haven't been in the best mood since I found that noose, and things got worse after it disappeared. This case is creepy, but I still love you."

His heart melted. "You *love* me?"

"Yes, Maxx, I love you, and I'm sorry I've stressed you out. What's crazy is I thought you were shunning me, so it's good that you called. Maybe we'll both sleep better tonight."

"I'd be happy to come over and lend some body heat. I mean, you don't have to get undressed or anything."

"As nice as that sounds, tonight isn't a good night. I've been so tired lately I'm gonna hit the sack early. Would you like to get together for dinner tomorrow?"

"I'd love to, assuming nothing derails me."

"Like what? Your new neighbor friend?" When he didn't laugh, she added, "I'm teasing, Maxx."

He paused, hoping she wasn't going to be possessive like some of his previous girlfriends. "We won a major battle with Captain Ryder today," he said, changing the subject. "He decided to give us more time, so Blaine and I are meeting Marv and Travis for lunch tomorrow. Blaine doesn't think Travis will show, but Marv seemed pretty certain he'd be there."

"How did you manage that?"

Watts laughed. "We cornered Marv in the parking lot where he works."

"What's so funny?"

"I had planned to stake him out and let him lead us to Travis, but instead of driving a car, he comes out of the bank pushing a bicycle. I cut him off before he could peddle away, and we had a conversation in the parking lot. It wasn't what I intended, but if Travis shows tomorrow, it will have worked out for the best."

"So, rather than stalking Marv, you bullied him into cooperating."

"Didn't I just say that?"

"I thought you hated bullies."

"I do, but in this job it sometimes has merit." Trying to end this conversation before it further deteriorated, he said, "Anyway, that's tomorrow's plan, and since I don't anticipate anything extending us beyond our normal shift, can we plan on seven?"

"Sure, seven sounds great."

"Oh, I almost forgot. We dropped in on Porgy this afternoon, and guess what?"

"He refused to see you?"

"No, actually our visit went better than expected, but he said the cops found that rust-bucket pickup we've been looking for.

Unfortunately it had been torched, so now Barbed Wire and Minnie Me will be that much harder to find."

"Well, maybe it's for the best. At least now you won't be craning your neck every time you hear a loud exhaust."

"I suppose," he said, still thinking about Porgy Mulberry in the hospital. "Sooner or later someone's gonna catch those bastards, and I hope they're better prepared than Porgy."

"Now you sound like you care about Porgy."

"It's not Porgy I'm worried about," he adamantly said. "He's out of the picture now. But those Skinheads have no respect for the law, and I don't want anyone else hurt. It's a shame they didn't find two crispy critters in the truck. That would have solved a lot of problems."

"Assuming it was *them*."

Watts clenched his jaw. Sometimes he forgot he was talking to a forensics expert who, under certain conditions, could be extremely anal. Sometimes it was difficult confiding in her because she scrutinized everything.

"Do you have any idea how beautiful you are?" he said, changing the subject.

"No, but thank you. You're pretty easy on the eyes yourself."

Relieved to have moved past their work-related topics, they spent the next twenty minutes flirting, talking and laughing. It was nice to end the call back where they were before the toy noose and theater haunting changed their lives.

Twenty Six

ALTHOUGH WATTS AWOKE EARLY at 5:30 AM, he slept well because he had stopped stressing over the deadlines. Rather than waste time in his apartment, he headed to work to review all he knew about Travis and Marv. By the time Spartan arrived, he was well prepared to compare notes for their lunch meeting at the Chuck Wagon Diner. He had already replaced the batteries and tape in the Sony and tested its operation. By 11 AM, they were heading to the restaurant and arrived before Marv and Travis.

Since Marv mentioned that the restaurant always held a table for him and Travis, Watts asked for the same table they had before. He hoped Marv had warned Travis they would be there. In his mind, he saw him bolt and head for the door.

The detectives ordered their drinks and took their time looking over the menu. When the waitress arrived with refills, they both ordered cold sandwiches. Their food arrived as Marv and Travis walked through the door. Sticking to the plan, the detectives pretended not to notice.

As expected, Marv and Travis sat at their usual table. Watts exchanged glances with the vet but neither spoke. Hoping to stimulate the conversation, he coughed and cleared this throat. He added, "I'm sorry, sir. I hope I didn't disturb you."

Travis didn't try to hide his smirk. "Son, if that's the best you got, I'm outta here."

Watts quickly straightened himself and set his napkin aside. "Okay, forget the ice breaker. Can we slide our table over so we can talk?"

"Do it."

When the detectives slid the table over, they left a small space between them so it was clear they weren't together. After doing this, Watts reached into his pocket and hit the record button. Its minute vibration confirmed his Sony was working. He noticed his partner eyeing Marv while he focused on Travis.

"Thank you for coming," said Watts. Not wanting to rush things, he bit into his sandwich, chewed slowly, swallowed, and sipped from his straw. "Travis, as I'm sure you're aware, your last conversation here is what got us interested in the Jeremy Delouse hanging. Since then, we've found evidence of rope marks where Jeremy allegedly hanged himself and a discrepancy in the ME's report. We've also checked your military record and saw you received a Purple Heart for your Vietnam service. Thank you for your sacrifice. I'm sure it was a difficult time. As homicide detectives, we'd like to resolve any questions about Jeremy's death, so what evidence did the police ignore in 1970?" He then took another bite and wiped his lips.

The waitress came and smiled at Marv and Travis, then noticed the tables had been moved. Travis assured her all was fine with a nod and wave.

Understanding this, she said, "The usual?" Upon receiving more nods, she hurried away.

Through bloodshot eyes, Travis sipped some water and stared at the detectives. His clothes smelled, his hair was greasy, and his breath could wilt a flower. Rubbing his face like it was a strain to be there, he said in a slurred voice, "Let me get this straight. You're saying you want to find the person responsible for a murder that took place over forty years ago?"

"That's right, Travis. There is no statute of limitations for murder."

He wiped his face once more and looked at Marv. When Marv gave a nod, he said, "You'd better get your notepads ready 'cause I'm only saying this once."

Spartan clicked his ballpoint. "Ready when you are."

"Well, since you've been checking my background, you must already know I was married to Betty Cerin. Marv tells me she works at the Scott Theater, so if you've been there, you've probably met her. Shortly after we married, I shipped out to Vietnam. The war took its toll on me just like it did on every other kid. As much as I tried to think about Betty, dodging bullets and killing Commies was a higher priority. And since none of us expected to live, we all smoked dope whenever we had the chance." Pausing to let a smile spread across his face, he said, "Mary Jane was killing so many brain cells that I was actually enjoying killing the enemy, young and old. You see, when you're a teenager watching your buddies get blown

130

away, revenge is all that matters. I suppose that's the premise behind war. It's all about attrition."

The waitress returned and set their drinks down, taking a quick glance at the detectives before saying their orders would be coming soon. After that, she promptly left.

"Anyway, one day I fucked up and stepped on a booby trap that shot a goddamned bamboo spike clear up my leg." Rolling up his pants and sticking out his battered limb, he said, "It tore me up real bad, and for a while they weren't sure they could save it, but they sent me home and the docs at Fitzsimons got everything working again. You always hear about Army docs practicing medicine until they get it right, but these guys were a cut above everyone else. I'm forever grateful for what they did."

Watts quietly nodded.

"Once I could walk on my own, they gave me some convalescent leave so I went back to Texas. When I learned they were gonna discharge me, I said no way because I was only half way through my tour. I mean, how could I abandon my buddies when I still had six months to go? So I talked the Army into sending me back to Fitzsimons for physical therapy so I could get another chance. I worked my ass off and eventually got the green light to get back to my unit, but by then a lot of my buds had been killed or shipped home, so it wasn't the same. Even so, I owed it to the dead to either finish my tour or die trying.

"Of course, all of this took its toll on my marriage and it became clear to both of us that it was a mistake. Since we had barely spent any time together, we had no problem getting it annulled. With nothing to lose, I volunteered for a second tour, which I finished unscathed.

"When I got back the second time, protestors were spitting on us and cursing, calling us baby killers and other bullshit names. Those candy-asses had no fucking clue what they were talking about either. But as the anti-war movement gained momentum, I started looking at the war from a different perspective and joined the Vietnam Vets Against the War. VVAW described itself as a national veterans' organization that campaigned for peace, justice, and the rights of all military vets. I believe those were their exact words. I wasn't real active, though. Mostly I joined protests to get sympathy, but when I saw my buds in wheelchairs with their legs blown off and no one gave a shit, I said fuck this and dropped out. I haven't paid a dime in taxes since nineteen seventy two because I refuse to support a government that played us like pawns and then forgot about us. And don't you dare call me a fucking derelict. I've always found work that paid under the table so I could buy whatever I needed. And now, as Forest Gump would say, that's all I have to say about that."

Watts glanced at Travis and then at Marv, who was giving him an "I told you so" look. Travis' tale verified what they already knew, but did nothing to answer Watts' original question.

"Mr. McLean —"

"Call me Travis or I'm gone."

"Okay, Travis. I was —"

He stopped abruptly when the waitress appeared with their meals. Once she left he was going to ask a question, but then Travis bit into his cheeseburger. When that happened, everyone followed his lead. Watts caught the waitress's eye by raising his empty glass. She nodded and soon returned to refill their drinks. He thanked her before she headed to another table.

As the tables filled up and the background noise increased, Watts was concerned Travis might raise his voice to compensate. He moved his chair a little closer to the vet, turning so his Sony could pick up the conversation. When Travis finished his meal, Watts asked the question that had bothered him the most. "Why do you say Jeremy Delouse was murdered?"

Straight-faced, Travis simply said, "He told me so."

"Who told you so?"

"Jeremy."

Watts nodded without showing the slightest hint of surprise. "How did he tell you this?"

"Check out the bags under my eyes, detective. Thanks to my fucking flashbacks, I can't sleep more than a few hours at a time. The shrinks called it post-war trauma or something like that, but to me it's a pain in the ass. It don't matter if I'm in a bed or lying on a park bench, it's always the same. The thing is I never had a problem sleeping until that spike destroyed my leg."

His eyes grew heavy and his head jerked backwards. Suddenly, his eyes opened fearfully and his head snapped back into position. Shaking it off as if nothing happened, he said, "My permanent state of exhaustion is why I've never sought a steady job."

Concerned that Travis was ready to fold like a losing poker player, said Watts, "You never explained how Jeremy told you he was murdered."

Travis was quiet for a moment and then slowly leaned forward. After pinching his eyes, he said, "Have you ever been so exhausted your mind is like mush, and you're not sure whether you're awake or dreaming?"

"I'm not sure. Why?"

"Well, I have. In fact, I feel buzzed all the time, and it's been years since I've had a drink. On the plus side, people see me coming and stay clear. The down side is I never feel human."

The vet paused, fidgeting in his seat as if he were sitting on a pebble. When Watts figured he had given him enough time, he said, "Go on."

"Okay, here's the thing. One day I read about this haunting at the Scott Theater, so I went to check it out. I read Jeremy's article in the lobby and pleaded for someone to show me the dungeon where it happened. The young man who volunteered to take me got called away unexpectedly. Since the stairs were right there, I went down and soon got chilled like I was entering a meat locker. Then I heard a faint voice say *murder* and *help*, and that scared the hell out of me. I looked around and no one was there. Then I was warm again like it was all a dream.

"I'd only been there for a minute or two before my escort was anxiously calling me back. I never saw a thing, but it had to be Jeremy's ghost. He must've recognized me and sought my help. I know it sounds crazy, but I'm telling you the truth. Then again, who's gonna believe some crazy ass drop out?"

Watts nodded, tapping his fingers on the table as he recalled his own experience there. What Travis was saying sounded perfectly plausible, particularly since neither detective had ever spoken of this to him. "Exactly where did you hear the words *murder* and *help*?"

"I was standing directly under the pipe where he hanged himself."

"How did you know that's where he died?"

"I don't know that for sure, but the newspaper account showed a photo and mentioned the pipe. Seemed reasonable to me."

He paused as if to analyze the detectives, then his fists clenched like he was ready to pound the table. "Look, I went there because they say Jeremy killed himself over my wife. It didn't matter how long it had been since he died – I had to see it for myself."

Then his fists relaxed and his chin began to tremble. "Look, guys, I realize you have no reason to believe an old pothead, but I swear to God, Jeremy's spirit spoke to me. It had to be him."

Spartan squinted at Travis. "You sure Betty wasn't the one who let you into the dungeon?"

"Aw, hell no," he said, waving an angry hand. "We haven't talked since the annulment. Like I said, some guy let me in."

Watts found that odd since Betty always seemed to be around. "How long ago did you hear this voice?"

Travis shrugged and stuck his lip out. "Maybe ten years."

"And that was the last time you heard a voice say *murder* and *help*?"

Repeatedly shaking his head, he said, "I constantly hear it, but I don't know if it's a flashback or Jeremy talking to me. But I swear to you the first time was real, and that's how I know Jeremy was murdered." Seeing Marv's reaction, he chuckled as he looked at Watts. "As you can see, Marv and I have had this conversation a lot."

"That's true," said Marv. "And frankly, I don't give a damn about Jeremy. As far as I'm concerned, he's nothing but an embarrassment to the family."

"I see," said Watts.

Spartan shifted in his seat. "Travis, has this voice ever said *noose*?"

Travis gave a quizzical look. "*Noose*?"

"Yeah, *noose*."

He made another face. "Nope. Only *murder* and *help*. Why?"

"I was thinking that since Jeremy was hanged, we thought *noose* might also come up."

"Like I said, no noose."

Spartan heaved a sigh and settled back in his seat. "Moving on, every time we've called or visited the theater, your ex-wife has been there. She's worked there continuously since 1969. Are you certain you didn't see her when you visited the theater?"

The vet's head dropped. "Okay, I admit it. Yeah, I spotted her the day I went into the dungeon, and every now and then I'll go back to check on her, but she has no clue it's me because I don't look anything like I used to, and I only go when it's busy. She's still so beautiful, and I miss her. I'm sorry things didn't work out between us, but letting her go was the right thing to do. If you tell her I've been checking on her, you will never see me again. Swear you won't tell her."

When Spartan looked his way, Watts said, "I'm not sure we can do that, Travis."

"Say it!" the vet said using his bullying voice. "Say you won't tell her."

"Fine. We promise we won't mention you to Betty. Now that

we have that out of the way, the paranormal investigators who visited the Scott Theater recorded more than one male voice and also some women. What convinced you that the voice you heard was Jeremy's?"

Travis smiled faintly as if he had been expecting that question. "One day Betty introduced me to him backstage, and I could tell he was flamboyant from the way he looked at us. Maybe we somehow bonded when we shook hands, and that's why I can hear his spirit. I can't offer a better explanation, but I know it's him."

Watts nodded, considering the possibility. Unfortunately, even Daisy couldn't help with that one. When the waitress delivered their checks, he reached for Marv's and Travis', but Travis grabbed his first.

"I told you I don't take charity."

"Me, neither," said Marv, taking his.

Watts shrugged. "Have it your way. I was just trying to say thanks for meeting us. Travis, where can we reach you?"

"You can't. If you need to talk to me again, let Marv know and we'll figure something out. Thanks for the trip down memory lane, detectives. It's been real."

With that, the two men rose from their table and approached the cashier. Watts knew not to follow, so he sipped his drink even though his stomach was sloshing. Belching helped, but he still felt over-stuffed. The waitress glanced at the detectives as though they had overstayed their welcome while she cleared Travis' table. Taking the hint, they got up and dragged their table back to its original location.

"I'm gonna hit the head," he said to Spartan. "I'll be right back."

"No sweat. I'll meet you at the counter."

Marv and Travis were long gone by the time Watts paid his tab. Spartan was leaning against the wall picking his teeth while waiting. After paying, Watts led the way to their car.

"So, what do you think, Blaine?"

Spartan flicked his toothpick in the trash and tucked his hands in his pockets. "It was an interesting meeting, but I can't say it was very informative. I'm not convinced Travis is a spiritual medium, but he does seem pretty straight forward. I can't believe they wouldn't let you buy his lunch. I thought it was a nice gesture."

"Thanks, but maybe pride is all Travis has left. That's a pretty ugly scar of his, isn't it?"

"That it is. Can you imagine a bamboo spike shooting up your leg like that?"

"Not really, but it's probably preferable to getting it blown off by a land mine. At least he's walking on both of his feet."

"Unlike his buddies in the wheelchairs. He sounds like he's still carrying a lot of guilt."

"Hard to say," said Watts, reflecting on Travis' Vietnam service. He needed to check with the veterans' organizations to see what they knew about his participating in anti-war protests. After what his father told him about the war, he certainly couldn't blame him. Who better to protest the war than those who had been there?

"Maxx, how are you gonna discuss this with Betty without compromising our word?"

"I think we can talk to her without mentioning Travis. In fact, now is probably a good time to pay her another visit."

"Okay, but are you gonna approach the boss?"

"We're not," Watts quickly said. "As best I recall, he gave us carte blanche authority, which means we're gonna keep digging until he needs us for something else."

Twenty Seven

DURING THEIR DRIVE TO the Scott Theater, Watts's bladder was feeling the effects his three glasses of cola. Trying to ignore the building pressure in his bladder, he wondered if Jeremy hung out in places besides the dungeon. He had hoped to use the restroom before seeing Betty, but she spotted them at the door and immediately greeted them.

"Nice to see you again, detectives," she said with a smile. "Where's the young lady?"

"At the office," said Watts, anxiously shifting his weight back and forth. "Betty, I really need to use the restroom before we talk. I had way too much pop at lunch."

"No problem. It's just down the hall."

"I'd better go, too," said Spartan.

They made a beeline for the toilet but Watts took his time returning because he wanted to see if his Sony might record another EVP. Before they reached the lobby, he said to his partner, "I haven't felt or heard anything unusual, have you?"

"Nope. Not a thing." Spartan paused and looked at Watts. "What, exactly, are you going to ask Betty?"

"I want to talk about her marriages."

Spartan eyed him suspiciously. "But you're not going to mention Travis, right?"

Watts cocked his head. "Of course I will, but I'm not going to mention he's been stalking her. I made him a promise, remember?"

Spartan let out a breath, nodding his head.

Betty was standing near the lobby's wine bar with her arms crossed like she was expecting bad news. She hadn't noticed them yet, and seeing her that way made Watts realize what a great actress she was. He hoped he hadn't insulted her by rushing to the restroom, but sometimes nature takes priority. Smiling warmly, he waved at her.

"Sorry about that," he said. "How are you?"

"I'm fine," she said, smiling again. "So, what brings you two back to the theater?"

"We were in the area and wanted to discuss your marriages. It shouldn't take long. Is there a place where we can talk in private?"

Her smile quickly faded. Glancing around, she said, "What's wrong with right here? There's no one else around."

Watts was about to say something when a framed newspaper article caught his eye. He was surprised he hadn't noticed it on the wall before, because it explained the legend of Jeremy Delouse and listed the Scott Theater as a haunted Fort Worth attraction. While staring at the photo of the dashing young actor, he noticed Betty's reflection in the glass.

"He was quite handsome," she said, now standing next to him. "The theater canceled two performances because his death was such a tragedy."

Watts nodded, watching her dab her eyes in his peripheral vision.

"I hear he was in love with an actress," he said. "That actress was you, wasn't it, Betty?"

As she lowered her head, a tear broke free. She hid it as best she could, but more kept flowing. When she turned away to wipe it, Spartan was there watching.

"Excuse me for a moment," she said, darting off to the ladies' room.

"That went well," said Spartan, looking disgusted.

Watts casually hiked his shoulders. "I didn't mean to hurt her, but her reaction tells me she and Jeremy had a fling while Travis was overseas."

"Okay. So now you're saying when Travis found out, he came back to kill Jeremy?"

"You can't deny it's a possibility."

"Maybe, but I'd be more inclined to believe it if Travis hadn't been the one who turned us onto this thing. Remember, he had no idea we would even be at the diner, not to mention sitting within earshot, taking note of what he was saying."

"So now you're assuming he didn't know we were listening? The other side is he saw our badges on our belts and wanted to plant a seed."

"I'm sure you're right, Maxx. That's why Marv's heard the story countless times."

Watts grinned. "Your sarcasm keeps getting better, Blaine. All I'm saying is, keep an open mind. Who knows how many sides there are to this story?"

"Noted."

They started to wonder about Betty when ten minutes had passed and she had yet to return. The halls were empty, and there was no sign of anyone else in the building. Air whistled through the vents, and somewhere in a back room, George Straight was singing on the radio.

Spartan was the first one to break. "She's not coming back, is she?"

Watts checked the time and shook his head. "No, Blaine, I think she bailed. Guess she didn't want to discuss her personal life after all."

"Can't say that I blame her. She obviously had strong feelings for Jeremy. You ready to head back?"

Watts nodded reached into his pocket for his keys and headed for the exit. Three steps later, he stopped and took another look, thinking Betty might be running after them. Seeing nothing, he opened the door and headed outside.

Neither spoke during their drive back to 350. Spartan seemed deep in thought, but he might have been angry, too. Taking advantage of the silence, Watts tried to fabricate a timetable in his brain but soon realized he needed the whiteboard. Whatever connection there was between Travis, Vietnam, Betty and Jeremy, he intended to find it. He had some thoughts, of course, but speculation was meaningless. He needed real evidence, and in a case like this, finding it would be difficult.

By reveling in his glory days, Travis McLean had given them more than he expected. From the way he described it, Vietnam was the last time he felt good about himself. Everything changed when he came home after his second tour. Watts couldn't imagine how it would feel serving your country and then being labeled a war monger and baby killer. Seeing his maimed buddies must have deepened his pain. But how did any of this tie in with Betty and Jeremy? If Travis was still watching over Betty like he said, then his feelings for her must be genuine.

It's too bad that Marv's parents were deceased, because they could have answered many of these questions. At a minimum, Jeremy's brother could have given a fresh perspective. As it was, they had encountered another dead end.

After arriving at the station, they went directly to the lab. Daisy noticed them walk in and met them at the counter.

"Hello, detectives. What can I do for you?"

Watts reached into his pocket, took out his Sony, removed the tape and slid it over. "If you can spare the time, I'd like you to play this tape on your fancy computer to see if we have any new EVPs. Don't worry about the interview with Travis McLean at the diner. I'm more interested in what was recorded at the Scott Theater. Today, Travis swore Jeremy's spirit has spoken to him, and a chill came over me when I was reading an article about Jeremy in the lobby. The only voices on the second half of the tape should be ours and Betty Cerin's. Anything else should be considered another EVP."

Nodding, she accepted the tape. "I'll get right on it. Anything else?"

Watts glanced at Spartan who was shaking his head. "No, I guess that's it for now. If you find anything, call us and we'll be right down."

"Will do. Blaine, let's check out our whiteboard."

Watts led the way back to his cubicle and grabbed a marker to trace Jeremy's blood line on the erasable board. "Let's begin with Jeremy Edward Delouse, born March 18, 1947, never married. His parents, William and Dolores Delouse, are both deceased from natural causes. Jeremy's brother, Warren Robert Delouse, was born on April 9, 1945 and married Grace Watkins in 1968. Grace was born on June 21, 1946 and gave birth to Marvin Delouse on May 2, 1970. Marv was their only child. Jeremy reportedly hanged himself at the Scott Theater on January 7, 1970 and was pronounced dead at the scene. Marv's parents died together in a car crash in 1987, so Marv has no immediate family.

"Next we have Travis McLean who was born on February 6, 1950. He married Betty Cerin on January 26, 1969 and was drafted into the Army on February 7, 1969. His Vietnam service ran from April 4, 1969 to March 30, 1971. He was injured on June 21, 1969 and returned to his unit on August 3rd of the same year. He had military leave from December 25, 1969 through January 23, 1970 which means he was in Fort Worth when Jeremy died. He also had military leave from August 15, 1970 through September 15, 1970. He received an Honorable Discharge on April 5, 1971.

"Betty Cerin was born on November 13, 1950. Her marriage to Travis McLean was annulled on February 27, 1970. She then married Justin McLaughlin on August 1, 1971 and was widowed on August 2, 1972. She was an actress at the Scott Theater from March, 1968 through January, 1970 and shows continuous employment to present day."

Watts stepped back to admire his handiwork. Keeping his back to his partner, he said, "This is everything from my notes. Do you see any discrepancies?"

After comparing what was on the board to what he had written in his notepad, Spartan shook his head. "Looks good to me."

"So, what do you take from all of this?"

"That Jeremy and Marv have a very unlucky blood line, and I'm grateful I'm not in their family."

"Very Funny," said Watts, staring at the board. The phone rang and it was Daisy. After hearing her brief message, he waved Spartan over. "Thanks, Daisy. We'll be right down." After hanging up the phone, he said, "Looks like we have another EVP."

"No way."

"She's serious. Let's check it out."

They rushed downstairs, and Daisy promptly took them to the electronics room. Dodging desks and piled paper, they seated themselves at the same table as before.

"Okay, Daisy, let's hear it," Watts eagerly said.

She handed them headsets and said, "Listen carefully and watch the digital display. I'll explain what's happening after we've played it a few times."

They nodded and donned their headsets. Watts wanted to adjust the volume because it was blasting his ears, but Daisy placed her hand over his to keep it where it was. Closing his eyes helped him picture himself standing near the framed newspaper article on Jeremy. Shortly after Betty spoke, a strange voice said what he believed was *help*. He immediately opened his eyes and looked at Daisy.

"Are you okay?" she said, stopping the soundtrack.

"I just heard a voice say *help*. It was much weaker than the *murder* we previously heard in the dungeon, but it's definitely there. Blaine, did you hear it?"

"I heard something, but I'm not sure what."

"Well, here's the deal, folks. Travis also heard a voice say *help*. I don't believe this is a coincidence."

"Daisy, did this EVP occur where the graph spiked?" said Spartan, pointing to the screen.

She looked at him, elated. "It did, and is has the exact pattern as the previous EVPs. I didn't want to tell you the word we believed it was until you heard it yourselves, but Maxx caught it on the first try. Combine *help* with *noose* and *murder*, and I'm a believer."

Spartan kept scratching his head. "Could you please play it again?"

"Sure."

After listening three more times, he still looked skeptical. "I guess your ears are better than mine. I mean, I see the spike on the graph where you say this EVP occurred, but convincing naysayers this is Jeremy's cry for help will be a problem."

"What about Travis and Betty?" said Watts. "They've both heard voices."

"Look, I'm not the one you have to convince. Attorneys like Hank Azar would have a field day if this ever goes to court. Come to think of it, every lawyer wanting visibility would be clawing to get this case, because it would be all over the news. Courtroom debates on ghosts would make great viral videos."

"I agree, which means we either need to find a paranormal expert who can testify on Jeremy's behalf, or find some solid evidence."

"Solid evidence seems unlikely," said Daisy. "Somehow I doubt a jury will be impressed with a few etch marks on a pipe, and that's the only solid evidence I've found."

Spartan nodded. "That's especially true, since everyone agrees he was hanged."

Watts sighed, pondering the evidence. While it was true that Daisy could print out the graph and they could play the tapes in court, few members of a jury would hear the words clearly or believe they came from a ghost. And as Spartan had pointed out, even if they convinced the jury these were legitimate paranormal events, who could say for certain Jeremy Delouse uttered those words?

"Well, since it's nearly quitting time, I'd like to thank Ms. Woods for her expertise and get someone to transcribe the tape. It's possible there's something else we're not hearing."

"You mean, like a ghost?" said Spartan, grinning.

"That wasn't what I was thinking, but it's a good comeback." Ready to end the day and spend some time with Daisy, Watts said, "I'm sure we could all use a break, so let's wrap this up and call it a night."

"Sounds good to me," said Daisy.

Spartan nodded. "Me, too."

"I can't speak for Daisy, but I'm leaving in fifteen minutes, and Blaine, I expect you to be finished before then."

"You won't get any arguments from me. Thanks again, Daisy. I'll see you tomorrow."

"Bye Blaine." She then whispered to Watts, "And I'll see you at seven."

Twenty Eight

WATTS WAITED IN DAISY's parking lot until 6:58, because he prided himself on being punctual. Opening the door the instant he pressed the doorbell was her part in the game. Giving her yellow roses was like old times, except this time she grabbed his hand and dragged him inside.

Once she had closed the door, she accepted the bouquet and inhaled its fragrance. "Déjà vu," she wryly said, "and yet somehow it's like we're starting over."

"Shhh," he said, pressing his finger to her lips. "We can't start over if it never ended. At the same time, I wouldn't mind pretending it's our first date. Yellow roses, dinner, conversation with no shop-talk..."

Smiling approvingly, she pressed her body into his and draped her arms over his shoulders. After giving him a quick smooch, she said, "I'd like that," and went into the kitchen to arrange her flowers in a vase.

While she worked at the sink, he slid behind her and wrapped his arms arms around her waist, kissing her tilted neck while she separated the rose stems. Then without warning, her head jerked back and hit his chin making him bite his lip. Before she could apologize and say she pricked her finger, he was leaning over the sink spitting blood.

After rinsing his mouth, he faced her with a goofy smile. "We're quite the romantics, aren't we?"

Her nervous laugh and head nod confirmed that. "I think it means we deserve each other. Who else would have geeks like us?"

The term struck him odd, but then he realized she was right. They could both be rather anal at times. "You up for some TexMex? I'm starving."

"That sounds great," she said, sliding on her leather jacket. "Is your lip okay?"

He kissed her gently and smiled. "I'm fine, but thanks for asking."

Watts looked for hanging objects as they stepped outside. Seeing none, he took her hand and started walking. He thought the blinds split as they moved past her neighbor's apartment, but he didn't mention it. Her sweaty palm proved she had her own concerns.

As always, Watts held Leroy's door open and assisted her in the truck. She looked sexy in her blue jeans and cowboy boots, but that black coat over her white blouse always turned heads.

Her inviting perfume had him running around the front and into the cab so he could be with her again. In no time they were back at their favorite Mexican restaurant. From the truck they could see there was a wait, so after checking in with the waitress, they went outside to sit by the pond. Water spilled from the fountain and laughter came from inside, but nothing could distract Watts from the woman he loved.

"Check out our reflections," he said, pointing to the water. "It's like a time machine that adds wrinkles to our faces."

She rolled her eyes at him. "Thankfully water ripples don't count," she said, feeling the corners of her eyes. "I have to apply daily lotion to minimize my crow's feet."

Watts looked at her face and cupped her chin. "Well, I don't see any, and no matter how old you are, you'll always be beautiful."

She kissed him and rested her head on his shoulder. "You say the sweetest things, Maxx. Your momma taught you well."

Staring at the water again, he said, "Whenever Dad got abusive, she'd remind me to always respect women. I'll never understand why she put up with him."

Daisy was silent for a moment, patting his chest. "I wish I could have met her."

Watts smiled back, covering her hand with his. "She would have loved you."

Seeing some kids dressed up as Halloween ghosts and goblins turned his thoughts to the paranormal. Did souls like Jeremy actually rise on All Hollow's Eve? If intelligent spirits like his were capable of communicating with the living, did he also have memories of childhood trick-or-treating or feelings for Betty?

"Maxx?" said Daisy, gently touching his shoulder. "You look lost. Are you okay?"

Suddenly aware of her voice, the moving water, the laughter and cigarette smoke, he blinked and smiled at her. "Sorry. I was daydreaming."

"Thinking about your mom?"

He hesitated before saying, "I do miss her." It was a true statement and kept him from sharing his actual thoughts. Before saying anything further, the pager in his hand vibrated. "Looks like we're up."

He stood up and then helped her to her feet. As they headed inside, the noise volume tripled, but the aroma of sizzling fajitas made up for it. Their window table overlooked the pond where they had been sitting. They noticed that a couple about their age had taken their spot. He hoped they appreciated them warming the stones for them. Smiling, Watts took her hand.

"This is perfect," he said. "Thanks for joining me."

Her eyes locked on his as she sipped her water. After setting her glass down she said, "So you prefer my company to your neighbor's?"

"Oh, please. I'm still trying to decide whether I should move."

Her laugher drew unexpected gawks. After waving her apology, she said, "Maxx, I was joking. You have nothing to worry about, okay? If she wanted you as a boy toy, she would've had her way with you while you were in her apartment."

He adamantly shook his head. "It never would've happened, Daisy. I'm not like that at all." Then he stopped and gazed into her eyes. "You don't think I'm like that, do you? I'm—"

"Relax," she said, sliding her foot up his leg. "I'm here, she's not – put her out of your mind."

"You're right," he said, noticing the approaching waitress. "Here comes dinner. Let's forget about her and enjoy the meal."

"Agreed."

They dug into their food, talking about the drought and how the wildfires ruined people's lives by reducing their homes to ash. This discussion led to talk about crime. Realizing they were approaching shop talk, they both laughed and changed to other subjects.

After paying for their meal, they left the restaurant arm-in-arm. Leroy lit up like a carnival ride after he punched his key fob. All went well until Daisy started to step inside, then she gasped and backed out, horrified.

"What's wrong?" he said, pulling her away.

When she couldn't speak he drew his gun and slowly peeked inside. Half-expecting a coiled diamondback, he was stunned to see the missing toy noose lying on the console, the loop pointed toward the passenger's side. After holstering his weapon, he raised the lid, dumped the noose inside, closed it, and locked his truck, having no idea how the noose got there or why. Guiding her back toward the restaurant, he said, "Feel like sharing a dessert."

Still trembling, she nodded, clinging to his arm as they walked, her vexed look spoiling the evening.

Twenty Nine

With only a few people still dining, there was no wait for a table this time around. Whether it was because they were preparing the restaurant for tomorrow, or the hostess sensed they needed to talk, they found themselves seated in a quiet corner. Daisy ordered a beer, while Watts stuck to his water with lemon. Neither was particularly hungry, but they ordered sopapillas anyway.

Watts didn't want to address the noose, but it had to be done. "Daisy, he said, looking into her eyes, "I swear I have no idea what happened. That stupid knot was locked in the glove box of my truck, which was also locked, and then it vanished. I did a thorough search and never saw it again until now. It wasn't there when you climbed out of the truck, and I've been with you all evening, so you know there's no way I could be pulling a cruel prank on you. I have no earthly explanation."

"I know, Maxx. But what worries me is that noose seems to have my name on it. First it shows up on my eave, and now it's in your truck pointing at me. Yes, it's just a stupid prop, but when you consider something felt me up in the dungeon, it's pretty freaky. It's like I'm being shadowed by a shadow."

Watts would have smiled except she was terrified. Was it possible she was being singled out by a paranormal force? Was it Jeremy or some idiot messing with her mind?

The waitress delivered their sopapillas and asked if they needed anything else. Simultaneously, they both shook their heads. Watts waited until she left before adding his thoughts.

"Daisy, I'm not sure what to do other than consult with a paranormal investigator. I mean, I doubt he's seen anything like it, but what do we have to lose?"

Steam rose from Daisy's sopapilla as she tore into it. She meticulously dripped honey on each piece before stuffing it in her mouth. After wiping her hands, she said, "Thank you, Maxx. That was tasty. Now I won't have to eat for the next twenty-four hours."

"You could always come to my place and dine on some low-cal pantry air."

She chuckled, patting his hand. "I really need to introduce you to a grocery store."

Smiling back, he closed his hand around hers. "Name the time and I'll gladly go."

Peeling her Corona label between sips, she slowly sipped her beer. The wait staff seemed to be getting noisier as they worked their way toward the only couple left in the dining room. Noticing that, Daisy polished off her drink and set it down.

"I'm okay," she said. "We can go now."

He calmly picked up the check and slid out of his chair so he could to take it to the cashier. He waited until she was ready before moving from the table. Handing his credit card to the clerk, he said, "Looks like you had a busy night."

"We're always busy," said the young woman, swiping his card. As the receipt printed out, she slid it to him along with a pen. Once he signed it, she punched some numbers into the register and made eye contact. "Thank you for coming."

He then nodded, smiled, and held the door open for Daisy. She didn't speak until they were walking toward the pickup.

"Maxx, I'm not into witchcraft, zombies, or any other weird stuff, but I'm open to any ideas this paranormal investigator may have. While you're at it, ask him if I should wear garlic around my neck."

Watts lovingly embraced her and gazed into her eyes. "Sweetheart, I'm pretty sure garlic is to ward off vampires. I believe a cross keeps evil spirits away."

"You're right," she said, her face suddenly brighter. "Thankfully I have one."

Watts intended it as a joke, but after her reaction, he wasn't about to admit it. As she climbed into Leroy's cab, Watts saw her looking for the noose. Thankfully, she didn't open the console. Instead, she took her seat, fastened her safety belt and and folded her hands in her lap. After starting the engine, he let Leroy idle his way out of the parking lot to minimize the noise. It crossed his mind that maybe he should go back to stock pipes, but the thought didn't last long. With that rust bucket pickup out of the way, Leroy was now the indisputable king of pipes, and he wasn't willing to give up the throne.

He turned on the CD, and it picked up where it left off with *Chicken Fried*. He liked how the upbeat song paid tribute to our soldiers, but with the next song being more reflective, he switched to the oldies station on his satellite radio. Hearing the sad song *Blue on Blue, Heartache to Heartache* made him turn it off and hold her hand.

"Daisy, you're always welcome to stay at my place. I promise not to bite."

With her staring out the windshield and not responding, he steered a course for her place. But the evening was not a complete loss. At least now he knew her moodiness was not the result of anything he had done. He was learning about her moods, but adapting wasn't easy.

After parking in her lot, he shut Leroy down and smoothed her hair. "Hey, kiddo, I'm worried about you. You have all these crazy thoughts running through that pretty head of yours, and I don't want them to bring you down. Sorry how it ended, but it was fun being with you."

"I had fun, too, and don't be such a dork. I love being with you, and you're not the least bit responsible for anything that's happened. Sorry I've been so quiet."

"It's okay, really. Can I walk you to your door?"

She dithered as she looked toward her apartment. "Sure, but just to the door, okay? I have a massive headache, and I need to get up early."

"I understand."

This time there were no nooses or split blinds – only a blank door lock awaiting a key. Seeing nothing disturbing, she hugged his neck, kissed him good night, and let him go. "Thanks for the nice evening, Maxx. You're the best."

"You're welcome." *I love you, too.*

Thirty

WATTS IMMEDIATELY WENT TO his computer when he got home to seek a rational explanation for the noose. One possibility came from an article stating that *all matter is composed of energy in the form of moving particles that are held within a solid state.* A paranormal orb came to mind when he read: *This solid state could be a body or in some form of energy. Since energy is always converting from one form to another, it is never static, but instead keeps flowing.* This may have explained how the orb appeared and disappeared, but how could this apply to a nylon noose?

The article went on to say: *Reality is composed of several dimensions. Some are visible to the human eye and some aren't. But as a species, humans tend to deny things they cannot actually see or hear because they can't relate to dimensions that are invisible or inaudible to them.* Did dreams fall into this category? If so, was it possible that an insomniac like Travis McLean could actually receive messages while in his zombie-like state? Watts scratched his head and read on.

Explaining the progression of modern science, the article suggested people should accept multi-dimensional reality as the norm, and that Quantum Mechanics had shocked the scientific community with its contrary-to-normally-held-theories in Physics. Tests had measured and quantified the ability for Extra Sensory Perception, or ESP, and spirits' voices had provided startling evidence by being successfully recorded. He knew this to be true because Daisy verified it in the lab.

Several web stories chronicled people's Out-of-Body experiences, while others discussed the sensitive machinery that scientists had built to study Ghostly Phenomenon. Many included photographs as proof of paranormal activity, but the website also cautioned that today's digital technology often produced fakes. His tired brain sought answers as to how a nylon noose could disappear and then reappear in a locked truck with a sophisticated alarm system. Before shutting down the computer, he e-mailed his question to his paranormal contact and then headed to bed, hoping his mind would allow sleep.

Morning came without incident, and he felt surprisingly refreshed. Most mornings he enjoyed singing in the shower, but today he used the time to think. He was okay admitting the EVPs were Jeremy's spirit talking, but the nylon noose explanation still eluded him. After shaving and brushing his teeth, he checked his phone. Not finding a response from his paranormal contact, he returned to the bedroom to dress and comb his hair.

Munching an energy bar on his way out the door, he deliberated over how he would sneak the noose into the forensics lab and have them examine it without Daisy knowing. Before climbing into Leroy, he inspected his doors to determine if someone broke in and left the noose. Seeing nothing obvious he climbed in, relieved the noose was still in the console. To avoid further contact, he slid his pen through the loop and dropped it into a sandwich bag, then tucked it in his coat pocket.

Spartan parked next to him in 350's lot. On their way inside, Watts brought him up to speed and then handed him the sandwich bag with the noose.

"Here's the plan, Blaine. At some point, I'm going to get Daisy out of the lab. If I can't get her to go out for coffee, I'm hoping she'll join me for lunch. Whenever that happens, I want you to take this to the lab and ask them to run every chemical analysis known to man. I need to know if this mystery knot has been subjected to anything abnormal. Only tell them the basics. If you were to explain how it magically disappeared and reappeared in my truck, they'd think we're nuts. Keep it on your person until you can get it to the lab. I don't want to chance losing it again."

"No sweat. What's your plan until then?"

"We keep digging into the Delouse family history, and this afternoon we'll give Betty another call. It'll be interesting hearing her explain yesterday's disappearing act."

"I take it you think she was avoiding us."

Watts gave him a sharp look as they approached the entry. "What else could it be? I'm beginning to think she could be the one who breaks this case. After all, she's the one who seems riddled with emotion."

"And you don't think Travis has issues?"

Watts held the door for his partner. "Let's stop speculating and get back to investigating. Something's staring us in the face, and whether

Jeremy was murdered or not is quickly becoming a moot point. I want to know what happened between all the players, and we need facts if we're gonna get someone to confess. It's quite possible this will turn out to be our most challenging case yet."

"Then I suppose we should get busy."

"Hmm," he said, surprised to find the transcribed hardcopy and two duplicate copies of his audiotape waiting on his desk. He quickly locked the original audiotape in his desk, snapped a fresh one in his Sony, and starting reading the dialogue. The results exceeded his expectations. Although little, if any, would be admissible in court, the transcript helped answer questions as well as document the EVPs they never heard while they were talking to Betty. He gave a copy of the transcript to his partner and then retreated to his desk to read his copy. He was particularly interested in Betty's emotional passages.

". . . What would you like to know about my deceased husband? That he died . . . one day before our first anniversary . . . That I inherited fifty thousand dollars? . . . That my happiness was robbed? . . . Forgive me for sounding bitter, but Justin [McLaughlin] was the love of my life." Watts had penciled in Justin's last name for clarification.

Comparing that with how she described her history with Travis McLean confirmed she had no emotional attachment to the Vietnam veteran. ". . . We were married on January 26, 1969, and he left for the Army on February 7th. . . he arrived in Vietnam on April 4th and was injured on June 21st . . . I learned he was at Fitzsimons Army Hospital . . . drove up there . . . he was terribly angry and told me to leave . . . he landed safely in Vietnam on August 3rd . . . I didn't see him again until December 26th . . . We spent most of the time fighting . . . He said I deserved better and he was back in Vietnam on January 23rd, 1970 . . . the fool opted for a second tour. We mutually agreed to have the marriage annulled and . . . I never saw him again. Perhaps now you can understand why I said I only had one husband . . . I have no regrets."

Watts felt like a news editor chopping words from an interview until it said what he wanted it to say. But Betty's passages contained some critical pieces of information, and her lack of mentioning Jeremy made it even more curious. She and Jeremy had been working together before she got married. What relationship did they have while Travis was in Vietnam? Was Jeremy ever drafted into the Army? Could a draft notice have driven him to suicide? What did Travis know about Jeremy? Was Jeremy the reason why Travis did a second tour in Vietnam? Watts jotted these questions down in his notepad and then sent a formal request to the Pentagon for Jeremy Delouse's draft status. For now, obtaining official records was one of the few tangible things left to do.

It was approaching the noon hour, so he decided this might be a good time to take Daisy to lunch. When he called down there, he was told she had stepped away from her desk, but they would have her call back when she returned. Almost immediately after hanging up, his phone rang.

"Hello, detective. What can I do for you?"

Resisting the urge to say something suggestive, he said, "Do you have any lunch plans?"

"Actually, no, but if you're asking me to go with you, the answer is yes. I can be ready anytime."

"Great. I'll meet you at the back door in five minutes."

Watts slid his chair back and tapped on his partner's cubicle. "I'm meeting her out back in five minutes, so you should have about an hour. I'll call to warn you if we're coming back early. Call down to the lab to make sure she's gone before taking the noose down there. Tell them it needs priority handling and that you don't want Daisy involved. I don't expect them to find anything, but you never know."

"Will do. Where you taking her?"

"Beats me, but I'm hoping she'll go for a burger."

"Have fun."

Watts skipped downstairs and out the door. Above him, crisscrossing contrails turned the sky into a game board while robins pecked at the ground. No sooner had the door closed than it swung open again and Daisy appeared wearing a smile.

"Hey, stranger," she said to him. "Long time no see."

"Yeah, it does seem that way. How'd you sleep?"

"Mostly on my side," she joked. "So, what's for lunch?"

"Anything but Mexican," he said, escorting her to his truck.

"Well, there's a kabob place not too far from here, and I'm pretty sure they have outside dining. Does that sound good to you?"

"Sure, I'm game."

This time she climbed into Leroy without hesitation. If she was still thinking about the nylon noose, she was hiding it well. As Watts drove Leroy onto the street, she sounded completely relaxed as she gave directions to the Lebanese restaurant. The patio was packed with men smoking, but when they went inside, wonderful smells enticed them.

Behind the counter, a chef shaved meat from a from a roaster column and stuffed it inside a gyro. After barking orders in a Middle Eastern accent, a waitress came over and scooped up the plate, dodging the hordes that kept coming in. Watts couldn't help noticing how few fair-skinned people were there. He frowned and quickly checked his pockets after a bearded man bumped him and didn't apologize. For a brief second he feared the noose was missing until he realized it was at the lab.

"You seem tense," said Daisy, touching his arm. "Is this place okay?"

"Of course. But if you don't mind, let's eat inside. I don't like breathing second-hand smoke."

"I'm not a fan of it either, so inside works for me."

After being seated at a corner table, they placed their orders and waited for their drinks. Watts was drawn to the artwork and tapestries, while the music reminded him of a desert harem. Imagining a belly dancer clinking and jiggling to the music, he smiled at Daisy. This is quite a place. How did you stumble onto it?"

"I heard about it from an Iranian friend. He said most of the tapestries in here are Persian, probably from Iran." As he nodded, admiring the hangings, she added, "The Persians mastered symmetry and used it extensively in their weaving. Their designs are as timeless as their craftsmanship is flawless. They influenced architecture all around the world. Pretty cool, eh?"

"Yeah," he said, letting his eyes roam the room. "I can't believe I've never noticed this place before. Then again, it has to be one of the most nondescript buildings around. I've driven by here more times than I can count and never knew what I was missing. Thanks for bringing me."

"You're welcome, but save your praise until you've tried the food."

His grin suddenly faded. "I hope you mean that in a good way."

"Of course I do. It's great."

Their drinks finally came, and soon after, their beef kabobs were delivered with jasmine rice and hummus on the side. While Daisy admired the presentation, Watts dug in, forking a slice of beef in his mouth.

"This is great," he said, still chewing. "Hot and full of flavor. I wish I could barbeque like this."

"I suspect they have some secret spices, too. Glad you like it."

Their waitress returned to refill their drinks, and when they had finished their meals, she delivered baklava. Patting his stomach, Watts thanked her for the excellent meal. She smiled back as she cleared the plates.

"That was really good, Daisy. I'm not sure I can eat dinner tonight."

"That's true because your pantry's empty, but you could join me for soup if you want."

"Sounds great," he said, scanning the restaurant again. "Have you noticed how few Anglos are here?"

"It's always that way. Middle East bias, ya know?"

Standing up to adjust his coat, he said, "If that's the case, it's their loss."

"I agree," she said, also getting up. "I come for the food, not the politics."

A glance at his phone confirmed there were no messages from Spartan. He took that to mean all must be well at the lab. "I suppose we should get back to the office," he said. "Captain Ryder's probably looking for me."

She turned her head and covered her mouth.

"You okay?" he said, giving a concerned look.

"If you must know, I had to burp. Now let's get going. We both have work to do."

Watts' gut reminded him he was keeping a secret from her. He hated doing it, and if the lab found something odd with the noose, he would certainly share it with her. But if they didn't, there was no reason to include her. He would simply lock it in his drawer for safe keeping.

They separated at the station and Watts headed directly to his desk. He found an e-mail from his partner, but still nothing from the paranormal investigator. Spartan's note said he was at lunch and that Tim Westin had the item of interest. Watts was glad to hear that, because Westin was one of the few lab technicians who worked outside the box. If there was anything special about this noose, he's the one who would find it.

Watts called down to the lab hoping Daisy wouldn't answer. Thankfully, Westin picked the phone up, but promptly put him on hold. The only reason for doing this would be if Daisy were near. When he came back on the line, his whispering seemed to confirm that.

"It's weird," the tech said, "but your noose is emitting a miniscule amount of energy, and I don't know why. It looks, feels, and burns

155

like a nylon rope, has human cells from where it's been handled but contains no odd chemicals, and yet it's electrically charged. It doesn't make sense. I mean, how can nylon conduct electricity?"

"Beats me. My only thought is that it may have retained residual energy from vanishing and then reappearing in my truck. I'm no expert, but I just read an article on Quantum Theory which said all matter is composed of energy that can be transported. Maybe that's what happened with the noose."

Westin chuckled. "You're way out of my league, detective. How about I give you my results and the noose, and you find a physicist who can explain the electrical charge? I want to get everything out of the lab before Daisy sees it and I'm forced to tell her about it."

Watts sighed, regretting giving him the noose. Then again, a physicist might consider this a breakthrough. But time was critical, and he was torn whether to pursue the noose issue or concentrate on Jeremy Delouse. If he had a coin, he would have flipped it right then.

While waiting for Spartan to get back from lunch, he browsed the Internet for information on Quantum Mechanics. Most of what he read was at a level he would never understand, but it did seem possible that the noose could have passed through his truck's doors by an unexplained force. Perhaps this is what charged the nylon with energy. If he believed in the paranormal, why not believe that, too? Of course, insane asylums don't care how crazy you might be. They simply lock you up and call for the shrink. At that point, Watts' only believers would be living down the hall from him.

His conscience begged him to forget this nonsense, but his gut told him to stay the course. Since his gut had the better track record, he called the physics department at Texas Christian University, hoping to speak to Dr. Farrentine, whom he had been referred to. Unfortunately, the professor was out, so he left a voicemail and hung up.

Spartan returned soon after and came into Watts' cubicle. "How was lunch?"

"Great," said Watts. He followed with an unsolicited restaurant review and smiled at his partner. "We'll have to go sometime."

"Sounds good. What about the rope?"

Grateful his partner didn't specify *noose*, Watts waved him closer and then whispered the details of what he knew, and how he was seeking a physicist's opinion. Spartan nodded, but his expression gave Watts the impression he should check himself into an asylum. The thought made Watts smile. Yes, he would miss Daisy, but living rent-free with three meals a day might be doable. Spartan's voice brought him back.

"Okay, so while we're waiting on the physicist, what do you want to do about Betty?"

Watts rocked his chair, thinking. Their last visit with her may not have gone as planned, but they did record another EVP. Unfortunately, they couldn't count on Betty's cooperation any more than they could Jeremy's. Still, there was no reason to hang around the office, so he double-checked his Sony and rose from his chair.

"Let's go talk to her."

"You want me to call and make sure she's there?"

Watts shook his head. "She made it clear the Scott Theater is her life, so I imagine she's there. Do you have something you'd rather be doing?"

"I always have things to do, but if you want to go, let's go."

"Fine. We're outta here."

The ride to the theater had become so routine that Watts found himself recognizing people on the sidewalks and dogs crossing the streets. One middle-aged woman even smiled and waved as he drove by. *So much for being incognito.*

As soon as they walked into the Scott Theater, they saw Betty Cerin turn and walk away. "Hold on, Betty," said Watts using his cop voice. "We need to talk."

Stopping to face them, a smile spread across her face as though she had just recognized them. Willing himself not to laugh, he slipped his hand into his pocket and turned on his Sony.

"Betty, what happened to you yesterday?" said Spartan. "You left us in the cold."

Raising her eyebrows, she said, "You were chilled, too? And here I thought it was hormones. I went to splash water on my face, and when I came back, they said you had left."

The two detectives exchanged suspicious glances. Spartan didn't appear any more convinced than Watts. Then again, nothing could explain the chill he experienced when he read Jeremy's newspaper account.

"Betty, we won't take much of your time," said Watts. "We just wanted to go over a few questions."

Standing politely with her arms crossed, she said, "Fire away."

"Very well. When did you first meet Jeremy Delouse?"

She paused, pressing her hand to her cheek. "Oh my, that was so long ago. As best I recall, Jeremy was working odd jobs in the theater before he became an actor, so I might have said hi to him a couple of times back in early 1969, but I didn't get to know him until we started working together on stage. He deserved more praise than he ever received, especially considering how his fellow actors ridiculed him for having been a custodian. Personally, I never saw what the fuss was about. He was just another guy trying to break into the business, and it eventually worked for him."

Spartan squinted with his head cocked. "What do you mean he was ridiculed?"

"Even community theater actors can be pompous," she said. "And several of them resented Jeremy coming in through the back door. But what about the actors who wait Hollywood tables hoping for a break? Isn't it the same thing?"

"I suppose," said Watts, wondering where she was going with this.

"Gentlemen, Jeremy was an excellent performer, and I respected him for working his way up. Unfortunately, he never got any praise until he died. Suddenly, they were gushing over him, saying how much he would be missed. It made me sick and I quit acting because of those hypocrites, but I still wanted to be involved in the theater. I've outlasted all those actors because I started doing administrative work. Seems I made the smarter choice, don't you think?"

Spartan nodded, keeping his hands in his pockets. "Can you tell us more about how Jeremy worked his way up?"

"It's quite simple, detective. He emptied the garbage and kept the place clean. Where are you going with this?"

Watts cleared his throat. "I think we're getting a bit sidetracked with how Jeremy got his job. Let's go back to 1969 and discuss your relationship with Travis McLean. How long had you been dating before you got married?"

Suddenly her body wilted, her face full of regret. "Maybe six months," she quietly said. My parents were furious about it, but they couldn't stop me because I was over eighteen and in love. Travis was a handsome charmer who could have had anyone he wanted. When he chose me, I was so infatuated that I wasn't thinking clearly. Being with him was like being on stage. Love at first sight, as the saying goes. But there's a big difference between infatuation and living together. We could barely afford food, because it took nearly everything we had to pay the rent. We had both been living with our parents until we got married, so living together was a big adjustment for both of us. What began as a fairy tale romance quickly became a nightmare. To be honest, it was a Godsend when the Army drafted him, because he then had a steady income, and we both had medical benefits. I felt guilty when Travis got wounded. I know it wasn't my fault, but it felt like I was the one who sent him overseas. How stupid is that? Marriage was difficult for both of us."

Watts nodded, stopping his pen. "I'm sorry you have to relive these painful memories, Betty, but while Travis was overseas, were you and Jeremy working on stage together?"

"Of course. He played Edgar Crocker in *Paint Your Wagon*. In the play version, Edgar falls in love with Elizabeth, which was my role. Jeremy did a nice job, too."

"I see," said Spartan. "What was your personal relationship with him?"

She cast a sly grin. "All I will say is Jeremy was good at everything he did."

Watts stuck out his lower lip, thinking about that. She seemed to sense where this was going and was twisting words to avoid answering the question. After chewing his lip for a second, he said, "Betty, I think what Detective Spartan was asking is, what was your off-stage relationship with Jeremy?"

Looking wounded, she hugged her chest and stared at the floor. "On stage Jeremy was my lover. Off stage he was nothing because I was married. I'm old-fashioned that way."

"So, you never went out for coffee or anything?" said Spartan.

Her hands fell to her hips as she met his gaze. For a second it looked like she was going to yell, but then her eyes softened and she slowly shook her head.

"It wasn't unusual for cast members to go out for coffee after a performance, but as for anything going on between Jeremy and me, I assure you that nothing was going on. I loved Travis and couldn't wait for him to get home. I wanted to grow old with him. I had no interest in Jeremy."

"Did Jeremy have feelings for you?"

Her face soured again. "How would I know? We never dated, and I certainly wasn't encouraging him." She paused to check out the people wandering the halls. Most had their backs turned, but some seemed curious about what was going on. Betty seemed disgusted with them. "Look, I don't mean to be rude, but as you can see, it's getting busy. Either wrap this up, or we can finish it another time."

"We'll do our best," said Spartan. "Do you know if Jeremy received a draft notice? Could that have been his reason for suicide?"

"I just told you I didn't know Jeremy other than on stage. If he received a draft notice, he never mentioned it, and I don't recall any reference to it in his suicide note."

"But the suicide note said he was killing himself over an actress."

"An *unnamed* actress," she said.

Watts nodded, jotting more notes. "Assuming the note was directed at you, did Travis know how Jeremy felt about you? Is that why he did a second tour in Vietnam?"

Betty gazed at him as though he was nuts. "What are you talking about? Jeremy killed himself months before Travis re-upped for a second tour, so if you're looking for a connection, you're sloshing through the wrong rice field."

"Perhaps," said Spartan, "but did Travis know Jeremy had feelings for you?"

"Travis had no reason to be jealous. I introduced them after a play, and I was so proud that my husband had been in the audience, I barely noticed Jeremy. And Travis was proud of me, too. It was one of the few times we were both truly happy."

"That's good to know," said Watts. "Now for a more difficult question. Why did you get so upset yesterday when we were talking about Jeremy?"

"Because I felt sorry for him. He had such a promising future. He was attractive, intelligent, talented, and yes, had I been single, I might have been willing to date him, but I made it clear that would never happen."

"And then what?"

Her forehead wrinkled. "As I said, if Jeremy was infatuated with me, that was his thing. I was never a participant. Now if you'll excuse me, there are people waiting to see me. Good day, gentlemen."

"Thank you for your time, Betty. Have a good day."

After getting in the car, Watts replayed his audiotape. Being able to listen without distracting visual cues made it easier to discern Betty's disposition during her questioning. He believed her pauses showed concern on her part, but that was pure speculation. What fascinated him was how well she spoke of Travis and how indifferent she was toward Jeremy.

"I hate to admit it, but maybe I was wrong about her," he said. "Before this interview, I was pretty sure that she and Jeremy were having an affair and Travis got wind of it, but now I'm not so sure. It's still possible she's delivering a stellar performance, but I'm pretty convinced she's telling the truth."

"I agree, said Spartan. "So, where does that leave us?"

Watts set his Sony aside and started the car. Another day was coming to an end without their being any closer to solving this riddle. There was a new homicide last night that Ryder assigned to someone else. But he was running out of detectives, which meant their turn was approaching faster than Halloween. In just a few days, ghouls, goblins and zombies would be running around in blood-splattered costumes, making it difficult to tell what blood was real and what was made up. More than once, police had found a body they initially thought was someone in costume. For some, All Hollow's Eve provided the perfect cover to bump someone off and get away with it. Spartan asked his question again, and he didn't have an answer. He set the car in motion still thinking about it during their drive back to the station.

Their return trip was agonizing because Jeremy's ghost kept haunting Watts. He was hoping his spirit would provide some sort of guidance instead of messing with his head. Not hearing back from the physics professor was another setback. He had hoped a scientific explanation for the noose's electrical charge would back up their evidence of paranormal activity, but now his hopes seemed dashed. His feet seemed heavier climbing the steps.

Back at the whiteboard, he and Spartan stared blankly at the evidence. But then Spartan's eyes got brighter as if he were onto something. He hadn't said anything yet, but he did make a few notes and rubbed his face.

Watts sighed and looked at his partner. "Okay, Blaine, what's going on?"

"Skilled actresses can turn on smiles and tears at will, and I believe Betty fits that category. So, what if she's lying about her relationship with Jeremy and Jeremy got her pregnant while Travis was overseas? Wouldn't you say that ups the stakes?"

Watts bobbed his head, hawking the board. "I've pondered that thought many times, and Kat Coulter proved that actresses are deceivers, regardless of age. Yesterday, Betty disappeared because she knew she let her guard down, but today she seemed better rehearsed. You have to admit that was a pretty nice recovery after she unsuccessfully tried to avoid us."

Spartan's lips curled slightly. "Sounds like we're on the same page, partner."

"Of course we are, and since we could get a new assignment at any time, what do you propose we do now?"

Spartan smiled. "I think the answer's been staring us in the face the whole time."

Watts cocked his head, squinting. "What are you talking about?"

"Maxx, every time we talk to Betty, I end up thinking about Marv. Haven't you noticed their eyes and his birth date? Betty would be a shoe-in to be his biological mother, and if that's the case, then Marv was conceived while Travis was in Vietnam. Considering that Jeremy died while Travis was home, I'm convinced Travis had ample motive and opportunity to kill him."

Watts locked his hands behind his head and leaned back in his chair. Spartan's theory was a long shot, but considering Betty's reaction, it was worth pursuing. Excited about the prospect, he shifted his weight and his chair leaned forward.

"For now let's put Travis aside and do a facial analysis on Betty and Marv," he said. "We should also check the *Fort Worth Star Telegram* archives for an old *Paint Your Wagon* playbill featuring Jeremy and Betty so we can add Jeremy to the comparison. It shouldn't take long to know if Marv is Jeremy and Betty's love child."

Spartan nodded, adding, "While we're at it, we should do a facial analysis of Marv's legal parents. If nothing else, we should be able to use their obituary photos."

"I like your logic, Blaine. You go after Marv's folks and I'll check on Betty and Marv."

The phone rang and Forensics Technician Tim Westin asked for Watts.

"What's going on, Tim?" said Watts. "You sound troubled."

"Daisy's been asking questions. I'm not sure whether she overheard someone mention the noose or not, but I wanted to warn you she's gonna be pissed if she found out."

"Thanks for the heads-up, Tim. By the way, I'm still waiting to hear back from the physicist on the noose."

"Would you mind passing on his explanation? I'm really captivated by this."

"Will do, and thanks again for the call." Watts frowned, cradling the phone. "Westin says the cat may be out of the bag," he said to Spartan. "We need to be more discrete next time."

"Forget it, Maxx. If Daisy asks about the noose, tell her I gave it to the lab for analysis. It's not a lie, so she shouldn't have a problem with it. If she asks why she wasn't involved, then you can honestly say it happened while she was away."

With pursed lips, Watts nodded his agreement. "As I said, I like the way you think. Now, let's get some work done." He spun his chair around and Spartan left.

The Department of Motor Vehicles database had current photos of Betty Cerin and Marv Delouse. Watts printed them out and then placed them side by side on the whiteboard. After a preliminary examination confirmed Spartan might be onto something, he took the photos to the lab.

Daisy gave him a stern look when she met him at the counter. He might have been concerned had Westin not tipped him off. "Hi there" he said, speaking before she had the chance. "I have another request for you." He quickly placed the DMV images on the counter.

She studied them for a moment and looked up. "This one's Marv and the other is Betty. How'd I do?"

"Perfect. What I'm looking for is a facial analysis on them. I'll e-mail these photos to you so they're a little sharper."

"No need. I'm pretty sure these will work. Come with me."

He followed her into the computer room where she scanned them and then opened a program that compared physical features. Pointing to the screen, she said, "Cosmetic surgery can change noses and eyes, but cheek bones and chins don't lie. I'll need an expert opinion, but from what I'm seeing, the family resemblance is strong. Is Betty Marv's aunt?"

"That seems unlikely, since Marv's last name is Delouse, not Cerin or McLean."

She thought for a moment and said, "Do you think Betty is Marv's mother?"

"It certainly appears plausible."

She nodded, studying their features again. "Do you think Marv knows?"

"Based on what we overheard at the diner, I'd say no. My guess is Jeremy is Marv's biological father, not his uncle."

Daisy looked dumbfounded. "We've certainly opened a can of

worms, haven't we? I mean, this could be devastating for Marv. If it's true, how will you explain it?"

Watts casually shrugged, shaking his head. "All I know is we'd better have our ducks in a row before we break the news to him. We're trying to find a suitable photo of Jeremy so we can compare all three of them. Blaine's also seeking photos of Marv's legal parents. If the computer matches any of them, then we might have something worthwhile. Please have your expert do an analysis on these two while we do more digging."

"Will do."

Watts was out the door before she could mention the noose. He felt lucky slipping away without a lecture. Then again, she knew she could do that over soup tonight. Suddenly, he didn't feel so smug.

When he reached his desk, he scanned the *Fort Worth Star Telegram* archives for a photo of Jeremy. It took longer than expected, but he eventually found one of the striking young man who had taken his own life. Not surprisingly, his obituary described him as a struggling actor who kept to himself. There was no mention of Betty. While Jeremy's photo printed, Watts got his partner's attention.

"Hey, Blaine, check this out."

"Hang on. I'm downloading photos of Marv's parents so we can complete this family reunion. We should probably compare Travis' features, too."

"Why? We know Travis wasn't around when Marv was conceived."

"Maxx, you always taught me to think outside the box. For all we know, Marv was a preemie."

Watts took that as a compliment. "Glad you're keeping an open mind, partner. Anyway, we'll go whenever you're ready."

Watts was about to open his e-mail when Spartan said he was set to go. They skipped down the stairs like kids eager to show off their artwork. Already expecting them, Daisy waved for them to join her in the computer room.

"Here's the rest of the family," said Watts, spreading the photos on the table. "This one is Jeremy, and these two are Marv's legal parents. As far as we can tell, Marv still believes Warren and Grace Delouse are his biological parents."

Daisy nodded, comparing the photos. She then scanned the photos into the computer and split the screen so she could view all of the faces at once. "This analysis confirms that Jeremy and Warren were brothers," she said. "According to this computer program, Marv shares the Delouse nose, but his eyes, ears, and hairline came from Betty Cerin. That means Betty and Jeremy are Marv's biological parents, not Grace and Warren."

"It certainly looks that way," said Spartan, reviewing the evidence. "But it's hard to believe Marv hasn't wondered why he doesn't look more like his parents."

Watts shrugged. "If he ever brought it up, we'll never know how his parents explained it, and I'm sure not going to ask Marv about it. Still, I agree with you that most kids are always looking in the mirror comparing themselves to their parents, wondering where certain features came from. But in spite of this, what kid would have the foresight to question whether the people who raised them weren't their own parents?"

Daisy nodded enthusiastically. "I don't share all of my parents' features, but I never questioned whether they were my biological parents."

"Okay," said Watts, stepping in. "The consensus is Marv Delouse is Betty and Jeremy's child, and based on his birthday, Betty was approximately three months pregnant when Travis came home on military leave. Daisy, how much does a pregnant woman show at three months?"

She looked at him like he was crazy. "How would I know? I'm a lab tech, not a gynecologist. Besides, I suspect it depends on the person. I mean, heavy people may not show at all, whereas a thin person might have a bump."

"Well, Betty's still thin so she was probably a hottie back in the day, but even with good acting, do you honestly think she could hide a pregnancy from her husband by saying she'd put on a little midriff weight?"

"Think about it, Maxx. You've been separated from your wife for months, you've been injured and finally get to be with her. Would you rather question her about putting on a few pounds or make love? I suspect Travis was so horny he never even noticed – at least on the first night."

"Maybe not, but on the second or third night and he felt her bulge, things probably began to click. Remember, how he said Jeremy looked at her on stage? It probably didn't take him long to realize they got busy while he was overseas. So when our battle-scarred soldier got the opportunity, he killed Jeremy, made it look like a suicide, and returned to Vietnam before anyone could question him."

Daisy looked repulsed. "I love how you turn romance into mattress dancing."

"Hey, I'm just keeping it short to make sure we're all on the same page."

Watts nodded to his partner. "Crude or not, I agree with Blaine, so let's shift our focus to finding evidence that supports our scenario. Let's start with finding hospital records that either proves Betty gave birth or that Marv's birth certificate is a lie. I'm not sure how Betty could have pulled that off, but my gut's telling me she did."

Spartan crossed his arms contemplating that. "I suppose it's possible."

"Of course it is." Watts quickly turned to Daisy, his mind churning ideas faster than he could speak. "Daisy, please find an expert who can verify your feature analysis. We need facts that will hold up in court, but more importantly, I need something I can show Betty that will force her to admit Marv's her child. I doubt she'll volunteer any information, but she might spill her guts if we catch her at a weak moment."

"We can only hope."

Watts nodded. "Well, let's get back to work. Thanks again, Daisy."

She gently patted his hand. "That's why I'm here."

Back at his desk, Watts searched his e-mail for anything that mentioned *noose*. No sooner had the list popped up than a new one came in from the TCU physicist to whom he had written. He eagerly opened the e-mail.

Detective Watts, I am Dr. Duane Wentworth, Associate Professor with the Department of Physics at Texas Christian University in Fort Worth. Regarding your question about Quantum Theory and the nylon noose, I have considered it for some time and bearing in mind there are no absolutes, offer the following:

Perhaps the spirit you have been seeking has figured out a way to connect the realities that are theorized to exist in the modern interpretation of quantum mechanics where systems can behave as existing in sometimes infinite possible realities. At some point, all of these realities may be realized, but in a way that none of them can connect with any other. In fact this interpretation, which is taken quite seriously among physicists, says that at any given moment, infinite universes may exist in parallel, while at the same time many more are being generated. Some of these worlds would differ only slightly, while others may differ significantly. As such, one might toy with the possibility of being able to "will" yourself into one of these parallel worlds to take advantage of something which happened in that world as opposed to the one you feel you are in.

Perhaps your aforementioned spirit possesses this ability to navigate between two parallel universes where one has a noose in the car and the other does not. This is not to imply you fell into an alternate reality. Remember that we are dealing with theory. It is more likely that the spirit you referred to may be transiting such universes and carried the noose. Perhaps this may offer a better explanation of the noose's disappearance and reappearance, although I have no idea why a spirit would choose your vehicle for such a task. Humans possessing traditional two-dimensional thinking would not notice what was going on, but a nylon noose carrying an electrical charge may add credence to its having taken a trans-worldly journey.

Remember that as a human, I can only explain your unusual occurrence in theory. If you would care to discuss this further, please drop me another e-mail.

Best Regards, Dr. Duane Wentworth

Watts re-read Wentworth's e-mail several times before calling his partner in. Spartan's eyes widened as he read the note.

"This is incredible," he said, leaning over Watts' shoulder.

"I agree, but as Dr. Wentworth says, it's theory, not evidence. Think about it, Blaine. If you were sitting on a jury, and some detective is testifying about some spirit transporting a nylon noose into another universe and back, would you believe him?"

"Probably not."

Spartan raised his arms over his head to stretch. After letting out a breath, he placed his hands on his lower back and leaned back.

"If I hadn't seen this stuff first hand, I wouldn't believe it myself. First it's EVPs, and now solid objects are being molecularly transported between parallel worlds. No, Maxx, if I were on that jury, I'd say it was a *Star Trek* episode, not a murder investigation."

Watts chuckled. "I can hardly wait to see Captain Ryder's face when we tell him about this."

"His face, or that giant Easter egg on the back of his head?"

Watts was laughing now. "Both, if he dares to show the back of his head. Anyway, it's time we filled him in, so gather whatever data you have and be ready to walk the green mile in five minutes. With luck, he'll tell us to boldly go where no detectives have gone before."

Spartan was chuckling now. "Okay, Captain Kirk. I'll see you in a couple."

With their evidence in hand, the detectives hastily walked to

Captain Ryder's office. Today, Watts didn't care about his farting shoe. He was more interested in seeing his boss's expression when they replayed the EVPs, showed him Dr. Wentworth's e-mail, and made their case about Marv's true biological parents.

As they approached Ryder's office, someone started coughing. Watts thought it was a colleague's joke until the smoker's cough worsened. Thankfully, it was coming from a nearby clerk and not their boss who was on the phone at the time.

Ryder hung up the moment he saw them and promptly waved them in. "We just got another homicide," he said. "Congratulations, you're up."

Watts set his evidence on Ryder's desk and nodded for Spartan to do the same. "We understand, but before you assign it to us, could we please go over our findings? I'm confident that once you see them, you'll realize we have established a strong murder motive."

The Captain's eyes narrowed as he gazed at the folders on his desk. "You do understand that we have a body downtown awaiting a homicide detective and that your vic has been dead for over four decades?"

"Yes, sir, but as you're always reminding us, there is no statute of limitations on murder, and Jeremy Delouse doesn't care about the other victim."

Ryder rubbed his meaty hands over his face and then stared at his desk. A few moments later, he picked up his phone. "You're up," he said to the unnamed detective. "The body's in the alley behind the food bank. Homeless male in his sixties with a gunshot to the head."

As Watts listened, he couldn't help thinking it was Travis McLean. Certainly plenty of homeless men fit that description, but considering all that was going on, it could easily be him.

"Captain, do you have the vic's name?" he said, interrupting.

Ryder raised a brow. "What difference does it make? Didn't I just assign the case to someone else? Do you suddenly want back in?"

"No, sir, it's just that our murder suspect fits that description."

Ryder leaned back in his chair, then abruptly sprang forward and leaned to one side.

Trying to avoid Ryder's bright pink bald spot, Watts looked at the floor. "Is there a problem?" he said.

Ryder angrily shook his head. "I keep forgetting that some bastard oiled my chair. I always found that squeak comforting. Anyway, you were saying about a murder suspect?"

"Sir, he's more of a person of interest with a strong motive," said Spartan.

"Go on."

The detectives spent the next fifteen minutes presenting their case. When they finished, Watts admitted they still had work to do, but they wanted to bring him up to speed.

Ryder had seemed impressed by their evidence, but his body language suggested he remained skeptical. "Here's my problem," he said. "If Travis McLean killed his wife's lover, why wouldn't he kill her, too?"

Watts mulled that over while gathering his things. Whenever his boss played Devil's Advocate, Watts knew he was on board, and knowing that gave him more freedom in what he would say.

"Sir, as ludicrous as it sounds, it appears we are getting direction from a spirit. Of course, I wouldn't mention that to anyone, but it does seem to be going that way. Once we've analyzed the rest of our evidence, we'll have another talk with Travis. In the meantime, we'll keep digging into those hospital records we mentioned."

Their boss kept looking at his chair as if waiting for a squeak. "Go find your ghost," he said, his face getting angrier. "Just make sure you find some solid evidence along the way. Otherwise, I'll be testing your noose's strength on your privates. Now get out of here before I change my mind."

"Yes, sir."

Watts beamed after he walked out the door. Ryder was the perfect boss because his threats were easy to ignore. That lack of fear probably came from Watts' abusive father. Once he overcame that, intimidation no longer worked on him. In this sense, he should have thanked his old man for giving him the spit in his eye like Johnny Cash's character in *A Boy Named Sue*. Nowadays, the only thing Watts feared was screwing up his relationship with Daisy. He never expected anyone to consume his thoughts like she had.

Spartan knew better than to say anything until they were clear of Ryder's office. He was also aware that everyone in the building recognized Watts' gate, and since the two detectives seemed to spend more time with the boss than anyone else, the office got real quiet as they retreated to their desks.

But Watts was in such a good mood, he couldn't resist spilling some bogus gossip. "Can you believe it?" he said, loud enough for others to hear. "He's gonna dock us two weeks' pay? We've been busting our asses on this case. It's not fair!"

Playing along, Spartan added, "I warned you it would come down to this, Maxx. I suppose two weeks' pay is better than getting busted down to Patrol though."

"Good point."

When they stopped talking, whispers became idle chatter. Before long, the office sounded like a hen house. Their noise reminded him of the *Hee Haw* re-runs his dad used to watch on CMT. In the most literal sense, *Hee Haw* was the corniest show on the air, and what was happening here reminded him of the *Hee Haw* ladies singing they weren't there to spread gossip so you'd better listen close the first time. Remembering that, he and Spartan wagered a buck on how long it would take for someone to confront them at their desks after they visited the boss. Watts went with five minutes, Spartan took ten. Detective Skip Parsons arrived in three.

Leaning over their cubicles, Parsons said, "So, the boss had your asses, did he?"

Watts gave a quizzical look. "What are you talking about, Skip?"

"Oh, come on. Everyone heard you say you were given time off without pay."

Accepting his winning dollar from Spartan and tucking it away, he said, "Blaine, do you have any idea what he's talking about?"

Suddenly Parsons' bunched and cheeks puffed.. "You bastards!" After wiping the spittle from his lips, he added, "Piss off!"

Watts and Spartan tapped their fists together as Parsons stormed off. Although detectives shared the common goal of catching criminals, there was always stiff competition to see who could solve the case. Certain that Parsons came to gloat, the joke turned out to be on him, so even if nothing else happened today, Watts would go home smiling.

Thirty One

THE REST OF THE afternoon was spent trying to trace Betty Cerin's medical history. Not having a warrant, this proved impossible due to countless privacy acts. From an investigator's standpoint, dead ends like this were frustrating. From a citizen's point of view, they made perfect sense.

Getting nowhere, Watts went back to Marv Delouse's birth certificate, which he was able to access. His document said he was born in Fort Worth's Harris Methodist Hospital on May 2, 1970 to Grace and Warren Delouse. Finding no adoption papers, he called Daisy for an update.

"I wondered if your feature analysis expert came up with anything on Marv?" he said.

"Well, he verified what I said – that it's extremely unlikely that Marv is Grace and Warren Delouse's, or Betty Cerin and Travis McLean's child, but it is highly likely that Betty Cerin and Jeremy Delouse are his biological parents."

"That's great, but it doesn't give us permission to tap into Betty's medical history."

"I'm sorry, detective. That's the best I can do."

An awkward silence followed. He could hear her breathing, so she hadn't ended the call. It seemed like she had something to say, except she wasn't speaking.

"Daisy? Is everything okay?"

"Actually, no. I meant to bring this up the last time we spoke, but it didn't seem like the right time. Maxx, why didn't you tell me you were taking the noose to the lab?"

Watts hesitated. Her voice may have been a whisper, but her tone was livid. Trying to ease her mind he said, "Everyone was trying to protect you. You freaked out after the last incident, and we didn't want to put you through that again."

After letting that sink in, he unlocked his desk drawer and briefed her on the physicist's thoughts about the noose's residual charge. Taking a glance inside he said, "Just so you know, it's still here and no longer carries a charge. Anyone looking at it would consider it a small replica and nothing more. Of course, Captain Ryder has threatened to test it on my nuts if things don't pan out."

He expected a laugh that never came, and now the phone was slipping in his palm. Pressing it hard against his ear, he said, "Look, Daisy, I'm sorry I didn't tell you, but as I said, our intentions were good. I promise not to do it again."

"Well, thank you for that," she finally said. "And for the record, I'm a professional and should always be treated as one."

"You're right, and again I'm sorry," he said, locking the drawer. "If you would, please e-mail me your expert's comments on the facial comparisons. I plan to confront Betty with them once our ducks are in a row. In the meantime, Blaine is trying to dig up dirt on Travis. We don't know who is keeping secrets yet, but we intend to find out."

"I suppose any or all of them could be. Regardless, good luck with it."

He nearly hung up when another idea came to mind. "Daisy, do you have any thoughts on who might have made the noose and stapled it to your overhang? Maybe it wouldn't explain its disappearance or reappearance, but it might explain how it got there in the first place."

"Honestly, I don't know. No one is putting up Halloween decorations, so I can't imagine it wasn't placed there without a purpose. Also keep in mind that it appeared the day after our first dungeon haunting experience. And while I can't explain how this rope could transport itself into another dimension and back, I refuse to believe that a ghost could fabricate a noose and then staple it to my building. That means a human is involved, and I want to know who."

"Well, Blaine and I are just as eager to find out." When she didn't respond, he said, "I'd better let you go, but for the record, I'm glad we had this talk."

"Me, too. Bye."

Watts studied their whiteboard after hanging up. Things near the top he left alone, but at the bottom he started a blood line for Marv with Betty and Jeremy as his parents. To the side, he noted that Travis was married to Betty, and also conveniently home when Jeremy died. From what he was seeing, Travis remained the likely killer, assuming that Jeremy was indeed murdered. But the one element that didn't make sense was Travis trying to convince his pal that Jeremy was murdered. Watts was still struggling to corral that one.

He rolled away from his desk and tapped on Spartan's wall. "I hope you're making progress, because I'm running into brick walls."

Spartan grinned back. "The good thing about brick walls is they can be torn down. I've practically memorized Travis McLean's military history. According to his training record, he excelled in hand-to-hand combat, although there are no awards or commendations that validate it. He survived two combat tours and then dropped out like he said. Since there are no current tax records on him, he's probably living on the streets."

"He did say he got paid in cash, so that may not be the case."

"True, but he could also be living under an alias."

Watts touched his lip and held his fingers there. When he dropped his hand, his flat expression remained. "Blaine, I keep wondering who benefits from solving a mystery from over four decades ago, and if Travis killed Jeremy, why would he be the one insisting it was murder. He may have his oddities, but I don't get the impression he wants to die in jail."

Spartan shrugged. "Maybe Travis is ill and wants to clear his conscience before he dies."

"Or maybe he feels sorry for Marv and wants him to know that Jeremy was his biological father."

"Maybe."

Watts reflected on this for a moment and said, "Travis' only reference to Jeremy was that he was murdered, so that doesn't fit." He pulled out his notepad and flipped through the pages. "Here we are. Travis claimed there was evidence of murder, but the ME ignored it and ruled Jeremy's death a suicide."

"But what evidence was he referring to? You've seen the photos. He was hanging from a noose with an overturned stool next to him. The ME said there was no sign of foul play. If we were the ones on scene, we'd probably support the suicide ruling too."

"I'd buy that if Doc Morton's report were error free, but it's not."

"Maxx, a minor error doesn't change the fact that Jeremy died from oxygen starvation to his brain."

"Perhaps, but the way Morton's been acting, I can't help thinking he missed something."

"Even if he did miss something, there's no way to prove it without Jeremy's records."

"I know," said Watts with a sigh. "I'm really starting to hate this case. It's like trying to solve JFK's murder, except in Jeremy's case, we're the only ones who care." After saying that, he rested his eyes, but soon images of Ryder slipping that toy noose around his testicles forced them wide open. Squirming in his seat, he added, "Let's forget about Morton and take a different direction. Travis made a statement about Jeremy being too emotionally weak to take his own life. Any ideas?"

Spartan didn't answer right away. Instead, he sat there looking dazed and confused. "I can't answer that because I never met Jeremy, but it does suggest Travis knew him better than he's led us to believe."

"Oh, I'm sure Travis' observations extended beyond his live theater experience. Of course, there's also the possibility we've been reading things into his statements. I mean, maybe he was referring to Jeremy being a weak actor, or maybe being overly sensitive is what made him an actor."

Spartan scratched his stubble as he scanned his notes. When he looked up, all he could give was a blank stare. "I'm stumped."

"Well, we know Jeremy wasn't gay because he was always having girl trouble, and although women can drive their men crazy, it's rare when a man kills himself over them. In fact, I'm willing to bet women are the ones more likely commit suicide over their men."

"If that's true, it's because men will murder their lovers before they'll kill themselves."

Watts nodded his agreement as he re-read his notes. He stared at the pages expecting his words to reveal something he hadn't considered before. When nothing leaped out, he placed his thumb under one particular passage.

"I keep thinking there's more to Betty's statement about actors dying on stage than meets the eye. Remember how she said they sometimes prepared for plays in the dungeon? What if Jeremy was talked into slipping that noose over his own neck as if it were a dress rehearsal, and then someone knocked over the stool?"

Spartan hesitated. "I'd say you're reaching because I've seen the play version of *Paint Your Wagon*, and I don't recall any noose. I mean, the show's a comedy about a bunch of gold miners who end up building a shanty town, and since the only attempt at order came from a loud-mouth preacher, why would they have a noose?"

"Hell, I don't know. I'm just tossing out ideas. We have no way of knowing whether Jeremy tied the knot, or if someone backstage used it to make the background more interesting."

"I'm sure Betty would know."

Watts moved on to another passage. "Okay, how about this? Travis claimed it would have been easy for any of the actors to plan their final exit in the dungeon, so did Betty tell him this, or was it his gut talking? And then there's his statement about how Jeremy was murdered and yet he never gives a name. Did he hold back because he committed the murder or because he knows who the killer is?"

Spartan raised his hands in surrender. "You're on your own with these rhetorical questions, Maxx. The fact is unless someone confesses to a crime, we're never going to solve this, so should we try Betty again or see if Marv can link us up with Travis?"

Watts mulled it over. They could probably see Betty today, but repeated visits might lead to claims of harassment. Then again, not seeing her was equally risky. "Blaine, what's your honest opinion of Marv and Travis – not as men, but as friends, and how they stay in touch?"

"I'm not sure, but I do find it curious how Travis doesn't seem to exist in our society and yet Marv seems to reach him whenever he wants."

"Exactly, so here's what I'd like to do. You ride your bike regularly, don't you?"

Spartan looked confused. "I ride my bike on family outings and my butt gets sore after a few miles. Why?"

"Well, I was thinking we could borrow one of the department's bikes, load it in Leroy, and get to the bank before Marv gets off work. Then you position yourself on the bike near the street where you won't be noticeable, but where you'll be ready to tail him. We'll stay in touch by cell phone so you can tell me what's going on. If for some reason he's driving a car, I'll tail him and you can catch up."

"Ah, yeah. Sounds great – unless he lives ten miles from the bank."

Watts gave a disapproving look. "If's he's pedaling to work in a suit, he can't live that far away."

Spartan sighed, tugging on his threads. "What about *my* suit?"

"Put some rubber bands over your pants so they don't get caught in the gears."

"Great, except that's not what I was talking about. If I'm on a bike and wearing a suit, don't you think *I'll* look rather conspicuous?"

"No more than any other tree-hugging commuter – now go check with whoever issues bikes. See if you can borrow some biker clothes, too. I'll meet you at my truck in ten."

Spartan left wearing a scornful look. Watts felt bad about giving him such short notice, but he had no choice if they were to get there in time to follow Marv home. As soon as his partner was out of sight, he called Daisy to brief her on his plan.

"I can understand why you'd want to take your truck to be incognito, but I'm not sure it's a good idea tailing someone while you're off-duty. Besides, what if he's not going home for the night?"

"Because whenever we ask to see Travis, Marv manages to arrange a meeting. I never saw Travis pull out a phone, so my guess is Marv knows where to find him."

"I see. Well, if you're not going to listen to me, all I can say is good luck. Call me with an update, and don't worry about being late for dinner. Soup can always wait."

Soup! Feeling like an idiot, it dawned on him that he had gotten so caught up in finding Travis he had forgotten about her invitation. "I'll call you when I'm on my way."

"Sounds good."

Watts shut down his computer, headed downstairs, and slipped out the door. Since detectives needed flexible hours to work a case, Captain Ryder would never question where he and Spartan had gone. Five minutes after getting to his truck, he saw Spartan pedaling his way over wearing black Spandex shorts, a black Spandex shirt, black helmet, dark sunglasses, *and black loafers.* Spartan's backpack covered the white letters on the shirt that said Police.

"Not a word, Maxx. Don't say one freakin' word," he said, leaping off the bike. After loading it in the back, he climbed into Leroy and glared out the window.

As his truck came to life, Watts passed on the ridicule and instead went over the plan. "I'll be letting you out on NW 22nd Street and then I'll park Leroy where we won't be overly conspicuous but I can still observe the bank's parking lot. Make sure you hide around the corner and be casual."

"You expect me to be casual while I'm on a bike that says Police? Great idea, Maxx. Knowing my luck, one of our Patrol cops will be quizzing me when I need to be following Marv."

"Why would he do that?"

"Hmm. Maybe because I'm riding a police bike in loafers and my gun, badge and suit are in my backpack. By the way, you owe me for the dry cleaning."

"Done. Anyway, keep your phone on you and don't hang up once I call you. Got it?"

Spartan squinted at his partner. "How can you not ride a bike?"

"I love running, never cared for biking," he said wearing his most sincere expression. "And I really do appreciate your doing this, Blaine."

Spartan glanced at his ludicrous outfit and rolled his eyes.

But the plan worked well. Soon after Spartan took off on his bike, Watts parked Leroy a block away from the bank's lot and pulled his binoculars from the console. Keeping them focused on the bank's exit, he waited for Marv to emerge. Once he could confirm his identity, he would pass the news on to Spartan.

While waiting, Watts listened to the The Beach Boys on the oldies station. The timing was good because he'd rather give chase to their *I Get Around* than Jan and Dean's *Dead Man's Curve*. Then again, his worst case scenario would more likely be a car hitting his partner.

At five minutes after five, Watts' phone rang and he relayed to his partner there was still no sign of Marv. Spartan must have understood because his call immediately dropped. After another ten minutes, Watts guessed the banker must have left early. He considered calling the bank to confirm that, but if Marv was still there, it might tip his hand. He decided to give it five more minutes. After that he would reconsider his options.

Finally, Marv wheeled his bike out the door. After alerting his partner, Watts gave Marv a head start and then keyed his ignition. Aware that his noisy pipes might draw attention, he waited until Marv was well clear and then pulled away from the curb using minimum power. He kept his phone line open so his partner could speak at will.

Word came back in a hurried voice. "He's a block ahead of me heading down 24th."

Watts hoped the degraded sound quality was because his partner tucked his phone down his shirt so he could control his bike. As Watts idled Leroy west on 24th, he waited for more words. Another update came within seconds.

"He's turning left on Prospect. You might want to pull into the parking lot that's on the northeast side." As soon as Watts acknowledged, Spartan added, "He turned into the third house on the right. Go check it out. I'm hanging back."

Watts parked Leroy under a shade tree shy of Prospect Avenue and raised his binoculars. He barely got them focused before Marv hauled his bike inside. He found that interesting, since the banker's legal address was miles away.

As one of Fort Worth's older sections, most of the clapboard homes were over fifty years old. Still, it appeared quite vibrant with trampolines, Doughboy pools, swings and kid toys. Strung clothes danced in the breeze, while two mangy dogs roamed like they owned the place. Smiling at the pooches, he muttered, "Nothing like dogs with attitude."

"Say again?"

Having forgotten his partner was still on the line, he quickly said, "I'll meet you at the parking lot on 24th."

"On my way."

Before leaving, Watts took another look through his field glasses. The home Marv entered was one of the smaller ones. Narrow and deep, it was surrounded by tall oaks with an empty driveway. The front door was shut and the blinds were drawn. He found that odd, since everything looked screened and the other homes had their windows open to allow fresh air. His first thought was Marv was running a meth lab on the side. He hoped that wasn't the case.

The Prospect address wasn't on Marv's driver's license, nor did it resemble a banker's home. Once Watts was convinced no one was peeking out a window, he drove Leroy to the lot of a two-story red brick building with boarded windows. The large driveway out front suggested it may have originally been a firehouse, perhaps built when cattle were still running through town. It was clean, in good repair, and the kiddie park out back suggested it had most recently been a day care facility. After parking Leroy in the shade, he spotted Spartan under a backyard awning retrieving his suit from his backpack. Watts was amused watching his partner pull his pants over his biker shorts and then replace his Spandex shirt with his own. The suit jacket was so crumpled that Spartan angrily returned it to the backpack, then knotted his tie, strapped on his gun, and fastened his badge.

"Wow, Blaine, it's like watching Superman in a phone booth. I should've filmed it for YouTube."

"That kind of thing goes in the category of *you can do anything once.*"

"Ooh, I'm scared," Watts laughed. "Get in the truck while I load the bike."

Watts lowered the tailgate and set the bike in. After climbing in the cab, he glanced at his fuming partner. "I've been meaning to ask how you got that bike and outfit so fast. I was impressed."

"Simple, said Spartan, rolling down his window and sticking his elbow out. "One of the bike cops wasn't feeling well, so I got his bike, clothes and backpack. I just had to agree to have everything cleaned and back by tomorrow."

"Cool. And what about the shoes?"

"He's a nine and I'm eleven. There was no way."

Watts smiled, staring out the windshield. "Okay, going back to our situation, we don't have a warrant, and Marv's driver's license didn't lead us here, so that leaves us in a rather precarious position. The way I see it, we either wait to see if Marv comes out, or we come back tomorrow while he's at work to see if anyone answers the door."

"What about double-checking Marv's legal address? It's possible it wasn't updated in all of the databases"

"I suppose, but let's worry about that in the morning. I'm sure Sandy would prefer having you home for dinner."

"I'm sure."

"And soak that Spandex. You must have worked up quite a sweat peddling those five blocks."

Watts was expecting a crude comeback, but instead Spartan laughed. As work days go, today wasn't too bad, but it was troubling that they still had more questions than answers. Even so, there was nothing pressing enough to keep him from seeing Daisy this evening.

Thirty Two

WATTS CALLED DAISY ON his way home to bring her up to speed. The more he explained his next plan to her, the crazier it sounded. First thing in the morning, he and Spartan would drive to the address on Marv's driver's license and then return to the mystery house on Prospect. People move all the time and don't notify DMV, but bankers don't normally relocate from a downtown condo to a neighborhood like this, even if the intent was to shorten their commute.

After listening to him ramble, she finally said, "Let's go bowling."

Her out-of-the-blue response left Watts speechless. Apparently her sudden bowling craving had replaced her soup invitation. Then again, a night of slamming balls into immobile objects might help him forget this crazy case for an evening. Bowling wasn't as fulfilling as blasting targets at the shooting range, but it could work.

"Pick you up at seven?"

"Make it six-thirty and you have a date."

"Okay. Six-thirty it is."

He shook his head as he ended the call, wondering what was so special about six-thirty. Either way, it gave him time to shower and change clothes. He took a polo shirt and blue jeans from his closet and slipped them on. The shirt fit fine, but sucking his belly in to fasten his pants made it clear his workout routine had slipped. He resolved that problem by changing into cords and accepted that his workout could wait another day.

As always, he stood by her door until his phone read six-thirty. While waiting, he examined her apartment building's overhang to understand how a noose could be stapled there without her knowledge. The ceiling was high enough so that it would have required a chair or a ladder, because climbing a rail with a fifteen-foot drop seemed unlikely. Like him, Daisy had neighbors on both sides with more around the corners. Both of their apartment complexes were sixties-vintage, had outside entries, courtyard pools, updated appliances and comfortable balconies. The only thing lacking was better security.

At precisely six-thirty, Daisy opened her door right when he pressed the bell. He extended his arms to give her a hug, but rather than fall into his arms, she spun around and locked her door.

"You ready to go?" she said.

Trying to hide his surprise over her abruptness, he smiled and took her hand. But as they descended the stairs, he feared their relationship was falling apart. They would need to have a serious talk if his gut kept giving him warnings like this.

Gingerly sliding his arm around her, he said, "I should warn you I haven't bowled in years."

She paused and made a face. "So what's that mean? Should I have them raise the bumpers?"

"No. I just wanted you to know so I didn't embarrass you."

His remark sweetened her sarcastic gaze. "Maxx, you have never embarrassed me. I love being with you, and if you'd rather do something else tonight, just say so."

"No, bowling sounds like fun. In fact, if I picture a few faces on those pins, I'll probably knock them out of the ballpark."

"I think you mean alley."

"Whatever. My point is, it's a great place to release tension."

She gave him that look again. "I hope I'm not the cause of your tension."

"Of course not," he lied. "But even with Captain Ryder's support, this case has been driving me crazy."

"What kind of support are you getting from Captain Ryder?"

"I guess I didn't tell you. He assigned us a new murder case and then retracted it."

"Really? That's awesome. When he hesitated, she added, "Isn't it?"

"Of course it is, but it also means we'll never live this down if we can't solve Jeremy's hanging."

He stopped talking, and for a brief moment considered admitting that her mood swings were driving him crazy, but her sweet face convinced him that nothing good could come from it.

Thinking about the case again, he said, "Let's not worry about it tonight. I'm sure we'll find the answers we need."

Her wrinkled forehead and delay in responding warned him she was still assessing his answer. He was amazed at how well she knew him, considering the short time they had been dating. Even worse, she knew how to read between his lines. Whether she took anything from his last comment, or he was imagining it, remained to be seen.

He unlocked Leroy's door and held it open for her. "You want to eat something on the way?"

"You know, after our big lunch I didn't think I'd be hungry, but now I'm craving greasy chicken fingers and a beer from the bowling alley snack bar. I know it's bad for me, but that's what I feel like."

Watts smiled. "Lady, it's your night. You can get whatever you want." He then closed her door and ran to climb in his seat.

He sensed things had changed the moment he started his truck. For whatever reason, their conversations had been getting shorter. If the bowling alley wasn't so close, he would have forced her to talk by singing off-key. Instead, he quietly moped as he held her hand.

The alley was busy, but there were still a few open lanes. Watts chose the one at the far end where they would have more privacy and then picked out his rental shoes. Tri-colored clown shoes weren't his preference, but he agreed to wear them so long as Daisy donned a matching pair. When he snapped a phone photo of her trying hers on, she reciprocated with a shot from hers. They repeated the process while they selected their balls. Before starting a game, Watts had her sit on the bench so they could compare phone photos. Her smile eased the knot in his stomach.

Tucking her phone away, she said, "How about that beer and chicken fingers?"

"You got it," he said, then hurried off. When he returned, he handed her a beer and kept one for himself. Recognizing her look, he said, "I figured one wouldn't kill me."

"I hope not," she said, tapping her cup to his. "Cheers."

He took a sip and wiped the foam from his lips. "Here's to whoever has the highest score."

She laughed and raised her drink again. "Why thank you, Maxx."

"We'll see about that."

He lifted his twelve pound ball, cradled it in his hands, carefully inserted his fingers, and stepped into his lane. Staring at the inlaid arrows, he glanced at the lane next to him to make sure the bowler there wasn't about to take his turn. Since no one was standing there, he glanced at the alignment arrows, took a few steps while his arm swung back, then kneeled and gently released the ball as his arm swung forward. Watching his ball roll down the center, Watts was certain he had bowled a strike. When the ball hit between the one and three pins, all ten scattered with a bang. Grinning like a fool, he casually turned around, walked back to the table, and took a sip of beer.

"I see," she said, her narrow eyes accepting the challenge. "Why do I get the feeling I've been set up?"

"No set up. Just a lucky shot. I actually expected a seven/ten split. I'm sure I'll see one before the evening is over."

Their food order was called right after he spoke, so he went to retrieve it. Still chuckling over his lucky strike, he handed her a chicken basket.

Casting a firm gaze, she accepted it and waved a fry at him. "If you know what's good for you, you'll wipe that smirk off your face."

Ignoring her, Watts took a bite of his chicken strip. "Hey, this is pretty good. I can't remember the last time I had these. I think I'll switch to Pepsi, though."

"Good idea, especially since you're the designated driver."

Sharing the laugh, they finished their food. Once they had wiped the grease off their hands, he gestured toward their lane. "We should probably throw some balls before they kick us out."

Eyeing him warily, she took her ball and approached her lane. After studying the pins, she set her ball in motion, and with a *bang*, all ten of hers flew just like his. Grinning wide, she turned around and swiped her hands together. "Take that, sucker!"

Watts laughed while high-fiving her. "For the record, I wasn't lying when I said it was a lucky shot. Call me a one-dimensional bowler, but I figure if I roll the ball down the center of a lane, it has a better chance of knocking pins down than if I try to angle it. I have no fancy moves or spins. I just release the ball and hope gravity keeps it on track."

"Noted, but excuses won't help your score."

Watts thought about that as he readied his ball. To prove his point, he decided to angle the ball this time. The result was the three pins on the far right skipped town, while the other seven stood defiantly. He spun around in surrender.

"You see? I told you it was luck."

Warily eyeing him, she said, "You'd better not be throwing the game."

"Nope. I'm doing the best I can. It's been at least two years since I've bowled."

"Yeah? Well I'll bet you a beer you get a spare."

"Make mine a Pepsi and you're on."

"I'll gladly take another beer, thanks."

Never one to back down from a challenge, Watts took his time, aimed between the one and three again and cleared the lane.

"Yeah, baby!" she said, enthusiastically wiggling her arms over her head. "That's what I'm talking about!" She quickly got up from the scoring table. "Okay, I'm buying. You still want a Pepsi?"

"Please," he said, perplexed.

One moment she was overly competitive, the next she was supportive and having fun. So, was he dating a nice girl or mean girl? Frustrated, he bent over to tighten his laces wishing he could stop himself from over-analyzing.

Since she came back smiling and handed him his soda, she seemed to be nice girl, and that helped put him at ease. Once again they toasted and sipped, exchanging awkward glances. Watts set his drink down with the intention of kissing her, but his uncertainty held him back. Instead, he smiled and caressed her face.

"Do you know how much I love being with you?" he said. "It doesn't matter what we do, so long as we're together."

She studied his eyes as her fingers traced his face. After outlining his lips, she cupped his chin in her hand. "I always enjoy being with you, Maxx." She took another sip, set it down, and calmly picked up her bowling ball, indifferent to his conversation.

Once again, Watts was dumbfounded. It was like watching a wild horse, beautiful, but impossible to tame. She had told him she loved him. She would cuddle and kiss him and say how much she enjoyed his company, but now it felt as though she had no deep feelings for him. Pondering that, he realized he fell in love too easily. After all, Daisy had never pushed him away. She just didn't want them moving too fast. And though she had never spoken of past relationships, he suspected she had been hurt, and from the way she acted, it was probably recent. But in spite of her quirks and sometimes elusive behavior, she still enchanted him. He focused on that as she readied her next ball.

Her release was the same, but this time it traveled right down the center. Eight pins flew, but when the sweep cleared, the seven and ten pins tormented her from opposite sides. Her face showed disappointment, but no anger. He clapped his hands to encourage her.

"Come on, Daisy. You can do it."

When her ball channeled back to her, she whispered something as she held it in her palms and then aimed it at the left corner. Miraculously, she nicked the outside of the seven pin and sent it sliding over to the ten pin. After wobbling for what seemed an eternity, the last pin finally dropped.

"That was amazing!" said Watts, running over to her. He picked her up and spun her around as if they were the only two there.

Hugging him back, she kissed him passionately. "You're what's amazing, Mr. Maxx." When they parted, she took a swing at his butt. "You're also up."

"You did that on purpose, didn't you? Nothing could ruin my focus more than your kiss."

Laughing, she said, "Deal with it."

"Yeah? Well, you must be worried about my winning if you're gonna sabotage me like that. Watch this."

With his mind wobbling like her last pin, he took his mark, studied the arrows, and carefully released the ball. Pins scattered with a thunderous crash, and when it was over, the same seven and ten pins stood tall.

"Bummer," she said, snickering under her breath. But then she put her hands together, clapping her encouragement. "Come on, Maxx. You can do it."

Ignoring her, he took his time lining up on the right side of the lane, positioning himself so his ball would hit the left corner. His release was smooth and all was looking good until the last second, when it fell into the gutter. Spinning around, he tossed his hands in the air with lackluster zeal.

"It okay," she said, looking at the scoreboard. "You get an A for effort."

Now that their bantering had ended, neither was concerned with their scores. They played three games in two hours and printed the results. Daisy won the first game 178 to 145, Watts took the second 165 to 163, and she won the last one 181 to 132. True to his word, Watts didn't throw a single point, and he was happy to be out-bowled.

When they left at nine o'clock, the alleys were full and people were waiting. They had barely changed out of their shoes before new bowlers were taking their place. After returning their equipment, they went to the restrooms to wash their hands and then headed outside.

Watts smiled as he climbed in the truck. After fastening his seat belt, he took her hand and held it. "Thanks for coming, Daisy. That was fun."

She reached over and gave him a smooch. "It was fun. Thanks for taking me."

They made small talk during the drive to her place, and when he got to her door, he gladly accepted another kiss. He opened his eyes half way through to see if she was looking at where the noose was hanging, but her eyes never opened. He quickly closed his and kept them shut until she pulled away.

With bedroom eyes, she rested her arms on his shoulders. "Would you like to come in?"

He didn't need to check the time. He knew it was early, but he also feared that going in could spoil the evening. All evening, her actions suggested she needed space and time, so her flirty invitation made him skeptical and nervous.

"I would love to except I really have to do my laundry."

Even though he managed to say it with a straight face, he didn't believe it himself.

"Okay," she said, unlocking her door. "Thanks again for a fun evening. Best fried chicken I've had in ages."

"Glad you enjoyed it." *I love you, Daisy.*

On the way back to his truck he kept thinking about how much easier life would be if she just said she loved him more often. Her lack of commitment made him feel like he was going through puberty all over again. Back then, all he could do was think about girls because he wasn't sure what to do with them. Now, whatever he did seemed okay, but not good enough to boost his confidence. To combat his feelings of inadequacy, he directed his thoughts to Marv Delouse, wondering what he was doing right now. Hopefully, morning would bring answers.

Thirty Three

WATTS ARRIVED AT WORK surprisingly refreshed. Last night had cleared up some things, while the bowling released some tension. Eight hours of sleep left him rested and prepared to deal with Marv.

Google Earth showed Marv's given address at 2600 West 7th Street was about equidistant to downtown or his work place, validating his bicycle commute. Spartan looked while Watts viewed the condo warehouse from the Google Earth's street level.

"He lives at Montgomery Plaza?" said Spartan.

"He does if his listed address is correct."

Spartan leaned in for a closer look. "Who wants to live in a converted Montgomery Wards store?"

"Apparently a lot of people, because their prices are as lofty as their accommodations."

"How so?"

Watts switched back to their web page and presented the images. "Let's just say they've improved the furniture section."

"Man, I'll say. That's pretty nice. Who would have thought?"

Watts tossed a hand. "Clearly, people with more vision than us. But what I don't get is, what the attraction would be for the apartments facing east or west. I mean, I could see living in an apartment near the top where you'd have views of downtown or the river, but the other directions?"

"I guess those people prefer the location and lifestyle more than a view."

"Maybe, but what's important is these apartments rent for over two grand a month, and that's probably in line with a non-married banker's salary and lifestyle. So assuming Marv lives in Montgomery Plaza, why would he have a key to the house on Prospect?"

"You mean we're going to knock on the door to find out, right?"

Watts shook his head. "First, we check out Marv's loft. Once we've confirmed he lives there, we'll go visit the Prospect house."

"Fine with me. What time you want to leave?"

Watts checked the time. "I'm assuming Marv has to be at work by nine, so we'll leave shortly after that."

"Sounds good. You know where to find me."

When the clock struck nine, Watts grabbed his partner and they were soon heading to Montgomery Plaza. Finding it was easy because the behemoth stood out like Big Ben.

Spartan stared at the building, shaking his head. "Okay, we're here. Now how do you plan to do this, since Marv isn't a person of interest?"

"Most places like this have mailboxes in the lobby. We know his address, so assuming the apartment numbers correspond with their mailboxes, all we have to do is stroll down the row and find his name. We should be able to do that without ever having to identify ourselves."

"I see," said Spartan, his face riddled with doubt. "And what if the lobby is locked?"

Watts' head cocked, then a thought came to him. Grinning, he said, "In a building like this, people are coming and going all the time, so when someone comes out, we'll waltz right in before the door closes."

"So in other words, we're going to break and enter."

"Not at all because the door will be open, and we're gonna look and depart without touching a thing. If Dad were around, he would call it no harm, no foul."

"That's great, Maxx, but Captain Ryder would call it breaking and entering because we're not guests or employees, and you don't plan on us identifying ourselves as police."

Watts paused to consider the repercussions for going through with his plan. Disappointed that his partner didn't think they could pull it off, he crossed his arms and presented a new plan.

"You have some valid points, Blaine, and since it might look strange if we both went in, I'll go in alone. No one's gonna question a man in a suit looking like he forgot something on his way to work. Wait in the car. I'll call if I need you."

Watts then climbed out and headed directly toward the lobby. Seeing that it had an electronic lock like his own apartment, he took out his card as held it like he intended to use it. As he neared the entry, he bent over to adjust his shoes until someone came out. When the door opened, he hustled inside while keeping his head down.

A jog to the left took him to the mother lode of mailboxes, which were arranged by apartment number. He went directly to Marv's, confirmed his name was still there, felt his pocket as if he had forgotten his mail key, shook his head in disgust, and then promptly headed outside. The entire operation took less than two minutes. After tucking his apartment key back in his wallet, he headed straight for the Crown Vic, grinning wide as he climbed in.

Spartan remained stoic. "Judging from your Cheshire Cat grin, I take it you got inside and Marv's name is on the mailbox."

"You guessed it. And don't worry about the security cameras. I kept my head down the whole time, not that anyone will ever review the footage."

Spartan sulked, scratching his neck. "Maybe hanging around these actresses has been good for you. Perhaps you should look into joining the community theater."

"Very funny," he said, watching Montgomery Plaza shrink in his mirror. The house on Prospect was only seventeen blocks away, so they should be there in no time.

Making no attempt to conceal their arrival, Watts parked the Crown Vic in front of the house. Once his partner had positioned himself out back, he headed to the front door like a salesman. The doorbell rang after he pressed it, and when no other sounds came from inside, he rang it again. Still, the house remained silent. Pounding on the door gained the attention of a large woman across the street. After flashing his badge, the woman ducked back in her home like a prairie dog.

Finally, he heard clumsy footsteps lumbering toward the entry, an awkward gate that he had heard before. The blinds split momentarily before shutting. After few more steps, the door opened slightly. Having already turned on his recorder, Watts smiled at the grumpy face.

"Hello Travis," he said, wedging his foot in the entry before the Vietnam vet could shut the door. "Got a moment?"

By this time, Spartan had come around front. He didn't do well at hiding his surprise.

Travis smirked when he spotted him. Looking back at Watts, he said, "I was wondering where your buddy was."

Spartan's face hardened. "Hello, Travis. We were wondering where you lived."

"And now that you know, you can leave."

Watts remained silent, wanting to see how this played out. Travis looked much worse than he did the last time they saw him. His eyes were red and swollen, his face worn and unshaven, his hair more tangled than a bird's nest, and clothes wrinkled like he had been sleeping in them. Squinting hard, Travis checked up and down the street before inviting them in with a head-tilt. He double-checked for nosey neighbors as he closed the door.

Watts looked around as he stood in the entry. The only way to make the place darker would be to paint over the windows. The musty smell went with the dated furniture and rabbit-eared analog television. The only magazine he saw sported a revolver on the cover. Sensing Travis' presence, Watts turned to meet his gaze. The big man didn't look happy.

"So whaddaya want, *detective*?"

Watts stepped back to avoid the vet's foul breath. "For starters, how about telling us about your Vietnam experience?"

He grunted and belched freely while looking like he could sleep standing up. A big yawn further tainted the air. Considering his condition, Watts was amazed he could remain vertical.

Scratching his belly, Travis finally said, "Vietnam was a lifetime ago."

"I know. My father was there in the early sixties, so I grew up listening to his stories. It was a difficult time for everyone, and whatever respect you guys got came far too late. My father was among those who died without ever receiving a thank you, but I want to say thanks for your service."

Travis nodded, unimpressed. "Did your dad kill himself?"

"In a sense, yes. Alcohol poisoning makes for a slow, ugly, agonizing death."

Travis nodded, then wandered into the kitchen. Plopping down in a chair, he gave another head-tilt for them to join him. The detectives quickly accepted his offer.

"Vietnam was like living in a New York sewer with rats shooting at you. Clever rats, too. They tunneled everywhere and laid booby traps for those who dared to find them. The VC deserves credit for creativity, though. I mean, who else knew bamboo could be such a viable weapon?"

Watts wanted to say the Japanese, but withheld his thought.

Travis rubbed the sleep from his eyes and then palmed his face. Suddenly he shook his head like an angry horse. He seemed lost, so Watts told another one of his father's war stories.

"Dad said Vietnam was the most screwed up war ever. It was like living two lives. One minute he was in his camp feeling relatively secure and the next, choppers had dropped him in some leach-infested rice patty where the enemy was shooting at him. One time after clearing the blades, his chopper took major hits and crashed a few yards from him. Parts were flying everywhere as the Huey ripped apart, and its crew never had a chance. He said the only good thing was the crash killed some Viet Cong, too."

Travis suddenly trembled like an addict going through withdrawal. Hugging his chest, he said, "We never should have gotten involved over there, and we sure as hell never should have stayed as long as we did. And now our guys are going through the same bullshit in the freakin' desert, while the assholes that sent them there eat steak and caviar and sleep in their own beds every night. It's like the old adage, the more things change, the more they stay the same. No matter who the President is, we're always getting fucked."

"That's exactly what Dad said, too." He paused, reflecting on his father. He didn't miss him, but he did respect his military service. "Travis, I know you were drafted, but you also elected to do a second tour. How many friends did you lose over there?"

Travis yawned, raising his shoulders. "You remember what I said about being drunk on sleep?"

"Yes sir, I do."

"Well, that's how it was over there except you could add pot smoking to the list. People were getting blown away every day, so after a while, you found yourself just stepping over their corpses because you had gotten so numb. That's why grunts are so fucked up, me included. There's no escaping war, detective. Closing your eyes won't hide images of flying body parts, blood-soaked clothes, and your fellow soldiers crying out to you while you aimlessly fire your weapon. So to answer your question, I have no idea how many people I saw die. All I know is it was a lot."

Spartan looked ready to speak, but chose not to. Perhaps it was because Watts had made a connection, and he didn't want to break the momentum. Watts gave his partner a quick nod of thanks and went back to the vet.

"Travis, did you ever kill anyone in close combat?"

"It wasn't the norm, but I did on occasion." He paused for a moment with his eyes closed. Soon, his eyes were open again and his lips were curling slightly. "Did you know that when you shove a knife up someone's ass there's so much pain they can't scream? It's fucking amazing. We called it the butt silencer. Of course, most

191

of the time we were shooting at foliage and tossing grenades to see if we got any return fire. If we did and it was intense, we'd call for air support, and with any luck they'd come in with five hundred pound snake-eyes. Napalm was cool to watch, but it was far less predictable than the bombs. It was always amazing how quickly the firing stopped when the planes approached. I'm sure the bastards saw them coming and hid underground, so our attempts at frying them was as effective as pouring lighter fluid on an ant hill and torching it. You may get some of 'em, but you sure as hell can't kill 'em all."

He paused again, stretched, and then rested his elbows on the table to prop his face up. "What about you, detective? Have you ever killed anyone?"

"Only once, and I'm not proud of it. I returned fire after I was hit in the shoulder. The lady with the gun wasn't as lucky."

Travis smiled wryly. "We had the same ROE," he said, his voice raspier now.

"ROE?"

"Rules of Engagement," he barked back. "Too often you had to wait until the shit hit the fan before you could counter. I guess that's the risk of being a peacemaker, right?"

"I suppose."

Feeling as though he had exhausted their Vietnam connection, Watts decided to introduce some more pertinent issues.

"Travis, would you tell us about your marriage to Betty Cerin?"

Suddenly alert, he quickly said, "It didn't work out."

"I suspected that was the case since it was annulled, but I'd like a few more details than that."

"Okay, how about this? I really loved her, but sometimes love isn't enough."

Watts nodded and leaned back in his seat, remembering that line from a song. He recalled how Betty had scurried away from the framed newspaper story in the theater's lobby, and wondered where Travis fit in this puzzle.

"Travis, are you saying you loved her, but she didn't love you back?"

"I suppose you could say that."

Watts nodded again, feeling more empathy for the vet than expected. "Was that a result of your wife having to cope with your existence in Vietnam? Did she send you a Dear John letter saying she wanted an annulment? If so, how did you react?"

"I never got a letter, detective. Only the boot. As for Vietnam, we didn't break up until I was home on leave, and in all honesty, the collapse was mostly my fault because I treated her like shit while I was in the hospital. We were practically strangers by the time we saw each other again. I started yelling, she kicked me out, and I left to stay with my folks. After signing the annulment, I volunteered for a second tour just to stay away. I started taking on the most dangerous assignments because I wanted to die a hero. Of course, the Devil keeps fools like me alive so we can live our Hell on Earth. Considering all that's happened over the years, Hell must be pretty damned crowded."

After saying that, Travis rested his head in his hands and closed his eyes again.

"Hell on Earth," said Watts, nodding. "I suspect we've all been there at one time or another. The key is to get out, and we'd like to help you with that."

"Don't worry about it, man. I'm old and I've gotten used to it."

Watts wasn't sure what to say next. He wished he could tell him that Betty said she loved him too, but that would be like salting a wound. He found it interesting that neither Travis nor Betty wanted to confront the issues behind their separation. Then again, he would probably be equally reluctant to reveal his personal life to a detective.

"Do you recall the particulars of your annulment?"

Travis marginally opened his eyes. "It says the same thing I told you – that we barely knew each other and we were incompatible. We were two kids who got married before we should have, and almost immediately after we wedded, I was sent overseas. After Betty told the judge how abusive I was, he signed the document with no objections."

"It's noble of you to accept the blame."

Travis grinned for the first time. "What the hell. Someone had to."

Watts acknowledged him and cleared his throat, signaling he was giving up the lead.

"Travis," said Spartan, "what is your relationship to Marv Delouse?"

The vet smiled, tilted his head back, and stretched his arms while yawning. His body reeked so badly that both detectives slid their chairs back at the same time. Ignoring them, he said, "My relationship to Marv?"

"Yes. To Marv."

"Well, whatever it is, I'm sure it's not what you think. You see, one day I was sitting on a bench overlooking the river, and this guy in a suit plops down next to me. Although I'd never met him before, there was something in his eyes that looked familiar. Rather than scare him away by staring at him, I struck up a conversation, and somewhere along the line, the Scott Theater came up. I nearly died when I learned Betty Cerin was his aunt. Can you believe it? My ex is his aunt? Anyway, after I told him about me and Betty, we were like best buds. Ten plus years later and nothing's changed. We argue a lot, but I'm not sure what I'd do without him."

"Very cool," said Spartan, nodding. "So, is Marv paying the rent on this house?"

After a slight hesitation, the vet's head slowly nodded.

"Okay, so you two became best buds," said Watts, cutting in. "What's your connection with Jeremy Delouse, the guy you claim was murdered?"

"Oh, *now* I get it," said Travis, his eyes wide open. "All this time I've been trying to remember where I've seen you before, and now I remember you're the bastards that eavesdropped on us at the fucking diner. God, I'm losing my mind! Fuck you both!"

"Easy," said Spartan. "We're homicide detectives, Travis. When someone mentions murder, we listen."

"Yeah, well it's all bullshit. I'm a drunk-on-sleep vet that desperately needs a nap. You'll do well to forget about it."

Watts watched Travis roll his hands over his head and then bury his face as though he wished this was all a dream. Right now he was probably wondering how they located him. That would be Watts' first thought, given the same circumstances. Then again, since he didn't share Travis' demons, he had no idea of knowing what the Purple Heart vet was thinking.

Watts and Spartan exchanged awkward glances while Travis held his silence. It wasn't until they heard snoring that they realized he was asleep. Watts whispered he would be right back and slipped out the door to retrieve something from the car. While there, he flipped the tape in his Sony to make sure he had a full side left. Travis was still snoring when he returned.

Setting his hand on the big man's shoulder, Watts shook it hard. "Travis, wake up. Travis!"

After several shakes, the vet's eyes opened looking puffier than before. He snorted, wiped his mouth, and squinted as though he had no idea who Watts was.

"Travis, we were discussing your buddy Marv Delouse when you dozed off. You were saying there was something familiar in his eyes so you decided to sit on the bench and strike up a conversation. Are you with me?"

He nodded, now staring at the empty table.

"How about I buy you a coffee?" said Watts. "Maybe take you to breakfast?"

The vet gently shook his head. "No, man, just tell me what you want and leave me alone." A wide yawn preceded him closing his eyes again.

Travis' random movements made him look like a disabled marionette. Even more surprising was how he could prop himself on his elbows and fall asleep without smashing his chin on the table.

Watts sighed and spread some photos on the table. "Okay, Travis," he said, "Here are some photos that might pique your interest." He didn't identify any of them, but the photos of Betty, Jeremy, Warren, Grace, and Marv were all taken at different stages of their lives. Those of Marv's adoptive parents were taken while they were in their mid to late forties. Betty's and Marv's were less than ten years old. Jeremy's headshot was from 1969. "Please look them over and tell us what you see."

Travis vigorously rubbed his face, opened his eyes, and then hunched over the photos. Within seconds he looked up and said, "I see five people, one of who's dead. Anything else?"

"Actually, three are dead," said Spartan.

"No kidding. I recognize Jeremy, but who else died?"

Spartan pointed to Grace and Warren and identified who they were.

"So those are Marv's parents, eh? How about that? He's mentioned their names a few times, but I've never seen their photos. Funny how you think you know someone and this happens."

Cueing off his partner, Watts tapped on Betty's photo. Once he was sure Travis was looking, he fingered Jeremy's and Marv's pictures. "So, what do you think, Travis? Notice any family resemblance between these three?"

Suddenly awake, Travis' face hardened. "Get out now and don't come back!"

Watts dithered, but then slowly gathered his photos. Before

leaving, he nodded politely to the angry man whose bunched fists looked ready to pound the table.

"Travis, I hate to say it, but Marv is Betty Cerin and Jeremy Delouse's child." After letting that sink in, he added, "Get some sleep, Travis. My card's on the table if you want to talk."

Thirty Four

As THEY LEFT, TRAVIS never raised his head, and Watts didn't care. It had been a good morning because they now knew where Marv and Travis lived, and Watts had planted a seed in Travis's shattered brain. At some point, he expected he would hear from him.

Spartan glanced his way as he climbed in the Crown Vic. "You think there's anything worthwhile on your Sony?"

"I doubt it, but I'll have it transcribed anyway. I should put in an expense report for all my tapes and batteries."

"Why not? In fact, I'm sure Captain Ryder would personally get you your money."

Watts grinned, knowing that would never happen. "By the way, I'm sorry if I dominated the interview, Blaine. I hope I didn't I cut you out."

"You didn't, but it usually works out for the best if you do the talking and I do the thinking, and right now I think we should find out who owns this house."

"Why is that?"

Spartan arrogantly rolled his head toward him. "Maxx, you have your gut feelings and I have mine. Right now my gut's telling me the title for this home isn't in either Travis McLean's or Marv Delouse's name."

"Okay, so what's the revelation? Marv and Travis know each other, and plenty of people rent homes in this neighborhood."

"That's true, but that's not where I was going."

Watts considered this as he twisted the ignition key. Glancing at the house, no blinds were split, no windows were open, but that didn't mean Travis wasn't spying on them. More likely, the vet was still at the kitchen table where they left him, staring at where the photos had been. Once the engine was started, he glanced over at Spartan.

"Blaine, you're damned good at running down leads, so I'll ignore your remark about how you do all the thinking. Feel free to check out the Prospect house title when we get back, and I'll work on getting this tape transcribed. Travis said he talks to spirits when he's exhausted, so considering his present physical state, I wouldn't rule out recording another EVP."

"Do you really think spirits follow Travis?"

Watts gave an annoyed look. "I don't know what to believe anymore, but I won't rule it out. Anyway, I'll worry about EVPs, you concern yourself with that Prospect house title. We'll compare notes later."

"Will do."

On the drive back, Watts was grateful they had aired their differences, but Spartan's comment about how he did the thinking still irked him. Whether he intended it as a joke or not remained to be seen. Still, his partner's instincts were usually good, so he was always open to suggestions.

"It's nice that all the places involved in this case are so close," said Watts, navigating the streets. "Sure beats the Coulter case where we were driving all over Dallas and Waco."

"You got that right. I'm guessing that Travis' house, Marv's condo, and the Scott Theater are all within a five mile radius of headquarters. And since Whataburger is in that grid, you want to stop there on the way?"

Watts smiled as he checked the time. Spartan was like Rolly in *101 Dalmatians* – always hungry. "Eleven o'clock seems early for lunch. Will you be okay for the rest of the day if we eat this early?"

Rolling his eyes, Spartan said, "Yes, Mom, and I promise to eat everything on my plate."

Watts made the short detour to the burger joint where smoke billowed from its orange and white striped roof. With the parking lot half full, he backed the Crown Vic into a spot where he could keep an eye on it and make a quick exit. He had been a detective for five years but still couldn't break this patrol day's habit.

"All right, partner, time to chow down."

Spartan flew out of the car, drawn to the scent like a seagull to scraps. The entrance door had shut behind him before Watts ever got to it. Moseying up to Spartan in the ordering line, he said, "I hope you hold the door open for your wife."

"Of course I do, but you're not my wife or my mother, so stop acting like a woman – you're driving me nuts."

The way he said it turned Watts' grin into laughter. "My goodness," he said, mocking his partner. "I had no idea you were so sensitive. I hope a thousand calorie lunch can turn that frown upside down." If he thought he could get away with it, he would have pinched his cheek, too, but Spartan started growling like a deranged mutt.

After placing their orders, they filled their drinks and found a corner table where they could see their car. Watts took a sip and then playfully smacked his partner's shoulder. "I'm sorry, Blaine, but you gotta admit you set yourself up."

Finally, a smile found Spartan's face. "You do realize that one of these days I'm gonna slam you and you won't have a comeback."

"One can only hope," he said, watching a server bring their meals. After thanking him, he added, "They're pretty fast here, aren't they?"

Spartan nodded while biting into his burger.

It only took them twenty minutes to consume their meals and belch their way back to the car. As Watts leaned forward to key the ignition, his belt dug into his stomach. He backed off to give his partner a serious look.

"If we don't stop eating like this, we're gonna end up like Porgy Mulberry."

Spartan laughed. "How ironic would it be if Porgy came back to work fifty pounds lighter and we've gained ten?"

"I'd shoot myself if that happened," he said, feeling his belly. "Next time I'm getting a salad."

"Sure, Maxx. Whatever you say."

Watts was eager to get back to the office so he could drop off his audiotape and check his messages. On his desk was a sealed envelope from Daisy. Tearing it open, he found a note saying she had re-checked the data on the nylon noose, and it lost its residual electrical charge within three hours of the lab taking custody. Her accompanying report supported the physicist's theory that an external force had removed it from Leroy's cab and then replaced it inside the locked truck. To Watts, the only rational explanation was that Jeremy was trying to make a point about his hanging, but after thinking about it, he wasn't sure how believable that was. Even if it were true, it failed to answer the question of who stapled the noose to Daisy's overhang. Watts drew the line at believing poltergeists could tie knots and squeeze staple guns. Everyone seemed to agree only a human could create and hang a nylon noose. If only he knew who was responsible.

He called Daisy and said, "I got your message – free of charge."

She wasn't laughing at his pun so he added, "Come on, Daisy. That was funny. Where's your sense of humor?"

"It vanished into another realm."

"There, you see? You just countered with a joke. But going back to the noose, I can't understand who or why someone would attach it to your overhang. I know we've been over this, but have you had any altercations with anyone who might want to mess with your mind?"

"As I've said numerous times, the answer is no. And as I've also said, Halloween decorations, nooses in particular, are not a tradition here."

He wished he could go downstairs and sit with her, maybe hold her hand to assure her all was well, but that wasn't going to happen, nor would she want it. Feeling he had to say something, he remarked, "Sooner or later this will all make sense." He quickly followed with, "On a different note, we made an interesting discovery this morning. You want to hear it?"

"Sure, fill me in."

"Oh, can you hang on a second? Blaine's trying to get my attention."

Following a brief pause, she gave a less enthusiastic, "Sure."

After reading the document Spartan passed to him, Watts nodded to his partner and said, "Get this, Daisy. The name on the title to Travis McLean's house is Arvid McAlister."

"Is that supposed to mean something to me?"

"Sorry." Watts took a few moments to bring her up to speed on the Prospect house situation and then said, "So Blaine's news means we have another name to run down. Frankly, I was hoping Marv's name was on the title." He felt a burp coming and quickly covered the phone. Unfortunately, he didn't cover it well enough.

"Did you just belch?"

"Guilty. Sorry."

"So I take it you already had lunch."

"Unfortunately," he said, rubbing his bloated belly. "Blaine held me at gunpoint and made me drive him to Whataburger. I didn't want to go, honest."

"Yeah? Well, if you don't stop eating there, you'll turn into a Whataburger, and then you won't be so pretty."

"That's what I was telling him, only I didn't say anything about being pretty. Anyway, I need to get back to work. Can I call you later?"

"I'd rather you call me Daisy."

Laughing, he said, "Oh, you are on today, lady. Talk to you later."

He hung up and went into his Spartan's cubicle, hoping to learn more about Arvid McAlister.

Spartan looked over his shoulder, shaking his head. "I hate being the bearer of bad news, but there's no one by that name with Texas DMV or in the national database."

Watts nodded, staring at the computer screen. After all that had happened in the last few days, the news didn't come as a surprise. "I suppose that means Arvid McAlister is an alias. Either that, or someone living outside the country owns the house."

Spartan didn't look convinced. "Not that foreign ownership isn't a possibility, but the Prospect house isn't exactly beach property. I doubt it's worth fifty grand."

"I know nothing about the home's real estate value, but I do believe the name is an alias."

"I know that look, Maxx. You're thinking that since Marv and Travis both have keys to the Prospect house, you believe one of them is using the alias. So, which one is it, and how are you going to get either one to admit it?"

"I'm not sure, but if one of them calls me, I'll ask him point-blank."

Spartan cast a suspicious gaze. "Do you really think that someone who just kicked us out of his house is going to admit to having an alias?"

Watts ignored the comment, so Spartan turned his back on him. After taking a few deep breaths, Spartan spun his chair around to face him.

"Okay, Maxx, let's say Arvid McAlister is Travis' alias and he's using it to find work. Have you noticed that whenever we see Travis, he smells like cleaning fluid? He also admits to keeping an eye on Betty, so what if Travis is secretly working as a janitor at the Scott Theater?"

Watts nodded enthusiastically. "I think you're onto something, because ever since we saw him this morning, I've been racking my brain trying to identify that smell – and once you said that, I remembered that smell from the janitor's closet in the Scott Theater's dungeon."

"Yeah, and the janitor who left the ladder walked like someone with a leg injury."

"Which, looking back, is how Travis walked when he answered the door."

"That would also explain why he stayed in the shadows so he couldn't be identified."

Watts' eyes widened. Things were finally making sense. "This is great, Blaine! Put yourself in for a pay raise."

"If only it were that simple. Besides, this is all theory. How can we prove it?"

"For starters, since no one seems to have any current photos of Travis, we'll both meet separately with a sketch artist and then compare the work. Between the two of us, we should be able to come up with a pretty good likeness of him. What do you say?"

"I'm game, but what do you intend to do with the sketch?"

"Circulate it among Scott Theater's employees, and if anyone identifies him as Arvid or Travis, we'll know he's been hanging around – no pun intended."

Spartan nodded, rubbing his chin. "That actually sounds like a good plan. Are you gonna tell Captain Ryder, or keep him in the dark?"

Watts patted his partner's shoulder with one eyebrow raised. "After all this time together, haven't you learned it's better to beg forgiveness than volunteer information?"

Spartan nodded slowly. "So, who goes first? Me or you?"

"Are you working on anything pressing right now?"

"Nope."

"Then you go. I need to talk to Daisy."

"Oh, I see. Well, tell her I said hi."

Watts feigned a smile as he slipped on his coat, but he wasn't sure Daisy was ready to hear what he had to say. Plagued by thoughts of the netherworld, he headed downstairs, his logical mind wrestling with his gut. As he entered the lab, he could taste bile in the back of his throat.

Daisy greeted him with less enthusiasm than he had hoped. Without wasting time on pleasantries, he again brought her up to speed, followed by his concerns about this case.

"So let's forget about ghosts and concentrate on Travis for a moment," he said, downplaying the dungeon's spectral phenomena. "If he's been working there as a janitor, he would know the place inside and out. Maybe there's an open-ended pipe running through the wall where he could have said *murder* to spook us. What if he somehow created those EVP's to distract us from the fact that he killed his wife's lover in 1970?"

"And I suppose Travis also figured out a way to suddenly drop the temperature and touch my thigh without being in the hall," she said, cutting him off. "Perhaps you're forgetting that you're the one who convinced Blaine and me this haunting is for real, and between the three of us, I'm the most analytical thinker. And never mind the evidence that supports our paranormal activity, or that if someone whispered *murder* through a pipe, we would have heard it while we were there and not just on the audiotape. Finally, you're forgetting that we searched and never found an open-ended pipe, hole, vent, or anything else where words could be funneled in. There's no way those EVPs were faked."

She paused to close her eyes and catch her breath. Several seconds passed before she blinked and opened them again. Leaning over the counter, she said, "Maxx, I don't have an explanation for what touched my thigh, but I can say that it was very cold. We all saw the orb come at us and heard the EVPs, so I'm not willing to write off Jeremy's ghost. That being said, it's certainly possible that Travis has been working there as a janitor using an alias."

Watts slowly bowed his head. "Those are all good points," he said, slipping off his coat, "but I really came down to have you examine this coat for hairs belonging to Travis McLean. His house was a mess, so I probably picked up some when I sat in his chair. If we can find Arvid and somehow get a hair sample, DNA should confirm whether Travis and Arvid are the same person."

"Maybe," she said, lifting his coat by the collar and holding it at arm's length. "But just so you know, I'm burning this if it has bed bugs."

Watts grinned. "No problem. Goodwill has plenty of them."

"Oh, aren't you a barrel of laughs today? I'll call you if I find anything."

Watts watched her walk away, still unsure where he stood with her these days. But what mattered now was that she was one of the finest forensics technicians on the staff, and if there was anything worthwhile on his coat, she would find it.

Thirty Five

SPARTAN WAS GRINNING WHEN he returned from the sketch artist. Watts didn't see how he could have created an accurate portrait in such a short amount of time. Then again, Travis' Army photo would have given him a sense of his strong jaw, deep set eyes and high cheek bones.

"Your turn, Maxx."

Watts nodded, slid his chair back, and went to meet the artist. Her office was no bigger than an interrogation room, bare except for a table with a computer, two chairs, a photo of the Tarrant County Courthouse, and the sketch artist herself. Watts found her courthouse photo an interesting choice, since it was within a stone's throw of 350. Maybe she found its architecture fascinating.

She was showing too much cleavage to put him at ease. If she were there to interrogate him, he would break within minutes. And while her long pants covered her shapely legs, when she crossed them and dangled her foot, Watts' eyes found them like a bass would a fly. Spartan returned so quickly, Watts wondered if this was the same sketch artist.

Her hand shake did nothing put him at ease. "Relax," she said, her strong voice erasing any illusions of a seduction. "I'm Julie, and if your description is anything like your partner's, this shouldn't take long."

Watts felt ashamed for acting like an infatuated schoolboy. What would Daisy think if Julie were to tell her about his behavior? To clear his thoughts, he looked around the room, envisioning the crime victims who had given descriptions. He couldn't imagine how difficult it would be watching their attackers come to life. Julie made a noise and he looked up.

Smiling, he clasped his hands together. "So, where do we begin?"

"I'm going to make this easy," she said, spreading three faceless heads in front of him. "One of these shapes matches your partner's description, and I won't tell you which one. Carefully examine all three and tell me which one looks like your man."

Watts immediately picked the one on the far right. "That's him."

"Okay," she said, making no mention of whether he had chosen the same outline as his partner. "Now let's move to the computer."

Watts should have known she wouldn't actually be sketching anything. He felt cheated until she punched some keys and several eye shapes came up below the faceless head. *That's how Spartan finished so quickly.*

"Okay, detective, now study these eyes and tell me which ones you saw on his face. Take your time. We can try as many as you'd like."

"Okay. Let's compare numbers four and five."

She nodded, split the screen, placed eyes on each of the heads, and looked at him.

"Great. Now leave the head on the left as is, but put set three on the right." After she did it, he stared hard at both of them. "All right. Keep the left, delete the right."

"Very well," she said, hitting a key. Now down to one image, she studied Watts' eyes. "Let's move on to the nose."

The same process was used for the nose, ears, mouth, hair and chin. Once these features were established, she added a beard. In less than twenty minutes, Watts felt like he was staring at an actual photo of Travis McLean, and that impressed him.

"Now let's compare yours with your partner's," she said, printing the image they just created. She placed Watts' copy on the table and slid Spartan's next to it.

His jaw immediately dropped. "They're virtually identical," he said, comparing them again. "Are you sure you didn't have pre-conceived notions as we went through this?"

Her face showed disappointment. "If I'm not mistaken, you were the one guiding me through the process and making the decisions. Not once did I make a recommendation. I could go on, but you already know the truth."

"You're right, and I apologize. I just find it remarkable that two people working individually could come up with such similar images."

Tapping a pencil to her lips, she gently shook her head. "First of all, being a detective means you have demonstrated certain identification capabilities. Secondly, some of the most notorious criminals were identified from police sketches because the witnesses had their images burned into their brains. The principles we used were the same as what sketch artists used sixty years ago, but the computer program makes it faster. Given the right tools and guidance, any sketch artist can assist a witness in recreating a criminal's face. Is there anything else I can do for you?"

Watts promptly shook his head. "I assume I can take these?"

"That's why I printed them out. I'll also e-mail them to you and your partner so they're on your computers."

"This is great," he said, getting up from his seat. "Thank you, Julie."

"Happy to help, detective. Good luck, and Happy Halloween."

Watts nodded as he ducked out of the room and hurried back to Spartan's cubicle. He did his best to mimic his partner's smug expression as he held up both images.

"Okay, Blaine, which one's yours? I'll buy you a cup of coffee if you get it right."

Spartan gave it a quick glance and trivially waved his hand. "Don't need the coffee, and mine's on the left."

Watts' eyes widened. "Is that your final answer?"

"Yes, that's my final answer. Did I win a million dollars?"

"No, because the one on the left is *mine*. But that should also make you feel good, because it shows we can show this image of Travis with confidence. Pretty cool, eh?"

"Yeah, cool. So, when do you want to head back to the theater?"

Watts checked the time. "After our last meeting, Betty might be upset with me, and I'm not ready to show her the image. Why don't you go in first and have her show you around the grounds? Once you're gone, I'll go in and see if anyone recognizes the man in the sketch."

"What are you gonna do while I'm inside? Hide behind a column?"

"That's exactly what I'm gonna do. Keep her outside for fifteen minutes, and I'll meet you at the car."

"Okay," he said. "If that's how you want to play it, I'm ready whenever you are."

"All right, then let's get out of here before Ryder shows up."

* * * * *

When they reached the Scott Theater, Watts parked between two pickups to avoid detection. He hoped fifteen minutes would be enough time to identify Travis as Arvid. His plan would fail if Betty came back too soon.

A pillar near the theater's entrance made a perfect leaning post for Watts to check his e-mail. He waited longer than expected, but eventually he heard Betty's and Spartan's voices. He made his break for the door as soon as they faded.

Once inside, he asked everyone he saw if they recognized the man in the image. Most glanced and shook their heads, but three people confirmed it was Arvid, although none had seen him today.

Seeing things fall into place made Watts happy. Travis/Arvid was clearly working at the theater, and the Prospect house was titled under his alias. But if Travis was a wage-earner, why didn't he have a Social Security number? That question became easier to explain when he learned the theater's manager just left with Detective Spartan. The revelation hit him like a cold splash of water. Until now, he had no idea Betty Cerin was the manager, and since she was the only one who could answer questions on employee pay, Watts called his partner asking that he bring her inside. When Watts spotted them coming his way, he hit the record button on his Sony and led them away from the entrance.

If Betty were surprised to see him, she didn't show it. She cordially shook Watts' hand and willingly walked with him. "I figured you must have been near when I saw Detective Spartan," she said. "What are you up to this time, detective?"

"Betty, we're still peeling layers, but we're nearing the center." For a brief moment after he held up the image of Travis, her face showed alarm.

Quickly recovering, she said, "Why are you holding a picture of Arvid? Has he done something wrong?"

"You're sure that's his name?"

"Of course I'm sure. Arvid McAlister has been with us for about ten years. He came here as a Vietnam vet looking for work. We had some odd jobs which needed to be done, so we gave him a shot. He did such a great job that we kept giving him part-time work. Why do you ask? Is he in some kind of trouble?"

Watts stared at her, amazed by her facade. Surely she could tell he didn't believe her. "Please look again, Betty. Notice his eyes and cheek bones, and picture your ex-husband. Are you certain this isn't Travis McLean?"

She studied it for several seconds, even slipped on her reading glasses, but then she let her glasses dangle from their cord and shook her head. "I do see some similarities, but this is definitely Arvid McAlister." She paused and tilted her head slightly while her hands found her hips. "Now please answer my question about why you're interested in him. What's he done? I need to know if it's safe to keep him around."

Watts bit his tongue to keep from smiling, thinking how wonderful she must have been on stage. "He's not in trouble," he finally said. "We just want to ask him a few questions. What kind of jobs does he do around here?"

Crossing her arms, she briefly looked away. "It's mostly clean-up duty, but not on a regular basis. Sometimes he'll pitch in with building production sets, too. It really depends on our needs and how he's feeling."

"How he's feeling? You mean he just sort of drops by when he feels like working?"

"In a sense, yes. Many Vietnam vets didn't have a choice in going to war, and when they returned, they were hated by their peers and ignored by their government. Our country hadn't been that divided since the Civil War. To make things worse, a lot of employers feared hiring vets, because so many were protesting the war. And since the government was discharging returning vets who didn't want a second tour of duty, the job competition was fierce. When Arvid came around looking for work, we were determined to provide for him, even though our budget is always tight."

Spartan glanced at the computer image and then back at Betty. "That's very noble of you. Would you mind showing us Arvid's closet or whatever he uses for a workshop?"

Giving them a strange look, she said, "After all your visits, I'd think you could show me the way. Anyway, it's near the stairs. You've walked past it at least two times."

The twitch in her eye caught his attention. She must have realized they were onto something and was struggling to downplay it. Rubbing only made it worse.

"You're right," said Spartan. "We could probably find it on our own, but would you please show us?"

Silent for a moment, staring at nothing in particular, she shrugged and headed toward the stairs. "I really don't have time for this, but let's go."

She led them down the familiar stairway to a dungeon room filled with cleaning supplies, mops, tools and the step ladder Daisy used to inspect the pipe. The single light bulb made it difficult to identify everything inside, but for a storage room, dim lighting was not unusual.

Watts slipped on some Latex gloves and went inside for a look. Glancing over his shoulder at Betty, he said, "Do you know if there's a flashlight in here?"

"I have no idea, but I'll find you one."

"Thanks, Betty." Watts waited until she climbed the stairs before speaking again. "I'm looking for anything that will confirm Travis and Arvid are the same person. Let me know when you see her coming."

"Will do." Leaning against the door frame, Spartan watched the hall. A few seconds later, he added, "You gotta admit she's a fine actress."

"Maybe, but we're here to gather evidence, not watch her perform."

"Noted. So what's next? Ask her how Arvid gets paid?"

Watts stopped what he was doing to think about that. "Good idea," he said handing Spartan his recorder. "Slip this in your coat pocket and turn it on before she gets here. Talk to her about his pay and whatever else comes to mind to keep her out of my way. I need more time to poke around in here, and I don't want her asking what I'm doing."

"Got it. By the way, she's coming down the stairs."

Watts casually stepped out of the room and waited for her.

"Here's your flashlight, detective. Anything else?"

"Thanks," said Watts, taking the light. "Detective Spartan has a few questions for you. If you'll excuse me, I still have some things I want to check out." He quickly ducked inside.

Staying close to the door so his partner could hear, Spartan said, "Betty, how does Arvid get paid for his work, and how much does he earn?"

"He gets paid in cash, and it works out to about ten dollars per hour, but you won't find any record of it because Arvid doesn't trust the government. He gets paid from our slush fund, and doesn't earn more than a few thousand dollars per year. The arrangement works well for everyone, because he doesn't receive any benefits."

Spartan nodded, jotting notes. "What happens if he gets hurt on the job?"

"Then he'd be treated like a visitor and would be taken care of. He's very careful, though. It's never been a problem."

Spartan nodded again. "So you'd deny he's an employee if he were injured."

She scowled. "As I said, the issue has never come up, and I'm asking that you not interfere in what has been a perfect arrangement for everyone. Necessary maintenance gets done, and Arvid works when he wants to. In the end, everyone comes out ahead. He won't take charity, detective, but he's always willing to work."

Spartan folded his notepad and smiled. "It's great you provide him with work, and we certainly have no interest in interfering. Has the Scott Theater ever assisted any other Vietnam veterans?"

"Not that I'm aware of, but then I'm not sure anyone else has come here looking for work." She paused to glance in the storage room before returning her focus to Spartan. "Don't misunderstand me, detective. The Scott Theater is not a charity organization, and as anyone will tell you, Arvid's situation is unique. Of course, whenever he decides to move on, we will probably look for someone who will keep a more regular schedule."

"I take it he's not very predictable."

She grinned. "Arvid is predictably unpredictable, but there's always work for him when he shows up."

Watts had been listening intently while he searched the room. Having found what he was looking for, he joined them and returned the flashlight to Betty.

"Forgive me for butting in," he said, "but I don't understand how your theater can work around Arvid's schedule like that. I mean, he seems more alley cat than employee."

Her face hardened, as it frequently did whenever Watts spoke. "As I told Detective Spartan, Arvid McAlister is not an official employee. He's merely a handyman who occasionally renders services. That's no different than any other contractor we'd hire."

"I suppose that makes sense." He took a moment to check the hall, wondering if Jeremy had been listening. Eager to hear the audiotape, Watts extended his hand to end their conversation. "Betty, we need to get going. Thanks again for showing us around. We sincerely appreciate your time."

"It's never a problem, detective. When should I expect you again?"

"Investigations are always open-ended," he said, herding Betty toward the stairs. Once they reached the lobby, the detectives bid their farewell.

Once in the parking lot, Spartan said, "What did you find?"

"Hair."

Spartan nodded. "Good thing Travis is messy."

"Messy doesn't come close to describing him. The guy sheds like a dog, and the flashlight made it easy to collect samples. The lab will need to confirm the results, but between the witnesses and these hair samples, as far as I'm concerned, Travis McLean is Arvid McAlister."

"I concur, but if he's only making a few grand a year, how can he afford to pay a home mortgage?"

Watts smiled at his partner. "Let's ask Marv about that."

"Okay. So, are we going to his bank or the station?"

"We're still lining up ducks, so for now, it's back to the lab. By the way, keep the Sony in your pocket until we get in the car. I have a feeling we're being watched."

Thirty Six

WHEN THEY ENTERED THE lab, Watts was grateful to have Spartan at his side, because it would keep him from kissing Daisy. Having listened to the tape before leaving the Scott Theater's parking lot, he was elated over finding another EVP.

Daisy smiled as she approached the counter. "My, my. You're certainly bubbly. What's going on?"

"For starters, I collected some hair samples from the dungeon."

She glanced at them quizically. "Okay. And?"

"Witnesses confirmed that the man in our police sketch goes by Arvid McAlister, and Betty confirmed Arvid works part time as a janitor at the Scott Theater. Of course, Blaine and I both know him to be Travis McLean – but neither Travis nor Arvid exist in the Federal system. However, the home on Prospect is in Arvid McAlister's name, and we're still trying to figure that one out. Anyway, I need you to match these hair samples to whatever you pulled off my coat so we can confirm that Arvid and Travis are the same person."

She looked at Spartan for an answer.

"We're still trying figure out if he's using a bogus Social Security number," he said, "But if he's not filing a tax return, it wouldn't matter, because he wouldn't be deducting the interest."

"And since he doesn't earn any reportable income, it's a moot point," said Watts.

"I think we're getting a little side-tracked," she said. "Travis must have had a Social Security number to be drafted into the Army. Can't you trace him that way?"

Spartan nodded. "We're still working on that."

She nodded and looked back at Watts. "What else do you have to tell me?"

"Jeremy says hi. We recorded him again, and he's still saying *murder* and *noose*."

Her lips pursed. "At least he's consistent. And I suppose you want me to verify your latest EVP while I'm comparing the hair DNA."

Watts smiled, leaning on the counter. "It's only because you're the best."

"Save it," she said, scooping up the items. "I'll call you when I know something."

Sounds good." Leaving the lab, Watts looked at his partner. "Somehow I thought she'd be happier."

Spartan placed his arm on Watt's shoulder as they headed upstairs. "Women are complicated, Maxx. Get used to it."

* * * * *

While Spartan was busy tracking down the Prospect house title, Watts reviewed Travis' military record for the fourth time. In 1969, a person's Social Security number was also their military ID, but identity theft issues eliminated that practice. In their attempt to correct that problem, the Army removed all Social Security numbers from their service records, thus further erasing Travis McLean from the government's reporting system. But the question remained why Marv would know his friend as Travis, if Travis was using the name Arvid McAlister at the theater. Did Marv know that Travis was married to Betty Cerin? Was he aware that Betty was his mother and that she and Travis had been married? It seemed far-fetched, but he couldn't rule it out. He rose from his chair and went into his partner's cubicle.

"Blaine, did you have any luck finding a Social on Arvid McAlister?"

"No, because the Social Security number on Arvid's title belongs to Warren Delouse."

A bird could have flown into Watts' mouth right then. "You're saying Warren, as in Marv's deceased adoptive parent, is on the title?"

"No, I'm saying Warren's Social is on the title next to Arvid's name."

Without thinking, Watts leaned on the flimsy cubicle divider and nearly knocked it over. After steadying it, he glared at his partner. "When did you know this?"

"Maybe a minute before you came in here. I was just about to tell you."

"Okay, so how does a man using an alias assume a dead man's identity?"

Spartan shook his head. "Travis never assumed Warren's identity, and for all we know, Warren may have lived in that house. Travis also never used Warren's Social to collect any benefits, and since he doesn't earn any recorded money, there is nothing to pique the IRS's interest. If Warren owned it and Marv put Travis in there, it may not even qualify as fraud."

Frowning, Watts stomped on a dust bunny, but rather than give up, the flattened dust ball hid under Spartan's desk. Smiling at that, he said, "If Marv inherited the property, why wouldn't he title it in his name so he could write it off?"

"I have no idea, Maxx, and I doubt Marv will volunteer an answer."

Watts shook his head again. "You know, when we first got involved in this thing, I figured we'd see some oddities, but I never expected this. Any ideas on what to do next?"

Before Spartan could answer, Watts' phone rang. Since it was Daisy, he raised his index finger to pause their conversation. "What have you got?"

"For starters, the EVP is legit and was recorded while Blaine was talking to Betty. Its wave pattern is identical to the previous EVPs, but there's no way to know if it was Jeremy."

"That's great. What about the DNA?"

"Still working on it."

"Okay. Thanks much."

After ending the call, Watts relayed Daisy's report and said, "Blaine, if this is really Jeremy talking, he seems very determined for us solve to his murder."

Spartan heaved a skeptical shrug. "I thought ghosts dangled chains and spooked people."

"Who knows? Maybe they do that, too, but what's important is *something* keeps repeating the same murder message, and considering Travis' physical condition when we left him, we may as well believe it's Jeremy who's talking."

Spartan responded by scratching his head and then smoothing it with his palm. Casting an odd look, Watts said, "What the hell was that about?"

"My head tingled, okay? Anyway, let's say Jeremy's talking to us. How do we write this up if we actually tie someone to his murder? And how is the DA supposed to present these EVPs so they're believable to a jury when Jeremy's spiritual existence is known as folklore? I mean, when you get right down to it, what we're doing is like trying Paul Bunyan for tossing his blue ox Babe around."

Watts rolled his eyes. "They're hardly the same, Blaine. In case you hadn't noticed, Jeremy Delouse was a real person, while Paul Bunyan and Babe are American folklore. Besides, we have scientific evidence that supports Jeremy's existence. As we've discussed before, this trial would be a media circus, but we can't worry about that. Right now, my money's on Travis as our murder suspect, but whether he would be tried as Travis McLean or Arvid McAlister remains to be seen. In the meantime, let's see what Daisy's up to."

"Sure, why not?"

As was her routine, Daisy was all business when she greeted them, so Watts made no attempt at humor or flirting. "I said I'd call you if I had anything."

"Sorry to bother you."

She waited until they were heading out the door before saying, "Which do you want to see first? The DNA results or the EVP?"

The detective slowly turned. "Either's fine," said Watts.

"Okay, follow me."

She led them back to the familiar computer room and presented the EVP comparisons. "As you can see, the voice is identical in all of these, but there is still no way to confirm that Jeremy Delouse is speaking from the grave. As for the hair samples, it didn't take long to confirm their DNA matches."

"Which means Arvid and Travis are indeed the same person," said Spartan.

"Correct. Doubters may take exception to EVPs, but DNA evidence is irrefutable."

Watts bobbed his head in concurrence. "This is all good," he said, "but let's think about it for a moment. We have evidence that points toward Travis being Jeremy's killer, but not enough to prove it. The Feds might be able to bust him for using a dead man's Social Security number, but if Marv argues the Prospect house is part of his family, and he authorized Travis to list it under Arvid McAlister, it wouldn't amount to anything. As for Betty and her slush fund misappropriation, that's an internal matter requiring someone in the theater to press charges, so in spite of everything, it seems we're still spinning our wheels."

"Which means we need a confession," said Spartan.

"I agree," said Daisy. "Without one, we have no case."

Watts' face filled with disappointment. He sighed heavily and patted the desk.

"Thanks, Daisy. You've done a tremendous job with this case. At some point, I hope we can use this evidence to convict someone. See you later."

He walked away wishing he had chosen better words. *See you later* sounded a lot like *good bye*, and he certainly didn't want it to be misinterpreted as a break-up. He wasn't sure why he was so tense around her lately. All he knew was, life was easier before they began dating. Still contemplating this when he got to his desk, he wondered which mystery he would solve first – Jeremy's murder or how much his girlfriend was committed to him.

Thirty Seven

WATTS SAT AT HIS desk staring at the whiteboard. Taping Travis McLean's police sketch near the top did nothing to answer how the house on Prospect ended up with Warren Delouse's Social Security number and Arvid's name. A person could write whatever they want on a loan or title application, but it wouldn't go through without proper credentials and a good credit rating. And even if it somehow slipped through the mortgage system, the Tarrant County Recorder should have caught the error. Pondering that, Spartan came in with more news.

"Here's another piece of the puzzle, Maxx. Travis McLean's house was paid for in cash about ten years ago, which is why the mortgage company didn't check the Social."

Watts chewed on that for a moment, barely acknowledging his partner. "I suspect that if you dig deeper, you'll find a withdrawal from Marv's account on or about the day the house closed, and as interesting as that may be, it won't provoke anyone's confession. What we need is DNA evidence that connects Betty to Marv, and getting that will be dicey."

"You don't think Captain Ryder will go to bat for us on that?"

Watts' expression soured even more. "Would you? I mean, we're talking about demanding DNA samples from a banker and a cultural icon. Any judge in his right mind would deny it, because on the surface, they're both model citizens."

"Unless he was convinced their DNA would prove Marv is Betty's son and Jeremy was his father, and that's why our hardened warrior killed Jeremy in the place where the lovers met."

"Even with that it's a tough sell," said Watts. Unsure what else to add, he glanced at his watch and then tapped the desk. "Anyway, we're wasting time sitting here, so if you're willing to get kicked in the teeth, let's go talk to the boss."

"I'm game, but shouldn't Daisy go with us?"

Watts shook his head. "We don't need her to provide evidence or use as a shield."

"I was thinking her forensics expertise might sway Ryder."

"Fine," he said, picking up the phone. "I'll call her, but don't expect miracles."

Spartan cocked his head and squinted. "Is everything okay between you two? I mean, you don't seem very buddy-buddy these days."

Tapping his fingers, chewing his lower lip, it took Watts a while to answer. "Blaine, I'm not sure what we have anymore. All I know is, the ball's in her court and if I don't start getting a warm and fuzzy soon, I may have to toss her back in the company pond." Stopping himself, he rubbed his face and then dropped his hands. "I'm sorry, that didn't come out right. I meant to say, no matter how things work out, Daisy's a great lady."

"That she is," he said, patting his partner's shoulder. "As I said, women are complex. Sometimes you have no idea what they're thinking, but that doesn't mean you should give up on 'em."

Watts slowly nodded. "Anyway, let me call her and see how much time she needs to gather her data – then I'll call the boss. Sit tight and I'll let you know when we're on."

"You got it."

Once Spartan was in his cubicle, Watts got Daisy on the phone. After explaining what he needed, she promptly ended the conversation by saying she would be up within fifteen minutes. He then called his boss and set up the meeting.

While waiting for Daisy, Watts reviewed his notes and tape transcripts, while Spartan did the same. Once Daisy joined them, they went over everything to ensure they were on the same page. By the time they started down the hall toward Ryder's office, Watts felt they were as prepared as they could be. Even so, once the boss waved them in, he couldn't shake the feeling they were gladiators entering the arena.

"Well, well, the Three Musketeers ride again," he gleefully said. "And what do you have for me today?"

"A simple request," said Watts.

Hands clasped, brows raised, Ryder didn't offer a seat. "Maxx, with you there is no such thing as a simple request, especially in the company of your entourage."

Ignoring the sarcasm, Watts got right to the point. "We'd like a subpoena to collect DNA samples from Betty Cerin and Marv Delouse."

Ryder's fingers unfolded and interlocked like tentacles seeking prey. He then tented them and brought them to his chin, silently studying his audience. Finally, he said, "Okay, detective, I'll forego my retirement pension and give it a shot, because this is the most bizarre case I've ever heard of. Never mind the fact that we have no body or medical records of the deceased, nor any actual proof that a homicide was ever committed. But there are so many intriguing sides to this story which demand explanation, I'm going to back you. Of course, it doesn't mean we'll ever find a judge who's willing to sign the order, and if we're successful and the media gets wind of this, things could go horribly wrong and put all of our jobs in jeopardy. So with that in mind, I want a yes from each of you that you want me to proceed."

Without hesitation, all three gave their verbal confirmations.

"Very well. I can't promise I'll have an answer today, but I will call the moment I hear something."

"Thank you, sir."

Watts quickly pivoted on his heel and led them out the door. Halfway down the hall, he said, "That went well, don't you think?"

"Time will tell," said Spartan.

Suddenly Daisy lost her color. "I feel sick to my stomach."

Watts stopped walking to look at her. Concerned, he said, "You don't look so good, either. Can I get you something? Drive you home?"

She shook her head and kept walking. "It's probably nerves."

Watts walked with her, hoping he wasn't to blame. He recalled how he had been treating her and wondered if he wasn't subconsciously driving a wedge between them. He wanted to pull her aside and apologize, but this wasn't the right place or time. It took all his effort to set his personal feelings aside and concentrate on the case.

Thirty Eight

As THE DAY NEARED its end, and with no word from Captain Ryder, Watts was beginning to think he had made a giant mistake. He found himself questioning the case, his relationship with Daisy, and even his becoming a detective. While his brain replayed his missteps, he wished he were more like TV's Detective Columbo, who always came up with answers. His partner's silence seemed to confirm he was having the same doubts but refused to discuss it. Right now, this case and their careers all hung on a judge's decision, and that made the minutes tick painfully by.

At four-thirty-two Captain Ryder called Watts on the phone. "It's your lucky day, Maxx. I have the orders on my desk, but you'll need to use absolute discretion. Give them the option of whether to donate hair or blood."

The news was electrifying. "Yes, sir!" Upon passing the word to his partner, he said, "Call Daisy to see if she can accompany us. We need to move fast, or Betty and Marv will be gone for the day. I'm heading to the boss's office to pick up the papers. I'll be right back."

His left shoe telegraphed his hurried pace as he headed for Ryder's office. When he got there, the captain wasted no time with words as he slid the document over. Watts thanked him and hurried back to his desk.

Spartan jumped up from his seat when he heard Watts coming. "Daisy should be here any second."

"We'll meet her in the hall. Let's get moving."

Daisy joined them carrying her lab kit. She looked better now that her color had returned, and she seemed as fired up as Watts and Spartan. Their first stop was the bank where Watts went in while the others waited in the car. He saw Marv's head pop up and then duck down as soon as he entered the building. Watts approached the counter and said he had an urgent matter to discuss with Marv without ever showing his badge. Assuming it pertained to bank business, the woman promptly left to speak to the loan officer. She soon returned saying Mr. Delouse would be right out. All seemed fine except Marv pretended to be busy, slowly flipping pages as if he were giving someone else his undivided attention. Watts stared at him, letting his eyes burn into Marv's head. It must have worked, because the banker set his papers aside and approached the counter.

Watts silently eased the subpoena over and waited until Marv had read it. "It will only take a second," he said. "A lab tech is waiting in the car."

For the benefit of his co-workers, Marv smiled and nodded, but his hands were trembling, and the tension in his face was undeniable. He told the clerk he would be right back and walked out with Watts. Spartan saw them coming and opened the back door so Marv could slide in next to Daisy without anyone noticing.

"What's this all about?" said Marv, his fake smile long gone.

Spartan guarded the door to make sure no one would run. "We just need to clarify some things," he said. "We can do it one of three ways. You can donate blood, pull out some hair in front of us, or Ms. Woods will cut some of your hair. It's your choice."

"And once that's done, you're free to go," said Watts, watching Marv check out Daisy's cleavage while she opened her kit bag and pulled on some gloves. Until now, Watts wasn't sure Marv was interested in women. Daisy was ignoring everyone.

"I suppose the hair around my ears could use a trim," said Marv.

"Very well." Daisy took the scissors from her kit and clipped a few hairs. After dropping them in a labeled dish, she clipped a few on the other side to even things out. "That's it. We're done."

Marv leaned forward to check her work in the mirror. He backed away looking disappointed. "That's not much of a haircut," he said, brushing his shoulder.

"But the price is right," said Watts. "Thanks for you cooperation, Marv. Make up whatever story you want, but if it were me, I'd say I had a client in the car who wished to remain anonymous."

Marv nodded and walked away like a scolded dog. He carried that look until disappearing inside the bank. Watts wondered if he would use the client excuse on his peers or tell them the truth. Either way was fine, since they got what they came for. He fired up the car and headed for the Scott Theater.

Like Marv, Betty tried to ignore them when they approached the entrance. She started to walk away and didn't stop until Watts called her name. At that point, she slowly turned and smiled as if she hadn't noticed them.

"Back so soon?" she said, like they were kids buying sweets.

Watts reached into his pocket and handed her the order. "It's just a formality," he said. "We'd appreciate your cooperation."

She read it over, reached behind her neck, and yanked out a few hairs, and handed them over. "Here you go. At my age, it's all falling out anyway. Anything else?"

Daisy accepted the sample, sealed it in another container, and nodded to Watts.

"I think we're good, Betty. Thanks for being so obliging."

No problem." She paused and clasped her hands. "You know, detective, as often as you come here, you should buy season tickets. We have some great performances scheduled."

Watts smiled warmly. "I'll give it some thought. Thanks again, Betty."

No one spoke until they were back in the car. Spartan was the first to break the silence.

"That went a whole lot better than I expected."

"I agree," said Daisy. "And I suppose you want me to analyze this as soon as we get back?"

"That would be great. If you need any help, I'd be happy to assist." He then turned to his partner. "Blaine, feel free to head home. No point in missing a hot meal with your family."

"You won't get any arguments from me."

Watts made a beeline for 350. Once the Crown Vic was turned in, Spartan headed for his car while Watts and Daisy headed inside. Watts wasn't sure whether he was more excited to spend time with her, or see if the DNA results supported their speculation. Turning their hair samples into DNA formulas would take time, but since neither had anywhere to go, time wasn't an issue. As the regular staff took off, Daisy's stomach growled.

"At this point it's in the hands of the computer," she said. "The building's secure and nothing will happen for a while, so if you'd like to get something to eat, it's my treat."

"Your treat? Really? What's the occasion?"

"That I'm dating the most amazing man on Earth."

Watts nearly choked. Here he was thinking she was ready to dump him, and she drops this on him. "Daisy, that's the nicest thing anyone's ever said to me. I'm not sure I deserve it, but thank you. And yes, I'd love to grab a bite. Where would you like to go?"

She shook her head and smiled coyly. "Tonight, all you have to do is sit back and enjoy. I'm driving, too."

If his grin got any wider, it would have reached his ears. "All right. Let's go."

Daisy briefed her co-worker on what was happening and instructed him to call her should the results finish before they returned. When they got outside, she slid her arm under his and then locked her hands together. "Trust me, Maxx, this will be great."

Watts patted her arm as they walked to her Toyota Tundra. It seemed odd opening the passenger door for himself, but he had no objections. She swatted his rear as he climbed in.

"Nice butt," she said, grinning. She closed the door and walked over to the driver's side just as he had done countless times, then fastened her seatbelt and looked sternly at him. "So here are the ground rules, Maxx. Don't ask where we're going or even think about ordering dinner. Most importantly, don't offer to pay. This is my night out with you, and I don't want you spoiling it."

Doing his best to hide his anxiety, he nodded and smiled. "Okay, I'll be your obedient slave for as long as you want. I must say, this is quite a surprise."

"Thanks," she said smugly, cranking the ignition.

Pointing her truck north on Main came as a surprise. The route was familiar, because they had just been to Marv's bank. It was also the initial route to the Prospect house. But true to his word, he quietly sat there wondering how long she had been planning this. His eyes opened wide when she pulled up to the H3 Ranch Steakhouse's valet parking.

"Really?" is the best he could come up with.

"Yes, really. Now, get out. The valet's waiting."

She didn't bother watching the driver whisk her truck away. Instead, she clung to Watts' arm and led him into Booger Red's historic bar, where they proudly served Buffalo Butt Beer. A buffalo's rear end mounted above the bar proved it.

Most of the bar stools were round and leather-wrapped, but the saddle stools added real flair. The neon sign over the entry read, *Booger Red's*. His portrait was painted on the rustic hardwood floor along with the words, *Women Want Me, Horses Fear Me*. Watts wasn't sure if the bar's tin ceiling was authentic, but the array of belt-driven ceiling fans certainly were. He didn't know of any other place in Fort Worth that had such Old West authenticity. This place must have gotten crazy when a cattle drive came into the stockyards. Except for belly laughs and clinking glasses, the background noise remained indiscernible.

Watts was blown away when they approached the dining room and Daisy gave the hostess her name. Only then did he realize this wasn't some random evening, but rather one she had been planning for some time. As he nervously followed her to the quaint table at the far corner of the room, he felt badly about asking her to run those DNA tests. Then sitting under the dim light and familiar atmosphere, he understood what this was about.

She ordered wine and then slid her hands across the table to hold his. When the waiter brought their drinks, she raised her glass in a toast. "Happy anniversary, Maxx. Today marks four months."

Wow! He had never dated anyone who even mentioned an anniversary. Clinking her glass, he said, "Happy Anniversary, and thank you." As they sipped with bedroom eyes, he added, "How did you manage to get the same table?"

"I'm glad you remembered. I wanted this to be as perfect as our first date." She took a long sip and set her glass down. "Maxx, I'm sorry I've been so bitchy lately. This isn't to make up for it, though. It's just my way of saying thanks for tolerating me."

"Tolerating you? What are you talking about?"

She noticed something on the table and started wiping it with her napkin. It was a distraction, of course, but Watts knew better than to say anything.

"I'm a pretty good investigator myself," she continued. "That noose over my door freaked me out, so I started asking around. I finally found the answer, too."

"Really?"

"Yeah. One of the residents said he saw a woman tack it up. He had seen her in the parking lot and at first thought it was me. But when he saw her profile, he knew it was someone else. Once he finished describing her, I had a sense of who it might be, so I confronted her and she admitted she did it."

Leaning halfway across the table, he said, "Who are we talking about? Betty?"

Daisy smiled, shaking her head. "Betty would never be threatened by me."

Before he could ask again, their waiter delivered some bread and stood ready to take their orders. She ordered for both of them, reciting their exact orders from their previous dinner here. Clearly enjoying the moment, she calmly tore some bread and buttered it.

"Well, don't leave me hanging," he pleaded. "Please finish your story."

"I will," she said, taking a bite. "Try the bread. It's excellent."

Since she wasn't talking, he tore a piece for himself. "You're right. It's just like I remember." After finishing his piece, he said, "So, who is this mystery woman?"

"Does the name Annie ring a bell?"

Watts squinted, thinking hard. He soon gave up and shook his head. "Should it?"

"Annie? Your next-door neighbor?"

"The one that fed me dinner?"

She nodded, calmly buttering another piece of bread.

"That's crazy. First of all, why would she do it? Secondly, how would she know where you live? And finally, how was she threatened by you?"

She took her time eating and washed it down with wine. "She's infatuated with you, Maxx. Always has been. You're just too blind to notice."

He felt the blood drain from his head. His emotions ranged from anger to confusion as he thought about his crazy neighbor. His next thought was to move as far away from her as possible.

"I don't get it," he said. "Until that night, I didn't even know her name."

"And that's a good thing," she continued, "because when I confronted her, I thought you were cheating on me. It took some coercing, but she finally came clean. The funny thing is, you were at home while I was over there and you never knew it. But even then, I had to back away until I was sure it was me you wanted. I'm sorry. I should have realized she was a nutcase."

"Yes she is," he said, holding his glass to his lips. "But how did she know where you live?"

"You can thank Leroy for that. Your truck is easy to follow, Maxx. One night she followed us when you took me home and watched from the parking lot to see which apartment I went in."

Watts set his drink down, shaking his head. "Maybe you should be the detective. It seems I'm clueless these days. And Leroy – well, I can't believe he let me down like that."

225

She waved her hand, snickering. "Oh, stop being so hard on yourself and your truck. Your problem is you're so focused on your work that you don't pick up signals from other women. She wanted to jump your bones the night you went over, but you wouldn't have anything to do with her. She laughed at how you high-tailed it out of there after dinner. I guess she figured that hanging a noose would scare me into staying in my apartment. Anyway, she's going to move, so you don't have to." She then raised her glass for another toast. "Here's to us, Mr. Maxx."

"Here, here."

Their waiter had impeccable timing in delivering their salads, and it was good that Daisy had cleared the air. But now Watts had a new problem with his crazy neighbor. If this evening taught him anything, it was to realize he knew nothing about women.

Thirty Nine

BEFORE THEIR STEAKS ARRIVED, Daisy got a call saying their DNA results wouldn't be ready for several more hours. Neither she nor Watts minded. They were technically off duty and were having fun catching up. In a vulnerable moment, Daisy admitted she left her previous job because she caught her boyfriend cheating, and because he was senior and worked in the same department, she elected to transfer to Fort Worth. Perhaps it was the wine speaking, but she continued to vent all the way through dessert and coffee. Hearing this explained a lot.

Watts glanced her way. "You realize we don't have to go back to the lab, right? There are a lot better ways to end an evening."

"I know, but we need to finish this."

She didn't speak again until they were inside the lab and she had read the DNA summary. Finding her smile, she presented the data.

"Well, here you go, Mr. Maxx with two Xs. This proves beyond any reasonable doubt that Marv is Betty Cerin's child. Now you can confront her about it."

"Lady, you sound pretty looped. I need to get you home."

"Why? So you can take me to bed?"

"No, so you can sleep it off. Let me worry about Betty, okay? If I can get her to admit Marv is her son, she might tell me what happened while Travis was home on leave. If we're lucky, she might even admit that Travis McLean and Arvid McAlister are one and the same."

"Well, good luck with that, Columbo."

Shaking his head, he said, "So, are you ready to call it a night?"

"Absolutely."

"There's no way I'm gonna let you drive, so should we go to your place or mine?"

"I'm not gonna let that crazy neighbor of yours get anywhere near you, so we're going to mine."

"Then your place it is, but we'll take my truck."

"Whatever works for you, buddy."

After he climbed in, she leaned over and kissed him. "Guess I shouldn't have done that. There are cameras around the lot."

"It's okay," he said, buckling her in. "The windows are tinted. But seriously, thank you so much for the wonderful evening. It really helped to learn more about you. It also helped to know about the noose lady. I promise I will never cheat on you."

"I know. And as for the noose, we still only know the first part of the story. Annie admitted to stapling it to my overhang but swears she had nothing to do with breaking into your truck and would never do anything to hurt you or Leroy. In a way, I feel sorry for her."

"Well, I don't," he said, pulling out of the lot. "Like you said, she's a nutcase. I can't believe she'd do that." He felt himself getting angry again so he said, "Anyway, we've already covered that. We have to be at work soon, so we'd better get some sleep."

She leaned into him and locked lips. "Sleep is boring."

"Maybe, but that's all you're gonna get."

* * * * *

By the time he returned from brushing his teeth, she had fallen asleep. As he slid under the covers and closed his eyes, Annie invaded his mind. He forced her from his brain by picturing Daisy. He felt her pain when she spoke of her cheating boyfriend. He rolled on his side and watched her chest rise and fall, hoping she was dreaming about him. Then he gently kissed her forehead and turned away, praying for a few short hours of rest. It didn't take long for sleep to consume him.

The buzzing alarm had Daisy climbing over him to turn it off. While she was on top, he hugged her tight. "Good morning, Sweetheart."

She slid away and ran her palm over her forehead. "Sorry," she said, shaking her head. "I didn't realize you were here. Did we – do anything?"

"No, you were drunk and we were both tired, so we slept for five hours. You want to shower first or second?"

"Second," she said, pulling his pillow over her head.

"Okay, I'll be quick."

Shortly after getting dressed, his phone rang. The caller ID showed it was Captain Ryder.

"Maxx, you're not gonna believe this, but we have another body hanging in the Scott Theater. I need you down there right away. You and Spartan have the case. You'll know why when you get there."

Stunned, Watts clung to the phone wondering what he meant by that. Rather than ask questions, he said, "Yes, sir."

Daisy was drying her hair when he poked his head into the bathroom. "Captain Ryder just called. We need to go, pronto. There's been another hanging."

She turned her dryer off and stared at his reflection. "Say what?"

"Daisy, I need to go. You want to come with me, or should I call you a cab?"

"Give me three minutes."

She was ready as promised, and they hurried out the door. When they arrived on scene, three patrol cars and an ambulance blinked near the building. He searched for a news van and was thankful none had arrived. With luck, they would be gone before any showed up, although that seemed unlikely.

He spotted a young patrol officer and thought about Porgy Mulberry. For reasons he couldn't explain, he wished that Porgy had been the officer on scene. Porgy could be a royal pain, but he knew how to do his job. Watts didn't have the same confidence with this rookie.

Showing the officer his badge, he said, "What happened?"

"Some old dude hung himself in the basement," the officer said, straining for a glance at Daisy who was staying out of the way. "I heard there's a suicide note. I'm not sure why they called you."

Watts's face turned to stone. "Son, the first rule in police work is to assume nothing is as it appears. That is especially true with suicides. You said the vic is an old guy?"

"That's right. Sixtyish I guess."

Watts nodded, glancing at Daisy while fearing the worst. "If the vic is who I think, this scene is more important than you realize. Have you seen Detective Spartan?"

The rookie shook his head. "Is she with you?" he said, still looking at Daisy.

Ignoring his inclination to deck the kid, Watts said, "Keep it professional. She's one of our best lab technicians."

The rookie gave her a nod and focused on Watts. "Okay, what can I do for you?"

"Same thing you were doing. Keeping this area secure."

"Yes, sir."

As Watts and Daisy approached the entrance, he regretted leaving his Sony at the office. If Travis was dead, Jeremy might be crying *murder* again. They were about to go inside when Spartan called his name. He turned around and saw his partner running.

"Hey guys," he said. Moving closer to Watts, he whispered, "Aren't those the same clothes you had on yesterday?"

"Actually, I have a closet full of identical coats and pants. Now, what have you heard?"

They spent the next few minutes comparing notes before heading to the dungeon. Badging their way in, the scene looked eerily familiar. Watts had seen Jeremy's dangling body too many times in his dreams, but now it was Travis hanging from a similar noose. He felt sad for the vet. While the theater's personnel may have known him as Arvid or "the janitor," to anyone who had met him, Travis was a hero who became a lost soul. Ironically, that was something he shared with Jeremy.

A strong urine smell came from Travis' moist pants. Watts looked for a liquid trail that might indicate he was killed somewhere else, but he didn't see anything. A small stool, perhaps one foot tall, lay tipped on its side like in Jeremy's crime scene photos. Looking up at Travis, Watts remembered his desperation as Porgy Mulberry held him under water. Nearly two decades had passed since that pool party, but the memory still hammered his heart. So why did Travis look so calm? Something wasn't right.

He nearly tripped on Daisy while she was inspecting the victim's shoes. While pulling on some gloves, he carefully stepped around her trying to get a sense of what happened. As he went through Travis' pockets, he realized the vet was also wearing the same clothes he saw him in last. Watts was joking when he said he had a closet full of identical garments, but he was sure that wasn't the case for Travis. He considered that as a crime scene photographer snapped photos. Making sure he was being videotaped, Watts carefully unfolded the suicide note, showed it to the camera, and read it aloud.

"Detective Watts. No doubt you are the first on scene. If I hadn't opened my mouth in the diner, I'd still be alive living my simple life. But you had to keep digging, so this was my only way out. Jeremy and I are laughing now, knowing our secrets are safe. May you and your partner rot in Hell. Cheers, Travis McLean, AKA Arvid McAlister."

When he finished, he dropped the note in an evidence bag and signaled for the camera to cut.

Spartan slid next to him. "I guess this confirms his alias once and for all."

Watts gave an indignant look. "Maybe, but don't you find it odd that his suicide note came from a printer? We'll certainly check his residence, but from what I saw when we were over there, everything in his house looked old and decrepit. Do you know anyone with an analog television set with rabbit ears?"

"Can't say that I do."

"Exactly, so I think it's safe to say Travis was not into technology. That's why it seems unlikely this note came from him."

Daisy looked up at them. "He could've used a library computer."

"Or one from Marv's bank or the Scott Theater," said Spartan. When Watts didn't respond, he added, "So, I gather you're not buying his suicide note."

Watts pinched his lips, shaking his head. "Not at all."

Daisy nodded her agreement. "I'll check it for prints when I get back to the lab, but if this was staged like you believe, his killer would probably make sure only Travis' prints appear. We can also identify the paper, although I'm betting it's generic."

"Anything would be helpful," said Watts, scanning the narrow hallway. Although the police and rescue people were staying ten feet away, whoever discovered the body had already contaminated the scene. "Everyone check the floor for drag marks, scuff marks, anything that might denote a struggle in the hall or a nearby room. Travis may have had trouble sleeping, but I don't believe he was ready to leave this world."

"Maybe we'll record another EVP," said Spartan.

"I doubt it," said Watts, unwilling to admit he didn't have the Sony with him.

While honoring the Purple Heart veteran with a final salute, he recognized Dr. Morton's voice as he complained about having to walk down the stairs. Before Morton got to the body, Watts gathered Spartan and Daisy together.

"Here's where I'm confused," he said. "Betty and Marv had both been looking after Travis for at least ten years. So if Travis were Jeremy's killer, why would they cover for him? It doesn't make sense."

"Because Jeremy killed himself when Travis learned Betty was pregnant," said Spartan.

Daisy nodded, watching Dr. Morton come closer. "Maybe Marv thought Travis was his biological father and wanted to take care of him."

Spartan nodded again. "Which is why Betty gave him work and paid him out of her slush fund."

Watts was silent as he considered the possibilities. What they were saying would have made sense if it weren't for the timing of the vet's death. Travis was not particularly pleasant when they saw him yesterday, but he didn't seem suicidal, either. He seemed more like the perfect fall guy to cover up the unfolding story about Jeremy's murder.

"Ms. Woods," he said to Daisy, "I'm going to request additional lab personnel to sweep every room in the dungeon. I'm particularly interested in finding hair samples and cleaning solutions."

"Whose hair are you looking for?" said Spartan.

"Marv Delouse's."

Spartan and Daisy looked at him like he was crazy, but he was already thinking about Betty. He thought she would have been here by now. Why would she pass up another opportunity to demonstrate her acting abilities when there was another hanging in her beloved theater? As cynical as that sounded, experience had taught him not to trust anyone. Perhaps that was another reason for his short-lived relationships. He forced Daisy from his brain so he could focus on the case.

By now, the ME had pushed his way through. Watts wasn't sure why Dr. Morton always arrived so late, but at least he was consistent. Morton stared at the body for some time before acknowledging the detective. His hands were shaking and his eyes barely moved. Watts moved closer to see if there was a problem.

"Is something wrong, Doc?"

"This is a nightmare, Maxx. As I told you before, Jeremy Delouse was my first case, and after we spoke in the morgue, I went through his medical records to see if I had missed anything."

Watts did a double-take. "Wait a minute. We left his microfiche out while we visited your secretary, and it was gone when we came back. Are you saying you took it?"

Morton eyed him like a pissed off warlord. "I didn't take anything, young man. I'm the chief medical examiner, and those records belong to me. However, I did find the microfiche library unlocked, and when I saw Jeremy's records on the reader, I tucked it in my lab coat."

"But why would you do that? Weren't you in the middle of an autopsy at the time?"

"I was, but my patient wasn't going anywhere, and my sinuses were giving me such fits I had to visit the restroom. I assumed you had left and didn't bother to clean up or lock up. Didn't Megan point out that we keep the Records Room locked at all times?"

Now Watts felt stupid. Transitioning from offense to defense, he humbly said, "She did, and I apologize. We had some questions, so we left the door cracked and went to see you. You were busy, so we went to Megan, and when we came back the fiche was gone. Didn't she tell you we were looking for his file? She spent at least five minutes with us searching for it."

"Actually she never mentioned it, but since that room is supposed to be locked, she probably thought I'd fire her if she admitted to it. I'll have a talk with her later."

Watts nodded, still feeling irresponsible. "Well, as I said, it was my fault, so please go easy on her. Anyway, can we go back to what you were saying about Jeremy Delouse?"

"Sure. After I finished the girl's autopsy, I went back to review his microfiche, and I noticed a discrepancy – nothing that would change anything, but still it was a discrepancy. As I read through his file, it was 1970 all over again. I saw him hanging on the pipe, just like this man here. His image haunted me as I read through his file, but in the end, I didn't find anything that would change my suicide ruling."

Watts nodded his understanding. The fact that Morton admitted his mistake without his mentioning it saved them both some awkward conversation. He wasn't happy with Megan either, but if she checked it before she went home and found it there, she probably figured we were all blind and forgot about it. Seeing that they had exhausted Jeremy's story, he said, "Doc, what can you tell me about today's hanging?"

Morton studied the pipe where the noose was tied and let his eyes fall to Travis' shoes. "At this point all I can say is he's dead, his hands and feet were not bound, and there are no obvious signs of a struggle. It also smells like he had been drinking heavily."

"Yeah, I smelled it, too. Between the urine and booze, I feel the need to shower."

Morton laughed. "I've smelled so many disgusting things over the years that my senses have been destroyed. Frankly, I'm surprised I can still taste food." He paused to look around. "Is there a ladder around here?"

"Actually, there is, but I don't want anyone touching it until it's been dusted for prints."

233

The ME placed his hands on his hips, gazing at the pipe that was beyond his reach. "Then how do you propose we get him down?"

"I guess we'll cut the rope."

Daisy suddenly looked up shaking her head. "I don't recommend that. We could lose valuable evidence if someone drops him."

"I agree," said Morton.

Mirroring the ME's stance, Watts felt constricted. He couldn't think because so many people were whispering among themselves. Making eye contact with a uniformed officer, he said, "I want this area cleared of all non-essential personnel. Secure the entry at the top of the stairs, and see if the department can round up a ten-foot step ladder."

"Yes, sir."

He then pulled out his pad and started jotting notes about the ME's admission to having Jeremy's records, his noted discrepancy from 1970, the unpleasant odors, the background noise, and the lack of cold sensations they had felt before. He directed the crime scene photographers, documenting with one film camera, the other one digital. While they filmed, he pondered Travis' suicide note and its reference to the diner. Besides his partner, Marv was the only person who knew about it. With Travis out of the way, Marv could sever his ties with the Prospect house and bury the ugly truth about his biological father. If anyone had something to gain from Travis' death, it was Marv. He held that thought as he cornered his partner.

"Blaine, Marv should be at work now, so I'd like you to go to Montgomery Plaza and see if the security folks will let you review their lobby tapes from the last twelve hours. If Marv was in and out in the middle of the night, we have reason to believe he had a part in this."

"You don't want to come along?"

Watts shook his head. "I'd like to stick around here to see what Doc Morton has to say, and at the rate things are going, this could take a while. Call me as soon as you know something. If you can't reach me, it's because I don't get reception down here, so please leave a message."

"No sweat. Mind if I swing by the station and pick up the Crown Vic?"

"By all means. But if you break it, you buy it."

"Sure thing, Dad."

Watts quickly turned his attention to Daisy. "What's your take on this?"

She lifted her shoulders and let them settle. "It's too early to tell, but if it was staged, someone did a good job. From all preliminary indications, it looks like a suicide."

"Maybe, but I still don't buy it, and I'm not sure the ME does either."

Busy examining the body, Morton said, "Maxx, I may be old, but I can still hear you. And I also agree with Ms. Woods that it's too early to tell anything."

Watts and Daisy smiled at each other, embarrassed at talking behind Morton's back. Watts excused himself and led her down the hall to the rehearsal room that was across from the janitor's closet. As soon as he entered the room, he detected alcohol and cleaning fluid.

"Let's sweep this room first," he said, searching for empty alcohol bottles. "If he was drinking with the intention of killing himself, I doubt he would care about cleaning up. I'm going to call Captain Ryder and brief him on the situation. Maybe he can expedite the forensics crew and the ladder."

"Sounds good."

Watts got his phone out and gained bars as he neared the top of the stairs. Sliding under the yellow police tape, he looked for Betty but didn't see her among the onlookers. While seeking a suitable place where he could speak in private, he spotted the trash bins out back. After briefing Ryder on the situation, he opened the recycling bin's lid and found it packed with alcohol bottles from the theater's bar. He immediately found another uniformed officer, instructed him to seal off the bin, then ran downstairs to find Daisy. Thankfully, she was still snooping around in the rehearsal room. She looked at him over her shoulder when his shoe farted.

"I'm back," he whispered so no one else would disturb them. "I need you to identify what kind of alcohol Travis was drinking as soon as possible."

Her face sank. "I can't do that without my lab kit, and even then it would be a best guess. Like you, I came here unprepared."

"I know. By the way, Captain Ryder says the rest of your team is on their way. I got the impression he didn't understand why they weren't already here."

"Well, we're not normally first responders."

"You're right, and it's not a problem. Anyway, back to the alcohol, check the large bin outside – it's full of empty bottles. If we know what type of booze Travis consumed, we have a chance of finding the bottle he drank from, and if we do that, then it's safe to say someone else dumped it there."

"Whew," she said, mocking him with a pretend brow wipe. "Those are a lot of words for a simple lab tech." She then laughed at his frowny face. "Come on, Maxx, lighten up. It's just the two of us here. I was kidding."

"I know, but what if Travis and Jeremy are watching? Have you felt anything touch your thigh lately?"

Now she was the one wearing a frown. "That's not funny."

"Sorry, I couldn't resist. Anyway, since I don't know much about alcohol, I'll settle for your best guess. Take a good whiff. Is it whiskey, bourbon, or Scotch?"

She grinned again. "Scotch is a type of whiskey, Maxx."

He raised his palms apologetically. "Like I said, I'm ignorant on everything except beer. Our house reeked of beer because that's what Dad could afford."

"Give me a minute."

"Take as much time as you need."

The room was bare except for some stacked chairs along the walls. The checkered floor could use a good cleaning, but it wasn't especially dirty. Watts stooped down to near-floor level looking for marks while she sniffed. "These scuff marks are consistent with actors and dancers moving about. Some sections of the floor are cleaner than others, perhaps from actors sitting down. I smell liquor, but I can't see where it's coming from."

"I know," she said, crawling on all fours. "And off the record, I agree that this scene is too clean for a suicide. I mean, if I were going to hang myself, I'd trash the place first. You know – make a statement. Then again, if I did that, I'd probably blow off enough steam to change my mind."

Watts looked at her, unsure how to respond. "Thanks for letting me know," he said. "And for the record, I'd appreciate it if you didn't kill yourself. If you're gonna do any hanging, then hang around with me."

"Oh, you're so clever."

"Very funny, but I know when you're mocking me. Now, come on and help me trace this scent," he said, sniffing the floor as he made his way around the room.

"I'm doing my best, but my nose isn't as sensitive as yours."

"Yeah? Well, consider that a blessing, especially on elevators."

Soon after making his quip, he pointed to a corner near the entry. "When your co-workers arrive, have them to do a chemical analysis over here. This area was cleaned recently, but I can still smell booze."

"I smell it, too, and to answer your question, it's Scotch Whiskey. Maybe Crown Royal."

Watts did a double-take. "How could you possibly know that?"

"I was a bartender in college, and you can never forget the smell of whiskey."

Imagining her in a clingy tank top juggling bottles and mixing drinks painted a whole new picture. The image vanished when two lab techs stuck their heads in the room. "Come on in," he said.

After giving them instructions, Watts went to find Dr. Morton. He expected to see the ME studying the corpse, but instead, he was sitting on the step stool doing not much of anything. Morton saw Watts coming and quickly got to his feet, speaking before the detective had the chance.

"I'm old and forensics said it was okay to sit," Morton said, offering no apology. "They dusted it for prints and didn't find anything. They also said grainy wood doesn't normally produce good prints. I assure you I haven't contaminated your crime scene."

Watts smiled. "The last time we worked together, you said you might outlive me."

Suddenly at ease, the doc smiled back. "It could still happen, you know."

"No offense, but I hope not. Anyway, sit if you want to. I'm still waiting on that ladder. By the way, we smelled whiskey in the other room, and it seems likely that Travis was drinking there before hanging himself. When you do your autopsy, please do a thorough check for alcohol content."

Morton smiled and placed his arm on Watts' shoulder as he escorted him away from the others. "Maxx, my boy, when will you learn that I know my job? I've been doing it longer than you've been alive, and checking the blood/alcohol content is one of the first things I do. I don't tell you how to do your job, so how about letting me do mine?"

Watts didn't like how Morton kept tightening his grip as he spoke, but he didn't want to make a scene either. Knowing others were watching, he smiled and nodded as if the ME just told a joke. Still grinning, he said, "Okay, Doc. Have it your way, but I need results as soon as possible. I have a bad feeling about this, and you're the only one here who can confirm it wasn't suicide."

Suddenly Morton wilted and his face paled. He started to walk away, but Watts grabbed his arm. "Hold on, Doc. What's going on?"

The ME looked up with a dour expression. "History repeats itself, Maxx. That's what the detective who found Jeremy Delouse said when he wanted to close that case. I was young and inexperienced and allowed peer pressure to influence my decision. Like you, I had doubts, but I couldn't find anything specific. I've lived with that guilt for over forty years, and even though I'm still convinced it was a suicide, I'm not about to make the same mistake twice. I assure you whatever ruling I make this time will be indisputable."

Since the ME's color had returned, Watts released his grip. "That's good to know, Doc, and I appreciate your candor."

Then a clank came from the stairwell. Watts spun around, certain it didn't come from Jeremy or Travis. Soon, the bottom of the ladder preceded a man in blue coveralls. Watts recognized him from 350.

"*Alto*," Watts shouted, trying to save the maintenance man some grief. But as soon as the man saw Travis' dangling body, his eyes became saucers and he dropped the ladder, running up the stairs as fast as his feet would carry him.

Watts couldn't blame the guy for taking off like that. Seeing a dead body, especially one hanging like a piñata, could be traumatizing. Since there was nothing he could do to change the situation, he picked the ladder up and positioned it near Travis. After briefing his police photographers on how he wanted things documented, he climbed the ladder to examine the rope. A simple clove hitch, two loops with the rope slipped between them, kept Travis suspended by the hangman's noose. It only took seconds to create these knots, but together they forged a lethal combination.

Enlisting the help of two uniformed officers, they raised Travis a few inches so Watts could undo the clove hitch that suspended the rope. Then they eased his body to the floor. Now that the body was horizontal, Dr. Morton removed the noose and called for the gurney. His staff quickly zipped Travis into a body bag and whisked him from the dungeon.

Watching them wheel the Purple Heart veteran out, Watts couldn't help thinking he might indeed have been responsible for his death like the suicide note suggested. With luck, Dr. Morton would find something to ease his guilt. Either way, he would never forget the man who fought in the rice paddies like his father.

Watts heard Daisy's voice and saw her waving for him to join her in the rehearsal room. Once he was inside, she closed the door and turned out the lights. Seeing others inside, he saved his wise cracks for later.

Using a special light, Daisy illuminated an entire section of the room. "I must say you have a nose for these things," she said. "What you're seeing is evidence of a fresh cleanup. There aren't any blood stains, but someone used solvent to mask the liquor and perhaps body odors. Everything matches what we smelled on Travis' clothes, so that means he was in here. We're still looking for hair samples, and there are people checking the dumpsters for any ditched items."

"Sounds good. Please sweep the janitor's room next," he said, lifting the phone from his pocket. "I need to check in with Blaine. I'll be right back."

Squinting into the sunlight, he listened to his voice mail. Two messages from his partner asked him to call as soon possible, so he quickly dialed, making sure no one was within earshot.

"I got your message," he said. "What's up?"

"That was a great hunch, Maxx. The Montgomery Plaza security folks have been real cooperative. It took longer than any of us expected, but their surveillance video shows a man in a suit matching Marv's description entering the building at 1731 local. Then at 0112, he leaves the building in a black Tee and dark jeans like we saw him wearing at the diner and then re-enters the lobby at 0421. At 0834, he left the building in a suit and hasn't returned."

"Super. Now we have a time stamp. Is there any indication that Marv might have been playing to the cameras? Surely he must have known they were there."

"That's something we'll have to ask when we see him, but he didn't have a nervous walk or try to hide his face. Other than it being the middle of the night, he may as well have been going out for coffee."

Watts rubbed his lips, thinking about that. He spent a few minutes briefing Spartan on what they found in the rehearsal room and said, "Sometimes it's what you don't find that's the most incriminating."

"How's that?"

"Well, the cleanup in the rehearsal room definitely lends itself to murder, not suicide. I also get the sense that Dr. Morton is leaning toward murder."

"Cool. So, what do you want me to do now?"

"Looks like we'll be here a while, so as soon as you can get a DVD of the surveillance video, join me here. We're gonna need it to confront Marv."

"Should we have Patrol bring him in as a person of interest?"

"Not yet, but call Captain Ryder to see if someone at the office can confirm Marv's at the bank. If he is, then have them do a stakeout to make sure he doesn't run. I figure we'll have one shot at this, and I don't want to blow it."

"I agree. See you in a bit."

When Watts returned to the dungeon, Daisy had moved to the janitor's room. She came out as soon as she heard him. Wearing an impish grin, she said, "You're smiling, so you must have found something else."

"Yup. Human hair from the ladder in the closet. Granted, a lot of people may have used the theater's step ladder, but there are at least two samples from different people. My guess is it was torn out when the ladder was folded. A lab tech is en route to the lab with the hair samples as well as swabs from the floor and walls."

Her news gave Watts another reason to smile. "This is great. Blaine just told me a man fitting Marv's description was seen exiting and re-entering the building during the wee hours of the night, so now we have motive and opportunity. We may not be able to solve Jeremy's murder, but it's looking like Travis won't be spending any time in Purgatory. Hopefully we'll be able to clear his name soon."

"I hope so."

Standing there facing each other with nothing to add, Watts smiled, rubbing his hands. Realizing that was Ryder's signature move, he stuffed them in his pockets and rocked on his heels. He stopped the moment his shoe farted.

"So, how much longer before you're finished?"

"One never knows. If you want to head back to 350, I'll catch a ride with one of the lab techs. I'll call if we make any new discoveries."

Watts gave a disappointed nod. She was right, of course. There was nothing more he could do here. "I'll call Blaine and have him meet me there. Thanks for the help, Daisy. I finally have a good feeling about this case."

"Me, too, Columbo."

Watts grinned and spun around. As he climbed the stairs, he mumbled, "What is it with women and Columbo?"

Forty

As many times as Watts had made the drive between the Scott Theater and headquarters, he felt like Leroy was on autopilot. Now that the morning traffic had thinned, it was just him and the crazies on the road. Braking for three mangy dogs along the way was the norm.

He called his partner to tell him about their change of plans but left out the details. Their timing worked out well because Spartan just left Montgomery Plaza. The two detectives arrived at their desks within minutes of each other.

Watts' first order of business was to review the security video with his partner. It didn't take long, since the critical times were all marked on the DVD. Because it was digital, the lab was able to enhance the image and confirm Marv's identity, and that made Watts feel better.

Leaning back in his chair with his arms behind his head, he said, "If I was a betting man, I'd say the hair on that ladder belongs to Marv."

Spartan nodded. "And that places him at the scene."

"Or at least confirms he moved the ladder at some point. Of course, I don't know why he'd do that unless he was involved in Travis' hanging, but his hair can't prove he was there at any specific time."

Running his tongue over the teeth reminded him he hadn't brushed. He quickly grabbed some gum from his drawer, stuck it in his mouth, and offered a stick to his partner. When Spartan waved him away, he returned the gum pack to the drawer.

Spartan waved him away so he tossed the pack in his drawer.

Trying not to smack as he chewed, he said, "Blaine, do you remember seeing any security cameras at the Scott Theater?"

Spartan shook his head. "But if this was murder and it was an inside job, they were probably turned off."

"Ah," said Watts, nodding. "So, you're thinking inside job too?"

"It has to be. Betty runs the place, so if Marv's involved and they have any cameras, she probably turned them off."

"First, you're making a big assumption thinking she's involved.

Second, Travis had his own key, so he could have gotten in anytime. If he was intent on killing himself, why turn the cameras off? I'd think keeping them on would make a bigger statement."

"And right now we don't even know if the theater has cameras," said Spartan, scratching his head.

"Well, since we still have people inside the Scott Theater, why not have them check out their security system?"

"Good idea. You want me to call?"

"Na, I'll see if Daisy can relay it."

Watts called, but her phone went straight to voice mail. Assuming she had no service, he called Dispatch to request a phone patch to an on-scene Patrol officer. When Officer Ray Sanders answered, he briefed him on what was needed and then returned to the whiteboard. Staring at the board, he and Spartan began connecting the players. When they finally agreed on the likely suspects, they devised a plan. What they still lacked was the DNA results to prove it.

While waiting for the lab results, they went to Captain Ryder's office to fill him in. After getting his blessing, Watts left another message for Daisy to call when she returned.

When Daisy finally invited them to the lab, the detectives rushed down like she was giving out free burgers.

"Follow me," she said, escorting them to the computer room. With everyone now familiar with DNA graphics, there was no need to re-explain. "As you can see, the hair samples from the ladder belong to Travis and Marv. Both were collected from the support bar hinge. The hair texture indicates it either came from their hands or their arms."

Watts nodded, recalling that both men's arms were fairly hairy. "So, are you're thinking Marv was lifting Travis when his hair caught in the ladder?"

"It's speculation, but yes. As for the liquor in the rehearsal room and on his clothes, tests confirm the alcohol was indeed Crown Royal. The rehearsal room swab samples also match his clothes and the cleaning solution in the janitor's closet."

Watts glanced at his partner. "She was a bartender in college," he offhandedly explained. "When it comes to booze, her nose is far more sensitive than mine."

"I'm impressed," said Spartan.

Watts' phone rang. Seeing that it was Dr. Morton, he held the phone from his ear so Spartan could hear without having to put it on speaker. The ME started talking before they had exchanged hellos.

"I have some news for you," Morton said. "Travis McLean's blood alcohol content was .14, and he died of asphyxiation, not alcohol poisoning. That in itself is not inconsistent with a suicide by hanging. What's important here is Mr. McLean was suffocated before he was hanged. Now, before you get all yippy, I want you to listen. First, I found traces of alcohol in his nostrils, which suggests he was blowing alcohol-saturated air through his nose while someone held a pillow or something similar against his face."

"Couldn't someone have poured alcohol down his nose?"

"I thought I asked you to listen. Besides, why would you pour good whiskey down a man's nose when you can drown him with water?"

The thought sent Watts back to the Crown Royal bottles they retrieved from the recycling bin. Their unique shape made them easy to find, but the neck design made it difficult to lift fingerprints. The ME never stopped talking, but Watts was missing most of it. The one thing he caught was that Travis was dead before he was hanged.

"You see, his capillaries didn't break like they would if his heart had been pumping blood when the noose tightened," Morton continued. "Of course, I still need to complete the autopsy, but from what I'm seeing so far, I'm convinced this hanging was staged. As for time of death, the liver probe places it between one and four AM. I'll send you a complete report once it's typed up."

"Thanks, Doc. That really helps." No sooner had Watts hung up than Officer Sanders was on the line. "Hello, Ray. Did you locate any security cameras in the theater?"

"No, sir. They have a monitored system but no video surveillance. One of the employees said that's to protect their clients' privacy. Apparently their philanthropists prefer to remain anonymous."

"Can't say I blame them," said Spartan.

"They're probably worried about ending up on Facebook," Watts added.

Sanders laughed heartily. "Chances are good they will anyway, since everyone has photo phones these days. Point, shoot and post. It's pretty amazing."

"Amazing and sad at the same time," said Watts. "These days it's tough for anyone to keep their private lives private." He paused and then added, "Ray, have you talked to an older woman named Betty Cerin? She runs the place. I'd be shocked if she weren't there."

"I've heard the name, but I haven't talked to her. Do you need to speak to her?"

"Not over the phone, but I would like you to escort her to my office at precisely ten forty-five this morning."

"Ten forty-five, eh? I'm not sure we'll be done by then."

"Ray, you guys are there to protect a crime scene, so I'm sure one of your buds can cover for you. My job is to solve this crime, and to do that, I need you to bring her here at exactly ten forty-five. Now, if that's gonna be a problem, let me know and I'll find someone else."

"No, it's no problem at all," he quickly said. "See you at ten-forty-five."

Satisfied, Watts hung up and dialed Dispatch to relay a message. "And now for our next player," he said to Spartan.

Minutes later he had Officer Amy Salem, the patrol officer who was watching for Marv at the Stockyards Wells Fargo Bank branch, on the phone. It didn't take long to brief her on his plan. He was ready to hang up when he added, "Please use caution and discretion. Mr. Delouse is stronger than he looks, and we don't want to upset any bank customers."

"Thanks for the concern, detective, but I'm sure I can handle him. See you at eleven."

Feeling confident, Watts ended the call and propped his feet on his desk. "Well, that's it, Blaine. Everything's set in motion."

"Good. Let's hope our packages are delivered in order at the proper time."

Watts nodded, glancing at his watch. They would be here soon. He dropped his feet so he could open his desk drawer and pull out his Sony recorder. After dropping in a fresh tape and batteries, he put it back and climbed out of his chair to stretch his back. "What a day, huh? I've got to get some coffee. You want any?"

Spartan shook him off, focused on the whiteboard. "I'm gonna hide this thing behind my desk. I don't want either of them seeing it."

"Good idea," said Watts, grabbing his empty mug. "See you in a few."

He headed to the break room contemplating his upcoming meeting. His day got even better when he spotted a fresh-brewed pot. He couldn't remember the last time time that happened. While filling his cup, he thought about Jeremy and figured if he were as involved in this case as their evidence suggested, maybe his Purgatory days would be over. Too bad he couldn't hold better conversations.

At precisely ten forty-five, Officer Sanders escorted Betty Cerin to Watts' desk. Spartan was there waiting. After inviting her to sit, Watts opened his desk drawer and pulled out his Sony recorder. He then opened a large file after making sure she could see Travis McLean's name on the label. Folding his hands and leaning back slightly, he looked like a school principal ready to expel a problem child.

"Thank you for coming, Betty. I'm sure you're upset over being here, so I'll try to be brief." He let his eyes drift to Travis' file, hoping it made her uncomfortable. "I must say, this has been a bizarre case. First, a legendary suicide hanging, then apparitions, accusations, a second suicide hanging, and revealing genealogy discoveries. Who knew you and Jeremy Delouse had a love child?"

She pressed her knees together and rigidly sat with her hands in her lap. "What on earth are you talking about? I've never had a child in my life."

"Betty, please don't lie to me. Your hair DNA confirms Marv Delouse is your child. Why do you think we collected samples from you two? Of course, at the time I had no idea those samples would lead us to Travis McLean's killer."

In an apparent effort to play it down, she confidently said, "Is that so?"

"Yup, and we have an airtight case against him. In fact, he's on his way here now."

Her expression changed when Officer Salem, a woman much beefier than Watts expected, paraded Marv to their cubicle. Watts let Marv and Betty exchange confused glances and then said, "Did you two want to say anything before he goes to jail? He'll be in there for a long time."

Betty's hands started to tremble. Soon, her entire body was shaking like an earthquake. "Why is he in handcuffs?" she anxiously said.

"I just told you that your hair samples led us to the killer, and that would be Marv. You see, his hair was intertwined with Travis McLean's on the ladder. It's an open and shut case."

"No it's not!" she said, then quickly lowered her voice. "Detective Watts, I think there's been a terrible misunderstanding. Is there a more private place where we can all talk?"

Watts and Spartan exchanged glances. *So far, so good.* "I'm sure

I can find a place, but be advised that everything you say will be recorded and may be used against you."

She glanced at his Sony and back at him. "Aren't you already recording me?"

Watts didn't bother answering. Instead, he leaned back in his chair and tapped his fingertips together like his boss. Shifting his gaze to Officer Salem, he said, "Would you please escort Mr. Delouse to the interview room? We'll be right down."

"No problem," she said, whisking him away.

Watts waited until he was certain Marv couldn't hear and then said, "Betty, before we join Marv, does he know he's your son?"

Through narrow eyes and a clenched jaw, she said, "I keep telling you I've never had any children. Marv is my nephew. His parents were Warren and Grace Delouse. They both died in a car accident many years ago. Since then I've been like a mother to him, but I assure you I am not his biological mother."

"Sure. If that's how you want to play it." He then rose from his chair. "Let's go."

Spartan lagged behind to make sure all went according to plan. For now he was to remain silent, but his turn to speak was coming.

The detectives had planned it so there were only two chairs in the interrogation room. Marv was in one, handcuffed to the stainless steel table. Watts seated Betty in the other one directly across from Marv.

"Officer Salem, you're free to resume your patrol duties."

"Yes, sir."

Watts looked around and then at his partner. "I do believe we need more chairs. Detective Spartan, would you give me a hand?"

"Sure." He then turned to Betty and Marv. "I apologize. Normally there are only two people in here at a time. We'll be right back."

When they returned, Watts planted his chair next to Marv's while his partner sat next to Betty. "You're not gonna give us any trouble are you, Marv?" said Watts. When the prisoner shook his head, he removed his cuffs and tucked them away.

Silently glaring at Betty, Marv rubbed his wrists. Though his contempt for her was obvious, Watts didn't want to address it yet. He allowed the tension to build for a moment and then pulled out his Sony, even though the interrogation room's recorders were already rolling. Addressing Betty he said, "You asked for a place where we could talk, and you can't get any more private than this. The floor's all yours."

"Thank you," she said, flicking her hair. "First of all, Arvid McAlister was very unstable. He rarely drank, but when he did, he drank to excess. I knew he was a mess when I took him in, and I tolerated his ludicrous work schedule because working here gave him purpose and kept him off the street. He had his own key so he could work whenever he was up to it. I had no idea he would abuse that privilege to kill himself in my theater, though. This could really hurt our attendance. It's a travesty."

"Interesting," said Spartan, chiming on cue.

"I agree," said Watts, impressed by how easily she used Travis' alias. "Marv, what do you have to say about this?"

"Do you have any idea how embarrassing it is to be cuffed in your workplace and hauled off in a patrol car?"

"Sorry about that, but you didn't answer my question."

Marv angrily shook his head. "What can I say about a bitter, hotheaded old man who hung himself? I fail to see why we're even having this conversation."

Watts smiled thinly. "Here's the deal, Marv. Travis McLean, AKA Arvid McAlister, was your friend. Secondly, he was murdered. Third, your mother here has—"

"My mother?" he said, glaring at her.

"Yes, Marv, your mother, and as I was saying, she's been lying to us for days and to you for a lot longer." He paused to address Betty. "Feel free to jump in at any time."

Not surprisingly, Betty chose to remain silent.

"Anyway, Marv, your hair places you at the crime scene, so that's a problem. We did appreciate your ineptitude, though. Had you slung the rope over the bar, slipped the noose around his neck, and then hoisted him up rather than tie a clove hitch first and then slide him up the ladder, we might not be having this conversation."

Marv stared at the table. "I don't know what you're talking about."

Watts nodded, tenting his hands. "Folks, I think it's time for a Come to Jesus meeting. By the way, I'll apologize now if anything I might say offends you." Then starting with Betty, he said, "We both know Arvid and Travis were the same person because DNA and his Army records prove it. And while on the subject of DNA, the hair samples we took from you and Marv also prove that you're related, as in mother and son. Now, here's the real revelation," he said, trying to sound enthusiastic. "Marv, your biological father is none other than Jeremy Delouse."

Spartan quickly leaned into Marv and whispered, "By the way, I think your biological aunt and uncle did a marvelous job raising you."

Ignoring his partner's comment, Watts said, "My mom and dad both always said war is hell on everyone. While Dad fought overseas, Mom dealt with everything stateside. Life can get real lonely while your spouse is away, and it can be easy to submit to temptation. No one can fault Betty for falling for a handsome actor like Jeremy, even though her husband was wading through rice paddies at the time. And no one would have known, had it not been for a baby boy, born a mere six months after Travis had been home on leave. So when Detective Spartan and I first began piecing things together, it seemed reasonable to think that Travis killed Jeremy out of rage. But our impression of him changed after we spoke with him at his house. He may have looked like a derelict, but he was proud in his own way."

He paused to glance at them both before locking eyes with Betty. "Now, here's where it gets weird. While we were looking into Jeremy's hanging, his ghost actually spoke to us on more than one occasion. The words he kept using were *murder* and *noose*."

Suddenly, Betty started laughing so hard her eyes welled. Dabbing them with her fingers, she said, "You're telling me that we're here because a man who's been dead for over forty years spoke to you from the grave?"

Spartan's shifting in his seat was their agreed upon signal for him to assume the lead. "Betty," he said, "You're here because you've been lying to us about your relationship with Jeremy and never having any children. I suspect part of the reason why you're so convincing is you've told these lies so often you actually believe them. In that regard, your best defense may be that you cannot differentiate between acting and reality."

Her smile gone, she said, "I want a lawyer."

"For what?" said Watts, cutting in. "You're not under arrest. Hell, people lie to the police all the time. In fact, I'd probably do the same thing if I were in your shoes. I mean, you managed to keep your son's family history a secret all these years. I can't imagine how frustrating it must be to see your whole world unraveling. By the way, you can thank your ex-husband for that. He's the one who got us involved in this case."

Like a thunderstorm ready to toss hail, her gaze became menacing. When her mouth looked ready to spit seeds, Spartan got in Marv's face.

"Tell us, Marv. Did you kill Travis because he was blackmailing you and your mother? I can't blame you if you did. I mean, that seems like a pretty good motive. Emotion sparks rage, and rage leads to murder." Spartan glanced at the actress and then leaned into the banker again. "Look, Marv, there are no more secrets, okay? We know Betty hired Travis about the same time you gave him a place to live. That must have driven you crazy, housing a bum like that." Backing off to laugh, he said, "Travis really did play you for the fool, though. He must have spent decades dreaming up this scam."

Watts gave a nod. "Here's another motive," he said. "What if you learned Travis arranged your parents' car accident?"

"That's insane," said Marv. "They were T-boned by a semi. Besides, why would Travis want my parents dead?"

"Because he knew the truth about you and wanted to raise you as his own. And before you say it's far-fetched, remember he drove a fuel truck during his second Vietnam tour. But then, you already knew that because he told you early in your relationship. Imagine all those years wondering if he drove that semi. And while you listened to his stories, you plotted your revenge. Still, you never imagined your mom would come up with the perfect solution. I'm sure your hatred for him helped you string him up. How am I doing, Marv?"

Suddenly the banker deflated like a punctured pool toy, slumping in his chair.

Spartan got up and stood behind Marv, bending so he was inches from his ear. "Here's a little lesson in murder," he said, barely loud enough to be picked up by the recorder. "If you're gonna hang someone, do it while they're still alive. At least that way you might have a chance at making it look like a suicide. Dead men hang differently because they don't struggle."

He then backed away and parked himself on the edge of the table with his arms crossed and eyes locked on Marv. He held the pose for a full minute and then got to his feet and leaned over the table without ever breaking his gaze.

"Here's what I don't get, Marv. During our talks with Travis, it was obvious he loved you as if you were his own son. In fact, I'd go so far as to say he loved you so much he may have slung that noose around his neck just to please you. But instead, you smothered him first and then strung him up like a side of beef."

Marv flinched and looked away.

"It's okay, Marv. You'll have plenty of time to think about it while you're on death row, waiting to be executed."

Staring at the table in front of him, the banker said, "This is bullshit and you know it."

"Not really," said Spartan, exhaling noisily through his nose. "Did I fail to mention we found whiskey stains in the rehearsal room and whiskey bottles in the recycling bin? That mistake really did you in. Had you been more careful, you might not be in such a mess."

Watts had been holding back because Spartan had agreed to be the warm-up act. They knew ahead of time that their best chance at a confession was to play the mother/son card. Now, while Marv stewed, he removed the facial recognition photos from the folder and spread them on the table hoping to wrap this up.

"Folks, let's have a look at your family album," he said. "Pay close attention to the eyes." When neither looked, he pointed out the similarities as he confronted the aging actress. "Come on, Betty. Even you can't deny Marv has your eyes."

Before she could speak, Spartan pointed at the pictures. "Hold on, Detective Watts. Marv's cheek bones and chin don't match Betty's. Where could they have come from?"

Pretending to have made a mistake, Watts then pulled out Jeremy's photo and set it on the table. "Sorry about that. I believe this is the missing link."

He then moved closer and arranged Betty and Jeremy's photos so they were together with Marv's picture below them. He intentionally placed Travis' photo next to his ex-wife, but separated by a few inches. "There we go. This clearly shows that Travis is not part of your family tree." He gave them a moment to show their indifference before adding, "Folks, I wouldn't be showing you this evidence if the DA hadn't told us it was indisputable. But what's sad is right when you are finally getting to know each other, Marv is on his way to jail. Not much of a reunion, was it?"

The banker looked ready to burst. Pounding the table, he said, "Fuck you!"

"Marv," said Spartan, calmly approaching him. "Believe whatever you want, but your condo's surveillance video has you leaving around one AM and then returning a few hours after Travis was murdered. Combine that with your DNA at the murder scene, and the photos become irrelevant. Right now the DA is finalizing his Murder One charges and says he will be seeking the death penalty.

On the bright side, you don't have to worry about being hanged, although in your case, that seems fitting."

While Marv's face reddened, his mother's lost color. Watts calmly rose from his chair and stood near the banker. "We've all had a nice chat, and now it's time we booked Marv. Betty, thanks for coming in. Say good-bye to your son." As he started to grab his arm, she abruptly raised her hand.

"Wait!"

Watts gave a confused look. "What? Do you have something to add?"

"Look," she said, rubbing her trembling hands. "Travis and I never should have married. Not because he wasn't a good man, but because we had so little in common. I loved the theater, and he loved the outdoors. That's why the Army was such a good fit, but even that changed after he was wounded. That bamboo spike impacted his life far more emotionally than physically. He was never the same after that. Even so, I was determined to make a go of our marriage, but he pushed me away saying I deserved better.

"As for Jeremy, you have it all wrong. I loved Travis, but it was very lonely with him gone. Since Jeremy cared so much about acting and the theater, we went out for a bite after a few performances, but it was completely innocent, and I never once kissed him. Then one day after an exceptional show, we decided to celebrate by having a drink in the dungeon from the bottle of Scotch he kept in the janitor's closet. I'm not normally a drinker, so I was buzzed before I knew it. After downing a second shot, I barely noticed his hands on my breasts. Following a third, I was naked on the rehearsal room floor. That's all I remember about that night. I woke up alone in bed thinking it was a dream, but then a few weeks later I found myself running to the bathroom to throw up. Thinking it was the flu, I finally went to the doctor and was mortified to learn I was pregnant."

She covered her face to hide her tears. After wiping her cheeks, she finally said, "I didn't know what to do. I knew Travis would be furious, so I didn't write him. When he wrote he was coming home, I concocted a scheme to make him think the child was his. The first night was dreamlike and we made love like it was the first time, but when I tried to seduce him on subsequent nights, he called me a whore. Naturally, I retaliated and called him a sick bastard. Rather than fight, he stormed out and spent the rest of his time at his parents' house.

Even so, we had a few sessions together, and I prayed that was enough for him to believe he got me pregnant.

"Of course, deep down I knew my scheme wouldn't work, because the baby would have been too big for him to believe it was premature. So I came up with another plan before I showed too much. My sister Grace and her husband had been trying in vain to get pregnant, so when I told her about my situation, she begged me to give her the baby so she could claim it as her own. This arrangement was truly a blessing for all of us. Everyone except Jeremy, that is.

"It wasn't long before he threatened to tell Travis he had fathered my child. He was so infatuated with me, I knew he was serious, so to keep him at bay, I started being extra nice to him, telling him to be patient, and that I would get an annulment so we could be together. That calmed him for a while, but then his advances got to the point where I couldn't work with him, and the understudy had to take over. Once he realized we would never be together, he hung himself, and as they say in show business, *The End*."

"The end or the beginning?" said Spartan.

She gave an inquisitive look. "I'm not sure what you mean, detective."

"It was the end for Jeremy, but it renewed your acting career."

Watching her expression, Watts took over. "Let's forget about Jeremy and focus on Travis," he said. "When did you get your annulment?"

"We filed almost immediately, but it wasn't final until he was well into his second Vietnam tour. He signed the papers while he was deployed, and the next time I saw him was decades later when he was using the name Arvid McAlister."

Watts turned to look at Marv. "But you only knew him as Travis McLean, right?"

Marv nodded. "That's how he introduced himself, and that's what I always called him."

"And you were unaware he also went by Arvid?"

"That's correct."

Watts tapped his lips with his pen pretending to think. When he figured he had delayed long enough, he said. "Marv, this may be your last chance. Would you please explain how your body hair got into the Scott Theater's dungeon?"

Marv tensed, clutching his hands. "I want a lawyer."

"That's fine. You don't need to talk to us. It's only your future that's at stake." Watts immediately angled his chair to face Betty. "When you first met Arvid, didn't you recognize him as your ex-husband?"

"Of course not," she said, as if he was stupid for asking such a question. "I hadn't seen Travis in over thirty years when he was lean and strong and handsome. The man who showed up at the theater had long, stringy hair, wore a thick beard, was heavy and smelled. If there was any resemblance between him and my ex, I never saw it. I assure you the man I took under my wing that day was Arvid McAlister, not Travis McLean."

Watts stared at the tiled ceiling to imply he knew she was lying. After a few seconds, he dropped his head to look at them both. "It's getting late, so I'll give you some choices. First, Marv will be booked for Murder One. Second, you both immediately submit to a lie detector test. Either that or you start telling the truth and don't hold anything back, and no, Marv, I don't have time to wait for a lawyer. Whether you talk now or not, the truth will eventually come out. It can be as easy or as painful as you want it to be."

When he finished, the only noise was his heart pounding in his ears and the nagging second hand from the clock. But the silence was wearing down his suspects, too. They fought hard not to look at each other, but they still shared furtive glances.

When Marv couldn't take it any longer, he said, "*She* killed him, not me!"

"Shut up!" Betty screamed back, raising her hand.

Watts grabbed her arm before it could swing forward. "Betty, you do that again and I'll have you removed." He let go and she pulled her hands to her face. Ignoring her weeping, he slid his chair next to the banker.

"Marv, I'm addressing you first, but this applies equally to both of you. You have the right to remain silent and anything you say can and will be used against you in a court of law. You have the right to consult with an attorney and to have that attorney present during questioning. If you do not have one, an attorney will be provided at no cost to represent you." After reviewing his Miranda card to make sure he had covered everything, he tucked it back in his wallet. "So, what's it gonna be, Marv? You understand your rights?"

"I do."

Swinging his head around at Betty, he said, "Do you understand these rights?" When she nodded, he said, "I need a verbal yes or no."

"Yes, damn it, although I don't know why you're looking at me."

"That's great, now don't say another word while I talk to your boy, or I'll have you removed." He then returned his gaze to the banker and calmly folded his arms. "Okay, Marv, your jail cell's waiting. Last chance to speak up."

The banker's eyes closed as he sighed. Slowly, his eyes opened and he started to talk.

"I got a call from Betty a little before one AM saying she was in trouble and needed me at the theater. She was crying but refused to say why. I immediately headed over there where she practically dragged me inside and led me to the dungeon. When we entered the rehearsal room, Travis was lying on the floor bluer than I've ever seen a man. The room reeked of alcohol, and a nearly empty bottle of Scotch lay tossed in a corner. Thinking that Travis had drunk too much I went over to attempt CPR, but Betty pulled me away screaming he was dead and we needed to do something or she'd be blamed.

"I couldn't believe what I was seeing, and when she told me to get the ladder from the janitor's closet, I did it without question. When I came back, she had a large noose in her hand and gave me an evil look. My head was so messed up at that point I didn't even ask where she got it.

"She told me to set the ladder under the pipe and then steady it as she climbed and tied the rope to the pipe. It was surreal watching her tie these knots. Then she started cussing like a crazy woman, exclaiming this was exactly how Jeremy died. Since I'd never heard her swear before, I couldn't believe it was her. I kept looking around expecting someone to come in, but no one ever did. Then she told me to slide Travis up the ladder, but I could barely budge him. Disgusted, she undid her knots and dropped the noose to the floor. After she climbed down, she slid the noose over his neck and then climbed back up and told me to lift his shoulders while she yanked on the rope. Amazingly, he slid up the ladder until his hand caught the folding arm. It only took a second to fix that, and once we had enough height, she re-tied the rope. We pulled the ladder away after she climbed down and set a step stool on its side. She wiped up the scuff marks while I put the ladder away, and then I joined her in the rehearsal room.

"While she worked on cleaning up the whiskey, I tossed the bottle in the recycling bin." He stopped for a moment as if a thought suddenly came to mind. "I bet you lifted my prints off the bottle, didn't you?" he said, his voice now full of vigor. When they said nothing, he fired another gaze at his mother. "God, what a perfect setup! I touched everything while you sat back and cleaned up. What a bitch! I'm glad you gave me away!"

"How dare you speak to me that way, you ungrateful bastard!" She tried to spit in his face, but he dodged it, and it went on the floor.

"That's enough!" said Watts, slapping the table. "Betty, you are now officially under arrest for the murder of Travis McLean, and Marv you are now her accomplice. Detective Spartan, I want you to cuff her if she so much as moves a muscle. After looking at both suspects to be sure they understood him, he said, "Okay, Marv, pick it up where you left off."

The banker took his time, turning until he could no longer see her face. "You saw me with Travis at the diner, and you're right, we treated each other like father and son. Arguing was only a small part of our relationship, and we never let it get the better of us. I took care of him when no one else would, and I wasn't lying when I said how we met in the park. His telling me he was a Vietnam veteran stirred memories of when I was a kid, so when he asked who my parents were, I told him. He laughed as if he had known all along and then started to wander off like he was done talking. I couldn't let him leave without hearing the rest of his story, so I took him to the Chuck Wagon Diner for lunch. While eating, he told me about Betty and how she got pregnant." Smirking at his mother he said, "I bet you never expected him to stay in touch with Warren, did you? He's the one who told Travis you were pregnant."

Betty's eyes narrowed to slits, but she never said a word.

Grinning now, Marv faced the detectives again and continued. "Travis told me he wanted to wring Betty's neck when Warren told him that, but after talking it through, he agreed she did the right thing by giving me up because their marriage was over. I really wished he had tried to be my father after Warren died."

"Oh, boo hoo," said Betty. "Don't judge me when you have no idea what my life was like."

"Well, it doesn't really matter now, does it?" said Watts.

"True," said Spartan, getting to his feet. "Then again, you'll both have plenty of time to reflect on everything while you're in jail. I'm still curious about why would you pay for a bum's house? You never did answer that one."

Marv's eyes narrowed and his body tensed. As Watts tried to cuff him, he yanked his hands away to slap the table. "Travis was a lot of things, but he was never a bum!"

255

"You'd better relax before you get hurt," said Watts, forcing Marv's arms behind his back. "But before I haul you away to the booking room, how about answering my partner's question? Why pay for Travis' home when you knew he wasn't your dad?"

Marv growled and leaned into Watts, his voice gravelly, his mouth full of spittle. "I did it because he fought for our country and needed help. The Government may have turned its back on him, but I couldn't. And for the record, the guy who killed my parents was said to be Hispanic – probably an illegal with no insurance. I realize you said it to get a reaction, but Travis did all his killing overseas. He didn't drive that semi."

Watts nodded politely and clung to Marv's arm feeling good about their session. Marv had countered his bluff and decided it was better to cooperate than be booked on a murder charge. Unfortunately, Betty had not been as cooperative, so he prolonged her son's cuffing to give her time to think. Before escorting Marv out of the room, he said, "Forget the semi driver and let's talk Vietnam vets. As I've said, I grew up with them, so I have a pretty good idea where Travis came from. Whenever my dad's buddies came over, they'd get drunk and swap war stories. They didn't want me around, but I was always close enough to hear them. My heart goes out to every vet who served over there, but I've never once had the urge to buy one a home, especially when I can't afford one for myself. So stop holding back and tell us why you let Travis into the house on Prospect. You're still going to jail, but at least it might rule it out as a murder motive."

Marv bowed his head and stared at his shoes. "I have nothing more to say."

Upon hearing that, Spartan gave Betty a disgusted look. "You two make quite a pair," he said, getting his cuffs out. "Then again, I suppose watching your son go to jail for a crime you committed is par for the course. After all, you've always resented him, haven't you?"

"That's not true," she said, returning his gaze.

"Look," he said, standing her up and cuffing her. "Detective Watts and I aren't soothsayers, but we're pretty good at solving puzzles, so this is what really happened. Jeremy raped Betty in 1970 and she was so angry that she lured him in, smothered him, and strung him up to make it look like suicide. Last night, for reasons yet to be determined, she repeated the act on Travis, except this time she had Marv as an accomplice. Betty, I can understand your anger toward Jeremy, but why would you want to kill Travis?"

Through narrow eyes she silently glared back, so Watts jumped in.

"Since Betty's not talking, I'll answer for her. When Travis reappeared ten years ago, he ransomed your secret for a job at the theater. Fearing your past could ruin your social status, you created work for him under the condition he went by Arvid McAlister, but then he befriended Marv as Travis McLean. You managed to hold it together until your slush fund dried up. That's when you snapped. In your defense, that's a lot to bear. Here you are, a successful theater executive when suddenly your ex shows up and is working for you against your will. It must have been extremely difficult to live this way, but is resentment ever enough to justify killing a man?"

Standing tall, she defiantly answered, "No comment."

Watts paused to study his notes before flipping the tape on his Sony. The clock ticked thirty more times before he looked at her. "Betty, it seems I forgot to mention that your prints were also on the whiskey bottle. I apologize." He then tucked his notes away and looked at his partner. "Detective Spartan, would you please have someone book these two on murder charges?"

"No problem. I'll be right back."

The suspects' eyes followed Spartan out the door and then returned to the table. In truth, Watts still lacked enough evidence to convict anyone. No doubt Marv's lawyers would argue this was entrapment, and Betty's would downplay her son's accusations, state she came voluntarily, and argue she was never charged until after she was coerced into a confession. His only chance was to continue to push their buttons.

"Marv, I'm sorry your mother involved you, but it proves Grace and Warren were better suited to raise you. I can't imagine your guilt over stringing your buddy up. Regardless of what happens in court, I hope you find a way to make peace with it. As I said, Travis cared for you immensely."

Watts let that sink in before facing the actress. "You know, Betty, what still amazes me is how much Travis adored you. When we talked to him at the Prospect house, it was clear no one ever replaced you in his life. I got the impression his biggest reason to seek you out was so he could watch over you. By the way, he covered for you by insisting you never recognized him. He was never really a threat to you, was he? I still find it ironic that he survived two combat tours only to die by his ex-wife's hands. Like Marv, you will also have to come to terms with it. May God take pity on both of you."

Marv kicked his chair over. "Even if you find DNA evidence proving she gave birth to me, she will never be my mother! Real mothers devote their lives to their children and don't give them away, and then doctor their birth certificate. I responded to her call for help, and now I'm being booked on murder? I don't think so. As for Travis, he was dead before I got there. Yes, I admit I positioned the ladder and helped lift him off the floor, but she did everything else."

"Shut up!" screamed Betty, grabbing her hair.

"Piss off, *Mom.*" He then looked at Watts. "I will gladly testify to what I just said if it will help put this black widow away." Just then, Spartan entered the room with two uniformed officers. The banker smirked as a cop approached his mother. "Enjoy prison, bitch."

But for once the glowing actress had no comeback. She made no fuss as the officer escorted her toward the door. Just before they went out, Watts stopped them.

"Pardon my manners," said Watts, "but I forgot to ask if either of you had any final words."

"Actually," said Marv, confidently raising his chin, "have someone from the DA's office meet with me so we can work out a deal."

"You bastard!" said Betty, lunging at him. Even with a guard restraining her, she still fought to get away. With her arms being held behind her back, she stared at her accuser, spitting as she spoke. "My son would have loved the theater and protected his mother, not cast her aside like a used rag."

"Yeah, well what goes around comes around, right mom?"

"Screw you!"

"You already did that, too." He then looked at Watts with pleading eyes. "Can you please take her away? I don't ever want to see her again."

"We're here to serve." Watts then nodded to the officer, but instead of taking Betty, Marv was escorted away.

With Betty now waiting in her escort's grasp, Watts seated himself again and stretched his legs out. He should have been elated, but the ticking second hand was like spikes to the brain. Slouching in his chair, he drummed the table with his fingertips avoiding all eye contact. He and his partner had made a pact that should they get to this point, they would both remain silent for a while. Although she had admitted to killing Jeremy, the odds of convicting her were slimmer than a cockroach's leg. Since she never admitted to doing anything to Travis, it seemed unlikely that Marv's testimony would be enough. Even so, she was now a mere shell of the actress who had walked into the interrogation room. He waited five minutes before looking at her and couldn't believe how she had transformed from stunning actress to the walking dead.

"Betty, did you ever wonder what your life would have been like if you had never met Jeremy Delouse?"

She shook her head in disgust. "I have never lived my life in the past, and I refuse to start now. Believe what you want, but we were never in love. That bastard stole my life when he forced himself on me, and he deserved to die. It was no accident that Travis died the same way, drunk and groping me. Neither felt a thing as they took their last breaths under the pillow. Too bad you got so nosy." She sighed and for a brief moment smiled at no one in particular. "Detective Watts, I made peace with God years ago, so I really don't care what happens to me, but I do hope they go easy on Marv. Everything he said was true. He only came because I called him."

The detective pursed his lips and blew air out his nostrils. "I have no idea how this will play out, Betty, but involving others to cover up a murder is never a good idea."

Her head dropped as if she had reached the same conclusion.

Once Watts nodded, the officer escorted her from the room. Now alone with his partner, he returned to his seat and gave a forlorn look.

"Why the sad face?" said Spartan. "I thought you'd be happy."

"I know, but I'm worried about the trial. It's such a bizarre case. At least you were present to hear her statement."

"Yeah, but it was also being recorded, and she understood her rights." When that failed to spark a reaction, Spartan added, "We did our jobs, Maxx, and we did them well. Everything else is up to the DA. Convicting her on two counts of murder should free Jeremy's and Travis' souls and rid the theater of ghosts claiming murder."

Watts snorted as he rose from his seat. "We can only hope," he said, wondering if their souls would rise on All Hallow's Eve. Tucking his Sony away, he smiled at his partner. "Another case closed, right Blaine?"

"I hope so," said Spartan, bobbing his head. "But the outcome could have been different if Betty hadn't repeated her MO."

"I know, and I won't rest until she's convicted. I'm worried she has some influential friends."

"Yeah, well so did Kat Coulter, and she's behind bars now."

"Good point. Maybe they'll become cell mates."

Slinging his coat over his shoulder, Watts smiled at the thought. "Love can sure be complicated," he said, thinking about his own relationships. "Seems it brings out the best and worst in people."

"Well, why not concentrate on the best and tell me how you and Daisy are gonna celebrate this victory?"

Watts took his time answering, as victory wasn't the word he would have used – not when his involvement got another man killed, as Betty and Marv both pointed out. But what really surprised him is how little he had been thinking about Daisy. He wasn't ready to read anything into it, but the thought did concern him. Trying to force her from his mind, he said, "I don't think we should celebrate anything until the DA has assured us we didn't coerce them into any confessions."

Forty One

WATTS DIDN'T RELAX UNTIL he received word their interrogation recordings were clean and no rights had been compromised. He needed that assurance before he and his partner marched into Captain Ryder's office. While playing Betty's recorded conversation for his boss, he reflected on how charming and witty she had been until the truth came out in the interrogation room.

While Ryder listened and skimmed through Travis' murder file, Watts reflected on Betty's confession. He could understand her getting Jeremy drunk as he had done her, but smothering him with a pillow and hanging him went beyond anything he could imagine. And the fact she had gotten away with murder for so long made it difficult to understand why she would repeat the act on her ex-husband.

So many things about this case didn't add up. He expected a response after saying Travis broke the theater's slush fund, but she never once flinched. It wasn't until he convinced her that Marv really was being booked for murder that she decided to come clean, and even then he wasn't convinced she was telling the truth. Still, it was good of her to back her son's story and admit he knew nothing about Travis until he saw him at the theater.

Even with her testimony, Marv would be facing a legal storm. He could have prevented it had he called the police when he first saw Travis' body. Instead he helped cover up a crime to protect the mother who deserted him.

As the tape ran on, Watts couldn't help feeling sorry for the banker. In the course of a single evening, Marv not only lost a friend, he learned the ugly truth about his heritage. The fact he hanged a dead man should reduce his sentence, but even minimal time would ruin his life. His best defense would be to claim he was so traumatized by seeing Travis' dead body he became a slave to his conniving mother. Whether his lawyer could convince the jury of that remained to be seen.

But how did Betty sway a son who despised her? Did she somehow convince Marv she gave him to Grace and Warren because Travis had been unbearably abusive? Reflecting on that, Watts noticed his partner's drifting gaze. Was he was having similar regrets about this case? The notion flashed him back to high school English class where they studied *The Rhyme of the Ancient Mariner*. In the story, the mariner kills the bird of good fortune and must wear it around his neck as a reminder. Now it seemed that Travis McLean was their albatross, their burden to carry to the grave. The thought chilled him more that any of the dungeon's spirits.

A squeak from Ryder's chair surprised him. Managing a curious look, he said, "Your squeak is back, eh, captain?"

"That it is, and you have no idea what it took to get it back. I must have spent half an hour experimenting, but there it is. Funny how much I missed it."

Watts nodded, thinking about Daisy. Squeaks were easier to fix than relationships, and he would never forgive himself if he lost her. Still smiling at his boss, he promised himself he would take her somewhere nice for the weekend – somewhere far from the theaters and parks where they had witnessed so much savagery. Spartan's nudge to the ribs hurt.

"You guys did good," said Ryder, setting the murder file aside. "Solving two murders at once is pretty astounding."

"Sir, we couldn't have done it without your support and Ms. Woods' expertise," said Spartan.

"Ah yes," sighed the captain. "The infamous Third Musketeer." He paused for a moment and folded his hands. "I must admit she's proven herself since she's been here. I'll send a letter to her superior noting that."

Watts suddenly sat up, surprised by his offer. "I'm sure she'd appreciate that, sir."

Ryder pulled off his reading glasses to stare at Watts. "Tell me the truth," he said, tapping the frame to his lips. "Do you guys really believe in ghosts?"

"Absolutely," said Spartan.

Watts agreed with a nod. "Don't you?"

Ryder chuckled and let his eyes drift to his desk. "I'm not ready to believe in spectral gallows, but I do promise to keep an open mind."

Grinning at his partner, the detective said, "That's all we can ask."

"I agree," said Spartan. "This investigation sure proved we don't know or understand much about other realms. I hope our actions will elevate Jeremy and Travis to a better place."

"I hear you, Blaine."

Ryder smirked at them as he set his glasses on his desk. "Gentlemen, it's Friday, and Halloween is two days away. You and that lab technician kept going when no one believed in you, and I commend you for your persistence. Once your paperwork is in order, I recommend you take off for the weekend, because I'm sure you'll have a new assignment Monday morning."

Forty Two

MARIACHI MUSIC BLARED FROM crowded waterfront restaurants as their dinner barge floated under a starry night. San Antonio's celebrated Riverwalk was a perfect weekend retreat for Watts and Daisy. As they drifted past the Alamo, Watts explained how his father promised to take him where Davey Crocket and Jim Bowie faced Santa Ana.

"Like so many of Dad's promises, this one came up empty. But seeing it with you is the best way to fulfill that childhood wish."

"Oh, Maxx, that's so sweet." She leaned her head into his shoulder and cuddled until the boat came to a stop.

As Watts stepped off, he had to brake for costumed ghosts and goblins rushing past. Once Daisy stopped giggling, they resumed their walk along the river, pausing frequently to admire the various street performers.

They arrived at the small amphitheater just in time to see ornately-dressed singers and dancers take the stage. When the colorful skirts stopped twirling and the stomping heels fell silent, Watts leaned over and kissed her. But in spite of this perfect evening, he still felt a void only time could heal. His time with Travis stirred unexpected memories of his father. Not all were bad, though, and while nothing could change the fact he was a drunken bastard, at least Watts understood him better. As they walked away from the amphitheater, Daisy's gentle voice caught him off guard.

"Are you okay?" she said, squeezing his hand.

Watts smiled back. "I am, now that we're together. Thanks for coming along."

"Are you kidding? Thanks for bringing me. I haven't seen the Riverwalk since I was a kid and this is the perfect time of year to visit. I love seeing kids in Halloween costumes and all the festivities. Most of all, I love being here with you."

"Thanks, but All Hallows Eve has a pretty dark history."

She backed away slightly and feigned a look. "How so?"

He shrugged watching his feet. "I remember a teacher saying hundreds of years ago they sacrificed humans and animals on that day to appease the gods, and much later, singers and dancers would go from house to house wearing blood-curdling masks and costumes to protect themselves from Evil. It's hard to believe the costumes and masks these kids are wearing evolved from that ritual."

"That's gross, Maxx. You brought me here to celebrate, so let's do that."

He smiled and led her down the Riverwalk, watching their reflections follow them. Across the river, kids skipped and jumped with various pails to collect their treats. There was joy on their faces and music everywhere. Suddenly he stopped and bent over to pick up a rock.

"What are you doing?" said Daisy.

After rubbing the rock in his palms, he said, "I just transferred my worries onto this rock, and now I'm gonna sink 'em." As soon as he said that, he tossed the rock in the middle of the river and watched the concentric circles spread. Before they reached the shore, another party barge drifted past and erased them. He then wrapped his arm around Daisy and kissed her on the cheek. "There we go. All better."

"I certainly hope so. You're far too precious to wear such gloom."

"Why, thank you, Ma'am." Walking again, he smiled at her once more. "And you're so precious to me. Why don't we find a quiet place and get to know each other?"

Smiling, she leaned into him and locked lips, as others maneuvered around them. When they finally parted, she cupped his face with both of her hands. "Mr. Maxx, I do believe that's the best plan you've had in a long time."

The End

Mark W. Danielson lives with his wife in Fort Worth, Texas. The second in the Maxx Watts murder mystery series, *Spectral Gallows* was inspired by a hanging that took place in Fort Worth's Scott Theater in 1970. Many of the paranormal events weaved into this story were documented by paranormal investigators at the Scott Theater. This theater is now officially listed as one of Fort Worth's haunted locations.

www.ingramcontent.com/pod-product-compliance
Lightning Source LLC
Chambersburg PA
CBHW060343030726
47497CB00003B/582